Zhara had [...]g comforting. S[...] should she care? She had enough problems of her own, and the man she was instinctively wishing to console was the source of most of them. Yet, there was something about his vulnerability that caused her to say, "It wasn't all your fault. I mean, I did a pretty dumb thing, letting go of my safety line. I panicked, and I shouldn't have."

Without any command from her conscious self, her hand stretched out and rested lightly on his arm. The effect was galvanic. Shock waves raced through her at ground zero, zinging, tingling. Her eyes flew open in surprise, meeting his, which were equally wide, equally surprised. She hadn't been prepared for the warmth of him; his solidity and his constant aggression had left her thinking of him as some kind of animated wall, a machine, Terminator made flesh. Yet, what she touched was a human being, and the unspoken communication that had passed between man and woman throughout the ages told her that right now, her touch was the one thing he needed to console him, more than anything else.

As with any other massive electrical overload, she found herself needing to break free of the source of all this terrible energy, but the power that raced from him and into her and back fused them as surely as if she had come into contact with a fallen live wire. With effort and a prayer, she tore her hand from his arm, jerking it back, expecting to see the skin on her fingers sear and fall away.

He inhaled sharply, nostrils flaring. Neither had the courage to speak before the other. Instead, they held each other's gaze, each aware of the other's erratic breathing.

"Detective," she began, at last.

"Cole," he corrected her. He still had not taken his eyes from her face.

She tried his name on her lips for the first time. "Cole . . ."

BOOK YOUR PLACE ON OUR WEBSITE AND MAKE THE ARABESQUE ROMANCE CONNECTION!

We've created a customized website just for our very special Arabesque readers, where you can get the inside scoop on everything that's going on with Arabesque romance novels.

When you come online, you'll have the exciting opportunity to:

- View covers of upcoming books

- Learn about our future publishing schedule (listed by publication month and author)

- Find out when your favorite authors will be visiting a city near you

- Search for and order backlist books

- Check out author bios and background information

- Send e-mail to your favorite authors

- Join us in weekly chats with authors, readers and other guests

- Get writing guidelines

- AND MUCH MORE!

Visit our website at
http://www.arabesquebooks.com

SOUL'S DESIRE

Simona Taylor

ARABESQUE
★BET
BOOKS

BET Publications, LLC
www.bet.com
www.arabesquebooks.com

ARABESQUE BOOKS are published by

BET Publications, LLC
c/o BET BOOKS
One BET Plaza
1900 W Place NE
Washington, D.C. 20018-1211

All Kensington Titles, Imprints, and Distributed Lines are available at special quantity discounts for bulk purchases for sales promotions, premiums, fund-raising, educational, or institutional use. Special book excerpts or customized printings can also be created to fit specific needs. For details, write or phone the office of the Kensington special sales manager: Kensington Publishing Corp., 850 Third Avenue, New York, NY 10022, attn: Special Sales Department, Phone: 1-800-221-2647.

First Printing: October, 2000
10 9 8 7 6 5 4 3 2 1

Printed in the United States of America

Soul's Desire is dedicated to my two American friends who have proven to me that friendship knows no barriers of distance or culture

For Debbie Wagner, of Fort Wayne, Indiana, who has been my most steadfast friend for over twenty-one years. Debbie, you're beautiful. You have enough guts for both of us. You'll walk on your own one day! You will!

For Judy Bernstein of San Diego, California, my cyber soul mate. Our passion for good books threw us together by accident, but our freshly minted friendship has taken us way beyond that. Thanks for the wise counsel, encouragement, company and support.

I love you both.

Prologue

"I'll tell you this," Brian Ames said, with his mouth full of hot dog, an annoying habit if ever there was one. "I've never seen you have such a thing for a woman."

Detective First Grade Cole Wyatt gave him a sour, sidelong look. "I have not got a *thing* for the woman," he protested. "I just want to get my hands on her. She's a thief. I'm a cop. Figure it out."

"Yeah," Ames agreed, sarcastically, "we're just here to serve and protect. Nothing personal *there.*"

In an effort to drown out his partner, Cole removed a plastic cup of coffee from its resting place in the cup holder of the car and took a swig of it. It had long gone cold, and the fake cream the salesgirl had poured into it had congealed into a gob of brownish scum that floated on the surface. It tasted like muck, but he wasn't getting out and walking three blocks to the nearest all-night convenience store for another—not on a foul, wet, chilly night such as this, with a nasty wind slashing all the way in from Chicago, picking up power as it swooped over Lake Michigan, just a few hundred miles away.

They were parked in an alley off the main financial district in the city of Medusa, an area where, it was joked, you were barred entry to any of the many five-star restaurants along Gibraltar Avenue if you pulled up to the curb driving anything costing less than twenty grand. On any other night, the bankers, brokers, and insurance executives would be striding around, literally claiming dominion over the very ground on which they trod, but it was late, and the miserable autumn damp that permeated the place had long sent them scuttling for the sanctuary of their sprawling suburban homes, far to the west.

Cole tapped his long, dark-brown fingers against his temple, keeping time with a song that only he could hear, as Brian went on. "But you'd be lying if you told me you weren't ticked off at her for giving you the slip every time you've come close—for what—three years? Don't tell me this ain't personal. And don't tell me if it was anybody but her, you'd be out here on a night like tonight eating crappy deli food, holed up with me for six hours, instead of being home with your son, watching the game."

Ames was right, which got Cole even more irritated than he was already. He shifted his huge bulk in vain, trying to find a comfortable place to settle, but the car was too short for his legs. His feet had gone to sleep an hour ago. He could see it now: the woman puts in an appearance, he leaps out of the car to give chase, and falls flat on his face because his feet are cramped up. Stakeouts were bad enough for an ordinary man, with spending half the night in a car with your knees pulled up to your chin. When you stood six feet seven, they were murder. He'd sell his maiden aunt for fifteen minutes alone with the creep back in Purchasing who had decided to issue all the detectives in the city with these dinky little Japanese vehicles instead of a *real* man's car.

Cole turned to look at his partner. Ames had a smear of mustard in his pencil-thin, red-blond moustache. This gave Cole a spark of malicious pleasure. He certainly wasn't going to tell him. "Look, this is *not* personal. She's a nuisance, and she's got to be stopped. Last I heard, cat-burglary was still against the law. I bring people like her in, and I collect a check every month. That's all." Only problem was, he wished he could believe that himself.

Ames snorted. "Who are you trying to fool, Cole? I'm your partner, remember? You're dying to smoke her out and haul her in like the prize boar at an archery contest. You're just miffed that a hot little thing like that has been running rings around you. Far as you're concerned, she's wasting that body climbing in and out of buildings, and those fabulous thighs weren't designed for slithering up and down rope . . ."

Cole raised a thick black brow. "You kiss your wife with that mouth, Ames? You know . . ." The crackle of the radio interrupted them. The air filled with electric anticipation as both men listened to the breathless, barked instructions. Cole felt a leaping in his veins. He tossed aside his half-eaten corned beef on rye and patted the small of his back to reassure himself that his weapon was there. Throwing open the door, he launched himself out of the car and was pounding down the sidewalk, three beats ahead of his partner.

The chase was on. Zhara Thorne was going down. Tonight.

One

Jail wasn't pretty. It stole your soul, wore you down, and robbed you of your humanity. They claimed it was designed to rehabilitate you—turn you into someone fit to reenter society—but that was just a load of bull handed down by do-gooders and politicians. Jail was punishment, pure and simple, designed to torture and humiliate—and that was why Zhara had made sure that throughout her entire criminal career, she had never been caught.

The De Boers building was silent. On the third floor, the janitor was busy emptying trash cans. On the fifth, his young female aide was thumbing through magazines, perched on the edge of one of the secretaries' desks. Out at reception, the overweight security officer dozed. During her second reconnaissance visit a week ago, Zhara had struck up a conversation with him. She'd sauntered in, looking much less than her twenty-three years, with her crazy black curls fluffed around her head like a halo and careful makeup giving her eyes a wild-eyed lost-soul look. Her cute button nose and soft, wide mouth added to the image of innocence. Her little ruse had worked; the elderly man had taken pity on the pretty young black girl who claimed to be from out of town and looking for work, and chatted with her for a good twenty minutes before sending her on her way. During that short time, the gar-

rulous old man had confided in her that he was hyper-
glycemic.

Tonight, while she'd watched from her observation post
across the street, he'd put away two iced doughnuts and a
mugful of what looked like hot chocolate. As she had expected, he'd nodded off within twenty minutes, drugged
by the sugar in his bloodstream, his shoulders, clad in his
ill-fitting blue security uniform, slumped forward over his
desk.

The business Zhara had to attend to was on the eight-
eenth floor, the penthouse where she now stood. The security officer's partner was all the way down on twelve,
making his rounds. At a rate of ten minutes per floor,
he'd be giving her plenty of time to locate the safe, open
it, and make away with what she was there for. Neverthe-
less, Zhara was enough of a professional to know that she
should not let her generous time frame make her com-
placent. She was here to do a job, and it was in her best
interest to do what she had to and leave. Self-assurance
was no excuse for getting careless; jail, she knew, was full
of careless people.

Her soft-soled, black leather boots made no sound on
the lush beige carpet. Zhara never did a job wearing anything other than fine kid leather; it was pliant and clung
to her, moving with her as she stole across the room. The
soft but sturdy covering protected her fine, nutmeg-col-
ored skin from the many nicks and scratches she could
have suffered as she pulled herself steadfastly up the side
of the building and down through the skylight. More im-
portantly, though, leather had no fibers, so she never left
behind any telltale microscopic traces that could lead a
sharp-eyed forensic specialist back to her.

The impossibly thick black hair that usually fell down
to the center of her back had been closely braided, and
then the entire skein carefully wound with a specially designed head-wrap, keeping it out of her eyes, and, of

course, preventing any strands from being left behind and
getting her into trouble. One thing she always boasted
about was that she wasn't sloppy.

Standing in the office of De Boers' Senior Vice President, Victor Chlumsky, she tried to get her bearings.
Heavy night-vision goggles allowed her to see clearly the
enormous mahogany desk, with its glass-like finish, free
of so much as a pen-holder or blotter. Behind it, a fat,
over-stuffed leather chair sat precisely in the center, as if
old Victor had measured off the exact middle and carefully placed his chair there before he left.

Her quick eyes cast around. Paintings she would never
be able to afford hung on the walls, nestled between a
gleaming brass sconce and a portrait of the current company president, as well as portraits of all the presidents that
had gone before him in the hundred and forty years of the
company's history. The United States flag hung on a polished wooden pole, beside the huge, frosted picture-win-
dow that screened out noise from the street far below. The
room looked every inch the office of a high-ranking em-
ployee in one of the most prestigious law firms in the city.

She made her way toward the walls, carefully looking
along each painting for signs of alarms or trip-wires. A
small, hand-held sweeping device told her that there were
no electronic traps lying in wait to trip off an alarm downstairs, or, worse yet, down at police headquarters. She put
her hands on her toned, athletic hips and shook her head:
lousy security for a company that did such sensitive business! They should be ashamed of themselves.

As she approached a glossy Japanese piece rendered in
black and red, a tiny beep sounded in her earpiece. Even
though she knew the source of the sound, it startled her
enough to make her step back sharply.

"Lizard?" she rasped. Her mouth was dry with nervous
excitement, as it always was when she was on a job. She
stuck out her tongue in an attempt to moisten her lips.

She tried finding her voice again, this time with more success. "Lizard, is that you?"

The voice on the other end of the wire was comforting; it held the absolute self-assurance that only the very young possessed. "Yeah. Who else? How are things going in there?"

"Just feeling my way around."

"Well, you had better hurry up. You've been inside nearly four minutes. Have you found the safe yet?"

She shook her head, even though her partner, who was up on the roof with all their surveillance equipment and climbing tackle, couldn't see her. "Nothing yet. Nothing behind the pictures."

Lizard laughed softly. "Look, Zhara, these are *lawyers*. No imagination. How well hidden could a safe be? Check the bookshelf."

She snapped her fingers. Of course; he was right. After the pictures, the bookshelf would be the most obvious place to look. She moved easily over to the vast rows of shelves that covered one wall. Law books—heavy ones, bound in fine leather and lovingly preserved—stood on every row. They were arranged alphabetically. That Victor Chlumsky was nothing if not neat.

She muttered to herself as she read the names off the spines: *"Accounting, Auditing and Financial Malpractice, Black's Law Dictionary, Legal Ethics* by Simeon Thorne . . . This last one stopped her dead. Against her will, her long-fingered, gloved hand reached out to lightly touch the deep burgundy leather spine of the thick book, and as she did so, her fingers shook. A vein in her temple throbbed a painful, staccato beat that was picked up in her chest. *His* book . . . the last book he wrote before he . . .

"Zhar?" The crackle in her ear snapped her back to the present, but for a second she was a little disoriented.

"Huh?" Damn that dry throat!

"Are you okay? Is something going on?"

She tried to clear her head. Her tongue felt heavy, but she managed to say, "I'm fine. Don't worry about me."

But he was growing worried. "Six minutes, Zhar." There was a note of urgency in his voice that couldn't be ignored.

"I'm on it." She tried to sound reassuring. "Don't worry." She continued her search for signs of a safe behind the books—and there it was: a little crack, a tiny seam in an otherwise perfect row of shelving. "Bingo," she breathed. Under the coaxing of her deft fingers, the wood paneling slid back, revealing a smooth metal rectangle just two feet by eighteen inches. An odd-shaped, complex hole awaited penetration by a special key—a key that only Victor Chlumsky possessed—and Victor just wasn't here right now.

Too bad, she shrugged. Whipping a flat leather pouch of tools from her belt, Zhara set to work. It was almost laughably easy. Again, she shook her head. To think that a powerful, reputable company like De Boers put up with a shoddy security system like this! What would the fine citizens of Medusa, moreover, De Boers' many wealthy clients, say if they knew?

The safe popped open like a toybox, and its contents lay before her, ready for the taking. "All done, Lizard," she gloated into her mouthpiece. Rifling through the piles of papers, small bundles of cash, and what looked like stock certificates, she was tempted to grab the whole lot and run, but she was there for a purpose. Her target was a small, buff-colored envelope made of thick, extravagant, embossed paper. For the person who had hired her, the small item was worth five thousand dollars; not bad for ten minutes' work. The envelope was easy to find, and as she stuffed it into the pouch that she wore around her waist for that purpose, she hissed quick instructions to her partner. "I'm out of here. Get the tackle ready, and open the skylight. Thirty seconds."

She paused, waiting for a response. None came. It took less than a few heartbeats for her to realize that something had gone terribly, horribly wrong. "Lizard?"

Nothing.

"Are you there?"

Nothing.

Oh God, Oh God, Oh God! Shaking, she tried to coax her stubborn hands to shut the safe and slide the bookshelf back into place, but all of a sudden her fingers were clumsy and, within the leather gloves, her palms began to sweat. She tried again, this time using her partner's real name. "Mickey, Mickey, for the love of . . ."

Zhara stopped. Something told her it was no use calling out to him. The room was suddenly very, very cold. She turned even before she heard the sound behind her.

"Zhara Thorne," the voice in the shadows said, "you are under arrest for burglary."

Zhara felt as if a bone was stuck in her throat. It was no use trying to make a sound. She knew none would come.

"I know you never pack a piece," the deep male voice went on, "so I won't draw on you. But let me tell you this, if you try any of your kickboxing crap on me, I'll drop you bare-handed."

She surveyed him warily. He was a shadow himself, dark and silent, unmoving. Her night-vision goggles allowed her to see him quite clearly, in spite of the almost total darkness. What she saw frightened her. He was a huge man, well over six feet, weighing easily two-fifty. The deep-gray overcoat that he wore made him seem all the more huge, and she hadn't needed to be told that its well-cut folds hid a weapon. His sharp features were cold and harsh, and his charcoal eyes had an eerie glow, like the moon in eclipse. She had no doubt that attempting to attack him would only lead to humiliating failure. Shaking with despair, wondering desperately what fate had befallen

Lizard before this man—this *cop*—had found her, she stood rooted to the floor.

The deep, booming voice went on, intoning the words that she had lived in fear of throughout her career. "You have the right to remain silent," the man began.

"Please, you don't understand . . ." The words were like shards of glass dragged from deep within her throat.

"If you give up this right . . ."

"It's not what you think . . ."

He steadfastly ignored her. "Anything you say . . ."

"I know what this looks like . . ."

"Can . . ." He continued implacably, reading off a small, tattered, white card that seemed almost consumed by his huge hand.

This was insane! The man was wrong about her. She had to stop him before he kept reading that awful, awful thing! "But I'm not . . ."

"And will . . ."

He wasn't listening. The man wasn't listening! She knew, just knew, that there was nothing she could do to make him stop. Miserably, she hung her head and let him continue to read her her rights.

"You don't understand," she tried again when he was finished. She held up her gloved hands, partly as a gesture of surrender, and partly in a plea for him to listen, just listen, for a second. "I'm retired." As she said the words, one of her thin, tempered steel lock-picking tools fell from her grasp and hit the thickly carpeted floor without so much as a sound.

Seeing it drop, and identifying the item immediately in spite of the low light, the huge man almost smiled. "That's funny," he said, and there was the merest whisper of humor in his voice, "you don't *look* retired."

Of all the stupid, stupid, stupid . . . ! She could have kicked herself. That sealed it. She was done for. Right now, she had two choices: deliver herself into this man's hands, like a lamb about to be slaughtered, or get out—fast.

High in her throat, her heart was suffocating her. Her gaze cast frantically around for a way out. There was only one, and that was through him—the huge, muscled, foreboding, dark bulk of him. *You never were a quitter,* she told herself, and bunched her strong, well-toned muscles in preparation for her last bid for freedom.

He read her mind—or simply noticed the shift in the tension of her body. With a commanding bellow, he raised a hand to halt her. "Don't even try it, Thorne. *Stop!*"

The surge of adrenaline fueled her determination, making it impossible for even such an unequivocal command to circumvent her decision. Her body was in flight almost before he could speak. She charged for the door behind him, and as she left her position by the safe and lunged forward, in those few nanoseconds that it took for her body to obey her brain's command, she saw his hand move, recognized his intent, and screamed.

"No!"

Too late. The big hand reached up, clicked on the light switch at his shoulder, and flooded the room with brilliant light. The last thing she saw was the horror on his face as he realized his mistake.

Night vision goggles work by drawing every particle of ambient light, even in almost absolute darkness, into the headset, magnifying it countless times. In a dark room, her eyes were given enough light for her to move safely around, perform small tasks, and locate her target. In bright light, the process was the same; the goggles reached out, caught every ray, every beam, and drew it in, magnifying it time and again, until the resulting flash was like a bullet to the brain, a supernova, filling her skull, her ears, her mouth, everything, with dazzling, paralyzing, blinding light. The effect was similar to staring directly into the center of the sun—at close range.

The man clicked off the lights almost instantly, but the damage had been done. Reeling, clutching her head, she staggered back, coming up sharply against Chlumsky's desk. Her gritted teeth would not permit her to emit the cries of pain that shot up from deep inside her. Her eyes were shut tight against the assault, and on the backs of her eyelids she saw dancing fireworks: red, gold, purple, green, blue. They hurt—they hurt so much! She whimpered.

Strong hands tore the goggles from her face, cupped her chin and forced her to tilt her head upward. "Let me look," the man said softly—amazingly softly—as if the monster that was bent on her capture a few seconds ago had been replaced by someone almost—kind. "You're hurt." His fingers touched her face, feeling her warm tears as they rolled down her cheeks, and for all the pain they caused her, they might well have been tears of blood.

But she wasn't giving up. Not now. Shoving her pain aside, she ducked left, feinted right, miraculously eluded his grasp, and was off and running. Python reflexes had him on her heels in an instant, following as she sprinted out into the hall and toward the skylight, guided more by memory and instinct than by sight.

He recognized her intent. "Thorne—no! Not the roof! You'll kill yourself!"

Ignoring his urgent warning, Zhara reached for the length of nylon climbing tackle that hung down from the skylight. It was the way she had come in, and it was the way she would leave. She was not a slender woman; her tall, supple body was that of a fighter, a natural athlete. With the sheer power of her arms, she launched herself upward, pulling herself up hand over hand, strong legs twining around the rope.

A hand grasped her black-booted ankle, but she kicked herself free. Then the sudden increase in the tension of the rope told her he was coming up after her. She was an expert climber, and one thing she knew was this: the rope wasn't strong enough to take their combined weights. It creaked a warning.

"Don't be a fool," he grated, just inches below her. "You can barely see."

"*You're* the fool," she panted. "The rope . . . it won't . . ." But there was no time for talk. She could feel the slim cord weakening under her hand. Her only hope was to get up, get up fast, before they both went crashing down onto the tiled atrium floor. With a triumphant lurch, she thrust her body up through the skylight.

Up on the roof, it was cold. The dismal October evening had deteriorated into a bitterly cold night, and a fine rain had begun to fall. She shook her head like a dog, grateful that her vision was slowly returning. Looking around, she scanned the wide roof for signs of her partner. She didn't have to look far. A few yards away, the young man sat with his back to the building's utility room, arms stretched painfully behind him, obviously cuffed. The albino's pale skin gleamed like the surface of the moon, and his eyes, the color of brackish water, were wide and panicked. A thin man with a shock of reddish-blond hair stood above him.

The grunt at her feet told her that the cop had made it up the rope and was levering his body through the skylight, as she had done. She stepped away from the hole as if the Furies were coming up through it and threw Mickey an agitated look. The problem was, if she left now, she'd be leaving him behind. Through a telepathy born of long association, he knew what was going through her mind, and nodded vigorously.

"Run, Zhar!" he shouted. "Go, go, *go!*"

Zhara ran, and the policeman was close on her panicked heels. As she neared the edge of the building, she heard him yell something, but the wind snatched the words from his lips. Their climbing tackle still hung over the edge, leading down all eighteen floors to the dark, quiet alley below. It was the only way down.

She grasped the rope in her hands and deftly clicked on her safety harness. Dropping to a seated position, she threw her legs over the edge . . .

. . . and was restrained by a hand grabbing her collar. "Give it up, Zhara." The intimate sound of her own first name on this man's tongue was like an electric bolt up her spine. For an agonizing moment, she was unable to move. He continued persuasively, voice low, so that only she could hear. "You'd never make it over the edge alive. Your eyes are shot to hell, and it's raining. Give it up. Come down with me. We'll take the elevator; it's safer. Come on. Think about the boy." He paused for two heart-beats, and then added, "It's over, you know." He said these last few words almost sympathetically.

She almost gave in. He was right. It *was* over. Something in her couldn't deny it. Then a movement she noticed from the corner of her eye caused her to look wildly around, in time to see the other officer approaching her from the side, weapon drawn and pointed at her. "Swing your legs back off the ledge," the blond man advised her, in a tone that brooked no argument, "and step down."

The first one let loose a curse. "Damn it, Ames, holster your weapon. I'm *handling* it!"

Ames hesitated for a moment, then lowered the gleaming pistol, and Zhara heard a soft click as the safety slid back on. Although he'd put his weapon away, he remained a few paces from them, waiting, ready to respond again if he were needed.

Pull a gun on her? Zhara's indignation boiled. A *gun*? The affront to her pride sent her innate stubbornness to the fore. Over? Not a chance! With the suddenness and agility of a cat, she twisted her head just enough to be able to close her teeth over the dark hand that still grasped her collar. She felt the skin split under the assault, heard the bellow of surprise, and felt herself being released. Without waiting to see how he would respond, she thrust forward with her body, and hurled herself into space.

She plummeted a good twenty or thirty feet into the wet night before her harness caught hold and pulled taut. Above her, two stunned faces peered over the edge, looking down. She saw the dark one say something to his partner, and then he disappeared. The other man stayed where he was, but, thank God, didn't draw his weapon again.

Zhara wasn't kidding herself. The man who had left could only be going one place: down. His best bet would be to make it down before her on the elevator and wait to catch her as she landed. And that, she decided, just wasn't going to happen.

Quickly, she began lowering herself, hand over hand, feeling the rope sway under the influence of her rapid movements. By the time she was parallel to the third floor, her guess was confirmed. Below her, the cop in the gray jacket stood, neck craned back, watching.

She hesitated and looked up again. The other man was still at the roof's edge. Her breath escaped her in a rush. She was between the devil and the devil. She clung to the rope, swaying in the chilly wind, mind whirring. *What to do?*

She lowered herself another few yards, just to give her body something to occupy itself with while she tried to figure this out. She, who had always prided herself on her intelligence and her ability to think her way through any situation, was thrown into a whirlwind of pure, giddying panic. She was in a whole lot of trouble; of that, there could be no doubt. *What to do?*

An idea that was so ludicrous that it would never even have entered her mind in a saner moment now loomed as the obvious course of action. If, and only if, she could lower herself just a little further to the second-floor balcony, she could get back into the building—smash her way back in if she had to—and make a mad dash to the back, where she could let herself out via the fire escape. It was almost laughably simple—but risky. And all she could count on was a few seconds' leeway before the cop was on to her. He'd be inside in a flash, and up the stairs behind her, or, if he figured out her intent, would simply race around to the back and be waiting under the fire escape. He was big, but she knew he was fast.

She looked down again. He was still there, still looking up, patiently waiting, like a hunter who had holed his fox and knew that sooner or later it would have to come up for air. The decision was made.

She let herself drop a few sudden, bone-jarring yards, until she was level with the balcony. The only problem was that she was a good ten feet from the railing; there was no way she could simply reach out and jump over it. Like a little girl on a playground swing, she began pumping her legs back and forth, building up her momentum until her entire body swayed like a pendulum. With each arc, she drew closer, until with one powerful thrust, she hooked a booted foot over the wrought-iron ledge.

The man below recognized her intent and let out an urgent shout. "No! Don't be a fool! It's too dangerous! Zhara, listen to me!"

She didn't listen. Pulling her body closer, she grasped an iron post with one hand. With the other, she clicked off the catch on her harness and let her umbilical cord go. She was loose, relying on her own physical strength and agility to survive. One leg was over the railing, and she was about to straddle it like a horse when—it happened.

Maybe it was the bright colors that still danced at the backs of her smarting eyes. Maybe it was the finger-numbing cold, or the rain, that by now, had increased from an annoying drizzle to an icy slanting assault. It could have been her confusion or her fear. Whatever it was, it caused her to make a mistake.

Zhara slipped.

The leg that still hung outside the railing failed to find purchase and, instead, skidded off the smooth metal, tugging painfully on her inner thigh muscles. Zhara found herself tilting sideways. In desperation, she clawed about wildly, but the wet gloves let her down, and the slick railing eluded her grasp.

The moment before she plunged headlong into the icy darkness, just before she hurtled into space to the cold cement two stories below, sending unimaginable pain tearing through her body, she heard just two things. One was the rushing of blood in her ears.

The other was the voice of the man below, who, powerless to break her fall, just had time for a single utterance: "My God."

Two

There were two places Cole often visited in the line of duty that he hated more than anything else. One was the hospital. The other was the morgue. He knew that it was only by the grace of the Almighty that he now sat on a hard, lumpy couch, ignoring his cup of coffee, in the former, rather than the latter. Exhaustion weighed on his shoulders. He rested his throbbing head in his hands as he tried to make some sense of what had happened tonight.

It had all gone so terribly wrong. It was supposed to be a good, clean bust—a simple arrest. No dangerous criminals—just a woman and a boy with a talent for finding their way into very high buildings. No drugs. No armed robbery. No record of assault. It should have been a piece of cake, but he'd fouled up royally, forced her hand, and look what it got her. Guilt: it was the cop's legacy. He wondered how long it would be before he could eradicate from his memory the sound of her body hitting the ground.

He rubbed the back of his neck wearily. After waiting patiently for three hours for some word, Brian Ames had gone up the corridor to find someone who would give him some information on how the surgery was going. St. Cyprian's was a good hospital, quite large for a city as small as Medusa, but adequately staffed. It was therefore surprising that there were so few people around tonight who looked as if they could be of any help, as far as information was concerned. But then again, Cole wasn't sure he really wanted an answer.

He flicked his wrist to check his watch. It was after one in the morning. His shift was long over, but he wasn't leaving until he knew the girl was out of danger. He drew a compact cellular phone from his pocket and dialed his own number. After too many rings, someone picked up. He heard his own voice on the other end of the line. "Hello?"

"I called three times, boy. Who were you talking to that you couldn't answer the call waiting?"

His son was silent for a moment. "Uh," he said, with a teenager's elusiveness, "nobody."

"Well, you better watch yourself, Omar, because I don't want 'nobody's' parents calling me up to tell me things about my son I might not want to hear, you read me?"

The boy laughed. "Sure. I read you. Don't worry. I got it all under control."

Cole shook his head. *Under control.* At that age, that's what they always thought. Too often, they were wrong. Not wanting to get into a lecture at this hour, he pressed on. "I'm just calling to let you know I'm delayed, and I won't be home for a while."

Omar snorted. "Surprise me for a change, why don't you?"

Cole smiled ruefully at that. It was true that there were too many times when he should have come home, but couldn't. He was lucky that Omar was patient, reliable, and had a good head on him. Still, absenteeism just wasn't the way to be bringing up a boy. He'd have to do better, somehow. "You made sure to lock up everything?"

"Yup," Omar said, good-naturedly.

"All the windows, too?"

"I'm not twelve years old, Cole," Omar said in exasperation. "Don't baby me. I locked the windows, the doors, and the gate. I turned on all the security lights.

I fed the dogs and watered the plants. I'm safe. Don't worry."

Cole sighed. Over-caution was *another* cop's disease. When you'd been this close to the criminal element, you learned really fast that "safe" is a very relative concept. "All right," he conceded. "I'll try to be home soon. You turn down that loud hip-hop a little, you hear?"

Omar protested. "But this group is *happening!* They're the best! You *got* to listen to them loud!"

Cole smiled at that, but he had to be firm. "Maybe, but I doubt Mr. and Mrs. Hung Wa next door share your opinion. From what I'm hearing over the line, you probably have their walls vibrating so much, all the clocks are falling off. Come on. Give them a break."

"All right," Omar conceded reluctantly, and was about to hang up before his father stopped him.

"Son?"

"What?"

"Just because you're almost as tall as I am doesn't mean you can go about calling me 'Cole,' you hear? It's still 'Dad' to you."

The boy laughed. "Yes, Dad."

"Take care. I love you, son."

"Uh." That threw him for a loop. At sixteen, he was at the age where "I love you" just wasn't cool—not coming from his father, at least. "Yeah," he finally said, and ended the conversation.

Cole folded his phone away and sighed again. He knew his last admission had made the boy uncomfortable, but he was always driven by the idea that he had to make him know it, by everything he said and did. He was the only parent Omar had. He owed him that much.

He was still deep in thought when he felt the weight of his partner settling in beside him on the squeaky vinyl-covered cushions. Ames looked as tired as Cole felt. He waited expectantly, but when Brian didn't seem ready to volunteer any information, he asked wearily, "News?"

Brian sighed. "Well, there's no damage to the internal organs, for starters. God knows how, but she's got no broken bones either. She's on a respirator now, but chances are good she'll be breathing on her own once the surgery is over. She took a nasty crack on the head . . ." He paused.

Cole had the ugly feeling that Brian had started with the good news and was just getting around to the bad. *"And . . . ?"* A muscle in his jaw worked nervously.

Brian shrugged. "There was some damage . . ." He paused and began again. "There was some damage to her skull. They're working on it." He couldn't go on.

Cole felt the blood drain from his face. "What do you mean 'damage'? Brain damage?" The mere idea of it made his body cold all over again.

Brian shook his head vigorously. "Not exactly. There was some bleeding inside the skull, between the membranes covering the brain. The blood collected there very fast, and put pressure on the brain. She was lucky they caught it so fast. The bleeding turned up on the MRI scan they did."

Cole's jaw worked. "And what's going to happen to her?"

"They're going in now . . ."

"Going in?" He didn't like the sound of that.

"They've got to relieve the pressure on the brain. They're going to pierce a small hole in her skull . . ."

"Sweet Jesus . . ."

". . . and drain the blood off."

"And what happens next? Is there going to be brain damage? What will happen to her?"

Brian shrugged. "No way of knowing. Not now. Not for days or weeks, probably. It's a head injury. You can never tell for sure with those. We'll just have to wait it out."

Wait it out? Cole was an impatient man. The idea of waiting to see if that bright, beautiful, young thief, who had almost been swift enough to elude him, would turn out to be somehow diminished, brain-impaired—it wasn't something he could bear to think about. He passed a hand over his brow.

Brian went on. "I called in to the precinct, so they could tell the boy, her partner, what's happening with her."

Cole nodded. It was the only humane thing to do. The young man would be spending an uncomfortable night in a holding cell. Leaving him in the dark about his partner's situation would be cruel.

"I called Eileen, too, and told her I'd be home late." Brian's blue eyes were miserable. He'd been married less than a year, and being away from his new wife any longer than he had to was pure torture. "She wasn't happy about it."

"Why don't you go on home?" Cole suggested kindly, although he hated the idea of facing this night alone. "I'll be all right."

Brian shook his head. He reached out and put his arm across his partner's tired shoulders. He was by no means a short man, but, given Cole's relative size, it was quite a stretch. "Don't be stupid. I'm staying here with you, man."

Cole didn't protest. He wanted company, and he was grateful that Brian would sacrifice a night in his wife's warm arms for a hellish stint in a cold hospital waiting-room. He simply nodded his thanks and then occupied his weary mind by watching the nurses bustle up and down the hallway and the people come and go. He continued to ignore his coffee.

Zhara awoke in a bank of clouds. Cool soft whiteness enveloped her, touching her cheek and cradling her head. In the stillness, she could hear her own breathing.

She realized she was afraid—of the strange pure whiteness of the place and of the fact that her body and her mind seemed separated from each other by an impossible distance. She opened her mouth to cry out, but before any sound could come, a dark angel appeared before her, hovering, his face just a shadow, but his presence very, very real.

Instead of crying, she whimpered, very softly, wanting comfort but unable to ask for it. Yet, somehow the angel seemed to know, because in that moment of terror and confusion, he spread his great ebony wings around her, like a diaphanous curtain, shutting her off from her fear. His comforting thoughts, his concern and empathy, penetrated her misty mind, calming her soul. Knowing that he was there to protect her, Zhara slept.

The next time she woke up, she wished immediately to be unconscious again, because her return to consciousness brought only excruciating, consuming pain. A shocked groan escaped her.

Then he was there again, her dark angel, standing at her bedside. Her drug-clouded brain struggled with the reality of his presence. Fighting to concentrate, she peered at the unearthly creature, and realized that the face she saw, though blurred, looked human.

"Zhara." The angel said her name, softly, in a voice that spoke of his own torment.

Was he calling her? Where to? Again, she tried to pierce the mist to clearly see his face, and something written on it brought back a memory that she knew was tinged with pain, but which she couldn't quite pin down.

He called her name again, with an urgency that scared her. She stared up at him, and the frightening idea struck her that he might be an angel of an entirely different kind. She swallowed painfully, her parched throat tearing at her from the inside. "Death?" she inquired fearfully of the specter.

Puzzled silence, then: "What? . . . Uh, no." He scratched his head as understanding dawned. "No, Zhara. Death isn't ready for you yet. Not for a long time." He said that with the determination of a person trying more to convince himself than his listener. "I'm Detective Cole Wyatt. We met up at the—the De Boers building." He struggled with what he had to say. "You remember? The roof . . ." He trailed off.

Clarity struck her with a blow so sure and precise that it would have jolted her upright, had her body not felt like it was weighed down by slow-drying cement. With the buzzing of bees in her brain, the images sped past: the elegant darkened office, the safe, the man in the shadows, and the blinding flash of light as fiery daggers slashed at her eyes. Then she was running like a madwoman, slithering up the rope like demons were after her, barely a whisper of air in her lungs, running, past Mickey lying on the ground, trussed like a chicken by those . . .

"Cops!" she yelled in panic, with all the remembered fear tumbling down around her like an imploding building. "Run! Run!" She was panting now, struggling to get up off the bed, but her feet wouldn't work and her head was a pain-filled gourd that would smash onto the ground if she tried to get up, shatter into a thousand pieces, and she would never be able to put herself together again.

She felt a hand on her shoulder. She flinched, afraid it might be the big, dark man who frightened her so much, but instead it belonged to a short, thin doctor with a long, sad face, who was flanked by a nurse in crisp white, with an equally long, sad face. The nurse was murmuring something motherly, while the doctor was insistently pressing her back into the pillows, telling her not to try to move.

"Why?" she demanded. How could this man be telling her to stay still, when Mickey was still up there on the roof

in the rain, and this dangerous, dangerous man was standing at her side, like a predator, waiting to claim her like
a spoil of war?

"I'm Doctor Narayan," the man was saying, with more
than a hint of an Eastern accent. "You've been injured in
a very bad fall, Miss Thorne."

Zhara stared at him. "Injured?"

He nodded patiently. "You fell from a building. You hit
your head very hard; we had to perform emergency surgery when you came in." A wave of his hand indicated
her head. "Please, try to remain calm. Don't try to move."

Zhara stared at him, mouth slack with horror. What did
he mean, hit her head? She tried to lift her arms to her
skull to feel the truth of his words, but, to her horror,
only one hand—her left—managed the strength to reach
up and encounter the turban of white gauze that surrounded her head. Her other hand lay limp on top of the
sheet, unmoving. Less concerned about her head than
she was about her unwilling arm, she tried to lift it.

Nothing.

"My arm," she gasped after a while. "Can I feel it?"

The man, the detective, leaned forward sharply. *"Can*
you?"

She shook her head, confused. "I don't know. I feel
something . . ."

The doctor intervened. "Miss Thorne, please. Don't try
to move anything. Don't try to feel anything. Just rest. It's
the only thing you can do right now."

Zhara watched as the sad-faced doctor hemmed and
hawed over a clipboard for a few moments, tapped his
feet nervously, and turned to leave. He couldn't! Not like
that!

"Wait!" she begged him. "What's happening to me?
Why can't I move my arm?" In anxiety, she tried to sit up
and throw her legs over the side of the bed, ready to
pursue the doctor as far as the door, if that was what it

took to get him to listen to her. Devastatingly, only one leg shifted. The other—her right—lay like a log. Bewildered, she looked down at her lower half and touched her leg gently with the hand that agreed to move at her command. It registered the sensation of being touched, but ignored her coaxing to move.

The doctor studied her solemnly for a few seconds, and then returned to the foot of her bed. Zhara felt her chest heave rapidly as panic clawed its way down her throat. The possibilities were more than she was willing to contemplate. "Am I—paralyzed?" she finally managed to ask, her very tone begging the doctor to tell her it wasn't so. She felt the tears begin to sting.

A large, strong hand landed lightly on her shoulder and squeezed gently. "Zhara, take it easy." The detective's voice was soothing in her ear, and the caring timbre of it alone calmed her slightly. But she insisted, repeating the question.

"Paralyzed?" The doctor wrinkled his brow. "I don't think so. Probably not."

The detective burst in. "*Probably* not—what's that supposed to mean?"

The doctor lifted a hand, addressing Zhara rather than Cole Wyatt. "You've suffered what is called a subdural hematoma—that's bleeding under the membrane encasing your brain. You hit your head very hard, after all." He turned an accusing look on Cole, who flushed guiltily, before going on. "When that happened, the blood probably pooled against the area of your brain responsible for motor control. You hit the left side of your head, so the corresponding side, your right side, will be a little weak."

"Weak?" Zhara demanded. "Just weak? Not paralyzed?"

"Probably not."

She didn't like the word "probably." She watched as the doctor withdrew a bunch of keys from his coat pocket and shifted aside the white sheets to reveal her bare legs.

Cole's black eyes flicked along them, just briefly, before respectfully focusing elsewhere. The doctor lifted her unmoving foot and scraped gently along the sole with a single key. It was like listening to fingernails drawn along a blackboard—a jangle on the nerves.

"Did you feel that?"

She nodded. He prodded her palm lightly, and she nodded again in affirmation.

He stepped away. "You haven't been paralyzed, Miss Thorne, but the area of your brain responsible for translating commands into movement has been affected."

"What does that mean?" Cole demanded.

"It means she will have difficulty moving for some time. Movement should eventually return." He shrugged. "In the meantime, she needs to get some rest."

He was leaving again! Zhara wouldn't let him until he answered another question. "How long? I want to get out of bed. Will it be days?"

The doctor said nothing, but his long face grew longer.

She tried again, more insistently. "Weeks? Tell me! Will it be weeks?"

Still nothing from the sad face, not a shift in expression, except maybe for a brief glimmer of pity that was gone so fast she wasn't sure it was ever there. Instead of confirming or negating her pathetic, hopeful query, he turned again to go. "Rest," was all he said before he made his way through the door. As the door swung open, Zhara caught a glimpse of a blue police uniform. The implacable sentry posted outside caught her eye but did not react. The door swung shut again.

Trapped. There was at least one police guard at her door, which was bad enough, but inside the room, right here next to her bed, was *that man*. She was a holed fox, and there was no way to escape. Then another thought came to her, one so cynically funny that she would have laughed if she could: she was being guarded, but if what the doctor had said was true, she couldn't have escaped even if she wanted to. What would she have done—leaped to her feet and dashed out the door?

Zhara lifted her leaden left arm up to her hot face—at least as far as the nest of wires and tubes that were attached to it would allow. The dryness of her mouth penetrated her down to her center. The rasp of her voice in her own ears was alien to her as she sobbed.

"Give her something to drink," the detective said, in a voice that would have no opposition. The nurse flinched under the commanding tone and immediately responded by fetching a glass from the nightstand next to the bed. The nurse's gentle hands helped Zhara to sip, and from the plain, standard-issue hospital glass, she drank the nectar of the gods. When she had had enough, she lay back onto her pillows.

Cole Wyatt leaned forward, his black eyes holding her wide, exhausted brown ones steady. "Zhara?"

She looked up, with venom and resentment in the thrust of her jaw, into the face of the man who was responsible for all this, the man who had hounded her like a common criminal up to the top of the roof, and said, "What, *cop*?"

He inhaled sharply, as if for a moment he had forgotten that they were on different sides of the legal fence, that he was some kind of crusading avenger with a badge, and she was, well—something else. He squared his shoulders and stood a little straighter, his concerned face losing some of the softness. "I wanted to say that I'm—sorry. Sorry that it came to this."

She snorted. "It would have come to nothing, if you hadn't chased me out of there like . . ."

It was his turn to snort. "You shouldn't have run," he said, self-control alone preventing him from shouting. "You resisted arrest. I ordered you to stop, and you resisted. It didn't have to be like this."

"Do you blame me? Do you blame me for running? You barge in on me like that, scare me, and don't expect me to run?" She laughed hoarsely in his face.

"You were committing a felony. A *crime*. It was my job to stop you. Do you understand?" The black eyes were on fire. He sensed that he was losing control, inhaled, deep chest rising, and stood back. As he struggled to get the better of himself, Zhara looked at him; for the first time he stood in light bright enough to see clearly by.

He was even larger in the light than he had seemed in the dark. The man's chest was a wall of muscle, and, even lying down as she was, she could tell he was uncommonly tall. His crinkly black hair was closely cut, and the walnut-toned face, far from being sculpted by a fine artist, was hewn from a tree trunk with an ax. Foreboding, indeed. She looked at her captor, searching for a weak spot that she could find and use to her advantage—anything to get herself out of this mess. She could find none.

"You've got this all wrong," she said, more to the stained hospital ceiling than to him. "I'm innocent. I wasn't doing what you thought I was, back there. I wasn't stealing. I'm ret—" She caught herself in midword. She was almost sure she had told him once before, but it made no sense compounding the error; wouldn't telling him that she was now retired simply confirm his ideas about her in the first place? "I—it's hard to explain."

He wasn't that easily diverted. "I know," he said, sarcastically. "You're retired. That's why you were in the De Boers building in the middle of the night, elbow-deep in someone else's safe, dressed up like a ninja when I found you."

She was too tired to fight. Exhaling through pursed lips, she closed her eyes. Then another concern forced them open again. "What about Mickey? What have you done with him?"

Cole bit his lip. "Mickey's still down at the precinct. He

was charged, and he's due to attend an arraignment hearing on Monday."

Zhara shook her head. Poor Mickey. What had she done? Why had she dragged him into this? At the time, it had seemed the only way. He was too young for jail—too *sick* for jail! With the sixth sense that only two people who had spent all their time together for years could have, she had an image of him, huddled on a hard bench, miserable face buried in his hands. Under cold institutional light, his pale albino's skin was almost translucent, echoing a fragility that only she knew he possessed. Mickey wasn't made to be locked up; all his life, and half of hers, they had been running from restrictions, shying away from walls and controls. And now he was in a locked cell with no one there to console him—thanks to Cole Wyatt.

She gave him a baleful glare. "Has he been in there all night?"

Cole looked confused. "All night?"

"Since you had him handcuffed in the rain last night. Have you had him locked up since then?"

She didn't like the way he looked at her. Something told her that what he was about to say wasn't anything she would enjoy hearing. She steeled herself.

"Zhara, that wasn't last night. You've been unconscious a long time. You fell three nights ago."

Stoically, she accepted this information, her face betraying not a glimmer of emotion. Better to reveal nothing than to let this cop see her cry.

"He's been asking about you. When I leave here, I'll go over to the precinct and tell him you're awake."

She didn't thank him. Another concern assailed her. If she had been asleep for three days, then . . . "Catastrophe," she muttered.

He leaned closer to her to be sure that he had heard her correctly. "What?"

"Catastrophe!" she repeated, more agitated now.

His black eyes were concerned again. "I know, Zhara. But you're very young. You'll heal. There are so many treatments available. So many ways they can . . ."

She interrupted, irritated. He'd totally misunderstood. "No, no, my *cat*. Her *name* is Catastrophe. She's alone in my apartment. If I've been here three days, then . . ." she broke off, not willing to make the poor creature's suffering any more of a reality by speaking it.

Finally, he seemed to understand. "She must be starving. And thirsty. Did she have much water?"

"She had a big bowl, but that'll probably be gone by now. Someone has to go help her." She turned her pleading eyes on him. "Someone has to go help her, fast!"

Cole whipped out a small notebook from his jacket pocket. "Give me the name and number of a family member, someone who you trust, and I'll call and explain the situation to them."

She shook her head. "I haven't got any family."

He was skeptical. "No one? No Siblings? Cousins? Aunts or uncles?"

"No," she said sadly.

He still held the pad in hand, ready to write. "What about friends, then? A boyfriend?"

"No," she answered shortly. Didn't he understand? There was no one. She had just two friends. One was in her apartment in the dark, dying of thirst. The other was in a holding cell, thanks to *him*. "Nobody."

He tried one last time. "A neighbor?"

She avoided his incredulous gaze. It was embarrassing to admit to a stranger that she had somehow contrived to live a life cut off from almost everyone. How could she explain that hers was a life of shadows, in which the only persons she made contact with were grocers and newsstand vendors, bus-drivers and librarians? That the sum total of her human contact involved simple, impersonal, mundane transactions, the purchase of the items she needed to survive, and casual, accidental meetings on the rare occasions that she chose to go outside into the street?

After so many years of running and hiding, knowing that one day those that searched for her would eventually track her down, how could she ever have found the time, the courage, the *trust*, to allow herself to get close to someone? How could she ever get into the habit of making friends? Even now, when her original reason for taking flight was no longer valid, she had somehow, along the way, managed to muck up her life so badly that she was still a fugitive, only now she was a fugitive of a different kind, and the consequences of her capture would be far more serious.

But what was she thinking? She *was* caught. She was this man's captive. The physical prison that made half her body immobile felt nowhere near as confining as the trap in which he held her.

She glanced up at him through her thick, sooty eyelashes. His eyes were fixed on her, and he was still holding the pad and pencil at the ready, waiting for an answer. "You don't understand," she began. "In my neighborhood, you don't see your neighbors much. I can't say I know anybody there. I mean I know their faces, but . . ."

He shut the book with a snap and put it away. "I'll call Animal Services," he offered.

She wailed in protest. "No! I don't want her put in some awful cage full of other cats. She'd hate that. She values her freedom too much. If they lock her up, she'll waste away."

The look on his face told her that he knew she was talking as much about herself as about the cat. He sighed. "This isn't exactly regulation," he said at last, "but if you like, I'll drive over to your apartment and take care of her for you."

It was crazy, but it seemed like the only sensible choice. She nodded. "Thank you." It galled her to be depending on her captor for salvation, but she had no other choice. Stubbornness, even hesitation, would only bring more moments of distress for her poor cat. "I would be grateful if you could—help." She looked down at her hands, one nervously twisting, the other almost immobile. Angry purple bruises covered them both.

The man nodded. "Tell me where your keys are, and I'll go there right away."

Zhara hesitated. "I don't have keys," she finally told him.

He looked as if he wasn't sure he'd heard right. "No keys? You don't have keys to your own apartment?"

She never carried keys, especially not on a job, so as not to leave any evidence around in case she dropped them, but she certainly wasn't telling *him* that! She hesitated. "I—uh—don't use them. I know a couple of ways in."

"I'm sure you do," he said dryly, and shrugged. "Well, I learned a few lock-picking tricks of my own along the way, so I suppose I can find my way around it. Any booby traps?"

She shook her head. He nodded, stepped away from her, and took a few paces toward the door before he stopped again. "Could I bring you anything from there? Clothes? Books?"

She shook her head, reluctant to ask for more help. She watched him open the door, again revealing the sentry that stood outside. "Wait!" she called him back.

Immediately he stopped short, head turned toward her, inquiring brow raised. "Yes?"

"I haven't given you my address."

He cut her off with an upraised hand. "Well . . ." He smiled almost sheepishly, and Zhara was amazed to notice that this man, this huge, tough mountain of a man, possessed a pair of dimples that would have graced the face of a cherub. Taken aback, she almost smiled in return.

"As for your address," he went on, "I've got a file on you an inch thick. I guess I could find it in there somewhere." With that, he bowed slightly and left the room.

A file, he'd said. An inch thick. She'd always imagined herself to be some kind of mysterious ghost, stealing in and out of buildings in the dead of night, undetected. She'd prided herself on her skill as a thief. Sure, there were always investigations. Sometimes she read about her own exploits in the papers, but she had never suspected that anyone had managed to make any connections between her and the spate of missing documents, stocks, bonds, and jewelry that seemed to be affecting high-rise buildings in Medusa over the past few years.

But this man had a *file* on her. It was a frightening thought. Her quick mind pieced things together; he wasn't just a cop investigating a call that night. He'd called her by name, and knew who she was. He'd been following her, perhaps for a very long time, waiting for her to make a mistake, and that night, she'd made one.

It was almost ironic. She'd been claimed by the streets— was it only seven years ago? She'd found herself engulfed, sucked down into them, without any tools for her survival other than her razor-sharp mind and agile body, first committing small crimes of necessity, later growing more ambitious, wreaking her own vengeance on the society that had cast her out by turning her stealth and speed into a career in crime, robbing from the rich.

In all that time, she hadn't spent a day in captivity. In all that time, she'd fancied herself to be moving undetected through the dark side. She'd even had a kind of arrogance about it, sure that she hadn't been caught because the police were simply too stupid. And now—now that she'd made the decision to climb back up out of the mire in which she'd wallowed for so long, bringing poor young Mickey out with her, she was trapped.

This time, she was innocent. The cop, Cole, hadn't be-

lieved her back in Chlumsky's office that night, but she'd
been telling the truth. She wasn't doing what he thought
she was—not stealing, not exactly. Rather, she was on a
mission that would pay her the money she and Mickey
desperately needed. Her quest had required stealth, secrecy, and deception, but it was all for the eventual good.
It wasn't a crime. The only problem was that there was
just one person who could save her, and that person
wasn't likely to step forward.

Air forced out between Zhara's clenched teeth. She'd
woven a very tangled web for herself, and something told
her that the spider who had finally caught her, in the
shape of Detective Cole Wyatt, wasn't about to let her go
without a fight.

Three

"You've finally lost your marbles," Brian Ames informed his partner, puffing slightly. He had to struggle to keep up. Impatient as ever, Cole was striding along the sidewalk, long legs hitting the paving with his characteristic, rhythmic pounding. "I've got half a mind to ask the captain to send you down for a psych. evaluation. The city shouldn't let crazy people carry guns on its behalf."

"Ha ha," Cole countered dryly as he strode briskly through Zhara's neighborhood.

Brian was insistent. "You've *got* to be out of your tree if you think you're just going to let yourself into a perp's apartment . . ."

"*Alleged* perp's apartment." Cole corrected him.

"Oh, *alleged* perp's apartment. Do you mean to say there's actually some doubt in your mind as to her guilt? You caught her in front of an open safe, with a belt full of lock-picking tools, in the dead of night, with a teenage lookout perched on top of the building. And enough climbing rope to hang half the state. And you're beginning to doubt she's dirty?"

The perplexed look on his friend's face prompted Cole to explain, even though he wasn't too sure himself why he was suddenly so touchy on the subject of Zhara Thorne. "I don't have the slightest doubt that she's guilty, Brian, but the law says . . ."

"I *know* what the law says." Brian brushed his explanations aside. "I just find it a little bizarre that you've been after this woman for years, and now that you've got her, and you have all the evidence you need to put her away, all of a sudden she's stopped being a perp to you. Furthermore, she seems to have got you under some kind of spell. I mean, look at yourself. Half an hour of conversation with her, and you're dragging me across the city to feed her *cat.*"

Although Cole would have been the last to admit it, his friend was absolutely right. For three years, this woman had been on his mind, a vague nagging, like a sore tooth, a discomfort that he couldn't silence but which he really couldn't pin down if he tried. On several occasions his sources had pointed to her as being responsible for a case he was working on, but apart from that, he had never had much more to go on than his gut instinct. All he had ever had that kept bringing his mind back to her had been a name, a description, and the desire to bring this particular law-breaker to justice.

Now that he had her, he felt not triumph but a niggling dissatisfaction, a kind of sadness that he could only ascribe to the ugly way in which the simple bust had gone sour. She'd been much younger than he'd come to expect (what was she, twenty-one or two?), so vital up on the roof, full of fire and fight (and he had still-healing teeth marks on his wrist to prove *that)*, and now there she was in a hospital room, looking pale, small and confused. The fire she'd faced him with in Chlumsky's office had gone out like a candle. Such a shame.

Of course! He pitied her; that's what it was! He might be a cop, but contrary to public opinion—and, obviously, *her* opinion—cops were human, and he did have feelings. He was partly responsible for the pain and distress in which she now found herself, and if his making a little trip across town could help her, well, there wasn't much harm in it, was there?

"It's just a cat, Brian," he said, in defense of his impulsive action. "It doesn't deserve to die of thirst. I wouldn't wish that on any creature."

"So you're doing it for the cat, then," Brian countered.

"I'm doing it for the cat." Cole hoped he was as convinced as he sounded.

"Uh-huh."

Partly to avoid any more pointed questions, and partly to get a little revenge on his partner for putting him on the spot like that, Cole stepped up his pace, leaving the shorter man several steps behind. He quickly glanced at the address he had scribbled in his black pocket notebook, although the gesture was hardly necessary; once he heard an address or number, he never forgot it. It was one of those little gifts that someone in his line of work learned to rely on.

Zhara Thorne's apartment was all the way over in Bedford, a neighborhood that wasn't exactly upscale. While it hadn't yet deteriorated to the level of skid row, it was only a matter of time. Around him, grubby, laughing children ran, skated, and skipped along the sidewalk in clothes that were too thin for this time of year. Storefronts were covered with aging but still brightly colored "Sale" posters, and speakers set up close to the entrances blasted music, trying to lure customers inside. There was little evidence of their succeeding. The entire area had about it an air of quiet, resigned despair.

He reached her aged brownstone building and stood, neck craned backward, looking up. For a second, he had a flashing image of Zhara, scaling down its side like some sort of Spiderwoman, but that memory brought with it another image, one of her slipping and falling to earth in agonizing slow motion, to an impact that would snatch her youthful agility from her like the shattering of glass.

Flinching, he shoved the guilt aside. He'd deal with that later, when he could think.

Brian finally caught up with him. "Seventh floor, huh?" he panted.

"Uh-huh. Walkup, looks like."

Brian shrugged in a way that said, *"Well, what can you do?"* He yanked open the heavy metal door that led into a small hallway that had seen better days. A single light-bulb was meant to illuminate the whole entrance, but failed at its job. Cole followed him inside.

By the fifth flight of stairs, Brian put into words the very thought that was burgeoning in Cole's mind. "You know, I don't get it. This woman has pulled off some pretty big jobs in the past couple of years . . ."

"Allegedly pulled off," Cole reminded him. As the words left his mouth, he couldn't believe he'd actually said them.

Brain went on as if Cole hadn't said anything. "She pulls off that government-bond heist down at the Trident Insurance place last year, and took those pearls from the Ainsworth Arms, the hotel belonging to that widow—what was her name?"

"Mrs. Ainsworth," Cole supplied with a smile.

"Yeah. Her. That and another dozen pretty neat jobs. Leaves no evidence behind, nothing we can use anyway, and somehow manages to make it through life unnoticed. All she's left us is rumors and speculation, and a couple of snitches who only *think* she might be connected, but nobody has ever found anything for sure. So she must be pretty smart. So tell me, if she's got all this money, what's she doing living in a dump like this?"

Cole had to admit he didn't have a clue. "I don't know, man. I was wondering that myself. Maybe she's doing something else with the money."

They were at the seventh floor at last. "Think she's a user?"

Cole gave him a serious look. "Drugs? I doubt it. Nothing turned up in any of those medical tests, and the only needle tracks I saw on her arms came from all those tubes they've stuck into her at the hospital. I know you can never be sure, but I don't think so. I don't pick that up from her. She was too healthy, too quick on her feet that night. I had a devil of a time keeping up with her."

Brian tried again. "Horses? Dogs? Cards?"

Cole shook his head. "She's too smart to be a gambler."

"What, then?"

Standing in the corridor at Zhara's front door, Cole whipped a small ring of fine metal tools from his capacious coat pocket, selected one, and inserted it smoothly into the lock. A few quick twists of his wrist and the door popped open. *Lovely*, he thought. Here he was, a detective on the way up the ladder, breaking into the apartment of a woman in his custody. This was one story he wouldn't be telling down at the cops' watering hole on a Friday.

He didn't have an answer to his friend's question, although he wished he did. The money she made obviously wasn't going into making herself comfortable, that was for sure. "Maybe she's one of those people who just can't manage money. They spend it as soon as they get it—you know, fancy clothes, restaurants, Caribbean getaways."

Brian didn't look convinced, but the question was left without further exploration when their attention was drawn by a high-pitched, plaintive wail at the back of the apartment. The cry was so much like a baby in distress that, for an instant, Cole was disoriented. Did Zhara have a kid in here, too?

The source of the cry came agitatedly out of a room at the back, running up to them with such desperation that neither needed to be fluent in cat-speak to understand her problem.

"Jeez," Brian breathed. It was the sleekest, most beautiful cat either of them had ever seen. The blue-point Siamese was obviously a purebred, with long, fine limbs covered in short, whitish, almost pale blue fur that darkened to deep blue at the ears, feet, and tail. Huge blue eyes took them in, flicking from face to face with a mixture of anxiety and curiosity.

Cole was nothing close to being knowledgeable about cats, but he did know that they didn't much take to strangers. This one, though, was distressed enough to forego the aloofness that usually characterized her species, and launched herself at his legs, meowing pitifully. She rubbed her big, beautifully shaped head against his legs with affection that one would only expect toward someone she had known and loved for a long time. The little display embarrassed him.

"Okay, animal. Take me to your water bowl." Amazingly, Catastrophe turned tail and glided hurriedly down the hall.

Brian was amused. "It speaks your language, Cole." He laughed. "Mr. Man's-best-friend-could-only-be-a-dog has found himself a kitty buddy!"

Rather than deign to answer, he followed the cat into a small room where, in the furthest corner, there were two empty bowls. One of them was a food bowl; he could tell by the faint dried line around the top edge that was all that was left of a meal that had been consumed three nights ago. The other bowl once contained water.

The animal paced at his ankles, growing more agitated by the second, until finally, unable to understand the unreasonable delay, it let loose the same distressed baby-cry that had greeted them when they arrived. Unwilling to see a living creature in such misery any longer, and anxious to fulfil the duty he had come here for, he acted.

Quickly, he strode through the doorway that opened onto a small bathroom, turned on the ancient tap, and filled the bowl with water. The cat fell upon it with obvious relief. He picked up the food bowl and returned to the sink, where he washed it carefully with a sponge that he found in the little cupboard underneath, one which he hoped was there for that purpose.

"I guess the cat food must be in the kitchen," he mused, making his way there. Brian followed and watched as he threw open the kitchen cupboards. Again, he was surprised at the austerity of its contents. There were quite a few cans, lots of pasta, but nothing to suggest that the woman spent much time cooking, at least not for any reason other than to keep body and soul together. Again, he wondered where her money went.

"Hell-*ooo.*" He had found what he was looking for. The surprise in his voice caused Brian to lean his fair head closer to take a look at the small can Cole held in his hand. The twenty or so neatly arranged cans of cat food were of a pricey deli brand, the kind pampered matrons picked up for their equally pampered cats down on Independence or Broad Street, the city's elite shopping district. He read the labels in amazement: smoked salmon, crabmeat, lamb . . .

"Cat eats better than she does," he commented.

"She must really love it." Brian voiced the obvious.

Cole nodded. "Better than she loves herself, maybe." The more he discovered about this woman, the more puzzled he became. He sighed and picked up a can of kitty pate de foie. "Well, let's feed the poor thing before it comes back out here and tells us what's what."

He returned to the bedroom with the now-filled bowl and placed it down in front of the cat, who had the good manners to signal her gratitude with a quick lick of her rasping tongue against the back of his hand before falling upon the food like the starving devil that she was.

Idly, Cole turned his attention to the apartment. A small bed and dresser were the only furniture in it. The bed was covered with a plain white sheet and blanket, with a single pillow tossed carelessly at the foot of it. He moved closer to the dresser, scanning the few items that were scattered on it. Two lipsticks, mascara, and a compact were the only evidence that she ever wore makeup. A large china bowl was filled with an assortment of hair ornaments, combs, pins, and barrettes.

He picked up a heavy wooden brush and held it speculatively in his hand. Like the cat food, it stood out from the austerity of everything else: its sturdy handle was made of a fine dark wood—perhaps mahogany. The thick black bristles were obviously natural, rather than the cheap plastic so much in use these days. Its back and handle were intricately carved, with deep, ornate curlicues inlaid with copper and mother-of-pearl, and even though the pattern was worn with constant use, it was obvious to Cole that it was an expensive item, possibly antique. Carefully, he put it down on the dresser again.

"No family photos," Brian remarked, glancing from the dresser to the bare walls. "No photos of any kind."

Cole turned his dark gaze on his friend, and for some reason there was a thread of emotion in his voice. "She doesn't have a family. That's what she told me at the hospital."

"Nobody?"

He shook his head. "A snitch I once had said she was a street child. Used to run with a gang up in Chicago. Didn't know much more than that."

Brian nodded. "Runaway, maybe." It was a story he'd heard too many times in his career before. Some young girl finds what she has to deal with at home so intolerable that the streets of a city the size of Chicago seem a better bet, so she runs and ends up being caught in a tangle of trouble far greater than the one she left. The heartbreaking thing about it was that no matter how hard they, as policemen, tried to solve the problem, they would never have the kind of resources needed to stem the tide.

Wordlessly, they moved to the only other room in the apartment. This time, there was contrast to the Spartan order and bareness of the room they had left. Clothes lay tossed everywhere: jeans, jackets, shirts, socks, and shoes covered the bed, the floor, and the table that stood in one corner. Posters of rock, rap, and hip-hop stars were taped to the walls, along with a monster print of the Sears Tower that dominated a whole wall on its own, and a huge CD player sat on a chair. It was obviously Mickey's room.

It was the same brand of player that Cole had given his son, Omar, on his last birthday. The posters on the walls glorified the same artistes that Omar worshipped. Cole swallowed hard. The boy he'd left in a jail cell waiting on bail that would never arrive was barely two years older than the boy who was at home, waiting from him to come in from work so that they could have dinner and perhaps play a few video games before bed. Two boys, with the same interests, but what different paths their lives had taken!

"The boy's room; Mickey's," Brian said, unnecessarily.

Cole nodded. He had always known that Zhara worked with a partner, but he had never been able to ascertain the nature of the personal relationship they had. He was not surprised to learn that they shared an apartment, but he *was* surprised to realize that he was relieved that they seemed to be sleeping in different rooms. Somehow, Brian homed in on his thoughts.

"Think they're lovers?" He stroked his red-blond mustache thoughtfully, as he surveyed the boyish chaos.

"No, I don't," Cole snapped. Then, he softened his response with, "The kid's barely eighteen."

Brian laughed. "Come on, man. We both know that's old enough. And there's only about four, five years between them. It's been done before, you know."

He knew only too well, but the possibility galled him so much that he refused to acknowledge it. "I just don't think so. I think she's set herself up as some kind of mother to him, or, at the very least, a big sister. She's very protective." He couldn't believe what he was hearing himself say. What did he care who Zhara Thorne slept with? Why would the mere suggestion that she could be involved in an intimate relationship with this boy irritate him so?

He was saved from the need for further self-interrogation by the re-appearance of Catastrophe, who, sated at last after her extended fast, came barreling into the room, licking her blue chops, almond-shaped eyes full of questions as to their purpose in Mickey's bedroom. She said this in so many words.

Under the barrage of loud, high-pitched yowls, Brian held up his hands. "Okay, cat. We've fed you, now we're out of here. You're ruler of the roost again, okay?" He turned to Cole. "Ready?"

Cole scratched his head, brow furrowed. "Damn," he muttered.

Brian rolled his eyes. "I don't like the sound of that." He waited patiently to hear what his partner would come up with next.

"What now?" Cole said, more to himself than to Brian.

"What do you mean, 'what now'?" Brian began, but by the time the words were out, he was speaking them to Cole's broad, receding back, as his friend was already halfway into Zhara's bathroom and rummaging around in a corner.

Brian watched in alarm. "Are you crazy? What are you looking for? Don't tell me it's evidence. We don't have a warrant. We can't just go digging through her stuff like that. Whatever you find, we won't be able to use it." He waited for Cole to stop digging. When he didn't, he tried again. "Are you hearing me? You come across anything in there, and the D.A. will have us for lunch."

Cole stopped and looked at him. "I'm not looking for evidence," he explained. "I'm looking for something to put the cat in." As if to bear out his words, he grasped a small wicker clothes-hamper and turned it upside down, emptying it of its contents.

"Put the cat in? Why?"

"Think about it," Cole said, trying to bring some semblance of order to the clothes he'd so unceremoniously dumped out onto the floor. "We fed the cat and it's fine now. But tomorrow, it's going to be hungry again."

"So you're taking it to the pound?" Brian sounded hopeful.

Cole opened his mouth, almost without intending to, and heard his own words come out of it. "No," he said, as he made his way back out into the corridor in search of the animal. "I'm taking it with me."

"You're . . . taking . . . it . . . with . . . you," Brian repeated slowly, just to be certain he was hearing right. "The cat."

Cole nodded wordlessly, deeming the question unworthy of a response.

"You, the man with the two biggest dogs in your neighborhood."

Cole had already made it into the kitchen, and was tossing cans of cat food into a white plastic shopping bag. "You'd rather I leave it here to die?" Brian was really getting on his nerves now.

Brian sighed. "Well, you always were a sucker for big brown eyes."

Cole lifted his head quizzically. A can of chunky turkey was clutched in his hand, halfway into the bag. "The cat's eyes are blue."

Brian grinned mirthlessly. "Wasn't talking about the cat."

Cole pursed his lips, not liking his friend's implication at all. He motioned Brian back toward the bedroom. "Stop giving me a hard time and get me the litter box."

This time, Brian put his foot down. "Listen, Cole, I love

you, man. I'd take a bullet for you. But that thing's got cat crap in it!"

Cole didn't even look around. "That's what it's for," he said, as he popped the surprised creature into the laundry basket and shut the lid fast. Brian made no move to do as he had been asked. Cole sighed. "Don't worry, I'll get it myself."

Brian sucked in his breath, patted his breast pocket for a packet of cigarettes, popped one in his mouth, and lit it. "It's your funeral," he told his friend.

Cole didn't say a word.

Four

The next time Zhara woke, it was daylight. Her foggy mind had cleared, in spite of the painkillers that the nurses had made her take the night before. She awoke with a feeling of sadness and despair as she had never before experienced, even in all the years of grief and isolation that had somehow conspired to lead her here, to this bed, with an injury that threatened to change her life.

On the nightstand next to her were a simple clock, a glass of tepid water, and a lamp. No flowers. No teddy bears with balloons and ribbons attached. No fruit baskets or hand-made get-well cards. The starkness of the room reminded her that few people knew she was in the hospital—and of those who did, nobody cared.

She was a prisoner, of her own body as well as of that man, Cole Wyatt. She thought again about Mickey. How was he handling his own imprisonment? It wasn't fair. Mickey was the kindest, gentlest soul she had ever encountered. Barring him up in a cell with criminals would be cruel.

Zhara pressed back into the pillow—a task that required delicacy, as her bandaged head still throbbed as if she'd been kicked by a mule—and sighed. She wondered how much of a respite her injuries would give her before Wyatt and his men turned up to interrogate her. When they did, she'd have to tell them that she was innocent. She hadn't been stealing—not exactly—merely retrieving an object on someone's behalf. The cop had just turned up at the wrong time and gotten the wrong impression. After she explained that to him, he'd let her and Lizard go— wouldn't he?

The remote possibility of her leaving the hospital a free woman almost brought a wry smile to her lips. Why would he believe her? As far as he was concerned, he'd caught her red-handed. He had even said he had a file on her, and that meant he'd been gunning for her for a long time. There was no reason for him to let her go, especially since she had no evidence to back up her pleas of innocence. There was only one person who could testify as to what she was really doing inside the De Boers building that night, and he sure wasn't going to talk, not when he knew that speaking up would jeopardize his own future. She was in serious trouble, and she couldn't see a way out.

The door opened, and, reflexively, Zhara stiffened, fearing that it was the detective. Seeing the round, soft, pink face of the nurse who had visited her most frequently so far, she relaxed. On her last visit, when she had come to draw blood from her for the umpteenth time, she had told Zhara that her name was Margie. She was in her early fifties, generously proportioned, and had her graying ash-blond hair drawn back and pinned neatly under her small white cap. Margie's bobby-pins were tipped with small yellow enamel ducks, an incongruity so startling against the sanitized whiteness that surrounded her that it caused Zhara to smile in surprise. It was the first time she smiled since she had arrived.

Margie came to the side of the bed and fussed with the white sheets, but Zhara had the impression that Margie really had no interest in them. Eventually, she asked, "What's the matter?"

"I thought you'd like to know that those two police guards have been moved from the door," Margie began.

"That detective, the tall one, called in and had them moved last night."

Zhara nodded. "I've probably convinced him that I'm not likely to run away," she said ironically.

Margie agreed silently, but said nothing. Zhara knew there was more. She waited.

"How's the pain?" The nurse motioned to Zhara's head.

It wasn't as bad as it had been at first, and Zhara told her so.

"I've got to change those bandages now. Ready to have a look-see?" Margie asked quietly. Zhara hadn't yet had the courage to ask how bad she looked, or even to request a mirror. The doleful look on the face of the doctor who had first visited her had been enough to dampen her usual stoic spirit. Look at her wounds—*now?* She didn't know if she could do it. She felt like a small child being encouraged by her mother to pull up the edges of the sheets and peep under the bed to see whether it really was inhabited by monsters.

"I don't know," she said, shaking her head. "It's too soon."

Margie ignored her weak protest and gently clipped away at the strips of gauze against her scalp with a narrow pair of scissors. Then, after carefully swabbing the area with antiseptic, she produced a pair of mirrors, offering one to Zhara, which she took with her left hand, and holding the other up to the side of the head wound so that Zhara could see the reflection in her own mirror. It was awkward, but it would work.

Zhara wasn't sure she wanted to look. Apprehensively, she rolled her eyes up toward the ceiling. What would she see? Her mind fed on images of incredible gore. What if she were bloody and gruesome? Suppose the damage was so bad she'd never heal? She, the natural athlete who could shinny up any building, any cliff face, who loved nothing more than the power of bare horseback pulsing under her as she raced across open fields?

It was too much. Against her will, her eyes clenched tight.

Margie laid a small, light hand on her shoulder. "It's not as bad as you think," she said, with half a smile in her voice. "And seeing it, knowing for sure, is certainly nowhere near as bad as wondering, and letting the demons of your imagination run amok. Look. Just open your eyes and look. Trust me."

Slowly, Zhara opened her eyes, first looking through her lashes like a small child afraid to stare fully at the screen during a scary movie, then, steeling herself, drawing the image in the mirror into focus, biting into her lip for courage.

Her face was a mass of bruises. Heavy purple welts loomed against her skin, like paint splashes on a cheap Halloween mask. Then her gaze traveled upward. A small patch of her prized dark hair had been shaved away, but the affected spot was so tiny that, if she were to undo her braids and comb her hair down, the patch would be invisible. Against her skull was a small, puckered scar that had already begun to heal. Was that all? Zhara didn't know what to think. She exhaled in surprise and relief.

"See?" the nurse smiled. "It's not so bad."

"But—my head feels like—like a block of cement. And my body! I feel like I weigh a thousand pounds. And I can't move my arm or my leg."

"You took a pretty nasty fall, unfortunately. But, we have good doctors here at St. Cyprian's. It will take some time, but with physiotherapy and patience, you'll heal." She took Zhara's weak hand in her own gentle one and brought her fingers up to her head. "I know it hurts, but it'll heal, too. You just need rest." She paused and smiled without a hint of condemnation. "And you need to give up this human fly thing of yours."

Zhara flushed. It was stupid how she had allowed herself to forget, even for a brief minute, how she had come to be here, and that everyone on the floor probably knew by now just who she was, even without the presence of the men in blue, who up 'till last night had been posted outside her room. She wished desperately not to be thought of badly by this kind, motherly woman.

There was worse in store. Margie took her time redoing the bandages before speaking again. "You haven't seen the papers since you've been here, have you?" she asked.

Zhara shook her head slightly, using small movements, afraid to cause herself too much pain. It wasn't as if she had any friends or relatives who would have provided her with things such as papers, books, or flowers. She'd had nothing for company except the walls around her and the endless reverberation of her own thoughts.

Margie dug into her deep pockets and fished out a tabloid, dated today, and handed it over wordlessly. Zhara knew the paper; it was a cross between a gossip sheet and a true-crime gazette. Its biggest advertisers ranged from bulk-rate supermarkets that lined the middle pages with clip-out coupons, to clearing houses for everything from "genuine" spy equipment to escort services. Not exactly the *Chicago Sun Times*.

It was opened at a page that was dominated by the photograph of a tall, dark-skinned man with a rough-hewn face, an almost frighteningly powerful physique, and a wide, full mouth: Detective Cole Wyatt. He'd been caught exiting the precinct building in West Medusa. Wind whipped at his heavy gray coat, blowing it out behind him like Dracula's cape. He was smiling at the camera, and again there was evidence of the pair of dimples that had caught her off guard the afternoon before. As before, the smile was at odds with the rest of him, which was nothing short of uncompromising.

Zhara shuddered, and, without being able to stop herself, held the paper closer and began to read. In true tabloid style, the headline was in bolder type than it needed to be:

> Another round to Cole Wyatt! Medusa's most decorated cop brings down a Lizard and a Cat!

With a churning stomach, she realized that the "cat" in question was she. She read on:

> Citizens of Medusa can rest easy once again, thanks to the skill and daring of the darling of their police department, Detective First Grade Cole Wyatt. While the rest of us slept uneasily in our beds, wondering who would next fall victim to the formerly unidentified feline burglar and her reptilian companion, long suspected of a series of high-rise heists across the city, Courageous Cole and his partner, Detective Brian Ames, risked life and limb to confront the sticky-fingered pair atop the De Boers building on Wednesday night. Sources say the two thieves were caught making away with large sums of money, stocks, government bonds, and checks when they made their desperate bid for freedom, firing several times at the two policemen while attempting to escape . . .

Zhara's mouth fell open. "I never stole any money!" she protested to Margie. Her brown eyes pleaded with the older woman for understanding. "There were no bonds, and I didn't have a gun! Nobody shot at anybody!" Horrified, she finished the article, which by the time it was over had painted her and Lizard as two hardened, dangerous career criminals, and Cole Wyatt as the nation's last crime-fighting hope. "They're lying!"

Margie smiled sympathetically. "Half the tabloids in the country will print anything," she told her, "if it will sell papers. It's a business, you know. Besides, most people just don't want to read the truth; it's too dull."

"But they make me sound so . . ." Zhara stopped. Why should she care what people thought of her? Why should it matter? Instead of going on, she folded the paper and thrust it back at Margie in disgust. "Typical of the man, I'm sure," she said, lips pursed. She'd heard of policemen who leaped at the opportunity to have their exploits lauded in the press. It helped their chances when it came to promotion time—not to mention what it did to their already over-inflated egos. An article like that every so often probably made him a real hit with the ladies.

"At my expense," she muttered.

"What?" Margie leaned closer, thinking she might be missing something important Zhara had to say.

Zhara shook her head. She was too tired to pursue it. "Nothing."

The story had made it sound as if she were at the top of America's Ten Most Wanted list. Yet this kindly woman was still extending a compassionate hand toward her. She felt ashamed—and grateful. She wanted to say that she really wasn't a bad person, to convince Margie that there was a reason behind all the bad things she had surely heard—a good reason, perhaps the best reason there was. Inexplicably, the woman's understanding seemed important.

"Margie," she began. The nurse had already begun busying herself, checking the battery of vials, dials, and tubes around the bed, but at the sound of Zhara's voice, she turned her head and her quick hands grew still.

"Yes, dear?"

"This may be hard to believe, but I . . ."

The door flew open, and Cole Wyatt strode inside, followed closely on his heels by the redheaded man who had pulled the gun on her that night. The paper had identified him as Wyatt's partner, Brian Ames. She scowled at them both. The words of explanation to Margie dried up on her tongue, and her mouth snapped shut. The last thing she wanted was for this man to know anything about her. What he already thought about her was bad enough. Some of it was true, she had to admit, but most of it was way off course. And so help her, she wasn't giving him the satisfaction of hearing her try to explain herself.

Instead, she tilted her face up toward him in defiance. Sensing the sharp rise in tension in the room, Margie made quick work of her tasks and scurried out.

Alone with the two men, Zhara waited. When last she'd seen Wyatt, he was on his way over to her apartment to rescue Catastrophe. For this small act of kindness, she was grateful, and her gratitude was enough to send the scowl that was forming on her face back into hiding. He'd done her a favor, she reminded herself grudgingly. She'd have to curb her resentment—at least long enough for her to find out how her cat was doing. She watched him, standing at the foot of her bed, and said nothing.

"Why didn't you tell me Victor Chlumsky was involved?" he began.

Zhara felt a hot ringing in her ears. Surely she wasn't hearing right. What could he possibly know about Chlumsky? How could he know? Had Lizard said anything? Did they wear him down until he talked?

She wasn't letting him enjoy the knowledge that his unexpected question had thrown her. With every bit of control that she could dredge up from within, she commanded herself to be calm. Holding his furious black eyes with her (thankfully!) steady brown ones, she spoke, measuring each syllable with care. "How is my cat doing, Detective?"

Cole looked like a bull that had been struck between the eyes with the business end of a sledgehammer. There he was, ranting about the circumstances of her arrest, and she was asking about a fussy Siamese? His surprise was almost comical.

To his credit, he recovered long enough to answer civilly. "Your cat is fine. None the worse for wear. As a matter of fact, it's being well taken . . ."

"*She* is," Zhara corrected him.

His brow furrowed. "What?"

"*It,*" Zhara explained carefully, "is a *she*. A female."

"And the second one in your household that's giving me a hard time," Cole muttered, still keeping a tenuous hold on the rage that had propelled him into her room. Behind him, Brian Ames struggled to quell a smile. Almost as if he knew he was providing his partner with a measure of humor, Cole wheeled round, froze the smile off Ames' face with a glare, and spun back to face Zhara.

"Listen," he said, "your cat is out of danger. As a matter of fact, *she* is at my house right now, giving my two retrievers a very hard time."

Catastrophe? At his house? For the second time in one minute, the man had managed to surprise her. She didn't know what to say next. "You took her home to your place? Why?"

Cole shrugged. "I wasn't prepared to cross town every day to change her litter box and top up her water, and from what you said, you don't exactly have anyone you could rely on to do it for you."

She stifled a retort at his obvious reference to her loneliness. Her resentment at his little dig was tempered by her surprise and gratitude. He'd done what she'd asked—taken care of Catastrophe for her. As a matter of fact, he'd gone above and beyond the call. She watched the hard, set face and marveled. He didn't look like the kind of man who'd take a cat home out of sheer kindness—and yet he had.

"Thank you," she said simply.

He nodded curtly and brushed the topic aside, as if it

were no longer important. With the relentless determination that had no doubt served him in good stead in his career, he dragged the conversation abruptly back to where it had been when he entered.

"Why didn't you tell me that Victor Chlumsky paid you to rob his own safe?"

Before she could speak, he took two steps closer to the bed, and, towering over her now, asked the question again. "Why didn't you say something about that before?" His angry black eyes held her rooted, and there was no evidence of dimples around the taut, hard mouth.

She, too, forgot about the cat. This was a question that could affect the course of her life. "I tried to tell you . . ." she began.

"When?" he interrupted loudly. "When did you tell me?"

Waves of anger rolled out of him and toward her, but she was not prepared to allow him to intimidate her. Her own temper began to rise. "Up there, in his office. Do you remember? I told you that I was . . ."

"Retired?" he asked, dryly. "Do you have any idea how often I hear that?"

"Well, it was true! You chose not to believe me! You chose to pursue me!"

"So why did you run?" he bellowed.

Her voice rose to match his. "Because I was scared! You turned up out of nowhere and arrested me! I tried to explain and you wouldn't let me! You chased me up the rope and cornered me—why *wouldn't* I run?" She could feel her nails digging into the palm of her hand, and the hot blood of anger flooded her face. The swine! He had made the mistake, he was the one who had refused to listen, and now he was asking questions? It almost made her want to laugh.

He made an obvious attempt to bring himself under control. His deep chest heaved as he inhaled sharply and swallowed. Drawing back, he began to pace. "Victor Chlumsky hired you to break in to his office, is that not so?"

Since he already knew this, she didn't see much point in answering. Goaded by her silence, he went on. "He hired you and your partner to retrieve an item from his safe . . ." Cole paused, and shook his head, almost as if he didn't believe it himself, *"as a test of the De Boers' security system?"*

Zhara wasn't going on until she found out whether this man had forced the information out of Mickey. "Who told you this?" she asked tightly.

Cole threw his arms wide in a broad, angry gesture. "The man himself, the Senior Vice President of the company you were caught robbing!"

She was unable to hide her shock. Chlumsky himself had told him this? At the risk of his own position with the company? "How?" she gasped.

Cole stopped pacing. "He walked into my office this morning and announced that he wanted to set the record straight. He said he couldn't let you go down for something you weren't guilty of. He told me that he was fed up with complaining to the Board of the poor security in the building, and that they didn't seem to believe him when he told them they were at risk. He said he decided to do something drastic, dramatic, to wake the company up, and that he'd heard of your—*reputation,* and decided to hire you to stage a break-in at the company and bring back a marked envelope to him. Then he'd have proof that the building wasn't safe." Cole stopped, and held her in his dark, angry gaze for such a long time that Zhara began to squirm.

"What?" she eventually snapped.

"I can't believe that anyone—anyone, would do something so dangerous, so harebrained . . ." he inhaled sharply, "and so stupid!"

"What's so stupid about it?" she shot back. "I told you, I'm retired. Mickey and I own our own security company . . ."

"Security company . . ." Cole repeated, sounding dazed.

"Yes, a security company. I've been straight . . ." she hesitated, since announcing that she'd gone straight was tantamount to a confession that she had indeed lived a life of crime, but there was no sense being coy. This man knew very well the kind of life she had once led. *"We've* been straight for a long time. We own a business. We show people how to protect themselves from theft . . ."

"By breaking into their buildings?"

She nodded slowly. "If that's what they want. Victor Chlumsky gave us thirty days to bring a sealed envelope back to him. He didn't want to know when or how we were going to retrieve it. All he wanted was the envelope, proof that someone could get in and out of the building—proof that the security of the De Boers clients was in danger. In return, he promised us five thousand dollars. It was easy money. Other times, for other clients, we just come in, point out all their weak points, and subcontract out to have security systems put in. But this time, the client wanted a special service, and we tried to give it to him. Why is that so stupid?"

"It's stupid," he explained slowly, like she wasn't smart enough to follow normal speech, "because it wound up putting you in a hospital bed."

"You helped put me here, Detective," she said, softly.

Her accusation was like a blow across the face. He winced visibly, and, before her eyes, his face took on a gray cast as the blood drained from it. His huge shoulders slumped, and he let his head fall forward into one hand. He seemed to be reliving those awful moments on the roof. Zhara almost felt sorry for him. Behind him, Brian Ames had not moved from his position against the far wall, but his sharp blue eyes were anxiously fixed on Cole.

Again, the telepathy that the partners seemed to have came into play. Without turning his head, Cole said softly to his partner, "Brian . . ."

Brian didn't need to be told anything more. He seemed glad to leave the emotion-charged room. "Sure, Cole," he said. He nodded politely in Zhara's direction. "Ma'am." *If he had had a hat,* Zhara thought, *he would have tipped it.*

Her lips twisted. The irony: a few nights ago, the detective was pointing a gun in her face. Now that she was cleared, she was "Ma'am". It was only good manners that allowed her to acknowledge his farewell.

They were alone. Zhara wasn't sure she liked that idea. As soon as the door shut behind Brian, she refocused on Cole. *Never let the enemy out of your sight,* she reminded herself. To do so would be fatal. What she saw threw her.

Still close to her bedside, he had not shifted or changed position. Yet his entire being, the angry aura of him, had ebbed, leaving in its place an almost broken spirit. She was confused. She peered at him anxiously. Was this a change of tactic? Was he simply gathering his strength for another attack?

Cole's silent head was still bowed—in deep contemplation or prayer, she couldn't tell. When he lifted it again, he was not the enraged bull that had charged into her room. Instead, there was guilt, sorrow, and pain etched on his face. The words came up from somewhere deep inside of him. "I'm sorry," he began, and then waved his own words away in frustration. " 'Sorry' doesn't exactly cut it, does it? I thought I was doing my job. I thought I was doing the right thing. Instead . . ." He stopped and looked away, aware of the inadequacy of words.

Again, Zhara had to struggle against the urge to say something comforting. So, he was hurting. Why should she care? She had enough problems of her own, and the man she was instinctively wishing to console was the source of most of them. Yet, there was something about his vulnerability that caused her to say, "It wasn't all your fault. I mean, I did a pretty dumb thing, letting go of my safety line. I panicked, and I shouldn't have."

Without any command from her conscious self, her hand stretched out and rested lightly on his arm. The effect was galvanic. Shock waves raced through her at ground zero, zinging, tingling. Her eyes flew open in surprise, meeting his, which were equally wide, equally surprised. She hadn't been prepared for the warmth of him; his solidity and his constant aggression had left her thinking of him as some kind of animated wall, a machine, Terminator made flesh. Yet, what she touched was a human being, and the unspoken communication that had passed between man and woman throughout the ages told her that right now, her touch was the one thing he needed to console him, more than anything else.

As with any other massive electrical overload, she found herself needing to break free of the source of all this terrible energy, but the power that raced from him and into her and back fused them as surely as if she had come into contact with a fallen live wire. With effort and a prayer, she tore her hand from his arm, jerking it back, expecting to see the skin on her fingers sear and fall away.

He inhaled sharply, nostrils flaring. Neither had the courage to speak before the other. Instead, they held each other's gaze, each aware of the other's erratic breathing.

"Detective," she began, at last.

"Cole," he corrected her. He still had not taken his eyes from her face.

She tried his name on her lips for the first time. "Cole . . ."

The door to her room blew open on gale-force winds, irreparably tearing asunder the fragile bridge that had formed between them seconds ago. Both she and Cole jumped guiltily, which was crazy, Zhara thought. What did she have to be guilty of? She craned her neck to look around Cole and see who or what could have burst so forcefully into her room.

The invader crossed the distance from door to bed in two strides and threw himself onto his knees at her bedside. Recognizing him, Zhara shrieked with joy.

"Lizard! How . . ." Her arm wound around his neck and she began to cover his cheeks with loud, enthusiastic kisses.

"They let me out an hour ago!" His pale-greenish eyes shone with excitement behind thin wire-framed glasses. "Chlumsky spoke up! He stood up for us! Can you believe it?" He laughed with boyish glee. "I swear, Zhara, I never told them anything. I kept my mouth shut, just like you taught me."

Unbidden, her eyes flew up over his head to meet Cole's. The brilliant fire in them had died; not even embers glowed. Again, there was nothing but cold, distant intelligence.

Following her gaze, Mickey noticed for the first time that they were not alone. Recognizing the other man, he bristled, withdrew his arms from around Zhara's shoulders, and faced him, ready to do battle, like a young fox throwing out a challenge to an intruding terrier. "What are you doing here?" he ground out, through teeth that were so tightly clenched that his jaw muscles bulged through his translucent skin.

Cole didn't rise to the invitation to rumble. Instead, he answered in civil, formal tones, "I simply came to inform Miss Thorne about what took place in my office this morning, Mr. Redding. And to let her know that all charges have been dropped, and that she's free . . ."

"Free to do what?" Lizard barked. "Get up and walk out of here? Not after the number you pulled on her up on the roof!"

Cole flinched, but, apart from that, showed no sign of emotion. He nodded in admission of the part he had played in the disaster. "I'm sorry. It shouldn't have happened. I promise I'll do anything in my power . . ."

"Your *power*?" Mickey spat out. "What power? Who are you? The Messiah? You're just a grunt on the city payroll—a *cop* . . ."

Zhara lifted a warning hand, anxious to intervene before the situation became any worse. "Mickey, stop."

Mickey's head snapped toward her at the sound of her voice. If there was one thing of which she could always be assured, it was his compliance with her requests. Not surprising, after all those years of being cared for by her, of having no one else to trust but her, Mickey was unquestioningly loyal. Thin chest heaving, pale face flooded with the blood of anger, he swallowed hard, forcing down the bitter stream of words that were striving to break free.

The conflict had been contained, but the sparks of anger still coursed through the air. Zhara was anxious not to let it go any further, and she knew that the only way of stopping it altogether was for one of them to leave the room. "Detective," she began. Addressing him as "Cole," as he had requested, would be unwise, considering their audience.

She didn't have to voice her request. He nodded. "Don't worry about your hospital expenses, or any therapy you might need. I'll make arrangements for all of it to be taken care of."

"Thank you." The cost of her care had been worrying her. The bill, which she was sure would be hefty, was one thing she certainly couldn't afford right now.

Cole gave a slight, courteous bow to each of them, and then turned to go. As he did so, he slipped one hand into his coat pocket and then stopped short. "Oh," he turned to her again, "I forgot." He withdrew an object and handed it over to her. "I thought you'd want to have this close to you."

It was her hairbrush. She took it, stunned into wordlessness. It was the only object she possessed that provided her with any link to a distant past in which she'd had all the things that children want and need: a home in which she felt safe and the security of knowing that she was taken care of, if not the comfort of knowing that someone loved her. Of all the possessions in her home, meager though they were, how could he have known that this was the only thing she owned that mattered? She ran her fingers lightly along the rough scrollwork on the back of the brush, eyes burning with the memories that flooded her.

Mickey was not as sentimental. He bristled again, ready to rush in to her defense. "Where'd he get that?" he demanded. Then he turned to Cole, eyes bright, and repeated his question.

"I retrieved it from your apartment yesterday," Cole answered levelly, aiming his response at Zhara, rather than Mickey. He was not letting the young man incite him into aggression.

"What the hell were you doing there?" Mickey snarled. "Did you have a warrant?"

Zhara thought it would be wise to intervene. "I gave him permission, Mickey. I asked him to go over and attend to Catastrophe. She had no food, no water . . ."

"So you let the detective that arrested you walk through your rooms? *Our* rooms? I don't even have to ask if I'll find everything tumbled when I get home. I'll bet he searched the place good."

"All I did was what I was asked to do," Cole defended himself. "I took care of the animal. I have no desire to carry out any illegal searches."

Zhara felt compelled to back him up. "He was doing us a favor, Mickey. Catastrophe would have died if someone hadn't gone to help her."

"And you asked *him* to do it?" Mickey was incredulous.

Zhara shrugged. "Who else would you suggest?"

Mickey swallowed hard. Even he knew that between

them they couldn't come up with anyone they knew who would be willing to do the same. He bit his lip and didn't speak.

With one last nod, Cole left the room. Zhara watched the door as it pulled silently shut, not sure if her anxiety was lessened or heightened by the fact that he was no longer standing at her side. Forcefully thrusting the treacherous thought from her mind, she focused her attention on Mickey. Holding out her arm, she invited him close to her again.

They held each other for a long time, lost souls finding anchors only in each other. Then she turned her moist eyes upward to his. "Are you all right? Was it horrible?"

He sighed. "It's a very dark place. Cold. And the waiting—for the sound of the guards' footsteps on the floor, for mealtimes, for anything that breaks the monotony of just being there and doing nothing." He shuddered.

Concern wrinkled her brow. "And the others? Did anybody frighten you?"

Mickey shook his head. "It's funny. I didn't wind up in a holding cell with the others. I had a cell near to the infirmary. It was quiet, and the bunk above me was empty. The other cells were full, but I had one of my own. Maybe someone up there likes me." He smiled weakly.

But, she knew that even in a small city such as Medusa, an empty holding cell was hard to come by. She doubted it was coincidence. A few people might have had the power to swing such an arrangement, but as far as she could guess, only one man would have had any interest in doing so. Mentally, she thanked Cole Wyatt.

For someone as gentle as Mickey, a crowded cell would have been awful; he didn't deserve to be subjected to the taunts and aggression of the others. With his angular features and closely cropped hair, the absence of skin color made it difficult to classify him as belonging to any particular ethnic group. Even Zhara knew nothing about his racial origins; she had never thought it important enough to ask. Still, they had both learned long ago that even in this enlightened age, an albino was the object of anything from clumsy, ignorant prejudice to outright rejection and hate. It was racism of a different kind. He had had to live with it all his life; she'd watched him suffer at the hands of others, and she was relieved that this time, in a place as dastardly as jail, he had at least been spared that.

"How are you feeling?" They both understood the reason for the concern in her voice.

"I'm fine," he assured her. "Honest."

Zhara knew her friend well enough to know that when he said "honest," he was being anything but. She laid one hand gently against his abdomen. "Any pain?"

He shook his head vigorously.

"What about your medicine? Have you taken it? You did have it on you when we left home, didn't you?"

Mickey avoided her gaze. "I haven't had it in a couple of days."

Zhara was aghast. "They didn't allow you to take it? Did they take it from you? If I find out they did, I'll . . ."

He stopped her with an upraised hand. "They didn't take it from me, Zhar."

"Then what? Did it fall? Did you lose it on the roof? What happened?"

His face was painted with broad bands of guilt. "I didn't have it with me. I didn't take it with me the night we left for De Boers."

"What?"

"I didn't need it." He shrugged. "It just wasn't necessary."

Zhara couldn't believe he was standing there telling her this. "What do you mean, 'not necessary'? Have you lost your mind? Don't you remember what the doctors said?"

"But I've been feeling fine!" he protested. "I haven't needed any pills in . . ."

"In how long? When did you stop taking them?"

He shrugged again. "Couple of weeks." He knew better than to look her in the eye right now. "Give or take."

She slumped back onto her pillows as if the air had been let out of her. "Mickey . . ." she began.

"Zhar, I don't need to get the lecture again, okay? I know it by heart. It's just that sometimes . . ." He stopped.

She understood. It drove her crazy, but she understood. She'd watched him during the times when he was so tired he couldn't get out of bed. She knew there were days when he went without food, because eating would only mean endless agonizing bouts of throwing up. Most of the times, it was the pills rather than his leukemia and all its related symptoms that caused him the distress. She didn't like it that he was cheating on his medication, but she understood, even though the price of his abandonment of his strict health care regime was a difficult price to pay.

Again, she looked down at her immobile body. They were so close to having the money to buy him the new life he had been dreaming of all these years. Although they had given up their walk on the dark side of the law, their legitimate work was still bringing in enough to get him what he needed—that is, until she fell.

It was something she and Mickey would have to discuss in detail later, but for now, he looked exhausted. He was wearing the clothes in which he had been apprehended: a leather suit similar to hers. Since they had both been drenched in the rain, the suit had shrunk and buckled. Now, it appeared to pinch and tug in a most painful way, and was as rough as cardboard to the touch. She was glad to see him, but she knew he needed rest.

"Mickey, I think you'd better go home now," she suggested.

He looked at her cautiously, like a reprimanded child. Sometimes, she forgot he was still a teenager. "You mad at me?"

She patted his cheek. " 'Course I'm not mad at you, Lizard. It's just that you must be tired after all you've been through. You need to get some sleep, rest up. You know that."

He had to agree that she was right. He didn't argue, but instead, kissed her lightly at the base of the bandage that was wrapped around her head, and prepared to go.

"One last thing." She stopped him before he walked out.

He waited.

"When you get home, take one of those pills. Please. For me."

She knew he was about to protest—would have loved to protest—but with effort he resisted, and instead nodded. "Okay."

"As *soon* as you get home," she emphasized.

"Okay." The only friend she still had in the world opened the door, went through it, and pulled it closed behind him.

And then she was alone again.

Five

"I think you have the wrong room," Zhara joked. Margie set down the huge bowl of pink anemones on the table next to her bed and grinned. "Nobody has *ever* sent me flowers."

"Oh, I don't know. They've got your name on them, and they arrived special delivery."

Zhara didn't have to look at the little card to know they were from Cole. In the past few days, he had lived up to his promise and was doing everything that he could to ensure that she was comfortable. He brought a small radio, which he personally set up and tuned to her favorite station. The next day he arrived with a couple of novels and a book of poetry.

She was grateful for the distraction from the pain and the boredom, but was not as certain about how she felt about his attention. She wasn't stupid enough to think that he was doing anything other than trying to assuage his guilty conscience; after all, he wasn't being nice to her, his prey, because he *liked* her, was he? She was just a loose end that needed tying up, and, meticulous as he was, he was doing it as carefully and as neatly as he knew how. In spite of this, she looked forward to hearing about how Catastrophe was doing; although Cole's visits never lasted more than ten minutes, he managed to fill them with stories of the ongoing battle between her cat and his two golden retrievers, Cain and Abel.

"Will the detective be visiting you today?" Margie asked, sniffing the flowers and smiling mischievously.

Zhara shrugged, not admitting that she had any interest in whether he did or didn't. "I don't know. It's getting pretty late in the afternoon. Maybe he's busy making the world safe from cat burglars," she said dryly.

"I'm sure he's only doing what needs to be done," Margie said sensibly.

Zhara sighed. "I'm sure." As much as she had to admit, even to herself, that she enjoyed his kind gestures, she never forgot that this man had a vested interest in seeing her pay for her crimes. True, he'd lost his hold on her over the De Boers issue, but he had a whole file on her—he himself had admitted that. What was to stop him from going back to the drawing board and trying to find another way to bring her down? She was simply a sick little mouse being brought trinkets by a large and dangerous cat. To let that knowledge slip from the forefront of her mind, even for a second, would be fatal.

As luck would have it, the devil walked in just as they were speaking of him. This time, he was not wearing his ubiquitous gray overcoat, but instead was casually dressed in a light blue sweat-top over darker blue jeans. His face and hair had the slightly damp look of someone who had just had a shower.

As he entered, both women were transfixed by the dangerous grace of the man, the suppleness and swiftness of his fit, muscled body. How could a man so large move with such confidence and precision? The bulging musculature that rippled under the close-hugging jeans, brought the unbidden speculation to Zhara's mind that if he looked that good *clothed,* well . . .

Cut it out, she admonished herself, but she had to admit that it was a pretty pleasant enigma. A quick glance at

Margie's suddenly heightened color told her that she wasn't the only person having such thoughts. Did he have this effect on every woman? Did he do it deliberately or was his unquestionable sexiness some kind of aura that he carried around with him unaware?

"Ladies," Cole boomed in greeting. He leaned over and gave Margie a light peck on the cheek, raising a girlish titter from the older woman. Having wreaked havoc with the nurse's composure, he turned to Zhara with an impish grin, as if enjoying the few seconds in which he was letting her wonder if she would receive similar treatment from those unbelievably well-shaped lips. Him, kiss her? Zhara dismissed the thought as ludicrous, but she was glad she wasn't hooked up to any device that monitored her pulse, because she was sure the sudden racing in her veins would have set off an alarm loud enough to bring half the interns in the building running in.

Cole came to the foot of her bed and looked at her without speaking. The fact that he didn't bend forward to her cheek brought both relief and disappointment.

"Nice to see you again, Detective," Margie simpered, like a schoolgirl. Then, disastrously, "Zhara and I were just wondering if you'd come today."

Zhara's mouth opened with shock. "Margie!" she began, but then embarrassment prevented her from saying anything more. It was one thing to admit to herself that she was looking out for him; it was entirely another for someone to tell *him* that she was!

Margie twinkled at them both like Puck in a white cap and scuttled out of the room. Zhara decided she would seek her revenge later.

Cole showed her both his dimples and stepped even closer. "Did you think I wasn't coming?" he asked softly.

She tried not to look at his face. "I just thought you were busy tracking down people like me."

He thought about this for a moment. "I'm beginning

to wonder exactly *what* you really are. I suspect that there aren't many people like you around."

She didn't know what to say to that, so she did the sensible thing and said nothing. She noticed that he held a small shopping bag under his arm, and in spite of herself, she began to eye it like an eager child.

Seeing the direction of her gaze, he changed the subject. "I brought you some magazines. I figured with all the time on your hands, you might be done by now with the books I brought you."

She accepted them gratefully. "You thought right." Taking the shopping bag from him with the hand that was still willing to move at her bidding, she fished inside and pulled out a dozen glossy publications, ranging from *Essence Magazine* to *National Geographic*.

"I wasn't sure what you'd like," he said sheepishly.

"So you got a little of everything." She smiled with pleasure, in spite of her resolution to be always on guard with this man.

He bit his lip, watching her as she rifled through her loot. A strange look flitted across his face, and she called him on it, brow furrowed. "What?" Had she gone and done something wrong again?

"That's the first time you've ever smiled at me." There was wonderment in his voice, as if he didn't know she was capable of it, but that the revelation was a pleasant surprise.

She shrugged, trying to sound offhand. "It's the first time you ever really deserved it."

"Back in a sec," he said suddenly, making an elaborate pretense of leaving.

"Where are you going?"

"Down to the hospital bookstore to get a couple dozen more magazines!" His laugh came up from deep inside him, and Zhara was only half surprised to note what a pleasant sound it was. The effect was stunning. His stern, rough face was transformed; he looked handsome rather than fearsome, broad features softened by mirth.

"Maybe I'll just read through these first," she suggested sagely.

"Maybe you should," he agreed. He stood next to her bed and watched her as she examined them. She came across one slim magazine and stopped in surprise. Cole Wyatt had done it again: somehow he had managed to home in on something that was extremely dear to her. How?

Wordlessly, she stared at the periodical in her lap. The issue of *Practical Horseman* magazine featured a splendid black thoroughbred jumping cleanly over a hurdle in what was obviously a contest setting. The young rider and the horse itself formed a single unit with a specific goal: winning the competition.

She stroked the horse's face with a light finger, drawing it down along the stately head to the powerful curve of his back. As memories rushed into her, her throat burned with tears that should have been shed years ago, but which never had been.

The change in her mood didn't escape Cole's watchful eyes. "Something wrong?"

"Why did you buy this?" she choked. It wasn't the kind of thing you just picked up when you didn't know what someone liked to read!

"If you don't like it, I can take it back," he offered anxiously.

"No, I—I just wanted to know what made you choose this. You don't know me; how could you . . . ?"

"How could I what?"

"How could you have known how much I love horses?" She turned her eyes up to meet his, then hastily looked away. He was proving to be much too good at guessing things about her; the less chance she gave him, the better.

He paused for a while. "I didn't know. I just thought you looked like a horse person. Have I offended you?"

She shook her head, trying to dismiss the dull pain that had enveloped her. He was only being nice; he didn't deserve to feel that he'd made a faux pas in his generous gesture, especially when there was no way she could tell him—no way he would ever understand the whole story. She tried to make her hurt less than it was, brushing it away with her hand.

"It's nothing. I owned a horse once. It just brought back memories, that's all."

He looked genuinely interested. "Tell me about it."

She sighed. "He was a silver gelding; his name was Windfleet. He was a jumper. We even made it to the Grand Prix. He had so much heart . . ." she couldn't go on.

His eyes, dark with concern, were on her trembling mouth. "Did he die?" he asked gently.

She shook her head. "Well, it was a long time ago, and I doubt he's still alive anymore." That thought alone was almost enough to send the tears prickling to her eyes, but she continued. "But that's not how I lost him. They—er, he was sold. My father . . ." She stopped, wondering how best to phrase her words to cause her a minimum of pain. "There were money problems, and he had to be sold." She threw up her hand in a gesture that said, "What else can I tell you?" and fell into a melancholic silence.

Cole seemed to think about this for a while, looking as if he wanted to comfort her, but didn't know how. "I'm sorry," he managed finally.

Again, she brushed it away. "It's nothing. Really."

They both knew it was far from nothing, but each was willing to let the matter drop. For the second time in a few minutes, Cole was obliged to change the subject.

"I see they took the bandages off your head." He peered forward to get a better look at her surgery scar. As he did so, she caught the scent of him—a sporty, woodsy smell that she knew with her woman's instinct was only half due to his after-shave. The rest of it, her quickly responding body told her, was all him. She swallowed hard.

"There's just a little scar," he told her, apparently oblivious to her response. "It looks pretty good. Your hair will grow back before you know it."

She flushed at the reference to her bald spot. Small as it was, it wasn't something a woman would feel comfortable having stared at, especially someone like her, who was so proud of her head of tumbling dark curls.

"How are you healing?"

"The tests have all come back okay," she told him. "No trace of blood still accumulating, and no sign that there's any permanent damage." But her tests were the last thing on her mind right now. She wished he would step away from her and let her have the luxury of rational thought once again.

But the wretch persisted, mouth still close to her ear. "Are your headaches gone?"

All of them except you, she wished she could say, but she settled for a simple "Yes."

At last, he straightened up. "The doctor told me you've started physiotherapy."

She grimaced. "The hospital calls the rehab room New Beginnings. The patients call it Purgatory."

"Is it that bad?" he asked sympathetically.

She didn't trust herself to answer. She knew she would have to start slowly, and she knew that getting back on her feet would be a long and arduous journey—if she ever got there. The alternative, permanent paralysis, was too awful to contemplate. The weakness down her right side was something she needed all her inner strength to put up with. It was humiliating, needing to be helped, to be taught how to move and to walk all over again, like a child—a big, overgrown, dependent child.

The mere prospect of being reduced to the misery she experienced in her childhood, subject to the whims and fancies of others, dependent on their kindness, made her doubly determined to tough it out and get back on her feet if it killed her. She'd found herself able to clench her right hand, and many of the empty hours sitting awake in bed were spent squeezing on a small, soft, blue rubber ball. At least that was a start.

He didn't press her for an answer. Instead, he turned on his heel and headed for the door.

"Where are you going?" she asked again, this time honestly afraid that he was leaving.

"Going for a walk," he answered cryptically.

Zhara wrinkled her brow. "You're going for a walk?" she asked.

"No," he corrected, *"we're* going for a walk." He disappeared through the door.

"Very funny," she said to the empty room. "Me, go for a walk. That's a riot."

She decided to discontinue her bewildered conversation with herself; her confinement was already driving her crazy. There was no need to add raving out loud to the list of symptoms from which she currently suffered. Instead, she forced herself to wait patiently as the minutes rolled by, trying to while away the time by flipping the pages of her new magazines, but discovering that she couldn't read and watch the door for his return at the same time, she put them away.

After a time span that her mind told her was only a few minutes, but which the rest of her contended was an age, he was back in, pushing a wheelchair ahead of him.

"You've got to be kidding," she protested.

He wasn't putting up with her protests. "It's perfectly safe," he said, firmly. "The doctors said it'd even do you some good."

She persisted. "There is no way I can get from here,"

she said, pointing to her bed, "to there." She pointed at the chair, which might just as well have been half a mile away, for all the good it would do her.

"There *is* a way," he insisted. Firmly, he slipped back the catches on the rails that ran along the side of her bed, sliding them smoothly downward. Lining the chair up with the bed, he leaned forward, arms stretched toward her.

"What are you doing?" Zhara hated the panicked squeak in her voice, but right now, she had to admit it was forgivable. He wasn't seriously thinking of *lifting* her, was he? *In his arms?* He was out of his mind.

"Getting you into your chair," he explained, unnecessarily.

"Like this?" She indicated his still-outstretched arms.

He withdrew them. "Would you like to try getting into it yourself?" he asked, with a hint of sarcasm.

"You know that's not possible," she scowled.

"Well," he countered reasonably. "I was offering you an alternative."

Some alternative, Zhara thought. The voltage of their last brief physical contact hadn't yet faded in her memory. She didn't think it ever would. "Maybe I'll just stay here," she suggested mulishly.

He smiled as he would to a recalcitrant child. "Come now, Zhara." The sound of her own name on his lips never ceased to make something inside her tighten. "Do you really want to spend another day holed up in here, staring at these old walls, cut off from the rest of the world? I'll bet you've counted the floor tiles a thousand times and the ceiling tiles a hundred thousand. Couldn't you do with a break?"

He was right. How many hours had she lain in bed praying, dying for a chance to just see something other than the tiny square of real life offered by her window? Was all the life that she would see until she left the hospital going to be screened off by the metal grillwork that covered that small opening? She sighed. He was right. She needed desperately to get out, if only for a few moments. And if getting out meant allowing herself into the devil's arms, well, so be it.

"I'd like to go outside," she finally said, and held out her arms like a little girl waiting to be lifted up by her daddy. She looked down at her right arm in surprise. It felt like lead, but it had moved! It fell onto her lap the moment she noticed it, as if too shy to try moving while it was being watched, but before it did, Cole had noticed it, too, and smiled approvingly.

The long, strong arms encircled her, and again the unbelievable power coursed from the one into the other. Remembering the way it had been the last time had in no way prepared her for feeling it again. A puff of surprised breath escaped her lips. He heard the soft gasp and looked directly into her liquid brown eyes. His own black ones held evidence that he was as affected as she by the contact jolt.

He remained holding her, not attempting to lift her. Each was transfixed by the other's gaze. His own breathing seemed to quicken; she could feel the exaggerated rise and fall of his dense chest against her own. The sudden flood of warmth between her thighs told her that her injury had in no way affected her sensation in *that* sensitive area.

Millennia passed. She wondered who would speak first, what would happen next, and if either of them would have the strength to break away and set them both free from this crazy magnetic bond.

"Um . . ." she began. Her fingers, still on his solid shoulders, could not resist roaming a few inches to his neck. "I'm told I'd be easier to lift if I—um, hold you around the neck." *That's good, Zhara,* she congratulated herself. *Remind him that the purpose of the exercise is to get you into the chair, not to set your very last hormone aflame.*

He found the breath to apologize. "Sorry. I don't know what . . ." She waited eagerly, but he didn't finish the thought. Instead, he lifted her, carefully and tenderly, and settled her delicately down into the well-padded chair. He peered anxiously at her. "Are you okay?"

She nodded, not wanting him to suffer the anxiety more than he had to. "I'm fine."

He didn't look as if he believed her, but instead knelt before her to move her footrests into place. As he did so, she looked down on his head and felt the urge to lay a hand on his close-cut curly hair. She could still smell him, and she wished to God he didn't smell so good. She thrust the hand behind her, into the small of her back, because she didn't trust it not to move toward him on its own; the first time she had touched him involuntarily was all the proof she needed that it was perfectly capable of doing so again.

Gentle hands helped her get her legs into position and her feet onto the footrests, and then, almost briskly, he rose and went to stand behind her, grasping the handlebars of the chair. "Ready?"

"Yes."

Effortlessly, he eased the chair out into the hallway. It didn't take Zhara more than a few glances around her to notice the stir they were creating. She couldn't figure out what was so strange about what they were doing; there were at least half a dozen other patients being wheeled along the wide well-polished hall, and there were many more on gurneys and crutches. What was so special about them?

Then the photo of a huge smiling man coming out of his precinct office, splayed all over a gutter paper, came to her mind. "The damn story," she muttered.

"What?"

She craned her neck to look up at him. "You know. The story. The one in the paper last week. That's why everyone's staring. They all know who we are."

The light clicked on in his head. "You're probably correct. It was an awful piece, wasn't it?"

She pursed her lips, not believing him. "Yeah, right. The way you were mugging for the camera, you looked pretty pleased with yourself."

He stopped short, put on the brake, and came round to face her, impervious to the stares of the orderlies, nurses, and patients around them, who suddenly seemed to have ample time to stop what they were doing to shamelessly catch the real-life detective scene unfolding before them. "Zhara, listen. I never authorized that story. Nobody called to talk to me, and if they had, I wouldn't have spoken to them. I don't believe in showing off to the media."

She still wasn't willing to believe him. "You didn't stop them from taking your picture, though."

He laughed at that. "It's an old photo, Zhara. It's from last year. I'd just come from accepting an award at the precinct. The photographer took me by surprise; I never saw her coming. It's most likely the only shot of me they have. They use it all the time."

She couldn't afford to let that one slip past her. "You're in the papers all the time?"

"Often," was all he would say.

She persisted. "For catching criminals?"

He looked at her for a long moment. "It's my job, Zhara. Sometimes," he paused, glanced at her wheelchair-bound form, and looked away, "sometimes, I make mistakes. But, usually, I do it well."

She nodded. She was realistic enough to admit that he was correct. "And the papers love you."

He shrugged. "Local boy makes good. It's a classic story, even if they do beat it to death. Everybody needs a hero."

"And you're it," she finished dryly.

He went back around the chair, released the brake, and set her in motion again. "Sometimes. There's nothing wrong with that. I think I'm a better role model for young men than the gangsters and playboys they usually tend to admire." He led them past gawking gaggles of onlookers and into an elevator. Behind them, their audience let loose audible, disappointed sighs. Their little snippet of excitement for the day was over. Moving as one, they returned to their duties.

Cole went on. "I'd rather have my son look up to me, or someone like me, than the whole host of other types the papers see fit to plaster all over the pages."

She was surprised. "You have a son?"

He nodded. "Didn't I tell you?"

Him, tell her anything? She shook her head. He was more interested in slyly trying to extricate information about her life. "No."

His face took on the look of an unmistakably proud parent. "His name is Omar. He's sixteen and almost as tall as I am. He wants to be a cop, like me." He sounded as if that was the greatest compliment his profession could ever have received.

A thought hit Zhara. "So then you're—married?" She hoped she didn't sound as disappointed as she felt.

The elevator doors opened, and Cole wheeled them into the lobby, out through the side gates, and into the brilliant sunshine of the hospital grounds before he answered. "No, I'm not married. I've never been married."

She hated to admit it, but she was dying of curiosity to hear the rest. So, he wasn't married, but was he living with someone? Omar had to have a mother; he didn't turn up in a cabbage patch. She realized she needed to know. But why? Why would it matter to her whether his son's mother was still in his life or not?

They began moving along one of the smoother,

broader paths. Even though it was autumn, the air was comfortingly warm today, and, thank goodness, the people who teemed around them seemed unaware of their well-publicized dual identities as Top Cop and Cat Burglar. The feel of the sunshine on her face was heavenly, after such a long time of dreary and lonely confinement. Once again, Cole had known exactly how to please her.

Just as Zhara had begun to think that Cole had let the matter of his son drop, he spoke up. "I was exactly the same age as Omar is now when he was born," he began. "I was an inner-city boy who never knew my father. I spent more time on the street than in school, shooting hoops and chasing girls. I was a worthless wretch; I'd be the first to admit it. The boys and I made a game of it, getting girls into bed with us. It was all for fun. We kept score."

Zhara could hear the tinge of self-disgust in his voice, but let him go on uninterrupted. "Omar's mother was two years older than I was. I was very successful with older women; I was six feet tall by the time I was fourteen and never stopped growing. As a matter of fact, I preferred older women; they were good for my ego. I used to go after women in their twenties and thirties. They made me think I was all that. I met Sondra at a block party. I never really got to know her, and I didn't care to, either. We went around for a couple of weeks, tops. She was a month away from taking up a college scholarship out west when she found out she was pregnant."

He sighed. Their movement along the shrub-lined paths slowed, as Cole seemed to grow more contemplative. "When she came to me, she was desperate. She didn't think she could handle college and a baby. She wanted my assurance that I would help her look after it. I was full of myself, like I said, and all she was to me then was a conquest, another number to add to my list and boast about to my friends. I told her to get lost." He stopped talking, consumed by guilt, amazed at his own behavior.

To her own surprise, Zhara felt obliged to offer comfort. "Cole, you were sixteen. That's still a boy. You can't expect to make a mature decision at that age."

He shook his head vehemently, unwilling to allow himself the luxury of an excuse. "I was old enough to know that what I was doing, all of it, was wrong. I didn't care. I left her standing there, on the side of the road, crying, and went off and played ball with my friends. I didn't see her or speak to her for years. I heard afterward that she gave up the scholarship and stayed home to have Omar."

"You never saw him when he was a baby?"

"No. My mother did. She sent that girl money throughout her pregnancy, and I never once offered to take on a part-time job to help her do it. She visited Omar when he was born and every Saturday after that for four years. And every Saturday when she came from Sondra's house, she berated me. She told me she hated what I was growing up to be, that I was wasting my manhood. She said I was heading down the same road as my father, the man who once told her he never wanted anything to do with her, when she told him she was pregnant with *me*. She warned me I was headed toward a life of oblivion. She cried and prayed for me, but for four years, I let her talk but didn't listen. I did nothing. I was smart, but I never applied for college. I didn't want a career. I was too busy having a good time."

Zhara listened in awe as this man poured out his own painful experiences to her. It hadn't occurred to her that the big, hard, righteous Detective Cole Wyatt could have had such beginnings. It shocked her to realize that she wanted to know more about him—much more. "What happened?" she prompted him. "What changed things?"

"I'd moved out of my mother's house by the time I was eighteen. I loved her, but was glad to get away from her endless pleadings to set my life straight. I thought I knew better. I took crappy jobs—jobs that never demanded I use my brain, but that was okay; they brought in just enough money to get me into the clubs on a weekend. I lived the way I wanted to live for the next two years, and it was killing me. Then, one day the doorbell rang. I opened it, and there was Sondra. She was crying. It was funny; the last time I had seen her she was crying, and now, four years later, there were the same tears in her eyes.

"She was holding this little boy in her arms, and from the moment I saw him, nothing was the same. I just stared at him. It was astounding. He had my eyes and my nose, my mouth and my hairline. It was like looking back at myself as a child. I couldn't believe he was actually before me in the flesh. I'd worked long and hard at pretending he didn't exist. I never wanted to look at any of the photos of him my mother had. I never wanted to hear any of the stories she always wanted to tell about him. Then, all of a sudden, there he was, my son, alive and breathing, and staring me down as hard as I was staring at him."

"Why was she crying?" Zhara wanted to know. They swung around a corner, and the path opened up onto a beautiful pond that glowed with the reflections of the trees around it, with their gold, umber, orange, and red leaves softly setting the autumn ablaze. Thousands more, long fallen, floated on the surface of the pond, chasing each other like tiny boats. It was the most beautiful thing she had ever seen.

"Would you like to stop here for a while?" he asked.

"Umm-hmm."

He guided the chair toward a long, ornate bench, braked it, and sat down opposite from her. Over his shoulder, she could see the beauty of the lake, but her eyes didn't drift that far. He was only inches from her, and as he went on with his story, she found herself mesmerized by the movement of his full, shapely lips.

"She was crying because she'd come to give him to me.

She was getting married to an older man and moving to Arizona. The man already had five grown children and wasn't prepared to go through child-raising a second time. He'd given her an ultimatum: find someone to take care of Omar, or there would be no marriage."

"I don't believe anyone would say something like that," Zhara breathed, shocked.

Cole shrugged. "Her fiancé did. Sondra didn't think she had much of a choice. I'd stolen her chance to go to college by abdicating my responsibility, and the few years in which she had to raise a baby alone hadn't been kind to her. She was still a pretty girl, but she'd lost that dewy look that she had. She looked tired and desperate. I realized just how big a part I'd played in her misfortune, and for the first time in my worthless life, I felt guilty. So I took him. God help me, I hadn't a clue what I was doing, but I took my son from her, let her hand me a suitcase filled with all his stuff, and wished her well. She stood and looked at him like she couldn't bear to leave, and it was the first time I had ever had any inkling of what it was like to hurt for someone else.

"After she left, I took him inside. He held my hand and followed me, never complained or asked what was going on or anything. He trusted me. I couldn't believe it. Zhara, I set that boy down on the kitchen table and stared at him all evening. I don't even remember if I gave him anything to eat; I didn't have a clue what he was supposed to eat at that age. But he just sat there on the table smiling at me."

Zhara watched Cole's Adam's apple bob abruptly, as he struggled to swallow his emotion. She knew better than to say anything at this point, but instead waited for him to speak again.

"Something changed inside of me that night. For the first time I saw myself for what I was: a waste. I thought about the time I had wasted in school, and the years that had gone by since school that I could have spent getting a degree or specialized training, or a proper job. I thought of all the nameless women I'd used for sport. I'd done to another woman the same thing my own father had done to my mother, and I was in the process of unleashing another fatherless boy on the world. Without a man's guidance, he stood a pretty good chance of winding up as useless as I was turning out to be. I was ashamed.

"I took my son in my arms and prayed for forgiveness. I told God I didn't have any idea how I was going to raise Omar, but if He gave me the guidance, I was going to do it right. I remember Omar wiping the tears from my face and saying, 'Why are you crying, Mister?'

"That shocked me. My own son was calling me 'Mister.' It was to be expected, of course; it was the first time he was meeting me. But it hurt. It took months for me to convince him to call me 'Dad.' "

"And then you joined the police force?" Zhara prompted.

He nodded. "Two months after Omar came to me. It was the best thing I could have done for myself. My mother was ecstatic. It was as if her years of prayers had finally been answered. I was finally taking up my responsibilities and becoming a man. She died less than a year after my graduation, but she died knowing that her grandson was loved and well looked after."

"Did Omar's mother—did Sondra ever come back for him?"

"She wrote and sent him presents for a few years, and then they trickled off. I've tried to look her up in Arizona, but she seems to have moved. I haven't really done all I can to track her down; I figured that if she wanted to be found, she would be. Maybe if Omar wants to see her when he's older, we'll try again." He inhaled deeply and let the air out with a rush. Telling such an emotionally charged story seemed to have tired him out. For a while he contented himself with watching her watch the water.

Eventually, he spoke again. "What about you?"

Zhara was immediately on her guard again. "What *about* me?"

He smiled. "I've poured out my life's story to you. You could at least give me something in return. You never talk about yourself."

With reason, she thought. "There's nothing to say."

"There must be. You didn't fall from the sky. You must have a family. You must have come from somewhere."

"No family," she said shortly.

"What about your parents?" he persisted.

"Both dead," she snapped. "Satisfied?"

"Far from," he answered. "How did it happen?"

She sighed. Was he anything like this in an interrogation room? Probably. "My mother died when I was a baby. My father—died later. I was twelve."

"Who raised you?"

"No one." She looked away.

"Someone must have," he insisted.

"That's what you think," she replied, stubbornly refusing to give an inch.

He tried another tack. "I know you're not from Medusa. Are you originally from Chicago?"

Her face reflected surprise. "How did you know I was in Chicago?"

"Your file . . ." he began, and then saw his own mistake. In a flash, they had fallen from their comfortable, if tenuous, rapport, back to their original status as policeman and prey.

Zhara struggled for the brake on her wheelchair, deciding that she didn't have to stay here and allow herself to be questioned. She thought he had been sharing with her all along, but he was really just attempting to lull her into giving him more information! "Maybe the answer is in your *files*, Detective. Maybe one of your informants can tell you all about me."

She didn't move more than two inches before he stopped her with one powerful hand. His face was dangerously close. "The things I want to know about you, Zhara, can't be found in a file."

She glared at him, eyes afire. "Things like what?"

He hadn't lifted his face from its menacing position so close to hers. "Who you are. I know your name, but I don't know *who* you are. What you are . . ."

"Oh, I think you've already made up your mind what I am, Detective," she retorted. She could feel his breath against her face, and the proximity was disarming. For her own protection, she injected an extra dose of pure venom into her voice.

"Running around in a leather catsuit isn't all you are. I can sense more to you in every look, in everything that you say. I want to know where you come from, what makes you get up in the morning, what made you . . ." he paused.

"Steal?" she sneered.

"Yes."

"Greed, maybe," she suggested mockingly.

"No."

"Thrills, then."

"No."

She pushed harder. "So book me. Go ahead. You know what I've done in the past. Go to your *file,*" she almost spat out the word, "dust off an old case, haul me before a court. Then you can ask me anything you like."

"You know that won't work." He sounded resentful, as if her elusiveness was a personal indictment on his performance as a detective.

Zhara smiled, knowing why, but delighting in the opportunity to rub it in. She lifted one dark brow. "Why not?"

"Because," he grated, "I have no evidence. Nothing. Nothing but a gut feeling about things you've had a hand in. You were smart enough to make sure of that."

She nodded at his grudging compliment, and he went on.

"So nothing you say to me or to anyone else will hold up in court. No evidence, no case."

She drove the advantage home with a triumphant smile. "Burns you to the very core, doesn't it?"

The hard, stony eyes glittered, and he seemed to think for several seconds before responding, as if he were weighing his options. She couldn't resist a shudder at the possibility that she had gone a step too far in goading him. He was so big, and she was so helpless, trapped in her chair. What if he decided to retaliate? What could she do to defend herself?

She drew a breath, about to speak, but was robbed of the opportunity when he closed the tiny gap between them, his head coming between her and the sun like an eclipse. The excruciating, astounding jolt caused by his mouth making contact with hers prevented her from saying anything more. All she could see was the image of his mouth, the beautiful, well-defined shape of it, an inch from her face, before her vision blurred as heat rose between them in sudden waves. Protest might have been the first thing on her brain's list, but it was the last thing on her body's.

Instead of pushing him away like she wanted to—like she should—she opened her mouth under his, like a desert flower at the first whisper of rain. His questing tongue pierced her mouth like a thin stiletto, parting her lips, flicking along her teeth. Each brief millisecond of contact left her yearning for him to stay in one place, but he skipped along, teasing, touching the inside of her lips lightly before dancing away. It was maddening.

This time, she did protest, not for him to stop kissing

her, but for him to stop teasing. Her arms wound around him (again, her unwilling arm moved!), both hands pressed firmly against the back of his head in an attempt to prevent him from stopping. She opened her mouth even more, allowing him access beyond the barrier of her teeth, and he accepted the invitation eagerly.

Her own tongue greeted his joyfully, and this time, their dance was a duet. Heat coursed from him into her, pouring into her center. She wished despairingly that she were not confined to her chair, that her disobedient body were whole enough for her to stand so that she could press herself fully along him and feel his excitement thrusting against her.

They broke the kiss, both gasping for air. Not prepared to allow themselves to lose contact, Cole snaked his fingers into her hair, twisting her long black braids around his hands and gently tugging her close again. His broad nostrils flared with hunger, and as they came together again, he whispered her name into her willing mouth.

It was broad daylight, but neither of them cared. She slid her stronger hand up under the dark sweatshirt and found her way through the crinkly nest of chest hair until she found a tightly knotted nubbin of flesh. How could he be so solid? The muscled wall under her fingers trembled as she roughly agitated the small, hard bump of his nipple. He groaned, almost losing his composure.

Each scratch of her fingernail brought a shudder of pleasure to him. She had an image of herself reaching out and enclosing one excited nipple in her teeth, torturing him, feeling his heart thump against his ribs and the crisp hair against her lips.

"Zhara, baby, please," she heard him groan, but she couldn't be sure if it was in real life or in her agitated fantasy.

Somebody behind them giggled. The spell shattered with the sound of breaking glass. Drunk with the kiss, they lifted their heads, but it was several moments before they had the mental clarity to realize that two teenage boys were standing just a few feet away from them, hands over their mouths, laughing.

Embarrassed, they drew apart. The boys ran off, perhaps for fear of reprisals. The magic was gone, and the warmth that had encircled them was replaced by a sudden chill in the air, as the sun slipped behind a cloud.

Zhara was aware that Cole was staring at her, but she couldn't bear to face him. How could she? Had she lost her mind? Furious, confusing thoughts circled in her head—bad memories and good, like bats swarming in their cave, angry at being awakened.

Cole was standing now, towering above her, hands still entangled in her braids, gently moving along her head, sliding down to the back of her neck, where light fingertips caressed her. Because of his height, she had a clear view of his torso and couldn't avoid seeing the agitated rise and fall of his chest, as he struggled to bring his breathing under control. She couldn't avoid, either, the clear—*the blatant*—evidence of his arousal printed against his form-fitting jeans.

The dryness in her mouth was balanced by the hot wetness below. Cole bent closer and whispered, "Baby, let's take this inside, where it's—more private."

She found her voice at last. "I want to go back to my room," she choked.

"That's just what I was suggesting," he laughed, softly. "I want to take you back inside, up to your room. The door has a lock, and as soon as we're alone, I want to taste that sweet, sweet mouth of yours again."

Frustration put an edge on her voice. "No, no, you don't understand! I want you to take me back—and then *leave!*"

The hypnotic rhythm of his fingers in her hair stopped

abruptly. "What?" he asked, as if he doubted what he was hearing.

It took all her strength to grasp his hand firmly in hers and thrust it away. This time, the tears that had been threatening all morning finally allowed themselves free rein. "You heard me, *cop,*" she said, more loudly than was necessary. "Let's move."

Wordlessly, he complied, leaving her alone with her agony and guilt. What kind of woman was she? Did she really find it so easy to forget, to allow another man to insinuate himself into her trust long enough to engender such a heated reaction from her? After all, Antonio, her first and only lover, her first and only love, was dead. Shouldn't she be loyal to his memory?

What made her treachery even more atrocious was that the man she had embraced so shamefully was a cop—and Antonio had been killed by a policeman's bullet.

Brian Ames was getting cranky. The traffic out of Chicago's O'Hare Airport had been in a snarl ever since they'd pulled out of the car rental lot, and that was an hour ago. Radio reports that the backup was caused by an overturned trailer that had cut across two lanes of the Kennedy Expressway didn't make the wait any easier. In fact, waiting was just about all they'd been doing all day—the flight out of Medusa had wound up being held in a holding pattern due to bad weather: what should have been less than an hour in the air had stretched to two. As he reminded Cole several times, spending his precious off-day lazing in bed with his wife, Eileen, was infinitely better than watching filthy gray exhaust belch out of the exterminator's van ahead of them on the road, and he'd been a madman to have agreed to follow Cole into another of his lunatic schemes.

"I say we arrest that guy in front," Brian suggested pettishly. "Throw every emissions law in the book at him, and send him packing off to a good muffler shop."

Cole smiled at his partner, set his coffee down in his cup holder, and pondered the wisdom of answering him. He decided that since Brian had given up his day to trek all the way out to Chicago on what was most likely a cold trail, the least he could do was be gracious. "We're not traffic cops," he answered, mildly. "And, besides, it's out of our jurisdiction."

Not to be deterred, Brian took a different tack. "Well, a citizen's arrest, then."

Cole gave him a humorous look. "A citizen's arrest for an emissions violation. That'll go down real well with the lieutenant."

Brian had to admit the image of two of Medusa's finest detectives leaping out of their cars in the pouring rain to arrest and cuff an exterminator over a faulty muffler wasn't exactly worthy of even the lamest episode of "Cops." "I don't think Lieutenant Dos Santos would find that amusing."

Cole agreed wholeheartedly. "Nope, I don't think she would."

They were quiet for another mile or two, and then Brian spoke up again. "Did you tell her why we're here?"

Cole shrugged. Brian took that as a 'no'.

"We *are* on our off day," Cole rationalized. "I didn't think we needed her permission."

"Well, I wouldn't say we need her permission per se, but, you know, Zhara Thorne is a suspect . . ."

"*Was* a suspect," Cole corrected automatically.

Ever the excitable one, Brian waved his arms in agitation. "Exactly! Zhara Thorne *was* a suspect. She is *no longer* a suspect. The De Boers case has been shot down."

Cole shrugged. "There's quite a bit of perfectly good jewelry still missing from some very high buildings back home, and stocks and bonds worth more than my pension mysteriously disappeared from half a dozen locked safes years ago. *Those* cases haven't been shot down."

"What they have been," Brian argued, although he should have known better than to disagree with Cole when he was in one of his determined moods, "is shelved. Our caseload is way too heavy as it is. We've gone over all this ground years ago and never turned up a thing."

"This time, we dig deeper. I'm going to find out all there is to know about Zhara Thorne."

Brian let the corners of his mouth curve a little, a rare concession for him. "All for the sake of the good people of this fair land, hmm?"

Cole took his eyes off the road, a perfectly safe act, since nothing had moved in five minutes, and gave Brian a quizzical look. "Huh?"

"You dragged me all the way out here to try to dig up her past because she's a menace to society, stuck in that old wheelchair as she is, right?"

Cole reminded himself that the man who was striking a little too close to home was his best friend in the world; it was the only thing that kept him from snarling at him to back off.

Brian persisted. "I mean, your renewed interest in her old cases wouldn't be fueled by a *personal* interest, would it? Not you, Mr. Cool." By now, he was practically grinning, something to which he was so unaccustomed that Cole half expected his face to crack.

Cole thought for a second. Why *was* he driving all the way out here, in nasty weather to boot, to pursue a suspect who was no longer a threat to anybody? *Was* it personal? Since that soul-wrenching kiss in the hospital garden (had he ever, even in his wild days, been so moved by something as simple yet devastating as a kiss?), he hadn't been able to get Zhara off his mind. What was she—calculating cat burglar or lost little girl? Where did she come from, and why was she so bent on blocking any attempt to pierce the dense veil of secrecy she had thrown over her past? And why did she resent his profession so much?

He was sure he could answer that last question himself. Zhara had been a thief. She herself had admitted to that. Thieves simply didn't like policemen. It was definitely nothing more complicated than that. Why, he couldn't fathom. She was bright, well-spoken, and had a good spirit—that he knew instinctively. She wasn't the arch-villain he had believed himself to be chasing all these years. She just *had* to be propelled by a motive greater than common greed. That motive, he was sure, would be unearthed in time, but for now, all the other questions didn't cease to teem about in his head like angry wasps.

All last night, she'd kept him awake, partly because of the heat she had stirred up in his belly, and the memory of the taste of her mouth on his lips, and partly because he was what he was: a cop, and a curious one at that. He had been presented with a mystery, and this was one mystery he was bent on solving, even if it proved to be the death of him.

So, once again, Zhara was under his investigation. This time, he had to admit to himself that his objective was to unwrap the enigma, find out who she was, and what had made her who she was. If it meant dredging up her criminal past by going to the last place his records had said she inhabited before moving to his hometown, well, so be it.

This, of course, was his idea. Brian was correct in assuming that their lieutenant, Lorna Dos Santos, would not be amused. Investigating a citizen on his spare time, for his own private purposes, wouldn't exactly rest well with their levelheaded, strictly-by-the-book leader.

So they simply hadn't told her.

Zhara didn't need Margie's medical know-how to interpret the complex columns, numbers, and lines on the sheets of medical results she had spread out for her. The numbers on the latest blood work were bad. The problem was getting worse, and it was getting worse fast. She let her head fall into her hands and exhaled so heavily that the pages on the cafeteria table ruffled in the gust.

Lizard tried to console her as best he could. "The results aren't so bad, Zhar. You're just being negative."

She pursed her lips. "Negative? How can you say something like that? This is serious!"

Lizard shrugged. The years of dealing with his rapidly worsening leukemia had made him almost inured to bad news. "You're taking it lots harder than I am. They're *my* tests. If *I'm* not worried about them, why should you be?"

The little prodding was all her nerves needed. She'd already lost too much sleep over that fiasco in the hospital garden—kissing Cole Wyatt as if she hadn't been kissed in years. Well, actually, she hadn't, but her shameless response to the simplest overture from a man she didn't even *like* hadn't gone down well with her self-esteem.

A sympathetic night nurse, hearing her still tossing and turning in bed well after three in the morning, had offered her a sedative, which she bluntly refused. Now, she wished she had taken advantage of the modern medical miracle that would have allowed her blessed respite from her tortured conscience for at least a few hours. But, she hadn't, and the ashy blue shadows under her tired caramel eyes and the claw hammer tearing away at the back of her skull were making her pay for her stubbornness.

As was his habit, Lizard came visiting quite early, and decided, as Cole had done before him, to allow her the chance to see something other than the four confounded walls that held her captive. After a stroll in the garden, Mickey's teenage appetite led them unerringly down to the hospital cafeteria, so that a mere three hours after a tasteless breakfast, Zhara found herself eating bland potatoes and sausages followed by wobbly lime-flavored gelatin cups topped with fruit—bananas! Didn't they know she hated bananas? And he was telling her that his new test results didn't matter.

Most people his age were lucky to survive three or four years after being diagnosed with leukemia, before the disease became so critical that life-threatening bone-marrow transplants were needed. Mickey was entering his sixth year. He'd been brave; he'd fought the disease hard. All the days he couldn't get out of bed, and all the times his cell count had plummeted deadly close to zero, and all the infections, the pain, and the therapy, had not daunted him in his determination to make it through life day by day.

Zhara remembered all the nights she had sat up next to him in uncomfortable hospital chairs, and all the times she had waited, watching the faces of the doctors as they conferred grimly among themselves before delivering their verdict on whether he'd live through this bout of infection or that sudden fever. She had cared for him as his own mother would have—or should have, since the yet-unknown woman who had borne him had never taken the time to know him before setting him down on the steps of the public library and walking away when he was a few weeks old.

He didn't have a birthday or a birth certificate, other than the ones made up for him later. Nobody knew where he came from, nobody knew who his family was. As far as the system was concerned, he didn't exist. But Zhara knew he did, and she knew that if he continued with the nonchalance about his health that he had suddenly adopted, his fiercely asserted existence would be in jeopardy.

The boy needs somebody to shake some discipline into him, Zhara thought wearily. Teenagers! Did they have to be so stubborn? Was she that bad when she was his age? She almost smiled in spite of the seriousness of the situation when she reminded herself that, not only was she as bad as he at that age, but she was also a wanted woman with a burglary record that she'd rather forget.

Lizard frowned. He'd come to patiently tolerate Zhara's ministrations and had grown as immune to her nagging as any teen would his mother's. But the sudden smile that toyed with the corners of her full mouth, right in the middle of one of her incessant lectures about his health, was just not like Zhara. "What?" he inquired, puzzled.

She tried to shake her smile off, but it spread outward until it filled her face, seeping upward to her eyes, giving them a glow he hadn't seen in a long time. Unable to stop himself, he began smiling hugely, even though he didn't yet get the joke.

Zhara decided to have mercy on him and let him in on it. "I was just wondering if I was as much of a pain in the butt at your age as you're being now."

He grinned. "And your verdict was . . . ?"

She shook her head. "I was pretty bad, wasn't I?"

"A proper monster."

She threw a plastic spoon at him across the table. "With good reason. I had you to take care of."

He grew serious at once. "And I would never have survived the streets if it hadn't been for you. They'd have eaten me up whole in no time, if you hadn't come after me." He got up from his seat across from her and came around the small plastic table to squat at the side of her wheelchair. Thin, pale arms, all angles and bone, launched around her neck, as Mickey pressed his cheek against hers. It struck her again how smooth and hairless he was. As far as she knew, he'd never had the need to shave. He was so young. And so very, very sick.

Her smile faded, and her mood descended to match his. She let him hug her. "I'll take care of you for as long as I need to," she vowed, pulling him closer to her.

He pulled away, frowning again. "Zhara," he began, and then stopped, thinking of what to say next.

Zhara didn't give him a chance. She pressed on. "I'm just scared that now that I can't walk, we might not be able to get the money we need to get you well again."

Mickey shook his head violently, like a swimmer trying to dislodge water from his ears. "Zhara, you don't have to carry my weight on your shoulders anymore. You sold your soul and stole for me, and that was bad enough. But now we're straight, and we have a good business. The business will survive even if you don't get . . ." He stopped, shocked at the direction his thoughts were taking, and then hastily amended, "I mean, *while* you get better."

Zhara struggled to quell the protest that rose to her lips. She *was* going to get better, wasn't she? This horrible metal prison couldn't be her destiny, could it? She shoved away the fear. "This isn't about me, Mickey, it's about you! You're getting worse, and we don't have nearly enough money to get you your bone-marrow transplant! Your medicine and chemo cost way too much already. Don't you understand?" She was agitated, her breath came in short puffs through her open mouth, and the eyes that were so full of mirth a moment ago had dimmed with anxiety. "Mickey, what are we going to do? What happens when the money's gone?"

In response, Mickey bristled. He stood up. "I'll work enough for both of us and keep the business going while you concentrate on getting better. I don't need you to steal or work to keep me alive anymore. *I* can work. *I* can see the clients." His fine nostrils were flaring, and the red flush of angry blood was evident just below his skin. His light-greenish eyes, which, characteristically of some albinos, habitually darted from side to side due to astigmatism, were even more agitated than usual. He pushed his thin, wire-framed glasses further back up on his nose. "I'm a man now. I can take care of myself."

"You're eighteen, Mickey!" she corrected him. Her

tone was as frenzied as his. "That's hardly a man." She didn't need to hear the angry snort to realize she'd offended him. He took two rapid steps away and looked down at her from that distance.

"I *am* a man, Zhara," he informed her, through a taut jaw. "When you were eighteen, you'd been on the street three years, with me in tow. You got us a place. It wasn't paradise, but it was clean and dry enough to sleep in. You made enough money that we didn't starve. You made enough to keep me alive and buy me the treatment I needed. You kept the pushers and the street hoods off our backs, and when you needed to fight to defend me, you fought. And you won." His voice rose steadily, so much so that one or two people at the neighboring tables stopped eating, hands poised on the way to their mouths, trying to catch the precious drops of the scandal that was obviously unfolding around them.

Zhara couldn't care less about the stares. Her attention was focused on Mickey, who had begun to pace, passing his hands along his closely cropped straw-colored hair, searching for the next words. She waited, silenced by her surprise at his passion, wishing she could stand, but instead she was confined to her chair, a prisoner of her own body, and had to sit there, neck craned backward, staring into her friend's inflamed face.

Mickey went on, lowering his voice and bending forward so that only she could hear him. "If you could do so much, if you could look after me and yourself for all those years, then why can't I? Why can't you let me take care of both of us?"

She pondered upon this for no more than a few seconds before answering, voice tremulous with emotion. "Because you're all I have. Taking care of you is my job. It's what I'm here for."

Lizard straightened and looked at her, eyes struggling to hold hers and failing; he was too upset to hold his

still, and she was too overcome to look him fully in the
face. Then, without a word, he turned and headed toward the cafeteria door. She let him go, knowing that
he would come back, looking at his thin frame as he
stalked away—so young, so boyish in his washed-out blue
jeans and T-shirt. *He'll be back soon,* she assured herself.
But his form disappeared among the bustling throng in
the hall ahead, and he neither slowed his pace nor
looked back, and panic began to slip its fingers around
her throat and squeeze.

"Mickey!" she shouted, shaky hands grasping the
wheels on her chair and clumsily wheeling herself away
from the table. Her right hand could grasp the wheel, but
it still didn't have the strength of the other hand, so that
her chair lurched forward awkwardly, its trajectory more
of an arc than a straight line. Several pairs of eyes turned
darkly on her in condemnation of her intrusion on their
peace. Still others were disappointed that the meaty conversation had fizzled to such an inconclusive end. Zhara
ignored them all.

Damn the stupid chair, and her unwilling body too!
Mickey had been the one to wheel her down here, and
now he was gone. Her arm ached, and from time to time
it flopped off the wheel and hung limply at her side. She
had to breathe deeply and wait until she had the strength
to lift it again.

She sucked her teeth in frustration, as she made her
clumsy way between the plastic cafeteria furniture. Who
was the idiot that set the tables out in the first place? Why
were they so close together? Didn't they expect that in a
hospital there'd be one or two people who'd need to get
between them in a wheelchair? She was halfway across the
wide room before she remembered that in her distress
she had left her bag on the little table. She swore as she
slammed into reverse, almost tipping herself over, and
slowly and laboriously made her way back to the table,

snatched up her bag, and tried her luck again with the table-and-chair obstacle course.

By the time Zhara had made it to the elevators, she was sobbing with anger and frustration. She had had no idea that it was this difficult to propel her own weight forward in a wheelchair. She'd done her share of biking, skate-boarding, and skating as a child. Why was this so different, so much harder? Again, she cursed the chair, her unwilling arm and leg, and added the elevator for good measure. At least someone had been thoughtful enough to put the elevator buttons at a reasonable height, she conceded. She hammered the button with a fist and the doors swung smoothly open. Maneuvering herself inside took such a long time that the doors began to close in on her, and, in her panic, she forgot that they were equipped with sensors that would prevent them from crushing her. The frightened squeak died in her throat as the doors swung open again.

She made it to her ward, a sweating, distressed heap, fiddled with the door of her room until she was able to close it behind her, and found that she was unable to get herself back into bed. Not even willing to risk the humiliation and pain of falling on her rear if she were to try to haul her body out of her chair and into bed with the power of her upper arms alone, she instead slammed toward the window and laid her head on the cool metal sill. She'd had enough.

What was wrong with the boy? What did he mean, he could take care of himself? He couldn't. He was a very sick child. Problem was, he didn't seem to be sufficiently aware of that, or at least he was not prepared to take the threat to his life seriously. It was all she could do to constantly remind him to take his medicine. Many a time they had had royal battles when he became due for chemo-therapy. Mickey hated it. That was understandable; people who had gone through it said it was one of the worst experiences a person could be subjected to, almost as dreaded as the disease itself. But it had to be done, and if she had to stick behind him all the way like a nagging parent, well, so be it. Take care of himself? Preposterous!

Zhara felt the acrid taste of bile mixed with the ghastly lime gelatin and bananas rise to her throat. Institution food. She never wanted to eat institution food again. She remembered with alarming clarity the thousands of mass-produced meals she had been obliged to eat during her awful years at the children's home to which she had been sent by a system that believed that as long as the hundreds of unwanted, abandoned, and lost children in its care were dry, clothed, and fed, it was doing its job. Her stomach roiled with the memory of acres of rehydrated mashed potatoes, creamed corn, spaghetti, and those ghastly desserts: alternating between gelatin and custard Monday to Saturday, and, as a special treat, hard, dry pound cake on Sundays. No wonder she hadn't been able to bring herself to eat any kind of dessert in all the years since she'd run away!

Through the blur of her tears, she saw her younger self, as if she were following her invisibly, walking into the loud and grimy hall of the Harbourmouth Home for Juveniles, led by the shoulder by a tight-faced social worker. Her father had only been dead a week, and with her long-deceased mother's relatives refusing to have anything to do with "that man's child," she found herself cast into the maw of the juvenile care system: an unnecessary child.

The few belongings that she had been allowed to keep after the banks swooped down on her father's property—no, she couldn't even think about *that* right now—were held in a single expensive leather case in her right hand. The social worker hadn't offered to help her with her burden, so she dragged it behind her with one long, thin arm. She was processed like a felon, signed in and shown to a hard, narrow bed in a long dormitory, following which she was marched back downstairs to what the authorities called a children's play area, but what she soon came to know as Bedlam.

Her horror, even after such a long time, was still fresh in her mind; there were children everywhere, fighting, playing, sitting in corners staring at walls, watching a single small-screen television that was bolted to a high wrought-iron stand in a corner. Zhara had been home-schooled all her life by tutors who were more interested in earning the lavish fees her father paid than in their shy, quiet pupil. She had, therefore, never walked across a school playground, never attended an assembly, never experienced the joys of study hall or a school lunch. The sudden assault on her senses was a shock from which she was sure she would never recover. As she turned her frightened, puzzled eyes toward the social worker, the acid-faced woman gave her a perfunctory half smile and turned, walking away to leave Zhara to the mercies of her new 'family'.

Nobody paid her any attention. As she walked, dazed, among the surging mass of noisy, juvenile humanity, picking her way between puddles of children who sat or lay around on the floor, her terror rose. *This* was her new home?

A thin noise, higher and sharper than the general hum around her, made her head snap to one side. Four tall boys, who looked to be around her age, twelve or so, were crowded around a strange, yellowish puppy that was cowering in a corner, twisted to protect itself, so that only its back was obliged to sustain the vicious kicks and punches the boys were raining on it.

As Zhara watched on from her wheelchair, she saw her younger self gasp in horror; she had always been a lover of animals, and this was no way to treat even such a miserable creature. She saw herself leap past groups of children and overturned furniture on long brown legs, tear the first young boy off his victim, and land a blow on his shoulder. She might just as well have been a gnat. He shrugged her off and she fell backward, banging her calf against a fallen stool and crying out in surprise. As the boy she'd attacked stood over her, as ready to fight as she was, the others gathered around him.

"What's your problem?" Bands of fat wobbled under his pugnacious jaw, and his spiky crew-cut bristled with aggression. Cruel eyes took in her long-limbed form and deduced that she would be easy to beat. He smirked.

"Leave it alone," she shouted, her outrage making her brave.

The boy blinked, surprised. As the heaviest and most vicious of the residents, he was used to the other children stepping away to make room when he walked. But this little pipsqueak, and a newbie to boot, was giving him lip. He didn't like it. He recovered enough from the shock to stick his aggressive face into hers and snarl, "Who're you?"

The shock that had propelled her into action had diminished somewhat, allowing her to realize that she had picked a fight with four big boys, and she didn't think she'd be rescued by an adult any time soon. But she wasn't prepared to back down. "I'm Zhara." She tried to keep the fear from rising to her voice.

"What kind of prissy name is *Zhara*?" The boy sneered. "I've never heard *Zhara* before!" Glad for the opportunity to display their solidarity with the alpha wolf, the rest of the pack hooted mirthlessly.

She wasn't prepared to let them intimidate her. She fixed her questioner with a stare and responded, "It's my mother's name, that's what kind."

Another boy snorted. "Your mother? If you've got a mother, what're you doing here?"

She blinked. Where she would normally have responded with reticent silence, she blurted out the truth. "She's dead."

The other boys grew strangely quiet. They all knew what that was like. "That why you here now?"

She shook her head. "No. She died while I was being born."

The boy, who had been standing at the ready to punch her if she proved difficult, gaped, almost impressed. "You killed your mother?"

Young Zhara let her head droop. She had struggled with this truth all her life. Nobody had ever come out and said it, but she knew it to be so. Her mother had died on a table, covered with her own blood, just when Zhara came screaming into the world. Her father had blamed her but had never openly admitted it. He had simply kept his distance, ensuring that she was cleaned and fed, and eventually suitably educated, but she never felt as if she were his child. In all of her twelve years in her father's huge cold house, she'd never been alone in a room with him for more than a few minutes. She'd never sat in his lap, never had a story read to her before she fell asleep, never felt a comforting hand on her hot brow when she had a fever. No, he had never actually come out and told her that he blamed her for his wife's death, but she saw it in every look he had ever given her.

Her mother's family blamed her, too, she was sure of it. That's why they didn't care to know her, never sent her a birthday present or a Christmas card. She came into the world a killer. Zhara felt her face begin to crumple in on itself, and she prayed that the aggressive gang wouldn't continue with their line of questioning; if they did, she knew she would begin to cry, and that was something she never let anyone see her do.

"She's just dead, okay?" She hoped the belligerence in her voice would daunt her determined inquisitor.

"And you're here because your father is punishing you?"

She swallowed. Her whole life as it had been was a punishment. Her arrival here was just another phase in her long, long sentence. But this time, it wasn't her father inflicting it on her—not directly.

"No. I'm here because my father . . ." She couldn't continue.

Miraculously, the same simplicity that makes children so prone to aggression also makes them prone to compassion. Instead of continuing to question her, or even inflicting on her the same abuse they had been meting out to their victim, who was still trembling on the ground, they all, as a unit, stepped away. The fat boy spat at her feet and growled to the others. "Leave her alone. She ain't worth it."

It was a battle won. Without affording her another look, the boys left her with the cowering figure in the corner, not even bothering to continue with their abuse. She stooped, reaching out to it with a compassionate hand, but drew back in surprise when it uncurled itself from its protective position to reveal that it was not a puppy, but a very small boy.

Zhara didn't know what to say. The child was tiny, underfed, thin—and had skin the color of a fresh mushroom. She peered at him. Thin wire glasses hung askew, and as he reached up to straighten them, she noticed his eyes. Pale green, they flicked about like marbles in an enclosed space. Briefly, she wondered if he could see, but her question was answered when he finally focused on her and smiled.

"Hello," the strange little boy said.

She helped him up, still staring. "Why are you so white?" she asked him, with the indelicacy of the very young.

He dusted himself off with hands that were covered with

livid bruises. "I was born that way," he shrugged, having answered that question a thousand times before.

She studied him for a while, taking in his straw-colored hair, transparent skin, and delicate features. "Cool," she finally said.

He looked surprised. "You mean that?" He allowed her to help him up.

"Yeah. You're the same color as my horse."

He brightened. "You got a horse?" He looked around as if he expected it to come charging in and rescue them both.

Zhara felt as if her eyes would fill up once again. Her head drooped. "Not anymore. They sold him."

Together they picked their way through the crowds of oblivious children and walked out to the narrow porch. He seemed to have recovered remarkably from his beating, as if it were an everyday experience. He was a bristling bundle of curiosity.

"Who sold it?" His legs were so much shorter than hers that he had to step double-time to keep up with her. The effect was almost funny.

She scowled. "The banks. They sold the house and all the cars. And my horse. They said my father owed them money."

For someone so young, he was quick. " '*All* the cars'? You had more than one car?"

Zhara wasn't prepared to go into the details about her father's properties. Why tell him you used to be rich if you weren't rich anymore? Luckily, the boy didn't wait for her to answer.

"I never been in a house with more than one car," he informed her, prattling on. "All my foster families only had one. And no horse, neither." He stared up at her, squinting, as if trying to figure out some puzzle.

"Foster homes?" She knew what they were. They were

people who got paid to pretend you were theirs. "If you were in a foster home, why are you here now?

"They keep sending me back. Nobody ever keeps me for long."

"Why?"

He shrugged but didn't answer.

"Did your parents . . . die, too?"

He answered offhandedly, "No parents."

"Don't be stupid. You gotta have, or you couldn't be born." She hoped she wouldn't be called upon to explain the birds and the bees to the kid.

He shrugged again, more elaborately this time. "I never did. My mother didn't want me. So they sent me to a home. And they sent me to another home. I've been all over the state." He sounded as if it were a point of pride for him.

She wanted to know something else. "What did you do to the boys?"

He didn't understand. "What boys?'

"The boys who were beating you up, stupid. What did you do to them?"

He acted as if he had long forgotten such a negligible incident. He waved it away. "Oh, that. Nothing. I didn't do them nothing. They just beat me up when they feel like it. Happens all the time."

She had never heard of anything like that. She was horrified. "Why?"

He flushed and looked away. "They don't like the way I look." Misery showed itself briefly through the thin layer of his bravado, and Zhara's heart tightened for someone who had to suffer like that at the hands of other children. She was old enough and wise enough to know that this irrational, unreasonable hate was something he would have to face for the rest of his life. She didn't want to add to this; as a matter of fact, she realized she wanted to do as much as she could to make it better.

She reached out and touched the skin of his cheek lightly. "*I* like the way you look," she consoled.

He beamed and then floundered around for something equally nice to say about her. He found it and brightened. "I heard you tell them your name. I think it's a pretty name. It sounds like Sahara." He waited. When she didn't say anything, he added, "It's a desert."

Still nothing.

He persisted. "In Africa."

"I *know* that." She brushed the information away. She didn't need a little kid to tell her where the Sahara was. What did he think she was—a dummy? But she liked the boy, so she tried to sweeten her irritated response by asking his name.

"It's Mickey, but everybody calls me Lizard," he said, proudly.

"Lizard? Why?" This funny little boy intrigued her.

"They call me Lizard," he stuck out his puny chest with pride, and beamed at her, "because I can climb anything. Walls and trees and hills and railings and houses. It's easy. Want me to teach you?"

They looked at each other for a long time, then grinned . . .

Zhara of the present sent Zhara of the past scampering away with her new little friend and sat back in the hard, cold wheelchair. The past wasn't something you dwelled on; it was something you accepted and put behind you. It was the only way to move on.

She turned her head and glanced at the radio on her nightstand, the one Cole had given her last week. The little digital clock on it told her she had been sitting at the window for an hour, remembering. It was time to shake herself free of all that.

She wondered if Cole would be coming soon. Again, the thought of his name brought the image of herself to her eyes, arms up around his neck, kissing him as urgently as he had kissed her. *If you're so embarrassed about it,* she asked herself, *then why are you staring at the door, waiting for him to walk through it?* She couldn't find an answer that could satisfy her.

Every day he had come at a different time. She would have sworn he was doing it to throw her off guard, keep her wondering, if she didn't know that his job didn't allow him to keep regular hours. Besides, why would he care if she were looking forward to seeing him or not? They both knew he was simply being nice, trying to make up for what had happened. Given the chance, Cole Wyatt would prefer to see Zhara in cuffs rather than in a wheelchair, but there she was, so he was just making the best of it. *Then why did he kiss me?* came the unbidden question. Again, the answer was obvious. He was just seizing the chance, like the opportunist he was. It had nothing to do with whether he liked her or not. Besides, she didn't like him, so why would she want him to like her? They were enemies who had an unspoken temporary truce, and that's all there was to their relationship.

She passed a hand over her braids to ensure they were neat and made a hurried check in the mirror. Her eyes showed their tiredness, and she wished she hadn't decided long ago that makeup just wasn't for her. She'd have killed for a little concealer and a pretty lipstick right about now. Not that she wanted to look *nice* for the man, she reminded herself hastily, but when he did come, she didn't want to be at the disadvantage of looking as if what he'd done to her in the garden yesterday had had any effect. She settled for splashing some water on her face and drawing her long, fine braids back in an elastic band.

The digital clock he'd brought her didn't tick—so why was she hearing the sound of the seconds and minutes crawling by? She glanced at it again. It was lunchtime, but food was the last thing she wanted to face right now. In a pre-emptive strike, she picked up the intercom and let the head nurse know she didn't want lunch. They brought it for her anyway, with murmured admonitions about keeping up her strength if she wanted to recover. Zhara thanked them politely and left it congealing on the tray where they'd laid it.

One o'clock found her pacing in her chair, rolling herself slowly and deliberately from one end of the room to the other. She consoled herself with the knowledge that she was at least learning to work the wretched thing.

Roll.

Stop.

Turn.

Roll.

Shadows lengthened, and an orderly came and took her tray away, scolding her like a bad child for not eating. Apart from this brief invasion, Zhara's vigil was uninterrupted. When her arms pleaded for mercy, she stopped her endless pacing and settled back with an unread magazine spread open in her lap. He'd come soon. She was sure of it.

Cole tapped his foot in time to the music grinding forth from the ancient radio that sat atop another, even older, nonworking radio, in the furthest corner of the pawnshop. In his impatience, his rhythm was a few beats ahead of the already zippy jazz piece. He didn't like waiting.

The wheezy old radio was surrounded by a dozen others, in all ranges of the spectrum from defunct to practically new. The haphazard collection was right at home with the rest of the décor. All around them, glass cases tried their best to display their contents but were prevented from doing so by a thick patina of dust that covered everything in the room, including the canary cage that stood in a corner. It had taken them several minutes to realize that the bird inside was not stuffed, as were the rhino's head and the moth-eaten owl on a half-rotted branch behind it, but very much alive.

Cole reflected briefly on the kind of mind that would install an owl, stuffed or otherwise, within the line of vision of the creature's natural prey. The poor canary was probably well on its way to a nervous breakdown, he thought wryly; as far as he knew, they weren't all that smart and it probably wouldn't be able to deduce that the owl had long shuffled off its mortal coil. It was most likely wondering every day if the owl, seated just a few feet away, would suddenly decide to strike. After just a few seconds' deliberation, and driven by instinctive compassion for the hapless bird, Cole lifted the large, dusty branch with the owl on top and moved it to a far corner, well out of the canary's sight. In this mess, the owner would probably never notice. Brian watched him with dry amusement. The canary sat dolefully on its perch, oblivious to the change in the demographics of his corner, and listened to the scratchy music with them.

"First you rescue a cat, now a canary. You're sure spreading that kindness around, buddy. Word's out the ASPCA's planning to honor you at their next Christmas fund-raiser."

Cole decided it wasn't worth getting into, so he shrugged expressively and let that one slide. Zhara's cat had taken to sleeping in his room, at the foot of his bed. He had tried locking it out once or twice, but the animal set up such a caterwauling outside his door that he eventually found it easier to just let it in so he could get some sleep. He was a dog man, he had never pretended to be anything more, but he had to secretly admit (only to himself, though) that the gentle snuffling of the cat as she slept and the occasional nuzzle at his toes, were comforting. At least he was spared the melancholic sensation of sleeping alone, even if his bedtime companion had four legs, rather than two.

In fact, he had discovered that the past few nights—with the exception of last night, when he hadn't shut his eyes even for a few minutes—he had drifted off to sleep thinking of Zhara, wondering if she had derived the same comfort from her pet's warmth and companionship. He shrugged off the thought. Zhara was a beautiful young woman. There was no reason for him to assume that she relied on a feline to keep her nights warm.

To his surprise, the idea that she might not be alone in her bare little room when darkness fell did not sit well with him. A curiosity stirred within him: what kind of lover would she choose? Would she settle for just one? Their kiss sprang again to his mind; the willing mouth and eager tongue could only belong to a woman who burned deep inside, who knew what she wanted from a man, and was eager to receive it. Something in him stirred, and he shifted uncomfortably, hoping his partner wouldn't notice his change in mood. Okay, so she wasn't a child, doubtless no virgin. Why would that have anything to do with him?

"Your face looks like a whole movie's just rolling inside your head," Brian remarked. "What are you thinking about like that?"

Cole shrugged. "Just wondering how much longer I'm going to wait out here before I jump the counter and go in search of the goodly Mr. Arismendez," he said lamely.

Brian shrugged wryly and let it go, and for this Cole was indebted to his friend. They continued to wait for the young shop assistant who had been minding the store to re-emerge with the owner, as they had requested. A buddy of his in the Chicago Police Department had recommended the pawnshop to him. The owner was notorious for ignoring a variety of laws, especially those that had to do with the legality of pawning items that you didn't actually own. After twenty years of busting him on a number of petty charges, the police had eventually settled on a compromise. Patos the pawnbroker was to keep his nose clean but his ears and eyes wide open. In exchange for his relaying interesting information about certain goings-on in his north-side neighborhood, they left him in relative peace.

"Probably thinks we're here to take him in for something," Cole suggested, as a possible explanation for the man's ten-minute delay in turning up. He was getting a little frustrated. This was their fourth stop, and so far, nobody they had spoken to remembered having any dealings with a beautiful, young, wild-haired girl and a slim albino boy. Convenient lapse of memory for them, but a pain in the tail for him.

Brian shrugged. "Why would we take him in? We're just out-of-towners looking for information. Besides, didn't your buddy say he was clean?"

Cole smiled ruefully. " 'Clean' is a relative term." He fished a pack of cigarettes from his pocket and tapped it against the back of his hand. Sometimes, all he really needed to do to settle his nerves was to hold the cigarette; lighting it was optional. He fingered the smooth white column thoughtfully. Belatedly, he remembered his manners and held the pack out to his partner.

Brian responded in the negative. "Thanks, pal, but I'm giving them up. Eileen made me. She'd have my neck if she smelled that stuff on me when I get back."

Cole was about to let fly a wisecrack about Brian not being the man he used to be before he gave up his bachelorhood, but, just then, Patos Arismendez, former fence and current proprietor of the fine establishment in which they stood, put in an appearance. His balding head was decorated with a scraggy fringe of hair that sparsely skirted his temples, but which was content to sprout copiously from his ears. His ruddy, leathery skin, covered with spidery red veins like byways on a road map, could have come either from years of too much sunlight or too much booze, and Cole did not peg him as an outdoorsman. Tiny eyes watched them carefully, and the man struggled to still an obvious twitch. He looked like a rat that had learned to walk on his hind legs. At no more than five feet tall, the man came up to Cole's breastbone. Cole immediately seized the advantage and stepped a few feet closer, forcing the already nervous man to crane his neck backward in order to see Cole's face. The psychological upper hand was now his; gleaning information might just be so much easier.

Trying not to betray his nervousness but failing badly, Patos rubbed his stumpy hands together and asked what he could do for the gentlemen.

Cole and Brian went through the motions of showing their credentials and mentioning the name of their brother-in-arms down at the local precinct, although it was hardly necessary. Patos' sharp, turned-up nose was finely attuned to the scent of cop, and right now, his nostrils were full if it.

"I ain't done nothing," he said at once, before Cole even had the chance to state his business.

Cole gave him a placatory smile. "I'm sure you haven't, Mr. Arismendez," he agreed smoothly, ignoring the impressive row of cameras, tape recorders, and other electronic items lined up on shelves behind the man's head. "I'm *sure* your customers all have sales slips for *everything* in your establishment."

Patos decided it was prudent not to respond, and, instead of speaking again, waited for the officers to play the next card. Cole withdrew his little black notebook from his pocket and opened it at the appropriate spot to show the shop owner a grainy old photograph of a teenage girl. The shot of Zhara was at least four years old, and a bad one at that, but it was all he had in his files. Short of whipping out a camera and snapping one of her back at the hospital, it was the best he could do.

The other man studied it closely, frowning. "Missing?"

"Not anymore."

"Dead?" He sounded almost hopeful.

"Very much alive. Do you know her?"

Brian stepped up to Cole's side, offering his partner the additional advantage of a second pair of eyes, boring into Patos' face. The man felt the increased pressure and flinched.

"Think hard," Cole encouraged pleasantly. "Take your time."

The man shook his head. "That's a pretty bad picture."

"It's a very pretty woman," Cole countered. "Hard to forget. Hair all the way down her back, thick and dark. Big brown eyes."

Patos shrugged and would have tried to back away but was prevented from doing so because he had foolishly allowed himself to be maneuvered up against the store counter. "I don't know. There's lots of pretty girls around."

Cole wasn't letting him get away that easily. "Yes, but this one's special. She had something the others didn't have. Think hard." He waved the photo back and forth before Patos' twitching nose. He was about to say "amazing body," but the thought of mentioning aloud the generous, soft curves he had pressed against his own hard body a day ago, of casting her pearls before this particular swine, seemed like sacrilege. Instead, he said, "Very young, but strong. I'm told she was a kickboxer." He leaned so close that he could smell the oil Patos had doused his hair with that morning. It made him queasy, but he persisted. "Liked to climb buildings. Tall ones. For fun and profit."

Patos sighed heavily. Cole had him, and he knew it. The last thing he wanted to do was get the cops set against him, since his home precinct had become so understanding of his situation. Cutting off the flow of information they needed so much would only result in things suddenly getting very uncomfortable for him in his business life. He caved in.

"Yeah, I remember her. She came in from time to time. Smart, knew how to negotiate a price. She always had this boy with her. Funny-colored kid—looked like Death. He followed her around like a puppy." He waited, as if hoping that was all the information he'd be called upon to surrender.

Cole and Brian stood, stony-faced. When you wanted someone to talk and keep talking, nothing worked like silence.

Patos sighed and went on. "She used to run with a bunch of street kids from over on Etna Street. Not a bad crowd, not hard-core or anything, but they were tight and they did what they had to do to survive, I guess." He shrugged. "The world ain't as peachy as we'd like it to be, some of us."

Cole nodded painfully. He tried to imagine the Zhara that he knew—strong, intelligent, vulnerable—as part of the kind of gang he and his colleagues were trying so desperately to remove from the streets of cities all over the country. Most of them were underage, runaways, some abused. Many of them fell into the hands of sexual predators. The possibility of that having happened to Zhara made him cringe. He waited.

Patos went on. "I knew she was supposed to be a pretty good kickboxer. I hear she was part of a dojo of some kind, a makeshift one, just a place where she and some others used to go to practice their moves. They said she could fight, but I never saw her in action. She and me was strictly business, you know? But she was kind of thick with another guy, Anthony or Tony or something, who used to fight for money in the clubs."

Cole stiffened. "What do you mean, 'thick' with him?" He didn't like the feeling his sixth sense was transmitting.

The little man shrugged. "I dunno, man. You're a detective, you figure it out. He was older, twenties or something, and sometimes he came in with her. He looked like he was the one in charge. When he was around, she shut up and he did the talking."

"She worked for him?"

Again, a shrug. "At first, they'd bring in the usual stuff—you know, radios, stereos. They just wanted money to eat and keep a dry roof over their heads, understand?"

Cole and Brian nodded encouragingly.

"But then, things got different. She and the boy, they wanted more. They gave up radios pretty fast, and next thing I knew, she was bringing in jewels, and papers, bonds and the like. So eventually I had to tell her I couldn't handle her no more. What's bonds and certificates got to do with me? I didn't know where to get rid of them. And the jewels, they weren't ten-carat gold with flyspeck diamonds—they were the real thing. She was onto something bigger. Word was she and the boy had started climbing into buildings. I heard she was good with a safe, too. She just started wanting more and more money."

Cole frowned. "Why'd she need all this money?"

Patos shrugged expressively. "There's things out there, man, that once they get their claws into you, you can't set yourself free."

Brian spoke the word that came to Cole's mind. "Drugs?"

"Who knows?" He lifted his hands helplessly.

"So you stopped buying her stuff?" Cole persisted.

"I couldn't afford it, man. She found somebody else, somebody bigger'n me."

"Who?" Cole realized that his heart was hurting in his chest. He had always known that Zhara was a thief, something in direct opposition to everything he believed in, but hearing another person confirm it somehow gave him a pain deep inside. How'd she ever get herself into this mess?

"Why you asking me? Chicago's a big city. One day I see her, the next day I don't see her no more. That's it. That's all."

Cole sighed. The man was right. Zhara and Mickey could lose themselves without effort in a city of this size. He stepped away, and as he did so, the pressure and tension oozed out of the ratty little man. "Where can I find this Tony guy?" Cole flipped open his notebook again, in readiness to take down an address.

Patos apparently decided he'd given them as much as courtesy required. "Look, I told you all I know. You want to know more, ask somebody else."

Brian spoke up hastily, and Cole was glad for it, because he was on the verge of getting just a little more aggressive with the slippery beast. "Tell us where we can find this hideout on Etna Street. Is it still there?"

"In a way. It's half fallen down now, and the city condemned it, from what I hear. It's a fire trap. There's hardly any kids left in there."

Cole took the address anyway, and they left the store to go into the chilly fall night. The rain had stopped, but the weather was still nasty. He checked his watch. It was later than they'd planned. The traffic jam had eaten up a few hours of their time, and they were due to fly back to Medusa tonight. He knew he would be coming back again if he didn't hit paydirt within the next two hours. His jaw took on a determined set.

"Etna Street?" Brian suggested, taking his turn at the wheel.

Cole nodded, glad to be able to mull over his teeming thoughts without the distraction of the road. Zhara filled his mind, the mystery of her, the paradox that she was. She was a puzzle that had to be solved.

"The kids who were there four, five years ago, when she was here, are probably all grown up and moved away by now," Brian warned him gently.

Cole nodded, and forced down the huge boulder in his throat before speaking. "I know. We can still try."

Brian didn't give him any lectures about going above and beyond the bounds of his duty, or ask again why he was still pushing this so far. Cole was thankful for his friend's discretion.

"Why do you think she needed all that money?" he asked Brian worriedly.

His partner glanced at him before putting Cole's own fears into words. "Maybe this Tony guy . . ." He paused. "Maybe he owned them, her and Mickey. Put them to work for him."

It was an ugly truth among runaways and abandoned children. The larger, older ones, even adults, often wound some kind of web around the younger, more impressionable ones, either through the threat of violence or gaining their loyalty by some other means. Once this was done, they set the children to work on a variety of petty crimes, even prostitution—Cole cringed—and sat back and let the children bring in the money. Things hadn't changed much since Fagin unleashed Oliver Twist upon the streets of London. It was a craven way to get rich, and Cole took a vow that should he find this Anthony, and should his suspicions prove true, he'd make him wish he'd never put a hand on a child in his life.

The streets were dark. Etna Street was, as expected, in a part of the city that people who didn't know how to defend themselves shouldn't visit, day or night. The shop-fronts were as dilapidated as the red brick apartment buildings. Unlike happier neighborhoods, where people would be out strolling, even on a chilly night like this, things were quiet, as if the residents lived under a self-imposed curfew. Drunks dozed in doorways and small groups of young men huddled against walls, the tips of their cigarettes glowing, watching the rented car

suspiciously as it rolled past. It might just as well have
had the word "Police" stenciled on the side.

"This must be it," Brian said softly, slowing down before
a dark behemoth that loomed at the side of the street.
They stopped and got out. Cole lifted his head to stare
up at the tall hulk of a building. Arismendez had been
right—the building was abandoned. Not a light shone
through the gaping windows. It was silent and cold.

"Doesn't mean there's nobody in there," he spoke his
hopeful thoughts aloud, and his partner nodded. Children went to ground anywhere, and were less queasy than
adults when it came to choosing their accommodations.
For all he knew, there could be a thriving community inside the apparently empty building.

As one, they strode through the doorless entrance and
clicked on the pocket flashlights that they each carried.
It was like walking into the belly of a whale. The dark maw
stretched into a huge hall, which led onto a warren of
other corridors. Paint hadn't touched the walls in years,
and rising damp became the perfect host for mold and
mildew. They didn't need their noses to tell them that
there were rats in the place; they were treading on the
evidence every step of the way.

Brian shone the light on his guano-encrusted feet in
disgust. "Three-hundred-dollar shoes," he commented.

"I'll have them cleaned," Cole assured him.

"You bet you will."

Cole walked over to the elevator shaft and peered up
into the blackness. The elevator had been torn out, and
all that was left were bare electrical wires. For the sake of
any children who might be wandering around the building, he was glad that the electricity had been shut off. He
tried to think of Zhara, young and vulnerable, coming
home to this every day, and he had to close his eyes to
shut out the hurt.

Together, they combed the place, moving methodically

from room to room, floor by floor. Nothing but cardboard boxes, empty soda bottles, and heaps of debris. Despondent, they made their way back to the entrance and stood on the sidewalk, contemplating their next step. Disappointment gnawed at Cole. This woman was filling his mind, expanding inside him until he was beginning to worry that he would never be able to free himself from her influence. He was sure that the only way to shake himself loose was to find out the truth—and here he was, at another dead end. He fished out the still unsmoked cigarette from his pocket and this time, lit it.

Brian waited until his friend had ground the butt under his heel before laying a hand on his arm and promising, "We'll come back, buddy. Next day off."

Cole shook his head. "No. I'm wasting my time. Yours too. The trail is cold. We . . ."

A noise stopped him from going on. Across the road, a metal window creaked open, and a head appeared, silhouetted against a faint light. Both men froze, hands ready to reach for their weapons. Gradually, their eyes were able to perceive the face of an old woman, hair twisted up into curlers, watching them steadily.

Cole relaxed his readiness stance slightly and let his hand fall to his side. He nodded politely. "Ma'am."

The woman leaned forward a little. "You narcs?"

Brian shook his head. "No. Why?"

Instead of answering, she asked another question. "Looking for the children?"

Cole caught his breath. "Yes! Do you know where they are?"

She shrugged. "Haven't seen many around since the place got condemned. Heard a twelve-year-old fell down the elevator shaft this spring. Since then, the cops have been making the building part of their rounds. The kids didn't like it, so they moved out."

"Where to?"

"Who knows? There's lots of places like this in the neighborhood. And you know children . . ." she waved her hand expressively.

"I'm trying to get information about somebody," Cole began.

She stiffened suspiciously. "I thought you said you weren't narcs."

"Not exactly," Cole explained. "We're detectives, over from Medusa."

"Same difference."

Cole didn't pursue the point. "I'm trying to get some information on a young man called Anthony, or Tony. He was here with some children a few years ago. He was seen with a young girl, very pretty, with long hair, and a younger boy . . ."

"Boy looked sick all the time?"

Hope leaped inside him. That had to be Mickey. "Yes." He tried not to let his eagerness show.

"This Tony feller, used to fight for money?"

"Did he?"

"Could be the one. Folks came from all over to fight him. People took bets on him. Heard he was something to watch. Some kind of Judo-something." She snapped her fingers, trying to find the right word.

"Kickboxing," Cole said. It was not a question.

"Yeah."

He inhaled through his nose and let it out through his mouth, trying to calm himself. "Where can I find him?"

She shrugged again. "God knows. He just disappeared. Some people say he got himself killed, and some say he left town suddenly. Some of the kids swear he's still down there, somewhere, appearing and disappearing, like the Phantom of the Opera. But then, kids'll say anything."

"And the girl?"

"She left right after he did. Maybe they ran off together."

This wasn't something Cole wanted to hear. What if Anthony had left Chicago with Zhara? Could she still be seeing him? He yearned to hear more, but the woman insisted that she had nothing more to tell them, so he gave her his number and asked her to call him if she remembered anything else. She promised solemnly she would, if the occasion arose, but he knew she wouldn't call. With a grinding of metal, she pulled the rusted window shut, leaving them alone again.

"Time to be getting back to the airport," Brian reminded him softly.

Cole rubbed the back of his aching neck. He withdrew the small cell phone from his pocket and flicked it open with one hand. "Give me a moment, okay?" Brian nodded and stepped aside to allow him his privacy. He was coming in pretty late; the least he could do was let his son know.

Quickly, he dialed some numbers, but instead of Omar's familiar voice, an echo of his own, a bored female voice answered. "St. Cyprian's Hospital, can I help you?" Cole removed the phone from his ear and stared at it in puzzlement. He had intended to call his own home number. Could it be that his fingers had instead led him to the woman who had consumed his mind all day?

The bored voice repeated its question, and then, when he still didn't answer, became a little irritated. "Hello? Look, if this is a joke . . ."

He cleared his throat hastily. "No, Miss . . . uh, sorry. May I speak to Zhara Thorne, please?"

He was patched in, and, to his relief, Zhara picked up on the third ring.

"Zhara," he said. Her name felt soft on his lips.

Silence. "Cole?"

"Yes." What was wrong with his throat? It was closing up on him, raspy, dry.

The sleepiness cleared from her voice at once and was

replaced by a chill wind that sliced into him in the damp night. "What do you want?"

He was a little taken aback. "I . . ." What was he going to tell her, that he had dialed her number by instinct? "I just called to see how you're doing."

"I'm doing fine." She sounded like she was speaking through clenched teeth. Obviously, she wasn't giving him an inch. He hesitated. "Is something wrong?"

"Why?"

"You sound so . . ." Then he remembered that their last parting had not exactly been warm, in spite of—or maybe because of—the kiss that had preceded it.

"How do I sound?" she persisted, archly.

He sighed. "Never mind. How are you feeling?"

She seemed to soften. "It's not bad. I'm learning to use the chair a little. I can move about now. It's just hard because of my arm . . ."

"I'm glad to hear it." He squeezed his eyes shut, picturing her lying stretched out on the narrow hospital bed, cursing her body for not obeying her instructions. That image alone was enough for him to forgive her testiness. Obviously, she wasn't having an easy time of it. All she could do during her endless hours alone was worry. He had to admit he was worried, too, only he was doing his best not to let her know. Adding his own fears for her recovery to hers would do no good.

"Where are you?" She failed to keep the tinge of curiosity out of her voice.

He hesitated. Better not to give too much away. Admitting he was out investigating her wouldn't exactly be smart. "Out of town."

Her voice cooled even further. "Pleasure?"

"Business."

"What business?" She sounded mildly suspicious, but maybe he was paranoid—or had a guilty conscience.

"Mine."

She ignored the snub. "Is that why you . . ." Her voice trailed off, becoming almost little-girl-lost at the end.

The light dawned. She was mad because she missed his visit today! The possibility of such a thing almost melted the chill her anger had breathed into his bones. ". . . didn't come to see you?" he finished softly. When she didn't say anything, he took it as a given. "Are you upset because I didn't come to visit?"

"Don't be stupid," she snapped.

A smile kissed his mouth lightly. "I'll come tomorrow. I promise."

She snorted. "Do as you like, Detective. Whatever happens, the world will keep on spinning."

Now, this was the Zhara he was coming to discover— prickly and full of fight. He laughed. "That's the spirit," he teased her. The line went resoundingly dead.

Still smiling, he got into the car next to Brian, and the two set off on the road. When he placed a second call on the cell, this time carefully dialing his own home number, Brian glanced at him questioningly, but didn't speak.

Six

The lack of something to do was the worst thing—far worse than the trauma of physiotherapy or the tedium of having to face the same awful food over and over. For want of anything else to distract her, Zhara set about loosening her braids. It was time for them to come out, and besides, she really only braided them so tightly when she was out on a job; braided hair didn't lose strands that could be left behind as evidence.

She sat by the window, taking advantage of the pale sun that bathed her shoulders, and began her task. It was difficult, especially when one hand trailed behind the other, and tired so often that she had to let it fall into her lap and rest every few minutes. The dozens of braids would take hours, but with the help of the radio that played soft ballads in the background, it was a better way to while away the morning than going out to one of the rehab rooms to watch the communal television. In her lifetime, Zhara had had all of the communal television she was ever going to watch.

She had just made up her mind that the soft music on the radio was making her a little too melancholy for such a nice day, and was about to wheel herself over to the radio to change stations, when the unmistakably woebegone strains of R.E.M.'s "Everybody Hurts" seeped into the room like soft tears. She stopped, wanting to click it off before it got to her, because it always got to her, but she was unable to move.

Unbidden, her lips formed the familiar words, and she mouthed along to the singer's sadness. His was the voice of a man in pain, who had suffered loss, and as always, she was convinced that he was speaking directly to her, and her alone. *Everybody hurts*, he crooned gently to her, *everybody cries*.

All well and good for you to say, she thought miserably, *you don't know how hard it's been, and what a struggle it is to hang on, hold on and not let anyone see you in pain.* As hard as she tried, and as determined as she was to push her body to the limit, to get up, force each step, teeth grinding, until she fell into the arms of her physiotherapist, gasping, she couldn't keep up a positive attitude all the time. There were enough hours in the day for her to spend one or two of them sitting and staring down at her bare legs, wondering if she would ever be able to look at them the same way again, as parts of her body that flexed and stretched at her command, rather than a mismatched pair of tools, one still eager to please, the other near useless.

And if that were not enough, there was the question of Mickey. Since yesterday, he had not come back. Repeated calls to their apartment brought only the sound of her own voice on their answering machine. Where could he be? She tried to force down the fear that nagged at her like an exposed nerve. Mickey liked to run away. No—he *specialized* in it.

Twice, at age nine and ten, he had run away from the Harbourmouth Home, tired of the torment he was constantly suffering at the hands of the brutish older children there. Twice he was hunted down and brought back. The third time he went missing, when he was ten and she fifteen, searches turned up empty. After six agonizing weeks of waiting, and of seeing the authorities of the Home do precious little to solve the problem, Zhara shouldered the responsibility for her only friend, and went looking for him. The looking didn't involve much speculation as to his location; she knew instinctively where he had run to, and there she headed.

Mickey had taught her well. Her newfound climbing skills made escape easy; as a matter of fact, Zhara slipped over the far wall with so little effort that she wondered if anyone truly cared about keeping any of them in in the first place. It took her five days to hitchhike to Chicago, sleeping in warehouses, sheds, and on dry nights, in open fields. She arrived tired, starving, but no less determined to locate him than she had been when she started out.

She found him right where he had always said he would be: in the tiny apron of a park in the shadow of the Sears Tower. A climber at heart, he dreamed perpetually of climbing it, always swearing that one day, he would. She knew he'd find his way to his Mecca, where he could lie on his back and daydream about one day reaching the top, defying death and the law, and be a hero.

They planned to go back to Harbourmouth eventually, but somehow that never happened. At first, they were simply too taken up with the barest necessities of staying alive, of finding food and shelter and avoiding the watchful police patrols and the interference of well-intentioned adults. Other children, older hands than they, taught them how to beg at the back doors of restaurants, and, where necessary, how to steal food and clothing. As cruel as they could be at times, children understood loyalty and solidarity, and the street children closed ranks around the two bewildered newbies, offering support, advice, and a family of sorts.

Then she met Antonio, leader of one of the many straggly groups of children that roamed the streets. Sensing their bewilderment and displacement, he lost no time in welcoming them into his herd, devoting as much time as he could to showing them the ropes and preparing them to face their first homeless winter. A little older, stronger, compassionate, and patient, he was the perfect target for her adolescent affections. These he accepted without vanity and eventually responded in kind. In him, she found a safe place to hide her wounded emotions, and close to him, she could forget about her father, the luxury that she had been cut off from when he died, and the mother she had killed on the day her own life had begun.

When Mickey first took sick, Tony helped. He showed her how to find the money she needed to make him better again. One thing was for sure, he'd told her solemnly, stolen radios and picked pockets couldn't pay for medical attention, not even the kind provided by doctors who didn't bother to ask where your parents were. He taught her how to plan and execute a heist, and showed her where to get the best prices for their haul. He put his own life at risk in an effort to help them achieve that objective. He taught her how to fight, and this she did gracefully, her long legs firing at the enemy, real or imagined, quick fists up before her face to protect herself.

All this he had done with a kind of calm that served to assuage her own guilt. It needed to be done, he had explained to her. It wasn't right, but Mickey was suffering, and friends didn't let friends suffer. Antonio always seemed to have the right answer. If he were here now, she wouldn't be struggling to prevent the tears from welling up inside. He'd have held her against his hard, slim chest and urged her softly to let them all out. When they finally spilled onto her cheeks and down her jaw, he'd have gently taken up a handful of her own hair and slowly patted them dry.

But Tony was dead, murdered by a boy in blue who should have thought twice before pulling the trigger, and all the crying she did, she did on her own. That kind of solitude was perhaps the most hollow of all. She laid her comb and brush on the windowsill and held her head, buzzing with all these bewildering thoughts and emotions, in her hands.

The door creaked open behind her.

Startled, she straightened up, dabbing at her eyes. "Mickey?" she asked, without turning. He was back! They never could stay mad at each other for long.

But the presence behind her was too huge, too imposing to be Mickey. The sheer bulk of him took up so much of the room that she was aware of a shifting in the balance of the space around her. She knew at once who it was, but, instead of turning to meet him, bowed her head in an effort to hide her damp eyes and the warm flush that rushed to her face as he drew nearer.

"Good morning." The voice behind her was low—and close.

"Cole," her voice rasped, and she coughed softly to clear her suddenly dry throat. She wanted to make another hasty dab at her wet eyes, but it wouldn't have helped. His sharp eyes wouldn't miss the streaks down her face anyway, so instead she continued to keep her head lowered, hoping he'd say whatever it was he had come to say and then leave. She still hadn't forgiven him for not coming to see her yesterday, even though her rational mind told her he was a grown man with a taxing job, who probably flew out of town on business all the time. Why would the fact that she had waited for him all day have made a difference?

"Come on," he said quietly. "Not still mad at me because I stood you up yesterday, are you?" He laid his hands lightly on the handles of her chair and turned her a little, so that she sat at an angle to the window, with the blade of sunlight cutting a swath across her face, falling on her half-loose hair. "Or because of our little kiss in the garden?" he added, with a dash of mischief in his voice.

Zhara didn't need to be reminded of that. It had been

a fiasco from start to finish, and the less she thought, the better. She didn't answer.

He bent forward even lower, perhaps with the intention of teasing her even further, but caught sight of her watery eyes, and concern wiped the idle smile from his lips. "Zhara?" He leaned uncomfortably close, and, in spite of her misery, she shivered at the scent of him: lemon grass and coffee and warm male. If he managed to hold her gaze in his, she'd be doomed. She looked down at her lap.

He persisted, anxiety edging his deep voice. "Are you hurting?"

Yes, she wanted to say. *Yes, Cole, I hurt. I hurt all over, but I'm not talking about my damn head. I'm talking about the fact that in a few days I'll be back home again, alone again, lonely again, with a sick boy to look out for, and nobody I can trust to share my hurt. I'm hurt because the only male arms that have ever drawn me close—until you touched me, damn you—are cold and still, and I ache deep inside but there's nobody, nobody at all who knows how to heal me.* But giving those words the tangibility of sound would be too humiliating, so she shook her head vigorously, afraid to open her mouth lest the floodgates re-open as well.

"That's not true," he contradicted her denial accusingly. "Why do you think you need to deny that you're in pain? Have you called the nurse? Has anybody given you any medication at all?"

"I am not in pain!" she shouted in frustration. Did he always have to be right? Why didn't he listen for a change, instead of always being the one to talk?

He heard her unspoken plea. "Well, if your body isn't hurting, your heart sure is. Then tell me what's bothering you." He waited, patiently.

Now that she had his attention, she didn't know what to do with it. Finally, she decided to articulate only her most immediate—and least vulnerable—dilemma. "It's Mickey."

"What about him?"

She sighed. "We had a fight. He left yesterday, mad at me, and I haven't heard from him since." In retrospect, it all seemed so silly. What *had* they argued about? It was nothing, a trifle that got blown out of proportion.

"Did you phone home?"

She looked at him as if he'd called her an idiot. "Of course I did. Don't you think that'd be the first thing I'd do? He wasn't there."

"Where does he go to? Where does he hang out with his friends?"

She shrugged. "Nowhere. Mickey and I don't exactly have friends. It's just us. That's all." She folded her arms around herself, shielding her body, and thus her vulnerability, from him.

The desolation in her voice rang loud enough for him to hear. "Come here." He laid his big hand on her shoulder and drew her closer to him. She stifled a sigh; he felt good, smelled good, and right now she needed the comfort of his touch—of anybody's touch—more than anything. She made the decision not to resist (it was, after all, just one time) and let him hold her, fitting her face into the curve of his neck and drawing warmth from him. From this close, she could see the faint shadow of his beard, recently shaven but already reasserting itself, on his chin. The hollow of his throat sank and rose with each breath, and collarbones made themselves known, pushing up gently against his dark skin. His size, and his crudely hewn features, gave the impression of his roughness from afar, but this close, Zhara could see and feel only sensual smoothness, and a warmth that threatened to envelop her, cozying her until she never wanted to crawl out of it again.

When he felt she was able to talk again, he said, "Do you want me go look for him?"

She flinched, pulling away. Cole, look for Mickey? He'd *love* that. "The last thing Mickey needs is to be hunted down like a dog by some cop," she countered acidly.

She might as well have slapped him in the face. He straightened, anger darkening his already black eyes to hard-edged onyx. "First," he began, icily, "I don't intend to 'hunt him down like a dog'. You were worried about him, and," he indicated her chair, "you're hardly in a position to go looking for him yourself. I was just offering to help." His rigid body shook almost imperceptibly, and Zhara wished she could have taken back her hasty slur. "Second," he didn't give her a chance to say anything, "I may be a cop, but I'm also a man and a father. I know what it's like to be concerned about someone. If my own son went missing, I'd have gone looking for him, too."

She hated to see the hurt in his eyes. What was wrong with her? He had been offering his help, that was all, and she had to go and offend him by throwing his offer in his face. She swallowed hard. "Cole, I'm sorry."

He didn't look mollified. "Look, Zhara. I'm a police officer. That's what I do for a living. You don't have to respect it, but you have to accept it. I don't respect some of the things you've done, either, but that doesn't mean I wouldn't help you if you needed it." A tight ball of muscle worked in his jaw. "So as long as you need it, my offer of help still stands."

She nodded, afraid to speak. Finally, she worked up the courage to repeat herself. "I'm sorry. I didn't mean to offend you. But I think he'll be back soon. Sometimes he . . ." she paused, ". . . needs to be by himself."

Cole nodded, and mercifully he let the subject drop.

As he stood there before her, unsure of what to do next, she let herself really look at him for the first time since he'd walked in. He looked fresh and clean, well-scrubbed, and sported a light jacket that somehow managed to comfortably sit across those broad shoulders. The front of it fell open to reveal a light blue linen long-sleeved shirt that topped off a precision-pleated pair of charcoal-gray slacks. He didn't look as if he were on his way to or from work. It occurred to her with sudden clarity that he had dressed this way to come to the hospital—to see her. Nobody had ever done that for her before. Surprised, she smiled.

Cole looked puzzled by her unexpected change in mood. "What?" he half frowned, perplexed, not sure if he should join her in smiling.

She waved it away. "Nothing." She watched him as he wavered from his usual stance of self-assured composure and tried to put him more at ease. "Thanks for visiting." He was still clutching a large, square package in his hand, and she was sure that it was another present for her. She couldn't take her eyes off it.

He followed the direction of her gaze and seemed surprised to find the package still in his hand. "This is for you. I got it—um—on my trip." He laid it gently in her lap and stooped again so that his face was level with hers.

Their tiff forgotten, she tugged at the wrapping, unable to avoid smiling up into his face with pleasure. She didn't often get presents, and his always thrilled her, but she would be a liar if she pretended that the box in her lap excited her more than the proximity of its giver.

Now that he was close up again, she could see how tired he looked. The intelligent eyes still held their watchful gleam, but the dusky smears under them spoke of no sleep. Again, she felt the tug of remorse. There she was, piqued because he hadn't been to see her, and he was probably holed up God-knows-where, all night. She really should think about the problems of others instead of her own, she scolded herself.

As she managed to peel the neatly wrapped paper off the package, a box of obviously expensive liqueur-filled chocolates came to light.

"Oh."

He raised a brow. "Oh?" he mimicked.

That wasn't very polite. She tried to look pleased. "I mean, uh, thank you. That's very kind."

He smiled ruefully. "You sound like your maiden aunt just gave you a cardigan for Christmas, when you really wanted a sled. Did I get the wrong brand?"

He was being so generous, she didn't want to offend. "No, I—thank you."

He pried the box from her limp fingers, looking hurt. "You already thanked me. I want to know if you like them or not."

"I'm grateful," she said, wetting her lips, "it's just that, well, I don't eat sweets."

He looked surprised. "None?" He didn't sound like he believed her.

She shook her head vigorously. "No."

"No candy at all?"

"No."

He was incredulous. "Ice cream?"

He was embarrassing her! "No ice cream."

"Not even cake?" He was aghast, as if life wasn't worth living without cake.

"Especially not cake," she informed him regretfully.

"Why?" He looked like a bemused twelve-year-old.

How could she explain to him that after encountering "dessert" as defined by the goodly cooks at the Harbour-mouth Home for Juveniles, she had no intention of eating anything with sugar in it ever again? She settled for an-swering "long story," and hoped he'd let it rest.

He didn't. "No chocolates? You must be out of your mind. I don't know about you, lady," he slit the cello-phane wrapping with a thumbnail, flipped up the box lid, and withdrew a plump piece, "but I think candy is Man's greatest invention." He took a bite, and the air filled with the scent of Grand Marnier. Then he held the other half between fingers dripping with liqueur and offered it to her.

She protested vigorously. "Cole, I *told* you . . ."

"I know what you told me," he said softly, holding her resistant gaze steady. His voice dropped to a husky whisper, "but sometimes the one thing you don't want is the one thing you end up tasting, and then when you do, you realize you keep wanting more and more." The piece of chocolate approached her lips, and, forgetting her protests, Zhara found them parting for him. Deftly, and very slowly, he placed it between them. The strong, sweet liqueur tasted like orange groves, the dark chocolate held a hint of coffee. Instead of withdrawing his fingers as her mouth closed, he left them there, at the edge of her full lips, so that the shock of the sugar—after all this time!— was replaced by a powerful, more visceral shock.

The chocolate melted fast, pooling onto her tongue in a flood of sweetness, and, to her horror, she realized that the tip of his thumb was insinuating itself further between her lips, until she was sucking on that instead. His fingers slid along her cheek to the curve of her jaw, where they lightly stroked her soft skin. She swallowed the purr that was rising inside her, but Cole heard it anyway.

"More?" he offered, tauntingly.

"I couldn't," she managed to say.

"Come on," he coaxed. He withdrew his hand—Zhara almost caught it in hers to stop him from taking it away from her face—and plucked another delight from the box. "Open," he commanded. She obeyed without resistance, mouth parted, waiting. Again, he bit into the round dark morsel before placing the other half to her lips. This time, her mouth flooded with amaretto, searing her tongue with its distinct toasted-almond taste. The heady alcohol—or maybe it was the power of his touch—went straight to her groin, infusing it with heat.

His forefinger claimed the space his thumb had last

enjoyed, and as her warm mouth engulfed it, he sighed. This time, to her delight, she discovered that it was she, not he, who was in control. His hands were huge, and the single finger was quite a mouthful. Grasping his wrist to ensure that he did not withdraw, and shocked at her own boldness, she drew him in, flicking her tongue against the tip. Sharp, almost vengeful nips punctuated gentle licks, and aggressive nails threatened to pierce the veins that pulsed in his wrist. After a thousand years, she pulled his hand away, but not to set him free. Instead, she blew lightly on the moist hand, cool air confusing his senses before she let him back inside her velvet warmth.

With his free hand, he rested the box down on the floor beside her wheelchair, and then settled fully to his knees. The light streaming in from the window framed his bowed head like a halo, and for a fleeting moment Zhara remembered her vision of him hovering over her that first night in the hospital, when she was convinced that he was a dark angel, spreading his wings above her.

She noted with almost malicious amusement that in his quiescence he was powerless; strength and might were laid low by her touch. He laid his heavy head on her lap and groaned against her thigh. His breath came in puffs against the thin material of her dressing gown, but then ceased, as if he were convinced that by holding his breath he could hold onto his sanity. She relished the moment, toying with him, growing brave after a while and allowing her tongue, pointed and hard like a blade, to tease at the webbing between his fingers before moving to engulf the thick shaft again. It was only when she realized that in torturing him she was torturing herself that she finally stopped, withdrew his quivering hand from its wet nest, and laid it lightly on her knee.

He was silent for a long time before lifting his head and staring at her. Shock rimmed his opaque eyes. "What are you doing to me?" he whispered.

"Punishing you."

"I deserve it," he confessed almost miserably. Painfully, with great effort, he rose to his feet. With her seated, and him standing, his bulging excitement was in plain view. Zhara tried not to stare. The man was big *all over.*

Without speaking, he moved around behind her and silently lifted one fine sooty braid in his hand. With deft fingers, he began to loosen it, taking up where she had left off. She let him work without protest, reasoning that it would allow them both to return to normalcy after what had just taken place.

What is it about this man, this man I don't even like, that makes me respond to him so? She couldn't bear to seek an answer to her own question. She squeezed her thighs lightly together. She didn't need to explore them to know that they were soaked with her heat, aching for attention after such an awfully long time.

That's it! She congratulated herself on her revelation. It was lust, pure and simple. Surviving three years without the touch of a man had seemed easy, because she had never encountered anyone capable of awakening such thoughts in her, even thoughts destined to reside in her private fantasies, never to see the light. Now she was at a low spot, vulnerable, facing an uncertain future, and in swaggers this man, who looks good, smells good, tastes good, and the dam of her pent-up neglected sexuality threatens to burst and spill forth, drowning her. It was all about sex—her need for it. She was, after all, a woman, and her body had needs that were more basic than her mind or her heart. He was sexy, and she was responding to that in what amounted to a simple reflex, beyond her control. It was ancient, visceral, all at the level of hormones. She didn't have to feel betrayed by her feelings, because her feelings had nothing to do with it.

Comforted by her rationalizations, she lifted a braid and began working on it, telling herself that it was okay if the quick, inadvertent contact of his fingers along the nape of her neck only increased the pooling between her thighs. As long as she remembered that it was purely physical attraction, she could handle it. She had mastered her body to allow it to perform marvelous feats on the back of a horse or up the side of a building; she could master it now, bring it to heel in the face of great temptation. No problem.

There was no telling how much time passed until they loosened the last braid. Cole had moved patiently from strand to strand, fingers working quickly, causing Zhara to wonder with just a hint of jealousy where he had managed to become so practiced. Neither spoke. When they were done, her hair stood around her head in a dense, dark fluff, thick and curly, responding joyfully to being freed from its weeks of confinement in braids.

He held bunches of it in his hands, weighing it, as if it were some rare silken fiber that he was about to purchase. Then, again with skill born of practice, he lifted her carved wooden brush from its place at the windowsill and with deft, even strokes began calling the unruly mass to order.

The sound of his voice after such a prolonged period of silence was strange to her. "Exquisite brush."

Zhara stiffened. She had become so used to not trusting him that any comment could mask an ulterior motive. "Yes," was all she said.

"Precious to you, isn't it?" he persisted.

She swallowed. Maybe it was her weakened state, or maybe she was simply growing fed up of resisting his probes for information about her, but for a change she responded honestly instead of withdrawing and turning him away. "It was my mother's. I'm told she had hair like mine."

He couldn't help but pick up on that one. "You're *told*?"

She tried to shrug casually, but halfway through, the shrug turned into a tremor. "I never knew her."

He waited.

What was he waiting for? Wasn't that enough? Why did he have to know everything about her? Again, she wondered if she was mad to share so much of herself with him, but there was something that urged her to speak, a tiny resident traitor deep inside that maybe wanted him to know her. She forced the next words out into the open. "She died in childbirth."

"With a sibling?" he asked, in a voice that told her that he guessed otherwise.

"With me."

His hands ceased their hypnotic motion against her scalp. Without turning, she knew that he was holding the beautiful, intricately carved piece up to his face and examining it, not for its artistry but for answers that it couldn't give him. "I'm so sorry," he said at last.

She nodded sadly. "So am I."

"For never having known her?"

The words in her mouth were like glass. "For killing her."

For the second time that afternoon he spun her around in her chair to face him. His eyes were wide with horror. "You can't mean that!"

"Why not?" she responded passionately. "She was fine until I came along. Everything was fine, and then she got pregnant with me. She was sick throughout, couldn't leave her bed, in pain half the time. Then there was this awful labor. Two days of it. I tortured her. And when I finally came, she was bleeding so much—"

"Zhara—"

"—she died on a bed, covered in her own blood—"

"—you can't—"

"—because of me!"

"—blame yourself!"

"Why not?" Her voice was shrill. "Why not? My father did! Her family did!"

He leaned forward, letting the brush slip onto the carpet, hands outstretched, offering asylum, but she went on talking, letting the agony that she had never shared with another human being spill out of her. "Her family never met me, never visited, never called. They hated me. *My father* hated me. He fed me and he bought me clothes, but he never touched me, never smiled, never asked me questions or read me a story or took me for a walk."

He let his warm arms encircle her, trying to shush her before she let her words continue to hurt on their way out, but she struggled against him. She needed to spit it all out, purge herself, get rid of the venom that had blackened her blood slowly all her life. "My father never kissed me, not once, ever. Not for my birthday, not for Christmas. I slept in a different wing of the house. He paid women to feed me and teach me. They bought my toys and filled my stockings on Christmas Eve." She was heaving as if she were about to throw up, but all that rose to her mouth were words and long-buried memories. "When I turned eight, he wrote me a check as a birthday present and gave it to my tutor to give to me."

Cole struggled to keep his anger down—blind anger at a man he didn't even know. What kind of sick dog would do this to a child?

"He died hating me. He died wishing I'd never been born . . ." She couldn't say anything more. She felt strong arms under her, gentle arms that lifted her with infinite care. Without thinking about it, she let her hand slide up to lock around his neck, and she was being carried over to the hard, narrow hospital bed.

Cole sat, lowering her into his lap, nudging her head down to his shoulder. Against his bulk, she felt small, like a girl again. Her sobs coughed up out of her, wet, pained,

and angry, and the sound of her own voice in her ears
was strange, much too high and weak.

But *his* voice, his was both deep and strong, soothing,
wrapping around her like a comforter on a winter's night.
When his lips were not framing murmured endearments,
they made low unintelligible sounds, like those of a small
mother creature crooning to her babies. The tears
wouldn't stop, couldn't stop, but then they did, leaving
her shaking and exhausted.

He had stopped speaking, and, instead, let his lips
smooth her eyebrows, kiss her eyelids, linger along her
wet lashes. She let herself go limp against him, as she
waited for her breathing to return to normal.

"Little one," he whispered, "sleep."

She slept.

She opened her eyes to find the sun gone from her
window, shifted to the other side of the building. To her
amazement, she was still seated in his lap; it must have
been torture for him, bearing her dead weight for what
was certainly hours. She made to slide from his lap, but
he held her fast. "No."

"But I'm heavy."

"You aren't."

"Cole, you must be so uncomfortable . . ."

"Be still."

She obeyed. She tried to gather her scattered thoughts,
remembering with shame how she'd let go in front of
him, spilling her agony, and he, almost a stranger. Not
even Mickey, her only friend, knew how deep her pain
ran, but she had told his man. She felt as if a barrier had
been breached. The knowledge that she had given him
had allowed him to know her more intimately, as if they
had made love, and, like a woman waking up to discover
a man she hardly knew in her bed, she was embarrassed.

She lifted her eyes to search his, looking for any sign
of mockery or contempt or any signal that this new knowl-

edge had increased the power he already had over her. But she saw neither glee nor contempt—only concern. Someone was concerned about her. The purity of his self-less emotion stole her breath.

"Come home with me," he murmured.

She squinted, not sure of what she was hearing. "What?"

"Come home with me, when you leave here. You're being discharged in a few days, and when you are, let me take you home."

This time, she slid successfully off his lap, and he made no move to restrain her. "I'm n-n-not sure I know w-w-what you're asking . . ." she stuttered in her confusion. His offer couldn't possibly come without strings, and if he was thinking what she *thought* he was thinking . . .

"No, no, it's nothing like that." He closed his eyes, re-hearsing what he was about to say next, to ensure he wasn't misunderstood. "When you leave, what are you go-ing to do? There's no telling how much time you'll have to spend in that chair; who's going to take care of you?"

"Mickey will."

"You live in an apartment seven floors up, with no ele-vator. How will you manage the stairs?"

"Mickey will carry me," she insisted.

"Up seven flights of stairs?"

He was right. She hadn't thought of that. "We'll move."

"Where? How? Do you have the money to move?"

She hesitated. She couldn't fight him with logic, and she wasn't sure if she was strong enough to cast about for another weapon. Could his offer really be as honest and genuine as it seemed? "Why are you doing this?"

"I want to take care of you."

"Why?"

"I don't know."

"Guilt?"

"No."

"What, then?"

"I don't know." His eyes, usually guarded or coolly assessing, were as puzzled as hers, as if he hadn't intended to invite her until he heard himself say it. "I don't know why, but I want to help."

"For how long?" she had to ask.

His brow creased. "What?"

"How long do you want to help me for? How long will it take before your patience runs out?"

He shook his head. "I don't under—" Then he stopped. Zhara could clearly see the comprehension dawn in his eyes.

She pressed home her point. "What if I never walk properly again? This isn't a little bruise I have, Cole, this is a brain injury. There are no predictions, no guarantees. What if it never gets better than it is now, with me tottering around, listing to one side like a wrecked ship? A useless arm and a useless leg. A burden."

"You'd never be a burden—" he began staunchly, but she cut him off.

"How can you say that? What if I'm still like this a month from now, or two months? What if I start to bleed from my head again—"

He opened his mouth to answer but never got the chance. The sound of the door made them both jump.

Mickey was still wearing the old grunge rock T-shirt and washed-out jeans he had had on yesterday, and Zhara knew at once that he hadn't so much as stopped by the apartment to shower. His pale skin was shadowed with a bluish tinge that told her that he hadn't slept, and the smudges of dirt on his clothing spoke of a restless night in the city. Her first thought was that he must be awfully hungry, but before she could voice her concern, he bellowed, "What's he doing here?" An irate thumb pointed accusingly at Cole, whose spine instantly stiffened against her back.

She remembered with horror that she was sitting on the edge of the bed next to him, thank God not on his lap as she had been mere seconds ago (there'd have been hell to pay if he'd caught them like that!), but close enough, still touching, still intimate. Guiltily, she pulled away, and the suddenness of the movement sent pain crashing along her bruised body, like a well-aimed sledge-hammer. The shock of the pain made her gasp, mouth open, eyes wide.

Mickey didn't notice; his attention was focused on Cole, who by this time was unhurriedly getting to his feet. The boy took a few menacing steps toward the much-larger man, like a Pekinese threatening a German Shepherd. "I asked a question, *Detective!*" He gestured aggressively at Cole with his pointed jaw. "Why are you here?"

With his cop's instincts, Cole knew at once that remaining calm and not rising to the bait was the best option. The boy looked tired, frazzled, and ill. It would serve no purpose to get into an argument, especially with an opponent who was obviously not up to the task. Slowly, without any inflection that could be misconstrued as an acceptance of his invitation to wrangle, Cole responded, "I was just visiting Zhara, as I do every day."

"On her bed?" He gesticulated at the narrow hospital bed as accusingly as if he had walked in and found it in libidinous disarray, sheets tangled, air above it steamy and pungent with the smell of passion.

Zhara cringed. "Mickey, please . . ." she begged. To be embarrassed in front of this man, especially after having allowed herself to be so vulnerable to him, spilling her deepest pain to him, would be too much. Mickey was always protective, always looked out for her best interests, especially where men were concerned, but today, he had moved beyond protectiveness to loss of control. She looked quickly and apprehensively from one to the other; Cole, ostensibly calm, but jaw working, so that it was ob-

vious that he was maintaining his control by an act of will,
and Mickey, reddening with each breath, adolescent voice
growing higher as the words spewed up out of him.

"Zhara," he demanded, spinning away from Cole to
face her, "what was he doing on your bed?"

Zhara was too miserable to speak. She let her head drop
to her chest, wishing they would both just go away and
leave her to her solitude.

A quick glance at her face was all Cole needed to tell
him it was time to intercede. He took a step to the side,
and the broadness of his shoulders was enough to eclipse
Mickey's view of Zhara. The low rumbling of his voice was
barely audible. "Son, I don't think she wants to answer
that question."

"I am *not* your son!" Mickey shrieked. Zhara had never
heard him so angry. What in the name of God could have
happened to turn her gentle, malleable companion
into—into *this*?

Cole took a step forward, hands held out in a placatory
gesture. "Your friend deserves her privacy," he advised.
"Why don't you just go outside for a few minutes until
you calm down. Can't you see you're frightening her?"

"I am not going anywhere!" Mickey folded his arms
across his chest and planted his feet far apart for balance,
daring Cole to move him. "*You* go outside!"

Before Cole had a chance to respond, Zhara cut in,
straining to see around the expanse of Cole's back.
"Mickey, stop it! What's gotten into you? Why are you
behaving like this?"

"Me?" He hammered his chest with both hands.
"You're the one who's . . ." he hesitated, not knowing
what to say next, "who's carrying on with a cop, *a cop*,
Zhara, on your bed in the middle of the afternoon!"

Zhara knew the guilty flush that flew to her cheeks betrayed her. Cole, who had turned in time to catch her
reaction, saw it, too, and decided it was time to leave.

Completely ignoring Mickey, he spoke to Zhara in even tones that were cool and non-threatening, and betrayed nothing of the range of heady emotions that had passed between them that afternoon. "I think it would be best if I left," he began.

Zhara knew better than to protest. She watched him silently, big eyes searching his for some hint of how he was feeling about all this. She found none.

"We'll continue with our discussion tomorrow," he went on, and without another word, he nodded with almost old-fashioned politeness, and strode past Mickey and out the door.

Cole's exit did nothing to mollify Mickey. "What discussion?" he demanded. "What were the two of you talking about?"

Zhara had more important ground to cover with Mickey than her conversation with Cole. "Mickey," she tried to keep her voice level. "I was so worried about you. Were you okay last night?"

"Fine," he answered noncommittally.

"Where did you spend the night?"

He gave her a weird, twisted smile. "In a park. It wasn't a problem. I've done it before, you know." He leaned forward, and she could see that his face had lost none of the aggression with which he had earlier faced Cole. "Now, my dear, tell me, what were you and our policeman friend talking about?"

Zhara felt her stomach chill. This wasn't the boy she knew and loved so dearly. This one was older, and much, much colder. She sighed. Might as well get it over with. She gulped in a lungful of air. "He asked me—he invited me to come home with him."

"What?" he bellowed.

"It's not like you think." She held up her stronger hand in an entreaty to him not to misinterpret what she was saying, to at least hear her out.

"What is it like?"

"He offered me a place to stay, while I heal. Until I learn to walk again."

"And what's wrong with our place?"

"Mickey," she sighed. She was tired, exhausted from the many emotional upheavals she had weathered throughout the day. She struggled to verbalize her thoughts as clearly as she could. "He's offering me a place where I can get about in my chair. His apartment is wheel-chair accessible. Ours is seven flights up."

"I can carry you up the stairs," Mickey asserted stubbornly.

She was incredulous. "Up seven flights? In your condition? Look at you, Mickey, you can barely stand as it is. You're sick. You can't take care of us both."

He shook his head. "Why is it that you always think you know what I can and can't do? First I can't run the business, now I can't take care of you. Why can't you believe in me?"

"I *do* believe in you," she sought to reassure him, "it's just that I don't want to be a burden on you, not while you're so ill. We both need time to regain our strength—"

"So you're telling me you've actually agreed to go live with this man?"

"I won't be 'living with' him . . ." she protested, then stopped. Had she agreed to take Cole up on his offer? She certainly hadn't had the time to accept or decline his invitation, not in so many words. But, slowly, it dawned on her that in her mind, she had already decided that Cole was right. It was the only sensible way to deal with her current physical limitation. The mere thought of actually sleeping under the same roof as Cole Wyatt shocked her. She'd already discovered that he was a dangerous source of fascination for her, and more than once she had come close, very close, to losing the tenuous control she held on her desires. And now it seemed that she was going to be closer to him than she had ever planned, for longer than she had ever imagined. The idea sent a shiver of anticipation down her spine; it was immediately followed by a shiver of apprehension.

Mickey was watching her intently. The blazing anger that had ridden him like a dark horse since he stormed into her room was replaced by something that looked like sadness, perplexity, and resignation combined. "You're going to do it, aren't you," he stated quietly.

She hung her head, not wanting her best friend to see the guilt in her eyes, and not wanting to see the betrayal she knew was written in his. Without a word, she telegraphed an affirmative answer to him.

He sighed heavily, all the fight leaking out of him like a slowly deflating tire. "Why?" was all he could ask.

She lifted her shoulders elaborately. "I don't know. I don't think I have much of a choice. I'd never survive in our apartment as it is. Even if we do get me upstairs, what happens if I have to go downstairs again? And what about my chair? I don't even think it'll fit in the hallway, and I know it won't fit in the bathroom. At least Cole is offering me a safe place to get over my injuries." She left it at that. There was no point in sharing her concerns about whether her injuries were such that she could "get over" them in the first place.

"So it's 'Cole' now?" He eyed her sadly.

Zhara put her arm around him and pulled him close, letting her face rest in the curve of his neck. She felt so badly. She tried her best to reassure him. "It's not what you think it is. It's not"—she paused, struggling to find the right word—"physical between us." *That's a lie,* her conscience admonished, *and you know it.* Everything about the man was physical. The way he walked. The way he looked at her. The way his tongue parted her lips, gentle, insistent, and exploring . . . She was glad Mickey couldn't see the flush that tinted her cheeks at the memory.

heart & soul's got it all!

Motivation, Inspiration, Exhilaration!
FREE ISSUE RESERVATION CARD

YES! Please send my FREE issue of HEART & SOUL right away and enter my one-year subscription. My special price for 5 more issues (6 in all) is only $10.00. I'll save 44% off the newsstand rate. If I decide that HEART & SOUL is not for me, I'll write "cancel" on the invoice, return it, and owe nothing. The FREE issue will be mine to keep.

Name _____ (First) _____ (Last)

Address _____ Apt.#

City _____ State _____ Zip _____ | MABR |

Please allow 6-8 weeks for receipt of first issue. In Canada: CDN $19.97 (includes GST). Payment in U.S. currency must accompany all Canadian orders. Basic subscription rate: 1 year (6 issues) $16.97.

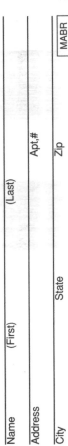

BUSINESS REPLY MAIL

FIRST-CLASS MAIL   PERMIT NO. 272   RED OAK, IA

POSTAGE WILL BE PAID BY ADDRESSEE

heart&soul

P O BOX 7423
RED OAK IA 51591-2423

She tried again. "He just feels badly about what happened, and he's trying to set things right."

"What about me?" His voice was imploring.

"You can come visit any time," she promised. She was sure Cole wouldn't mind. "He has a son almost your age . . ."

"I don't want to meet his son," Mickey interrupted, "and I certainly don't want to visit you at that man's house. He's our enemy. Can't you see that?"

She wished there were some way she could make Mickey see that he was wrong. "He's not the enemy. He's trying to help."

Mickey snorted and pulled away from her. "He'll help, all right. He'll help until he finds enough information to nail us both. Then he'll be the hero cop again, and we'll be behind bars."

Zhara wished she were confident enough in Cole to deny *that* accusation. As far as Cole's job was concerned, she couldn't be too adamant. One thing was certain: if it ever came down to a choice between their tenuous friendship and his profession, she had no doubt that she would wind up the loser.

Instead of answering, she forced him to look her in the eyes. "Mickey, let me promise you this: whatever happens, I'll never stop being your friend. We've been through some really rough times together, and I promise you, I'll always be there for you. Okay?"

Inexplicably, he looked disappointed, waiting for her to say more. When she didn't, he nodded resignedly and stood up, pulling away from her. "Maybe I ought to get some rest," he suggested.

"And some medicine," she reminded him. "You look awful."

"And some medicine," he echoed, but still didn't lift his head or look at her. He slumped toward the door, opened it, and closed it quietly behind him without a fare-well.

"Good-bye," she said to the shut door. By now, the room was completely dark. Zhara didn't bother to turn on the lights.

Seven

Cole decided it was time to talk to Omar. Ever since Zhara had called him to let him know that she was accepting his invitation, he'd been reduced to a bundle of nerves. Why, he couldn't imagine. It wasn't as if she was going to be his first houseguest! As a matter of fact, he could barely remember a six-month period since he had been on the force that his guestroom wasn't full.

Since that night when he had taken his vow before God to become a fitting father for his son, his fathering had not ended with Omar. Whether it be on the job, or during his part-time basketball coaching down at the community center, or on his many stints as Big Brother for a number of boys' homes and charities, he had always found himself drawn to some young man on the edge of destruction, whose willing spirit yearned for parental intervention before he became lost to the world. And Cole had always stepped in, most often taking the boy into his home for weeks or months, so that he could offer the time and guidance that could make a difference between a life of drugs, crime, and low self-esteem and a life that was worthy in the eyes of society.

Sometimes, he had failed, and from time to time wound up having to bust a boy he had tried to save—or even worse, identifying him in the morgue. But, usually, his outstretched hand, patient attention and no-nonsense surrogate parenting were enough to save a youth from self-destruction. Those were the times when he thanked God for saving him from himself, and he was grateful that he had the means to show his gratitude for that salvation in a way that mattered.

But this time, with Zhara, would be different. He wasn't so stupid that he couldn't see that for himself. Sure, she needed help, and sure, she was desperately trying to turn her back on whatever demons of the past had haunted her and led her to crime. But that was where the similarity between her and any of his other protégés ended.

First of all, Zhara was older than any of the youths he had helped. She was already an adult, not a child with no place to go. Second, she was definitely, tangibly female. At the mere thought of her femininity, Cole inhaled deeply, his mind clouded for a giddying moment by the scent of her skin against his. *Definitely* female! He shifted in his squeaky leather chair, realizing with shock that he was hard as a rock. Three seconds. That's all it had taken—three seconds of thinking of her, and he was as aroused as he would have been if she had been seated before him, lush, curly hair loose around her shoulders, full lips open, waiting for the impression of his own against them.

Which brought him, unfortunately, to his dilemma. He wasn't just motivated by generosity. Kindness and concern for her well-being were not the only sentiments that prompted him to invite her to convalesce at his home. Part of him was scared that if he let her be wheeled out of the hospital, she'd also be exiting his life, and that was just too soon. He didn't know her yet, not half as much as he wanted to know her . . .

So was it right? He was a cop; she was an ex-criminal that he had hunted but never truly caught. And now she had agreed to sleep under his roof, in the room next to his own. For the next few weeks, months even, however long it took for her to heal, she would be dangerously accessible. There were maybe ten feet or so from his bed to his own bedroom door, another five to her door, and maybe another ten to her bed—all he would need to cross to find himself there on impulse one night would be a mere twenty-five feet, one foot in front of the other, and there he would be, standing at the foot of the bed of the most fascinating, enigmatic woman he'd ever met.

And would she let him in? Or when she turned those gorgeous eyes on him would they be full of contempt or disgust? He wouldn't frighten her, would he? One of the drawbacks of being a man of his stature was that women sometimes found him—overwhelming. Then he remembered the daring flick of her tongue along his finger that day in her room, and he was sure that the smoky flame that burned deep inside that beautiful woman was big enough to accommodate even him.

The image that flashed across his half-closed eyes caused the front of his pants to grow even more taut, if such a thing were possible. In pain, he stood and began pacing the small space, hoping that the pounding in his temples and groin would soon subside. The door to his study was thrown open and a band of yellow light cut through the shadows.

"Dad? You wanted to see me?" The outline of Omar's head stood out against the light. At his ankles, Catastrophe rubbed herself up against the doorframe. Cain and Abel flanked Omar, casting occasional foul glances at the cat. The two retrievers hadn't taken the intrusion of the wily feline lightly, and since she had been here, many a lamp and vase had fallen victim to their skirmishes. But there wasn't much that could be done about that, was there? Dogs would be dogs, and cats would be cats. He was only grateful that the small civil war hadn't yet resulted in any casualties; and he couldn't confidently bet that if it did, the loser would be the cat.

To hide his embarrassment, Cole sat again, praying that in his state of intense arousal, he would be able to speak in a normal voice.

"Why are you sitting in the dark?" Omar hovered, waiting to be invited into his father's private room. Catastrophe had no such reservations. She covered the space between herself and Cole with a yowl of greeting and sprang onto the desk to kiss his face.

Cole cleared his throat and then managed to say, "Just thinking something through." He motioned the boy in.

Omar came in and sat in the chair he usually chose, stretching his long legs out before him. He was wearing the team shirt of his favorite basketball team, and on his feet, of course, were the sneakers his favorite player was touting on television this month. "Were you thinking about whatever it is you want to talk to me about?" Omar wanted to know.

Cole nodded, wondering where to begin.

"This isn't about drugs again, is it?" Omar began, with the impatience of youth, "because if it is, I've heard this speech a thousand times, and I swear to you I'm not hanging out with any users, or pushers, or drinkers . . ."

Cole interrupted him, smiling. "I know you're not. I know I can trust you. I'm proud of you."

Omar flushed at his father's praise, but was too embarrassed by it to bask in its glow for more than five seconds. "So, what is it then?" He paused and then frowned. "You're not stopping me from going away to basketball camp, are you?"

"No, no, I'd never do that to you." Omar had won a place at a leading basketball camp upstate, and for the next ten weeks he would be spending his weekends, from Friday afternoon to Sunday evening, away at camp. Cole was proud of the boy, and was looking forward to Omar having the chance to see if his passion for the game would lead him to the state youth league championships next season.

Omar was getting impatient. "What, then?"

Cole took a deep breath. "Someone's coming to stay with us for a while," he began.

Omar smiled broadly. "Is that all? The Cole Wyatt Rehabilitation Center is taking in another boarder?" That was the nickname Omar and Brian Ames privately held for Cole's guestroom.

Cole smiled. "Something like that."

Omar knew his father well enough to tell that there was more to the story. "And . . . ?"

"And this time, it's not a he, it's a she."

Omar stared. "A girl? You're kidding! This never happened before!"

Cole shrugged. "Well, I've never found myself in this situation before."

"She pretty?" Omar was, after all, a teenage boy.

Cole snatched up a newspaper off his desk and threw it at his son in mock umbrage, causing the cat to look from one to the other in alarm. "Very. But she's too old for you, so don't even think it. Do you think I'm crazy enough to take in a teenage girl with you and your hormones roaming the house at night?"

Omar shrugged. "Worth a try. So who is it?"

Cole braced himself. "Zhara Thorne. She needs a place to stay that's wheelchair accessible, while she gets over her injury."

His son's mouth fell open. "The Cat Lady? The climber? She's coming here?"

"Unless you have any objections." Cole waited.

"Why would I have any objections?"

"It's just—different from what we're used to, that's all. I just wanted to know if you'd mind."

"Is she really a jewel thief?" Omar looked intrigued, almost impressed.

"She was."

Omar shrugged. "Well, we've had all kinds of people stay here. It won't be the first time." Then, a shrewd look came over his face. "Do you like her?"

Cole's voice caught in his throat. He didn't know what to say. "Yes," was all he could manage.

His son gave him a look that was older than his years. "I mean, do you like her 'that way'?" The boy was smiling.

"Yes, I guess I do." He waited for a reaction.

"Cool." Omar lifted the cat into his arms and began ruffling the fur on its belly. It didn't look amused. Cain and Abel looked even less amused—they looked like, given half the chance, they'd take the hairy blue-eyed interloper out back and teach her a thing or two.

Cole lifted an eyebrow at this surprising response. " 'Cool'? How can you say that? She's everything I've fought against my entire career. She broke the law. I'm supposed to thwart people like her, not . . ." He was going to say "fall in love," but he stopped himself just in time. The mere suggestion that such a thing could possibly have happened was a load of rubbish, and he knew it. Instead of saying anything more, he scratched his head in puzzlement and waited for Omar to tell him he was right in being reticent.

Omar shrugged eloquently. "The way I figure it, you aren't a stupid guy, and you've got one of those instincts, cops' instincts, that'll tell you if someone is okay or not. So, if you like her, then she probably deserves it. Go with your gut, Cole."

Cole was so overwhelmed by the depth of his son's faith in him that he let the "Cole" business slide. Instead, he realized to his horror that his eyes were becoming moist. *What a great and wondrous miracle it is,* he thought, *to be blessed with a son this special.* He reached across the desk and playfully gave his boy one of the elaborate, convoluted handshakes that Omar was so into.

"Omar," Cole began, "I—"

Omar interrupted him, all teenage machismo again. "I know, I know, you don't have to say it."

"—love you," Cole finished, unable to stop himself.

"Aw maaaan!" Omar was flushing all over, embarrassed.

Cole laughed loudly. "One day, son, you'll be saying it to a child of your own, and you'll understand why it's so important to say it whenever and wherever you can."

"Yeah, right," Omar mumbled. He set the cat on the floor and made for the door. The dogs got up and followed him, but Catastrophe seemed content to stay where she was. "You want me to fix dinner?" he asked over his shoulder.

"Nah, get your coat. We'll eat out." He was in a good mood again. All was right with the world.

Mickey refused to help Zhara check out. Instead, he came the Wednesday evening before she was due to leave, shouldering a black canvas duffel bag filled with her clothes and toiletries. He seemed fully resigned to the fact that she wasn't going to be with him for quite some time, and although it was clear he didn't like it, he didn't seek to change her mind. Zhara was grateful to him for that.

They sat side by side on the edge of her bed for hours, not saying much, Zhara quietly munching on the burger and fries that Mickey had smuggled in to her, against hospital regulations. The burger was cold and the fries limp by the time he turned up, but it had been so long since she had eaten anything that hadn't been checked and cross-checked by a nutritionist (who Zhara was convinced was a humorless sadist), that she ate it up like a five-star meal.

When Mickey finally left, he hugged her like he wasn't sure he would see her again, and Zhara had to remind him again that he was free to visit her at Cole's place whenever he pleased. This time, he didn't protest.

Next morning, she was dressed and ready much too early, nervously twisting at her hair and staring at the door, waiting for Cole to stride through at any minute. By midday, when he still hadn't shown up, she was beginning to get nervous, and the confidence with which she had begun the day, and the determination that she was doing the right thing—or at least the only sensible thing—began to fade.

Her phone rang late that afternoon, and a penitent Cole was on the other end. "Zhara," he said softly.

There it was again, her name on his lips, like a call from somewhere primitive inside of him, and, as had happened every other time she had heard it, something inside her answered, silently. She took a deep breath before speaking. "Cole, if you don't think this is a good idea, I understand. I can call Mickey—"

He cut her off hastily. "No, no, sweetheart. It's just work. I've been out in the field, and I didn't even have time to call. I'll be over as soon as I can. I don't know when that will be, but I promise you I will be there, okay?"

What could she say? She knew him well enough to know that when he promised something—verbally or otherwise!—he delivered. "Okay."

There was a silence, a pause, and the sound of a breath being drawn, as if he wanted to say something more, but then the phone went dead in her ear. It was only after she had placed the receiver back onto the cradle that she remembered what he had called her.

Sweetheart.

Now, what in the name of all the saints was that supposed to mean? Unbidden, her thumb found its way into her mouth and she began methodically stripping away at both nail and cuticle.

The endearment seemed to have popped from his lips without so much as a conscious thought. Had he even realized that he'd said it? It wasn't the first endearment of his that had reached her ear; he'd called her "baby" once before, out in the garden the first time he'd kissed her, but that was in the heat of sexual arousal, when his husky voice had urged her to return to her room with him so that they could continue stoking the flames they had lit out by the lake.

But "sweetheart"—that was different. That was the kind of thing a man said to a woman when he was thinking with his heart, not with another, less discriminating part of his body.

Zhara began stripping away at another fingernail. Only one man had ever whispered such endearments to her, in a voice filled with emotion and underlying passion, and that had been years ago. The space in between had been long, cold, and empty, and now, here she was, waiting for a man to come for her, and knowing, not hoping or dreading, but *knowing* that the proximity in which they would find themselves would lead them down a path to giddy, soul-searing pleasure.

Her nipples tightened painfully, and between her legs she could feel a second pulse. She and Cole Wyatt, her pursuer and tormentor, savior and protector, were going to make love, and it was going to be soon. Terror and exhilaration alternated with the rapidity of a strobe against her closed eyelids. She might not have had much experience with sexual matters; after all, having had just one lover at her age was more of an anomaly than anything else these days. But she knew her body and her mind well enough to know that nothing, not loyalty to Antonio's memory, not fear of the repercussions, nothing, was larger than her need for him right now.

Instead of being disappointed at Cole's delayed arrival, she began fervently to hope that he'd be held up for at least another few hours.

She needed the time to learn to breathe normally again.

"You've lost your mind," she chided herself aloud. "This man is dangerous. Can't you see he's dangerous?"

But rational thought proved to be a dull blade. Instead of succeeding in talking herself out of the madness that she knew would unfold between them, she was shocked to find herself shaking with the eager anticipation of someone who was about to embark upon a delirious and exhilarating journey.

When the door opened an hour later, the tremors still rippled through her body. She looked up, eager anticipation in her eyes, only to be forced to hide the rush of disappointment when Margie entered the room. The anticipation that took a nose-dive swooped upward again when Cole stepped in, close on her heels.

The plump, maternal nurse, who had given so much of herself during Zhara's darkest hours of pain and despondency, seemed even more cheerful than usual. Today, her graying hair was swept up in its usual style, but her little white cap was affixed to her head with large bobby pins tipped with shiny plastic ladybugs. The sight of them cued a bubble of laughter to pop out of Zhara.

"Glad to be out of here, huh?" Margie beamed at Zhara like she was a favorite niece.

Zhara nodded, unable to deny her relief at finally being free of the walls that had held her captive these two weeks. "I'll miss you, Margie," she said, shyly. In her past experience with institutions, she hadn't become so attached to anyone or received so much attention from anyone before. Her gratitude for the simple, kind gestures that Margie had made to her during her stay only threw into stark contrast the coldness of her own friendless world.

Margie was already picking up Zhara's bags and placing them in the open doorway. "Oh, no, you won't," she answered briskly, as if she herself didn't like the idea of giving in to any emotion, at least not outwardly. "Not when you have this kind, handsome gentleman to help you get better. I'm sure he'll be able to fill all your needs, much better than I ever could." She shot a sly smile at Cole, who returned her innuendo with a wide and innocent stare.

"I'll do my best to make sure she feels welcome." He circumvented Margie's obvious attempt at matchmaking by deliberately taking her provocative statement at face value.

Margie chuckled, but held her peace.

Before Zhara could speak, and she was glad she didn't have to, because she was sure she would trip over her own tongue in confusion, Cole covered the small distance between them and swept her up into his arms. She couldn't prevent the gasp that escaped her at being lifted into his arms again. She could feel the hard muscle of his flat belly against her hip and thigh, as he effortlessly held her high, with one large, hard arm supporting her back, and the other under her firm, round bottom. Her blood hummed. Under her thick, black lashes she looked up at his face, hoping to see evidence that their brief contact was also giving *his* blood pressure a few bad moments, but to her disappointment, his roughly sculptured face revealed nothing.

Gently, he laid her in the chair, slipping the footrests into place with smooth clicks. He was about to lift her right foot, the weak one, onto the rest when she stopped him, showing him that she could lift it and place it there on her own.

"I've been working hard at getting it moving again," she told him proudly.

His eyes caught hers, full of genuine, honest-to-goodness happiness for her. "That's very good, sweetheart. I knew you could do it."

She tried not to look too pleased.

Margie hugged and kissed them both before hurrying down the corridor wiping her eyes, and then, too quickly,

Zhara and Cole were outside and heading toward his car. She was on her way to his house, where inevitably she and he would be alone. The idea both scared and excited her.

Cole watched Zhara and his son chattering away like parakeets as Catastrophe purred away on her mistress's bosom. In twenty-four hours she and Omar had fallen in sync as easily as if they had known each other for years. They seemed to have discovered a taste for the same music; the knowledge that Zhara preferred the noisy, exuberant hip-hop his son favored to the blues and jazz he liked to listen to reminded him that she was, in fact, closer to Omar's age than she was to his. This made him cringe.

The first night, they'd sat around the table after dinner and talked, three of them at first, until the conversation segued into a two-way chat between Zhara and Omar, and Cole found himself leaning back in his chair, watching the two of them in an animated argument about the relative merits and demerits of West Coast and East Coast rap. He didn't have a clue what they were talking about, so rather than open his mouth and be thought a fool, he contented himself with quiet observation.

It was very rare that he ever brought a woman home. Somehow, he didn't think it was right to let his motherless son become too attached to any of his girlfriends, since he was well aware of the alarming statistics on cops' romantic relationships. It wasn't fair to allow Omar to grow to like someone who, inevitably, would fade from his life as soon as she started resenting his late hours and dangerous work. But, seeing Zhara at his dinner table in active conversation with his son somehow seemed so—right. What that meant was anybody's guess, and Cole just wasn't prepared to investigate his own thoughts too carefully right now. All he cared about was his instinctive knowledge that a woman's presence, *Zhara's* presence, was proving to be good for Omar.

This afternoon, judging from the racket emanating from Omar's room, Zhara was there with him, keeping him company while he packed for his weekend at basketball camp. Cole looked at his watch. They'd been up there over an hour, and from the laughter and chatter, he was sure that they were doing more talking than packing. But it was time to get going, or Omar would miss his train. He strode into the room to find Zhara in her chair by the window, with the sun setting the tips of her dark, curly hair on fire, and Omar sitting on the edge of his bed with his bag zipped up and placed on the floor at his feet.

"I thought you were going to give me a shout as soon as you were all packed," Cole chided his son gently. "We're going to be late for the station."

Omar looked surprised to see his father, as if he had forgotten he was even in the house. "Oh, Cole—uh, Dad. We just got to talking and we kind of, uh—forgot the time—"

Zhara interrupted. "I'm sorry. It's my fault. I was talking too much."

Cole took in the excited flush on her face and forgave her at once. From what she said, she didn't often get a chance to laugh and chat with anybody. Suddenly he realized that her presence here might be good for his son, but his son's friendship was proving to be good for her, too. "Not a federal offense," he joked, and realized too late that his little quip was the worst thing he could say, since he was finally succeeding in getting Zhara to forget their former relationship as cop and quarry. He bit his lip as she flushed, and Omar stood awkwardly, offering his hand to Zhara in polite farewell.

"See you when I get back, Zhara," he said, solemnly, almost as if it were a question, as if he were reading the tension between her and his father well enough to know that the tide could turn at any moment, and he could just as easily return from camp to find that she'd upped and left. He gave her a worried look that begged for consolation.

Zhara couldn't offer any, as she, herself, couldn't give any guarantees. She nodded in response to his farewell, but didn't say anything. She fidgeted in her chair.

Cole took his leave of her, promising to be back in half an hour. "Just down to the station and back," he promised her.

In the car, he avoided his son's pointed gaze and concentrated on his driving a little more than was necessary.

"Ouch, Dad," Omar said.

" 'Ouch,' what?" he prodded, although he knew very well "ouch what."

"I know your tongue got away with you, man, but d'you think you could try to put this cat-burglary thing behind you? She's not doing it anymore, you know. She told me she went straight years ago."

"It was just a slip of the lip," Cole defended himself.

"What you just said, yeah, but don't tell me what she did all those years ago isn't still in the back of your mind. It's coloring your judgment so much, you can't even see for yourself how much you care about her."

Cole nearly ran the car off the road. This was a sixteen-year-old talking! Out of the mouths of babes. But Omar was right. If she worked in a department store, or taught, or made cakes for a living, he wouldn't be caught up in the overwhelming struggle that had been dogging him ever since he laid eyes on her. His judgment was colored by her unorthodox career. No doubt about that.

Omar was still laying on the pressure. "Why can't you just forget what she *did* and start finding out who she *is*? Maybe if you discover that, what she did will make sense, and then you'll be able to forgive her."

Cole protested. "It's not up to me to forgive her for

anything, Omar. I don't pass judgment. I just obey the law and do my job."

Omar wasn't letting himself be swayed. "You *have* passed judgment on her. I saw it all over your face last night. You were sitting there, wondering how she could be so nice and so smart and so funny and still be a thief. And you're so bothered by that, you can't just accept her for the person that she is."

Cole made a right turn and pulled up smoothly in front of the station, where he switched off the engine and twisted in his seat so he could look his amazingly wise son in the eye. "You're saying I'm wrong for holding on to my values? How am I going to be a fitting father to you if I teach you that right and wrong can be shifted to suit your circumstances?"

Omar let his hand fall on Cole's arm, emphasizing his point with a gesture that said they were both men together, having a serious discussion. "You *are* a fitting father to me. And I don't think that right and wrong should shift. I just think that sometimes good people have good reasons for doing bad things. And maybe if you knew what the reasons were, then you'd understand her better. And then you wouldn't think she's a bad person anymore."

Cole swallowed hard. His son was dishing out fatherly advice, and all he could do was listen.

Omar pushed open the door and hauled his tall, thin frame out onto the pavement. Cole stepped out the other side and the two of them watched each other over the top of the car.

"So, where are you taking her for dinner?" Omar wanted to know.

"Dinner?"

"You going to make her sit around the house all weekend?"

He couldn't stop himself from smiling at his son's auda-

cious assessment of his situation. "I guess not," he had to
admit.

Omar rolled his eyes in exaggerated frustration. "Jeez,
Dad. What do I have to do next? Give you a talk on the
birds and the bees?"

Cole decided it was time to put his foot down. "That,
I don't need."

Laughing, Omar shouldered his bag and headed for
the station doors.

"Have a good time," Cole yelled at his receding back.
Omar waved without turning around, and Cole watched
him until he disappeared.

He leaned against the car door, pulled out a cigarette,
and lit it, but stared at it for a long time without putting
it into his mouth, trying to get his mind around Omar's
observations. He sighed deeply. The issue *was* an issue of
forgiveness. Was he big enough to forgive Zhara for not
standing up to his ideals? He stood still for a long time,
remembering the kind of man he had been in his own
youth and the wasted life he had lived and the girls he
had hurt with his selfishness and callousness—most nota-
bly Sondra, Omar's teenage mother. He'd been a bastard
to the nth degree, and he was the first to admit it.

But he'd asked for and received forgiveness for his
crimes, and he became a changed man. Zhara was struggling to bring about the same change in her own life. If
God had been big enough to forgive Cole and help him
put his past as far behind him as east is from west,
shouldn't he, Cole, be big enough to forgive Zhara?

He closed his eyes, trying to get his racing emotions
into perspective. It was all so clear now. What she *was* was
so much more than what she had *done*. She was bright
and sweet, sensual, fragile, and right now, she needed
someone. And so help him, he wanted to be the one she
needed.

Cole stared at his cigarette until it burned down to his

fingers, and then he tossed it down and ground it out. With a tremendous emotional shove, he pushed his prejudices aside, and then discovered to his shock that they left behind a huge, gaping space in his heart—one that waited to be filled. He knew it could be filled with anything he chose; but he wanted it to be filled with the surprising and wonderful emotions he had been pushing to the background since he had come to know her—respect, warmth, a desire to protect, a desire to touch, to embrace, and to engulf himself in her, and, perhaps, even . . . love.

He jumped a little, startled by the word that had surfaced unbidden. Love. It wasn't a word he used with anyone other than his son. It wasn't a word he ever remembered applying to, or saying to any woman he had ever been with. "Like," certainly, "admire," sure—but "love?" It had a new, fresh taste in his mouth and a sweet bright scent in his nostrils. To his shock, he discovered he was smiling.

Zhara watched Cole across the rough, country-style, wooden table with something akin to suspicion. He had changed somehow, subtly, but radically, and it unnerved her. She was used to his cool demeanor, his slow, evaluating stares, the way he always seemed to watch her as if she were a tough case he needed to crack in order to save his own honor as a cop. But tonight, there was none of that. Instead, he was acting almost as if they were—on a date!

He'd come back from the train station in a somber mood, his stare distant, his brow furrowed. At first, she assumed he was upset with her for engaging Omar in a lengthy conversation and almost making him miss his train, but he had brushed away her apology as if that matter were of no importance. He had shuffled off to his den like a distracted bear, only to return an hour later with an almost shy invitation to dinner. Stunned, she could do nothing but accept, so here they were, just the two of them, finding things to talk about across a restaurant table.

Around them, the hum of the other diners' voices melded with the soft strains of Spanish guitars. The tiny *bodega* to which he had taken her was more than half an hour's drive outside of Medusa, but Cole had promised her that it was well worth it, and he had been right. Steaming helpings of paella and blood-red house wine, served in cool, stone carafes, beckoned invitingly in the light of the pale, flickering candles that adorned their table. She listened attentively while he told her story after story about raising an obstreperous son single-handedly, trying not to puzzle too much over what seemed to have changed within Cole. Whatever it was, she told herself, it made him less suspicious and guarded, and more open, warmer. That was good enough for her.

The waiter took their empty plates away, while Cole was finishing a funny anecdote about the time he took Omar to Madrid on vacation. The restaurant they had gone to served him calamari marinated in the creature's own purple ink, and Omar, at age seven, had climbed up on his chair and loudly accused the waiter of trying to poison him.

Zhara laughed heartily, enjoying the gleam of fatherly pride in his eyes and the softer, more intimate glow that reached out and touched her every time his eyes held hers. He refilled their glasses so gracefully, she almost didn't notice he had done it, and then reached out across the table and took her hand.

Zhara looked in surprise, first, down to the big hand that almost hid hers, with its thumb lazily stroking the fine bone that pressed up against the skin of her wrist, and then up to those black, black eyes that held a mystery.

"Zhara," he began, and then paused, searching.

She waited.

He pressed on. "I want you to give me something."

She frowned. What could he possibly want of her? "What?"

"You. The truth about you. Who you are. Where you came from. Anything. You can't remain such a mystery all the time. It's driving me crazy. Just give me something— no hiding, no pulling away. Please."

She struggled to retrieve her hand. Now, why did he have to go and spoil things like that? What did he want to go digging up her past for? Why couldn't he just have let things lie as they were, and go on telling her stories for the rest of the night? "Why?"

Cole's grip around her wrist tightened, gently but firmly. He wasn't letting her go. "I want to know you. That's all. It's not about my job, and it's not about trying to make you feel bad. I just want to know who you are. In return, I'll tell you who I am. Then we can work from there."

This was all going terribly wrong. "Work from there to what, Cole? What do you want from me?"

"I don't want anything *from* you. I just want *you*."

She opened her mouth in surprise and then closed it again. What did he mean, "want her"? She had known from the start, ever since she agreed to go home with him, that they were moving unavoidably toward a point where he and she were going to come together in a searing collision of their bodies. She was prepared for that; she hungered for it. But now he wanted *her*, her mind. When did that become part of the bargain?

"Start slowly," he suggested. "Tell me where you're from, where you grew up. Tell me how you wound up on the street."

He called *that* starting slowly? The look on his face told her they weren't going anywhere until she talked, so with a deep breath, she began.

"You know about my mother dying—"

"Wasn't your fault," he interrupted.

She didn't argue. Bringing it up the last time had been devastating enough. She went on, keeping her voice steady. "My father was a lawyer and a writer. He wrote books on law, legal ethics . . ."

Cole gasped. "What was his name?"

"Simeon. Simeon Thorne."

He slapped his forehead. "Your father was *the* Simeon Thorne? The writer? I don't believe it! I studied his books in law class. I've got everything he's ever written. He was one of my idols. I once hitchhiked all the way to Atlanta with two of my buddies from class to hear him speak. He was amazing." Then he stopped. "If he was your father, then you must have been very—"

"Rich." Zhara nodded. "I grew up in a mansion, with twenty acres of blue Kentucky grass all around me. We had pools and cars and horses. But, like I said, I never saw my father. He was always out on the book-tour circuit or on the college-lecture circuit, but even when he was there, he wasn't." She sighed. "Not for me, anyway."

He reached out and imprisoned her other hand. His eyes grew grave. "Simeon Thorne . . ." he hesitated, ". . . killed himself."

She winced and nodded. "After a while, he got bored with what he was doing. I think he wanted some thrills. He started playing the stock market, wildly, and taking big risks. And most of the time he lost. Then he had to take bigger and bigger risks to make up for his losses. And then he started, well . . ."

"The insider trading scandal. I remember. I was a rookie on the force when the news broke. He was using information he learned from his clients for his stock deals. Then he started milking their trust funds to buy the stocks. The day they put out a warrant for his arrest—"

"He walked into his study, put a gun in his mouth, and

pulled the trigger," Zhara said miserably. "I heard the gun go off. It was just a little pop, but it scared me. I *knew*, I just knew what he had done, and I couldn't face it. I ran down into the laundry room, curled into the clothes drier, and hid. I spent nine hours in the drier, too frightened to get out, before the investigators found me."

He let go of one her hands, reached out, and touched her cheek. "What happened then?"

"We lost everything. *I* lost everything. The banks closed in and repossessed the property and the horses—including Windfleet. I remember the day they took him away. He fought them; he knew they were taking him away from me. They had to shoot him full of sedatives before they could load him on the trailer. I just stood on the balcony and screamed." Tears began to sparkle for her lost silver horse, where they hadn't for her father.

"And you?" he prompted.

She shook her head in wonderment. "Nobody wanted me. My father's relatives didn't want anything to bring the scent of the scandal into their homes, and my mother's relatives, well, you know." She didn't want to go into the whole painful story about them blaming her for her mother's death all over again. That would be more than she could stand.

He nodded.

"So they sent me to a home. I was twelve. That's where I met Lizard. I mean Mickey."

"And you ran away. Why?"

She shrugged. "*I* didn't. Not really. Mickey ran away, several times. The other children picked on him because of the color of his skin. I tried to protect him, because he was so small. But, when I couldn't, they beat him. Badly. And nobody seemed willing or able to do anything about it. So he ran away. And the last time he did, they couldn't find him, so I went looking for him."

"You found him in Chicago?" Cole guessed.

Zhara nodded. "I walked and hitchhiked from Kentucky. Took me five days. He was camped out at the foot of the Sears Tower. I knew he'd be there. We both liked to climb." She paused at this, looking for condemnation in his face at this reference to her modus operandi, but she only saw a patient willingness to listen. She went on. "He had this fantasy that one day he'd climb it. He had pictures of it stuck up over his bed, and he used to carry a little battered postcard of it in his pocket."

"And you never went back to the home."

She shook her head emphatically. "We hated it. It was horrible. And there was talk of me going to a foster home. If they did that, we'd be separated. We'd have died without each other. We were all we had. The streets of Chicago are full of homeless children, invisible children. Nobody sees them because nobody wants to. We became invisible, too."

"And you stole to survive?"

Zhara hoped the shame didn't show on her face. "The other children taught us how to pick car-locks and boost radios. We begged for money or food outside of fast food restaurants, and when the owners chased us away, we just picked another spot. We took clothes off lines, and we slept in empty buildings. It was a pretty simple life—hard, but it was a routine."

Cole let her hands go and leaned forward, and as he did so, Zhara felt as if an anchor she had been holding on to had slipped. "But you didn't stop at car radios. You started wanting more money. Why? What did you want it for?"

She knew from the look on his face that he was hoping in his heart that she wouldn't confess to needing the money for something that violated his strong code of ethics, like drug use. She reassured him hurriedly. "It's not what you think. It was Mickey. We needed the money for him. He was sick. He's had leukemia for a long time, and his treatment was costing more money than we could ever make by begging."

"So you started climbing."

"So we started climbing." She prayed he would understand. She didn't think she had the energy to withstand his pointed questions and the burning scrutiny of his eyes much longer. She fidgeted as he stared at her, his eyes scanning her face as if he had suddenly found something written there in a very fine hand, and he was committing every word to memory.

With a rush of escaping air, he sighed heavily and sat back, head against the back of his seat, staring upward at the ceiling. Zhara could hear the wheels of his mind turning. As she watched him, she chided herself for having told him more than she had ever meant to. He had assured her that his curiosity was personal rather than professional, but ammunition was ammunition, and if he ever chose to use it against her, there would be nothing she could do.

"So you *did* have a good reason," she heard him murmur, so softly she was sure he hadn't meant to utter it aloud, and certainly not to her.

She frowned. "What?"

He straightened. "Nothing. Something my son said to me earlier." He brushed it away with his hand. "Forget it."

She nodded glumly, waiting to see what he would do or say next. He looked as if he had a hundred more questions, but the trepidation on her face must have registered, because instead he smiled ruefully. "Have I tired you out with all my questions?"

He had, but she denied it politely.

He knew she wasn't being truthful, but he let it slide. "I won't ask you anything more tonight, okay? Let's just enjoy each other's company."

She *was* enjoying the evening, with the soft candles, the

good food, and with the quiet, contented glow that pulsed gently between them. She would have died rather than admit to him that at that moment, there was nowhere she would rather have been, and nobody she would rather have been with right now. She toyed with her glass, watching as the tiny flame on the table struck fire off the swirling liquid, and closed her eyes, wanting to draw every precious moment of this wonderful evening into her body through every pore.

"Dessert?"

She opened her eyes. He had a twinkle of mischief in his, knowing she had sworn to him that she never ate dessert. She declined with a shake of her head.

"Still not eating candy, eh? I thought after the time we shared that box of chocolates in your room, you'd be more open to another sweet treat."

She was glad he had decided to lighten the tone of the evening. She countered with the same levity. "Oh, I don't know. Maybe the little taste I got last time wasn't sweet enough to leave me wanting more." She smiled wickedly.

He winced. "Ouch. An unkind cut!"

She shrugged elaborately. If it hit him where it hurt, well, good.

"Maybe you just didn't have all I've got to offer. You can't tell how good a dish is if you just nibble at it. You have to eat the whole thing, relish it, indulge your senses. *That's* how you eat dessert." As he spoke, she couldn't take her eyes off his lips. Sweetness indeed.

Their eyes met, and the levity died. In its place, a fire they had both been doing their best to douse sprang up, its warm glow beating into second place the candle that burned low on their table. "Give me tonight, Zhara, and I'll make a believer out of you."

She didn't trust herself to speak, but her parted lips and heated flush was all the answer he needed. Abruptly, impatiently, he stood up, tossing a few bills on the table in payment for their meal. The tip was grossly out of proportion to their check, but he certainly wasn't hanging around waiting for change.

Zhara let him wheel her out to the parking lot, her whole body so tingly with impatience that she was sure she could leap out of her wheelchair and beat him to the car. As he fumbled for the keys, she stood shakily, relying on the strength of her unaffected leg to compensate for the weakness of the other. Propping herself up against the car, she waited as he folded the chair and slid it into the trunk. Instead of holding open the door for her, though, he grasped her firmly and effortlessly lifted her into a seated position onto the silver metallic hood of the car. She shivered in the cool autumn air.

"Are you okay there?" he asked, worried that he'd hurt her.

"Fine." She watched him, puzzled. What was he doing? Wasn't he taking her home?

"Just a little taste," he explained. "To whet our appetite. I can't wait till we drive all the way home before I kiss you, Zhara." His descending head obscured the dim lights of the parking lot, and his mouth found hers unerringly in the dark. The naughtiness of the public kiss, with patrons coming into and leaving the lot and idle busboys taking a cigarette break twenty yards away, excited her as she never would have imagined. It was sophomoric, maybe, but stealing a kiss in full view of everyone sent a thrill through her. She lifted both arms around his neck, her weaker one just as determined to press against his skin as her stronger one, fingers gently grazing the low-cut hair at the nape of his neck.

The pressure of his mouth was undemanding but curious, slowly exploring every tiny curve of her lips, every soft, moist corner of her mouth. One hand supported her back while the other slid down to her knee, shifting it slightly apart to allow him to insinuate his bulk closer against her. The cold metal of the car against her bottom penetrated her skirt and panties, a stark contrast with the warmth that was kindling inside her and radiating outward. The wandering hand took it upon itself to go exploring, up along her thigh, under the soft fall of her skirt, to the elastic strip against her hip. It lingered there, torturing her with its indecision, a fingernail grazing the line of fine skin that trembled at the point where her underwear ended and her flesh began.

In her mind she begged him, *Cole, please, please, touch me,* wishing he would go past the elastic frontier into territory that had lain undiscovered for too many years. But the treacherous adventurer withdrew, sliding back down her leg.

As he stepped away, she groaned, stubbornly restraining him with a hand on his arm. "Cole . . ." Her breath on his face was Sirocco-hot.

"Enough with the public display," he muttered gruffly. "What I want to do to you next, we certainly can't do out here."

"One more kiss," she pleaded, half laughing. "For the road."

"If I kiss you again right now," he growled, "I wouldn't stop at your lips. That would be like having the topping and pushing aside the cake. I'd have to taste the buttercream satin of your skin and dip my tongue into the sweet, warm syrup pooled in the hollow of your throat, and then I'd get greedy, and reach down here . . ." He let his fingers slide down from her throat to the soft valley between her breasts, stopping at the point where her button held her blouse closed. "I'd have to peel open this wrapping and hold each sweet little kirsch cherry . . ." the finger tapped one taut nipple, and something deep between her legs screamed, ". . . in my mouth." He went on, voice thick, "And, then, when I'm drunk with the taste and smell of you, I would have to go lower," the hand descended further, between his hard body and her pliant one, to rest lightly at the aching point between her thighs, "and feed my body and soul on your sweet, warm mulled wine, inhale your spices, and drink my fill, until . . ."

"Stop," she begged him. His low, husky voice, rich and deep with desire, had her mesmerized. Her thigh muscles quivered involuntarily. She didn't know how much longer she could stand the torment. She'd never felt this level of insane desire before. "Cole, please stop."

"Why, my sweet?" he taunted, nipping her sharply on the ear as he whispered. "Calorific overload?"

"Just get us home," she gasped.

Without another word, he lifted her with one swift movement and placed her into the front seat, to scattered applause from the bored busboys, who trailed back into the kitchen and shut the door, their break having been a tad more interesting than normal.

Effortlessly, he levered his tall body in and buckled up. "I knew I should have chosen somewhere closer to home," he muttered to himself as he slid onto the highway.

Zhara laughed, giddy with the knowledge that he wanted her so much. Her laughter helped drown out the tiny voices that jostled for attention in her head, voices that asked questions like: *What are you doing? Are you crazy? Don't you know this man is your enemy?* Others, not to be outdone, taunted: *Do you think you can satisfy him? Hasn't he had so much more experience than you, with your one teenage romance? Don't you know that when he eventually rolls out of your bed, all you will see on his face will be boredom and dissatisfaction?* She shoved them into the back of her consciousness, gnawing at her lip, frowning.

Cole took his eyes off the highway to glance at her, and immediately laid a gentle hand on her now nervous, clammy one. "Scared?" he asked softly.

She shook her head in denial.

He was smart enough not to believe her. "I won't hurt you, Zhara, not with my body, not with my actions, not with my words. Believe me, as long as I am with you, nothing will harm you. I'd take any hit, shoulder any pain, anything, if it meant it would spare you hurt. I promise you."

She looked up at him, puzzled. Could he possibly mean that? How could he mean that? His eyes were fixed on the road, yet the determined cast to his jaw told her that he was adamant in what he said. She was amazed. Cole Wyatt was promising to protect her. Why?

He persisted. "Do you believe me?"

She couldn't answer. She didn't know if she *could* believe him.

"I hope I never have to, but I'll prove it to you if necessary," he promised vehemently. "I'll do what it takes to make you trust me."

Zhara was silent, but clenched his hand hard and didn't let go until they drew up to his garage and the engine died. As he clicked open the lock on his door, she tugged on his arm, mutely begging him not to get out yet.

He turned toward her, eyes full of questions. "Still scared?" he asked, concerned.

She gulped in mouthfuls of air, unsure of how to convey the new fear that had risen to the forefront of her mind. "Cole, I . . ."

"Tell me," he encouraged.

"My body," she tried to explain, "it's . . ."

"Beautiful," he supplied reverently.

"Awkward," she corrected. "I'm so afraid I can't, uh, move the way you'd want me to." Her face was hot with embarrassment. "I mean, I don't want to be just lying there, flopping about like a dying fish . . ."

He laughed so loudly she was almost taken aback. This was serious business! What did he have to laugh about?

"This is your last warning." His dimples danced. "Stop

worrying. Stop complaining. Stop trying to talk me out of it, or I'll . . ."

"I wasn't trying to talk you out of it," she protested, but for the life of her she couldn't prevent his infectious smile from taking over her own lips.

"Good," he grinned, and let the matter drop. He launched himself out of the car, strode round to the other side, and opened the door for her. Shakily, she stood, waiting for him to take her chair out of the trunk and prepare it for her. It was a lengthy process; it had to be unfolded and set flat, and a number of clips and clamps had to be set in place. Again, her immobility galled her.

"Never mind the chair," he muttered. In two strides he was at the house door, unlocked it, and was back at her side.

She took two slow steps forward. "I'm strong enough to make it to the door, you know," she asserted. "I've been exercising."

But before she could take a third step, she was up in his arms. "Save your strength, darling. You'll need it for what I have in mind." With that, he strode through the door, locked it, and headed for the corridor leading to the rooms.

"Yours or mine?" he inquired impatiently.

"Whichever's closer," she answered, equally impatient.

He all but kicked in the door of his own room, holding her steady with one powerful arm as he flicked on the lamp by the side of his bed. "We won't do this under cover of darkness," he asserted. "I want to look at you and see every shudder of pleasure ripple through your body."

With infinite care, he laid her on the bed, and before she could cast a curious eye around to take in the room where this mystifying man slept, he was on his knees at the bedside, slipping her shoes off her feet, and letting the tip of his tongue trail his hands as he tugged at the buckles. His hands were big enough to circle each foot, as he brought them to his lips, first one, then the other, pressing light kisses on their soles. His thumbs stroked the bones of her ankles, hand sliding up to her calves, and then a howl of surprise escaped her as her little toe was engulfed in his hot mouth.

Sensation raced through her, barreling along her system, sending hot blood rushing to her extremities with mind-numbing speed. As fast as her brain had time to register the exquisite pleasure of the act, it was over, and she could only fight to regain her breath before he lifted one of her legs, tilting his head so that he could place a nerve-jarring kiss at the back of her knee. The delicate flesh quivered at the gentle assault.

Again, before she could connect act with rational thought, he had shifted his attention to her soft wrap skirt, and was tugging at the fasteners at her hip, impatiently, until she began to fear the fine material would tear under his questing hands. Before she could help him, the clasp snapped open, and the veil of fabric was thrown back, revealing a very thin, very damp pair of panties.

He pulled back, eyes greedily taking in the shadow of dark hair that was barely visible behind the lacy material, and the starkness of her cinnamon skin against the bone-white cloth. Then, he leaned forward again, this time working at her blouse. In short seconds, this, too, came away under his determined hands, and now she lay under him, in nothing but her underwear, feeling more naked than she ever had in her life.

He stared, eyes moving slowly but voraciously down the length of her body, making her squirm; his gaze was as tangible as the fingers that trailed behind it. "You are . . ." He paused, unable to find a word to adequately convey his awe. He tried again. "Zhara, you're . . ." He gave up, instead opting to show rather than say.

Sharp teeth grazed a hard nipple through the stretchy

fabric of her white bra, and each hand grasped a rounded, firmly muscled globe of her bottom, causing them to quiver like a horse's flank after a long, hard ride.

Zhara yearned for the feel of his lips against hers again; he hadn't kissed her since they'd left the parking lot. She managed to wet her lips enough to allow her to speak coherently. "Kiss me."

He ignored her, moving to the other nipple, as if she hadn't spoken.

She burned with the need to be comforted by his kiss. "Cole . . ."

"You'll wait," he taunted, and returned to his pleasant task.

A third time, she managed to entreat, "Please, kiss me. I need you."

Instead he laughed, and his dark head bent toward the lace-covered triangle between her legs. The effect was galvanic. He neither removed the garment nor tugged it aside; the simple unheralded contact of his lips with the sweet-scented, moist spot at her center was enough to send a white-hot ball of sheer pleasure hurtling to her solar plexus, bringing about the most powerful spasm she had ever experienced. His name burst from her mouth, and then she had no air left to do anything but whimper, trembling fingers buried in the bunched muscles of his shoulders.

Smiling broadly, he stretched himself out over her, taking care not to make her bear the full burden of his weight, yet letting her know in no uncertain terms that she wasn't going to be getting up without his say-so.

He waited until her breathing approached normal levels again, and then said, "You asked for a kiss?"

She nodded, unable to answer.

He gave her what she had been begging for, softly, sweetly, his restraint belying the storm that had swirled around them moments before. Her mouth opened like a

fern tendril, unfurling, inviting. Her hands roamed his
broad back, relishing the roughness of the jacket that he
had not had the time to discard. It was her turn to be
curious about his body; he had her almost naked—surely,
he was obliged to return the favor!

Impatiently, she tugged at the offending item of clothing, sliding one hand under it and around his waist while
the other began to slip it off his shoulders. He shifted,
allowing her to have her way, and, as the jacket fell from
him, she explored his broad back, delighting in the rise
and fall of his tense muscles—then she felt something.
Something wasn't right.

Her fingers encountered an object hard and cool to the
touch, nestled in the small of his back. She didn't need
to see it to know it was a gun. Zhara went rigid.

Cole sensed with his body the change in hers. He lifted
his head, eyes still dimmed with desire. "What?"

"This . . . thing . . ." she began. With the slamming of
doors, her body began to shut down, cooling rapidly, as
if a sudden north wind had blown in.

He shook his head confusedly, not understanding her
for a moment, and then realization hit. "Oh, my gun.
Lord, I'm sorry, I forgot—let me—" He pried her fingers
away, removing the weapon from the leather holster, and
unbuckling the holster from around him with a swift, practiced hand. She watched him intently as he stood, checked
the safety, and then strode to the dresser, where he slid
the instrument into a drawer, locked it, and put away the
key.

By the time he returned to the bed, she was sitting up,
both arms doing their best to cover her nakedness, staring
at him in horror. He stopped short, unsure. "Zhara?"

She couldn't understand why he was so puzzled.
Couldn't he tell? If she needed anything to remind her
just how stupid she was being, allowing herself to be pleas-

ured by this man, this *cop*, his gun was it. She felt about frantically for her clothes.

He was horrified. "Sweetheart, what's wrong?" He glanced from the dresser to her ashen face. "Did it frighten you? Are you afraid of guns?"

"Only cops' guns," she snarled, eyes accusing.

He still didn't look as if he got it. The room was still hot from their frenzy, and the air lightly perfumed with the scent of her body. He hadn't fully shifted his mind over to accept the cold fear that now filled the space between them. "*Cops'* guns?" he echoed. "What, do you think I'd hurt you with it? Oh, Zhara, baby, I'd never."

The stress, the shock, were too much. Sudden tears pricked at her eyes, like tiny shards of glass, and she let her head fall into her hands as she began to weep. He was at her side, arms around her, rocking her, not saying anything, but letting her cry.

"Talk to me." Her tears had run their course, and now she was limp and quiet in his arms. "Tell me what's wrong."

"I'm an awful person," she tried to explain, head bent in shame. "I betrayed him—with you."

"Who did you betray?" he asked softly.

"Antonio."

She felt him flinch, and then, carefully, neutrally, he asked, "Who's Antonio?"

She turned her eyes up to his face. "I loved him."

Cole inhaled and then seemed to be thinking. "Was he a street child, like you?"

She nodded miserably. "He taught me everything. He was good to Mickey and me. He took care of us."

He prodded, gently. "And what happened? What does this have to do with my gun?"

She let him hold her, unresisting, while eyes that had seen too much horror stared off into the distance. "He was a boxer, a kickboxer. We had a dojo up on the north side. Not a real dojo—just an empty hall where we used to meet, and Antonio taught us, about twenty of us, survival skills. Martial arts. Just enough to help us stay alive on the street. Then the community council wanted to renovate the hall and asked us to stay away. But we kept going back, because we didn't have any other place big enough to practice. So, eventually the council called the police to clear us out, round us up and get rid of us, so they could have their building back.

"It started out peacefully, with half a dozen cops parked outside, telling us to leave quietly. They weren't even going to arrest us; they were just going to shoo us away and warn us not to come back. I can't remember what happened, but one of the children threw a stone, and then the others followed. Things got out of hand, and lots of people started shouting. Then one of the cops threw a smoke bomb. We all started screaming, running, and one of the kids tripped a cop and started hitting him with a piece of wood. Antonio held me by the arm, trying to get me to safety, when he looked around and saw the officer on the ground, trying to protect his face, and this boy beating him with a plank.

"He pushed me behind a pillar and told me to wait for him, and ran back in to save the cop. All he had to do was tell the boy to stop, because the children always listened to him; he was the eldest, our leader.

"But this cop, this rookie, thought he was coming to attack. I looked round the pillar and saw Antonio running toward the other boy with his arms above his head, shouting at him to let the cop up. Then I saw his body jerk backward and the look of surprise on his face, and then he was down and bleeding, with a hole in his chest." Zhara stopped talking, eyes fixed on Cole's, begging him to understand.

Cole watched her gravely. "The cop killed him."

She nodded miserably.

He tilted his head back, staring at the ceiling as if seeking inspiration, then looked back into her face. "Did you love him very much?"

She nodded again.

"He was the only lover you've ever had," he stated rather than asked, surprise in his voice.

She was puzzled. "Yes, why?"

He hung his head. "Oh, honey, I'm so sorry. I thought you were more experienced. If I'd only known, I would never have been so—aggressive."

She didn't answer. What could she say?

He seemed to be thinking again. After another long pause, he spoke again. "Zhara, I'm so sorry this happened. I know I would never be able to fathom exactly how hard this must have been on you, and I can't understand what could have gone through another officer's mind, to pull a gun on an unarmed boy. He was wrong. But I didn't shoot your friend. You can't blame my entire brotherhood and me for what happened. It's not fair. Can't you see that?"

Of course she knew that, but there was a place within her, ruled by emotion, where logic could never go. "I know. But I find it so hard to forgive . . ."

"*I* didn't do it," he reminded her again. "Forgive me for what happened on the roof, forgive me for your fall, but please, don't blame me for something I had no part in." He pointed at the dresser. "My gun is just a tool of my trade. I'm a cop. And I understand how everything you've ever been through could have tainted your judgment, but aside from what I do for a living, I'm also a man. Can't you just give me, the man, a chance?"

Did he know what he was asking her to do? She had lived in fear and exile for so many years, walking on the shady side of the street, yearning for light but afraid to go to it, longing for companionship, but afraid to take that risk again. Did he have any idea how hard this would be? "I don't know," she ventured to say.

"At least give it some thought." He stroked her hair, loose and tousled around her shoulders. "And please, don't ever think that what we did is a betrayal of your lover's memory." Zhara watched as his face twisted with the effort to speak, as if this concession was a hard one for him to make. "You loved him, but he's gone. Making yourself suffer won't help. You're young and beautiful, and you need to be touched as much as anyone else. I'm sure that denying your needs isn't the kind of sacrifice he'd have demanded of you. So no guilt, okay?"

She watching him searchingly, looking for evidence that he was simply trying to manipulate her back into bed again.

He saw the look and rushed to disabuse her of the idea. "And I'm not just saying that because there's nothing I'd rather do right now than make love to you."

Carefully, she turned his words over in her mind. Antonio had been generous and kind. Would he really have wanted her to suffer for so long? She accepted Cole's words, reluctantly. "Okay."

He grunted and stood up, stretching his cramped muscles. "I'll take you back to your room now," he told her. "And then I'll go back out to the car and bring you your wheelchair, okay?" He held out his arms to her, waiting for her to crawl into them.

She didn't move. It was well after midnight by now, but there were still many hours left until dawn. She wasn't sure if she really wanted to be alone for the rest of the night—not after having been dragged hurtling along such a roller-coaster ride of emotions.

Cole was still waiting. He didn't let his arms fall to his sides. "Zhara?"

How do you ask a man to let you spend the night in his bed? She bit her lip, grinding it between top and bottom teeth, afraid to begin to speak, because she was sure that whatever she said, it wouldn't come out right.

Cole spoke for her. "Do you want to stay here tonight? With me?"

Her face grew hot again. She nodded.

He looked into her face, his emotions a mystery, and then slowly began to undress. He kicked his shoes off, then tore off his socks. Zhara watched him, hypnotized, as he quickly popped the buttons open on the dark-green shirt, peeling it down off his powerful arms and tossing it carelessly over the back of the chair. He tugged open his belt and then the zipper of his fly, and soon, the heavy material fell to his feet and he stepped out of it.

It wasn't an undressing, but an unveiling. Dense, dark skin was pulled taut over rippling muscle. The breadth of him was almost frightening. He was a wall—no, he was flesh, warm, firm flesh that gleamed in the pale light that bathed the room. He watched her watch him, a half-smile on his face. "Pleased with what you see?" he asked, half teasing, half abashed at her frank appraisal.

All she could manage was, "Uh-huh."

"Good," he said softly, "because I like what I'm looking at very much."

She squirmed. Mercifully, he kept his undershorts on, and climbed into the wide bed, pulling her against his chest as he settled down. His chest was like velvet over steel. Her head fit perfectly into his shoulder, and one of his fingers toyed idly with a lock of hair that had tumbled over her forehead.

"Are you afraid?" he asked after awhile.

"Yes," she admitted, glad that he was kind enough to ask.

"Don't be. Sleep."

She closed her eyes.

At dawn, she stirred. Pale lilac filaments of light breaking through the gap in his curtains tickled the room. Her head was still nestled in his shoulder; she had fit so perfectly that she hadn't even shifted during the night. His chest rose and fell rhythmically, and the hand that had found itself nestled in the dark hair on his chest bobbed like a petal on a wave.

She lifted herself onto her elbow, looking down at him through eyes heavy-lidded with sleep. In repose, his face lacked the hardness it usually had. She wasn't surprised. She was discovering that the roughness of his features was more of a physical trait than a personal one, and that he was more kind, more patient, more pensive than she had ever imagined him to be. Maybe he was right. Maybe she *was* allowing his profession to cloud her judgment of him, as a man. Maybe if she forgot long enough that he was a cop, she'd be able to see the man clearly enough to love him properly, like he deserved.

Her eyes flew open; she was wide awake now. Love? Who'd said anything about love? She certainly hadn't. She cast a suspicious eye about the room, looking for the mischievous entity that had dared to whisper such a treacherous word into her ear. She didn't love this man! To do so would be madness! She needed him, yes, but that need was only temporary. In a while, she would be on her own feet once more, strength regained, and she'd be able to fend for herself. She wanted him, surely. He was attractive, and every time he touched her, he left her questioning her sanity. As a matter of fact, she was sure that her desire for him would hold the cure; if they did make love, maybe the abrasion of their bodies would erode the stupid idea that what she felt for him was anything more than intrigue and desire.

"Good morning."

She looked into his face, startled. She hadn't realized he'd awoken.

"What's going on in your mind?" he wanted to know. "You're frowning. Did you sleep badly?"

"No."

"Did I snore?"

She smiled, in spite of the seriousness of her problem. "No. Did I?"

"Like a rotary saw."

She punched him in the arm, hard. "I did not!"

He shrugged, pulling her down to him. "Well, you purred, at least."

"Purred?" She smiled into his face, curved lips just an inch from his and being drawn closer by the second, as if he carried a magnetic charge that she couldn't resist.

"Like that ratty little animal asleep in her basket in my study."

She was about to rise to her pet's defense, but as he pulled her closer, she discovered that her indignation was not the only thing rising. "Oh," she gasped.

"Yes," he agreed fervently.

This time the teasing, tormenting kisses of the night before were softer, sending messages of comfort and reassurance. If she had had any reasons to protest, she couldn't remember what they were.

Without breaking the kiss, Cole managed to unhook her bra and slide it off her, turning her to her side so he could feast on the sight of her breasts. Her panties followed, and then his shorts, and bare skin touched bare skin. Her body ached with the accumulated need of years.

One hand slid between them, down across her belly to a place where another, more insistent heartbeat had struck up an agonized staccato rhythm. His exploring fingers took up where they had left off the night before, searching, finding. The right hand, knowing full well what the left was doing, stroked her spine from the base of her neck downward to the point where her body swelled into two full, round mounds. Then, after protecting them, he slipped his hand under her bottom, tugging her to him.

As he slipped easily into her, his eyes held hers, en-

suring that he shared every flicker of her emotion at the
breach of her last line of defense. She closed her eyes
to shield herself from his probing gaze, but his whispered entreaty for her to look at him, share the moment
with him, made her open them again. His wide, deep,
black pupils spoke to her words his mouth never could.

They moved together, urgently, hungrily, forgetting that
they had both meant to take this one slow. There'd be
lots of time for that. Right now, friction and contact were
all that mattered. Faster than either of them had expected, the insane pleasure that drove them escalated into
a shattering pain, throwing flesh and bone and muscle
into electric confusion.

She opened her mouth and a song came out, high and
loud. He joined her, his deep bass melding with her cry.
Their eyes, which throughout the hurricane had never
looked away from each other, closed, as if after such a
searing collision they needed to be alone in their private
space for a while. His heart thudded against his chest; she
could feel it under her fingers, beating so hard she was
afraid for him, until she realized that hers was just as frantic. They struggled for breath, unable to waste precious
air on speech, and clung to each other like lost souls.

Eight

Cole sat in his den, both feet resting on the wide wooden desk that took up most of the room, with his eyes closed and his finger stroking his furrowed brow, thinking of Zhara. Catastrophe lazed on his lap, with his other hand held captive between her paws, tail idly flicking. On the floor, Cain and Abel sat, keeping a resentful eye on the blue-point Siamese. She was getting a little too comfy in the house by far, and they didn't like it one bit. The cat threw them a triumphant glance that let them know she was taking over, both house and master, and they'd better just learn to live with it.

Cole was oblivious to the little inter-species power struggle going on around him; his mind was full of the sound, taste, and smell of the woman still sleeping in his bed. They'd made love for hours, satisfying both desire and curiosity, touching each other in wonder, until all he could feel was her. His vision had narrowed, blocking out everything in the room, everything, until all he could see was her. He put an awed hand to his cheek; even though he had showered and shaved an hour ago, he was convinced he could still feel the sticky traces of her tears, drying.

How could he possibly have been so wrong about a person? He'd been convinced for years that this woman was hard and selfish, a menace, everything that he despised, a disease he was mandated by his badge to cure. But he'd pushed aside the barriers of resentment and mistrust, looked inside her, and found only a soft, sweet, frightened girl who was fighting with every weapon she had to help her friend hang on to a life that could slip away at any moment, and to hide herself from the pain of a childhood nobody should ever be forced to endure.

Then there was her lover. Not Anthony, the modern-day slave-driver his own imagination had conjured up, but Antonio, a young man who was as lost as she had been, and who had only sought to help make things better for her and the other children that had formed her make-shift family. Impulsive sorrow, pity for her having to deal with violent loss at such a young age, was replaced briefly by jealousy at knowing that this man had once touched her, physically and emotionally, so deeply that she had never dared to allow any other man to touch her since.

Cole shoved away the thought. He was resentful of a dead man. How low could you go? But dead or not, Antonio had Zhara's love, and that was something Cole could never hope for. He glanced in the direction of his room. Sure, she'd allowed him access to her body, but as sweet as that had been, he knew that her heart was a closed door on which he wouldn't even dare to knock.

Coward, a scornful voice mocked. The voice was right. He wanted her so much but hadn't the shadow of an idea how to go after her. He was pretty sure that the last thing she wanted in her life right now was him. And even if he decided to try, what could he possibly do to get her to trust him? She'd trusted him with her body and trusted him with the silent tears of loss and pain and exhaustion that had leaked from her heart as he held her close. But the warmth of the night had a notorious way of chilling in the brilliant sunshine. He had no guarantee that when he saw her next, the first thing he would see in her eyes wouldn't be the shock and horror of having let a moment of weakness trick her into doing something she sorely wanted to undo.

If, God forbid, that happened, Cole was sure he would lose his mind. This strange emotion, this love—because that was what he had finally acknowledged it to be—was so new that it left him unsure of what to do to stop it from dying. All he knew was that right now it was as fragile as Zhara herself was, and if he needed to hold it in both hands like a newly-laid egg, keep it warm, and hold it close until it was strong enough to fend for itself, well, that was what he would do.

The phone buzzed, startling both him and the cat. In true cat fashion, she got up lazily, stretched, yawned, and strode over the table, whereupon she sat on the receiver just as Cole was reaching for it. Cole disentangled the handset from her possessive claws and put it to his ear, mildly irritated at being torn from his contemplation of such a huge and serious dilemma. "Cole Wyatt," he barked.

"Cole, where've you been?" Brian Ames' voice crackled with anxiety. "I've been calling you all morning. Why haven't you picked up?"

Cole's eyebrows shot up. Brian had been calling? He hadn't heard the phone ring a single time. With good reason. He almost smiled as he thought of him and Zhara, drowning out any sound the phone could possibly have made. "I—uh—I guess I overslept a little," he lied uncomfortably.

"Is Zhara nearby?" Brian brushed the excuse aside. Obviously he had more important things to talk about than Cole's reasons for not answering.

Cole stiffened. "No. Why?" he asked sharply.

"Oh, man, you'd better get over to the station. Something's going down, and you'd do well to hear it first hand."

"*What's* going down? Talk to me, Brian."

"Couple of the officers busted this guy, called Oliver Mason, on a customs scam. All kinds of stuff. Booze, porn, Cuban cigars, cases of them, smuggled across the border through Mexico. Something like that. They fly them by light aircraft to him here in Medusa and he has this little underground distribution network . . ."

"Get to the point."

Brian sighed. "I *am* getting to the point. Mason got squeezed, really hard. Seems they got so many different charges against him, it's enough to put him away so long he's going to miss his grandkids' college graduation . . ."

"And . . . ?"

"So he's done a deal with the D.A. He's giving names, dates, places, in exchange for lesser charges. This guy's singing like the Vienna Boys' Choir."

Cole realized he had a massive headache. He rubbed his temple with two fingers. He didn't have time for any more preamble. "Brian . . ." he began.

Brian hurried up. "I was there; I heard him talking. He claims he used to be a fence." He paused and inhaled sharply. "In Chicago."

Cole felt as if someone had reached into his chest, caught hold of his heart, and squeezed. Hard. "Zhara's name came up," he finished for Brian.

"Hers and Mickey's. Four years ago."

"Is it really bad?"

He could almost see Brian shrug. "Nothing very big, and they were both minors at the time, and it's out of your jurisdiction. But the information's being relayed to Chicago. It's an old, stale case, but it's the first time any-one has ever found a witness with evidence on her. You never know . . ."

"If they decide to open up the case . . ."

"Yeah." Brian sounded uncomfortable, and Cole had the distinct impression that Brian was beginning to figure

out that his commitment to Zhara ran much deeper than
his desire to make up for that awful night on the roof.

"I'll be there in half an hour," he said decisively.

As he reached out to slap the phone back down, he
heard Brian's voice, tinny in the distance. "I'll be waiting."

Cole struggled for breath. In his head, huge boulders
rolled, slamming into the sides with force. The veins in
his temples felt as if bubbles of air were expanding there.
He was beginning to get physically ill with fear for Zhara.
He knew the system well enough to know that old cases
like that rarely got followed up, not if they didn't involve
violence or murder. Burglaries were a dime a dozen, here
as well as in Chicago, and no cop had the time or the
resources to delve too deeply into a case that was deep-
sixed four years ago. That was the reality.

But, it was also reality that some bright spark up in Chicago might take it into his head to make Zhara a pet case,
maybe a young officer bucking for promotion, or trying
to impress his superior. Maybe an officer with a grudge,
one who hated to let sleeping cases lie. *Not too far-fetched,*
Cole thought wryly. He himself was guilty of the same type
of obsession with Zhara's case, a nagging unwillingness to
let an elusive mystery rest. Now, with a real live witness,
this case could rise from the dead, and Zhara and Mickey,
who were both trying so hard to put their past behind
them and join the ranks of the law-abiding, would be nothing but grist for a huge and horrifying judicial mill.

This new development wasn't good. It wasn't good at
all.

Zhara let the water rise up over the soft mound of her
belly and then her breasts. She sank slowly, easing back
against the smooth, pale blue porcelain bath with a sigh.
Cole surrounded her; the smell of his sweat clung to her

skin so that even the translucent bubbles popping around
her could never remove it. She had opened her eyes to
find herself alone in his wide, heavy bed, amidst tangled,
damp sheets, with pillows and clothes, both hers and his,
scattered on the floor. Her wheelchair was placed carefully
next to the bed; he had obviously gone down to retrieve
it for her while she slept. Of course, once she managed
to clamber into it, she could easily have wheeled herself
back to her own room, to wash off the traces of their
passion in her own bath, but she rationalized that his bathroom was as disabled-accessible as hers, so it didn't make
much of a difference where she bathed.

But she was honest enough with herself to admit that
she stayed where she was out of a need to find out more
about him, and piercing the intimacy of his bathroom was
as good a place as any to start. Only good manners had
stopped her from poking around in his medicine cabinet.
As she lay in the warm water, appreciating the manly scent
of cedar and sandalwood that wafted up from his bubble-
bath, she let her curious eyes take in the details: the thick-
piled navy towel that he had carelessly tossed on the floor
after he had used it earlier, the dressing-gown that he was
obviously too impatient to use, hanging forlornly from a
hook, the washbasin and countertop strewn with hairbrush, shaving implements, cologne. Everything in the
room bore his stamp—including her.

She flushed at the thought of it. The man had
branded her like a heifer at a rodeo—with his eyes, his
fingers, his lips, his tongue, his . . . she squirmed, glad
for the warm water that eased away the soreness between
her thighs. She was amazed at herself, abashed at the
memory of herself urgently whispering in his ear, "More,
more, please . . ."

Well, she'd asked for it, and he'd given it to her. She
didn't need to look to know that there would be faint lilac
bruises blooming on her inner thighs and along the curve

of her bottom, where he'd gripped her in the final cataclysmic moments of their union. She smiled triumphantly, treasuring both the marks and the memory of how they'd gotten there, like trophies. They were proof that her body wasn't dead, after all. She'd tried to shut herself down, close herself off to men and desire and all the complications one suffered when both those elements were brought together in the same place and time. But this morning was proof enough that she was a woman, alive with need and desire and wonderful passion.

Her mind turned to Antonio, poor Antonio, so young, so fervently devoted to her. She'd loved him, as ardently as any teenager could love. His death had meant a kind of death for her, one that found her denying any need to be close to another man. With surprise, she discovered that she didn't feel guilty. She didn't feel as if she had betrayed his memory; that was still alive in her, and it always would be.

But something new and brash and wonderful was taking the place of the void left behind by Antonio's loss. Something huge and frightening and inevitable, and at the center of it was Cole. The satisfied smile that played around her kiss-swollen lips faded, and her mood became serious. What in the name of heaven was this man really doing to her? Sure, he'd plucked at her strings, producing notes she'd never heard before, but it was the effect that he had had on her mind and her soul that was frightening.

No, she corrected herself, the achingly beautiful morning in bed had not caused the emotions that stood out starkly in her mind; it had simply made them visible, like churned-up water at the seashore suddenly becoming quiet, so that she could look down and clearly see each shell and pebble and time-worn piece of glass on the sandy floor. She loved Cole. Not the way she had loved Antonio; there was nothing soft and sweet and timid and youthful about this awesome emotion. This

love was huge and frightening and delicious and wonderful and improbable—no, impossible. Just *naming* it
was flying in the face of God.

How dare she? How dare she have the temerity to look
into the center of the turmoil that Cole raised in her just
by walking into a room, the fear he instilled in her when
he fixed her with his deadly keen black eyes, the anguish
he left in her when he didn't call at the appointed time,
the breathlessness, the shudder that took her over every
time his face loomed in her mind's eye late at night when
she should be sleeping—how dare she call it *love*?

But it *was* love, wasn't it? She wrinkled her brow. A love
that could be either blessing or curse, depending on
whether he proved worthy of her trust or not. She loved
him as a doe loves a hunter that holds out a sweet apple
in the palm of his hand. The goodness that he showed
her could be genuine kindness or a trap that would prove
lethal.

Zhara strained to remember the details of the night
before. He'd spoken to her in the car, while they were on
their way home, before everything had blurred into sound
and touch and taste. What was it that he had told her? *I
won't hurt you, not with my body, not with my actions, not with
my words. As long as I am with you, nothing will harm you.*
Genuine words or words designed to seduce? Worse yet,
were they words designed to calm her, stop her in mid-
flight, distract her long enough for him to make his case
against her and finally haul her in, so that the Great Decorated Detective could once again make the local paper?
It wasn't inconceivable; words cost nothing. They said that
cats, both big and small, purred while they brought their
prey to the ground, not out of the pleasure of killing, but
in order to soothe their victim, lull it into a comfortable
place, stop it from defending itself. Then the cat would
rip its throat out.

She shuddered. Cole couldn't be that unkind. She

forced herself to remember the way he'd touched her, the murmured endearments, the caresses that had spoke volumes. *You're a fool,* she whispered to herself. *Why are you so worried? Can't you tell he feels the same way about you? It's there every time he looks at you. It's in his touch. What are you afraid of?*

Feeling better, she hugged herself, and the warmth and gladness came rushing back in, dispelling her fears and irrational worries like cobwebs. She was in love, grown-up love, for the first time, and she knew, she was *convinced,* that the object of her affections felt the same way about her. Her life was back on the right track, and with sheer determination, and the understanding and support of a strong man, she would be able to forget the past, cut it away like a sack of stones tied around her ankles, and rise unhindered to the lake surface where she could breathe clean air again. What could be better?

With renewed strength, she tried to rise from the water, leaning heavily on her stronger side, with her weaker leg, getting stronger every day, following suit. A hot thrill of hope rushed through her. Today, she'd try to walk again. She'd practiced in her room, in private, and had made two or three steps before sinking to the carpet. But today she felt she was strong enough to go farther—across the room, maybe. Cole would help her. And perhaps afterward, he would hold her close and tell her how proud he was of her for trying so hard. Maybe then would be the right time to share her feelings for him, and when those wonderful words, "I love you, Cole," were past her trembling lips, she would hold her breath and wait, to see if he would return them in kind. It was going to be a very, very good day.

She was halfway out of the tub when she heard a tentative knock on the door. "Zhara?" His voice was faint, almost timid.

Sheer surprise made her lose her balance, and she fell

heavily back into the water, a tidal wave washing up and over the sides and onto the floor. She looked down at the mess ruefully. "Pretty clumsy, Thorne," she muttered to herself.

The knock came again, and then the door opened slowly. A smile of pleasure rose to her mouth as she turned toward the broad-shouldered shape that filled the doorway. It was the first time she was seeing him since those final breathless moments before they'd both fallen into exhausted sleep earlier that morning, and she felt a combination of shyness and eager anticipation.

"Cole," she breathed, seeking out his eyes, holding one hand outstretched for him to touch. "Come here," she coaxed, surprised at the seductive timbre of her own voice.

He didn't move, but instead stood half in and half out of the room. The water in which she lay suddenly became very, very cold. The splash that had sent most of it overboard had lowered the level so much that it now failed to cover her breasts, and her nipples lay exposed, gemstone hard, to his view. But the man who hours before had buried his face against them like a contented nursling now averted his eyes, hastily, with something that looked a little too much like embarrassment.

Zhara felt her insides contort into a hard, uncomfortable knot. This wasn't happening. He was looking everywhere except directly at her. Where was the light that had shone from his eyes this morning? Where was the glow and the naked pleasure and honesty? His face now held the closed, guarded look of a poker player. Zhara called his name again, softly now, voice almost a mew.

In response, he sighed heavily and took a long, deep breath. "I—have to go in to the station. Now."

She frowned. "Isn't this your day off?"

He lifted his shoulders. "Brian, uh, asked me to come in. That's the way it is sometimes. I may be off duty, but I'm always on call."

She felt a wave of panic. She didn't want to be alone in the house, not with him walking out with that look on his face, like a depth charge had gone off inside him. "Why?" she persisted.

"It's, uh, a case I'm working on." He stared down at his feet. "Big break."

Her eyes narrowed. "What case?"

He shook his head. "I'm not at liberty to tell you."

"Why not?"

He sighed. "Because that's the way I work. I'm a detective. Confidentiality is part of my job."

She knew there was more to it than that. Dread prodded her in the chest with long, bony fingers. "This 'case,' " she asked, carefully, choosing her words slowly, "is it mine?"

He shook his head mutely, but couldn't hold her gaze.

She wasn't letting him get away that easily. "Cole, look at me and tell me again. Does this case have something to do with me?" She wished she could get out of the icy water and get dressed, instead of being naked and vulnerable in front of him, but she'd rather freeze in the now-chilly room than allow him to see her weak and naked and fumbling. "The least you could do is look at me. Is it my case?"

He lifted his head, and his black eyes were dull and flat, but they held hers steadily. "No."

"What, then?"

He didn't flinch. "Nothing important. Just routine."

"But important enough for you to leave the house on your day off, right?" She knew she was getting shrill, but she didn't care.

He nodded stiffly. "That's right." His lips were clamped so tautly that they were rimmed with a thin gray line.

She knew he was lying, and hated him for it. She'd been right—he'd held her down, purring, and she'd allowed herself to cease struggling, to trust him, even to love him.

And now he had her where he wanted her, and he was moving in for the kill. What other explanation could there be?

The alternative came screaming to her brain, and shame rippled over her, sticky and dank. Forget the cloak and dagger theories, the real explanation was so ordinary, so mundane, that it almost made her laugh. He was experiencing morning-after regrets, pure and simple. He'd realized that he'd lost control, maybe said more than he'd meant to, certainly *done* more than he'd meant to, and he stood there before her now, too abashed to hold her gaze, wishing to hell he hadn't made love to her.

This was what it was like, waking up to a man who felt nothing but remorse for having let his guard down with you. This was what it felt like when passion was replaced with aloofness. He didn't need to go in to the station; he just needed to be away from her.

She didn't know what to say, where to look. So much for her stupid little pipe dreams about being loved and loving him in return. She was nothing but a perp, a bust gone bad that he was trying to make up for by being nice to her. Only he'd been a little *too* nice to her, and now he wished he could undo it all.

She sniffed, trying to sound uncaring and aloof, warning herself that tears now would be her undoing. She didn't give a damn anymore if he saw her naked and clumsy, flailing around like a wounded bird. Gingerly, she stood, turning her back on him so that the pain on her face wouldn't diminish the contempt she threw into her voice. "Very well, Cole," she tried to sound distant, uncaring. "Go off to your work. I'll be fine."

She groped for her towel, and was filled with resentment when he found it and placed it in her hand. Wrapping it around her, she plopped into her chair, wet as she was, knowing that later she would regret it, as she would be forced to wheel around on damp upholstery until it dried. But so what? Her chest felt as if it had been forced open by huge steel jaws, and her still-beating heart torn out and tossed on the ground like offal.

"I'll be back as soon as I can," he promised softly. He had mustered the courage to enter the room fully now, and was hovering anxiously over her, as if expecting that she would need help to wheel out of the bathroom and into her own room.

Who needed his help? Angrily, she thrust forward, deliberately running over one of his feet in the process. "Sorry," she said unrepentantly, and maneuvered herself through the door, past him, and out of the bedroom. She was getting good with her chair, and if she was obliged to use it as a weapon, well, fine.

He followed. "Zhara?" He didn't sound very sure of himself. She ignored him and kept on going. His long legs allowed him to meet up with her in three strides. He laid a hand on the back of the chair, not exerting enough force to prevent her from moving into her own room, but almost imploring her to stop. "I'm sorry. I have to go. I won't be long, I promise."

She twisted in her chair so she could look up into his troubled, closed face. What did she care how long he was gone? His return would only mean more misery. Shaking her head, she thrust herself through her own doorway. He didn't try to follow her. "Just go," she told him raggedly as she let the door swing shut behind her. Breath coming in short sharp puffs from the exertion, she stopped, listening. He stood there for a long time, hesitating, unmoving, and then, after an agonizing pause, he turned, and she could hear the sound of his shoes retreating down the hall. A few moments later, the front door opened and then slammed, and then his car engine roared to life.

* * *

Cole had a headache going on three days now. It was
the kind of pain that grabbed at the back of his head like
claws, sinking its nails down into his neck, slowly increas-
ing the pressure on his shoulders until he had to struggle
to square them and walk upright. He knew that pills
wouldn't solve the problem, nor would sleep—as if he
were getting any anyhow.

He couldn't stand the way Zhara looked at him—the
way her brown eyes followed him around, full of fear and
hurt, only to shutter themselves as soon as he turned to
face her, becoming carefully guarded and blank. After
their morning of loving, she was entitled to expect him
to be more open with her, to keep on touching her as he
had then, to share himself with her as their lovemaking
had implied that he would. But there was no way he could
be forthright with her, or strengthen the wonderful new
bond that had formed between them that morning, unless
he dealt with his immediate problem. He was too methodi-
cal to leave such a huge and dangerous loose end dan-
gling while he pursued her as a woman. In the meantime,
he hoped he wasn't hurting her so badly that the damage
would be irreparable by the time the crisis was over. Oh,
he knew that she was suffering, and wished to God he
knew what to do to make the pain stop.

But he couldn't. He'd hated lying to her about his
emergency case not being hers, but he was a cop, and
sometimes, stretching the truth was called for in the performance of his duties. Evidence against her was surfac-
ing; there could be no denying that. And the fact that it
was his case meant that he had to examine it judiciously
and without bias, whether he liked it or not.

He sat in his den, listening to the pounding of rap emanating from his son's room. Omar had returned from basketball camp, sized up the chill that had settled upon the
house like a snow flurry, and resorted to his room. Cole
was well aware that Omar sensed the tension between him-

self and Zhara, and he knew that the boy was confused
and uncomfortable, and that, too, pained him. But he
couldn't discuss his information with his son, either. He
was hurting the two people he loved most by his silence,
but the demands of his job—no, his calling—wouldn't
have him handle his problem any other way.

He closed his eyes and let his head fall back on the
padded leather headrest of his chair. Years ago, he'd taken
a vow to be the kind of man his son would be proud of,
and that definition, in his own mind, included being the
best he could be at his job. Not too long afterward he'd
taken *another* vow, at his graduation, to uphold the law
without fear or favor. Surely that vow dictated that he was
to be as meticulous about his work as he could be, even
if the woman that he loved lay at the center of his case!

He'd watched the new witness, Oliver Mason, being interrogated by his colleagues, and he'd listened to the
tapes, alone in his office, again and again. Zhara was
plainly incriminated. True, Chicago was out of his jurisdiction, but copies of the tapes had been forwarded to
his brothers in blue in that city, and it was only a matter
of time before they decided whether they were prepared
to reopen a case that was years old.

He wasn't naïve; in a city of that size, burglary cases
were a daily occurrence, and few cases that had gone as
cold as hers had were ever reopened, not unless there was
some political or personal motivation to do so. His logical
self told him that was hardly likely, because Zhara had
been a teen at the time, a street child, and thus merely
an annoyance to the authorities. It would probably wind
up dead, filed away and forgotten while more pressing
matters were dealt with.

But what if it didn't? It would break his heart to see
Zhara and Mickey dragged through an indifferent justice
system, not now, when they were both trying so hard to
start new lives. Therein lay his dilemma. He knew several

people in Chicago—people with the power to ensure that her history was buried and forgotten. A phone call would be all that it would take, a favor or two called in, and Oliver Mason's testimony against her would never see the light of day. In an attempt to save his own slimy skin, Mason had fingered many fatter fish than Zhara, enough to have both police and prosecutors in a tizzy for a long time to come. So what if a little case like hers turned up missing?

But the thought of making such a call revolted him; his very spirit rebelled against it. It was simple enough to actually do: pick up the phone, dial the number, make the request. But at what price? Zhara would be saved, yes, but Cole knew that her freedom would come at the cost of his own soul. For him, being a cop meant being a *clean* cop. He'd been offered many bribes, but he had never taken any. He'd had a variety of trinkets dangled before him: watches, cars, vacations, cash—his, if only he would look the other way, but every time he had done what was right in the eyes of the law. It was the only way he could sleep at night. It was the only way he could look his son in the eye every day.

If he were to make that call, there would be a stain on his fingers by the time he set the receiver back down into the cradle. A tiny stain for a tiny misdemeanor, surely, but a stain all the same. A blot on his pristine copy book. If he did that, would he ever feel the same sense of pride he always felt when he polished his badge? When he looked in the mirror, what would he see?

On the other hand, what good would his manhood be if he lost Zhara? Who would he have to share his pride in himself with? He rose heavily to his feet and began to walk back and forth from one side of the room to the other. He was convinced that the walls were getting closer and closer to each other as time passed by, crushing him, forcing the air out of the room so that he would eventually be unable to draw another breath.

This dilemma had the devil's own horns. Love or the law? What could he do to keep both?

He sat again, deep in thought. There must be another way. Somehow, some way, he had to save her. But how? If only he knew her better, knew more than she so reluctantly shared with him. In spite of his desire to spare her, he had to admit that a huge part of himself wanted to know everything about her, things that Mason's tapes didn't hold, things about her lost youth that she refused to tell him.

After long and painful deliberation, he lifted his head to stare in horror at his arm, which, without any conscious instruction from him, reached out toward the phone on his desk and began dialing a number that he knew by heart.

"Zhara, Zhara, no. Tell me it isn't so." Mickey stared at her, face ashen. "You're not really in love with that *cop*, are you?"

Zhara slumped in her wheelchair. Oh, she was beginning to hate this chair! It was as much a prison as her body was, holding her back, when all she wanted was to get up, run, and keep on running away from Cole and his deathlike silence, away from the house that he was letting her use out of kindness but nothing else. Away from Mickey and his accusing, shocked looks.

She focused miserably on her fingers twisting in her lap, unable to look into those pale, agitated eyes. It had taken her days to convince Mickey to visit her at Cole's house, and, even so, he had promised her that he would come only when both Cole and his son were out of the house. They faced each other in the living room, she, of course, seated, he standing. In spite of the heat emanating from the radiator, and the warm sweater that she pulled defensively around her, the room felt cold. Pale October sunlight filtered in through a window but offered no additional heat.

Mickey pushed his glasses up on his nose with a frustrated hand. He looked bad, very bad. Zhara was sure that his throwing up had started again, because his usually lanky frame was downright thin, and his skin was sallow and dehydrated. Her heart ached for him. How much more could his fragile body take before it gave in to the leukemia? He was existing on a diet of dry food, crackers, and toast, mainly, as his nausea had become so persistent that even the scent of a cooked meal triggered his vomiting, in spite of the anti-emetics he was taking with his medication.

At least, she reassured herself, he had remained true to his reluctant promise to start taking his medicine again. It would help contain the rapid decline in the functioning of his immune system, although this was just a stopgap measure, and what he really needed was professional treatment. Which brought her to the reason she'd asked him over in the first place.

She took a deep breath, unsure of how to broach the subject of his health; Mickey was so touchy about his illness and the way in which it limited his freedom. "Mickey?"

He watched her balefully, both hands shoved into his pockets. "What?" he grunted.

"How are you feeling?"

His colorless eyebrows shot up. "What?"

"You're throwing up again, aren't you?"

"What does that have to do with anything? Don't change the subject! I'm asking you about that man, who you seem to think you're in love with."

Not *think*, she wanted to protest, *know*. But discussing Cole would be painful and useless right now. Mickey was her best friend, but she couldn't even bear to get into that with him. She brushed the name away as if it didn't matter. "I don't want to talk about him," she stated firmly. "I want to talk about you. I asked you how you're feeling."

He grunted, but let the red herring pass. "Fine."

She wheeled closer to him, wishing he were seated as well so she didn't have to take the vulnerable position of looking up at him while she was trying to be firm. "Not fine, Mickey. You're very sick."

He shrugged, but did not answer.

"I want you to go back in to Chain of Hope and start taking chemotherapy again. Sign up to get on their waiting list for bone marrow transplant donors." Chain of Hope was a chain of small government-funded clinics across the country that specialized in helping cancer patients under twenty-one. With contacts all over the country, they would surely be able to use their network to find him a suitable donor. More than a year ago, she had convinced Mickey to attend for a while, because the service was free. But as soon as they had begun probing into his background, Mickey had run scared, refusing more treatments. He had still been a juvenile at the time, and knew that if he was pegged as a runaway, he'd be turned into Social Services, and in all likelihood they would be separated.

She hadn't liked the idea then of him choosing to remain with her and suffer over being returned to the social system and continuing to receive medical attention, but she had respected his horror at the idea of losing the autonomy he had fought for for so long. So everything they had had been poured into private medical care, and their earnings from their new security business had gone into paying for doctors who would provide adequate treatment but wouldn't ask too many personal questions.

But the time for that was over. They simply didn't have

the money, and waiting for more to come in while Mickey suffered would be nothing short of a death sentence.

Mickey didn't seem to see it that way. "Chain of Hope? Are you crazy? Why?"

She tried to stay calm. "Because you need them. Because we tried, but we can't pay for your medical attention, and Chain of Hope is free."

He scowled. "We went there before, and it didn't help—"

She cut him off. "It didn't help because you didn't stay in the program long enough for them to help you, remember? You pulled out when they started asking too many questions."

"If I hadn't pulled out, they'd have sent me *back*," he countered passionately.

That was true, she acknowledged, but it was no longer the case. "Mickey, you're eighteen now. Nobody's sending you anywhere. But you're still sick. No," she paused. "Sick" didn't cut it. "You're *worse*. You need help. It's the only way."

He shrugged, indifferent to his own fate. "I'll think about it."

Zhara was aghast. "Don't *think* about it, Mickey! *Do* it!"

"Why?"

"Because if you don't, you'll die!" The words burst from her lips before she could stop them. They both fell silent. The concept of his death had always hung between them, suspended in the air, cold and harsh, but never vocalized. For years they'd discussed his illness, and turned over in their minds all the treatment options that faced them, but, as far as she could remember, neither of them had ever spoken the word "death." And now that she had, it had solidified, becoming almost a person, and stood in the shadowy corner of the room like a specter, watching them with chess-player's eyes, waiting on their countermove.

"Would you care if I did?" he asked softly.

Her mouth hung open. Her mind searched for something to say. Would she care? How could he even ask such a question? "What do you mean? What do you mean, 'would I care'? Of course I would. You're all I have. I wouldn't know what to do without you. I love you."

He looked at her sadly, face much older than it should be. "Do you?"

"You need to ask? After all this time?" The pain that such a question caused her was like a samurai blade, clean, sharp and white-hot, between her shoulders.

"Then tell me. Say it." Each hand was placed on an armrest of her wheelchair. His face was very close, eyes stock-still for once, penetrating hers. He had stopped breathing and was just waiting.

"Mickey," she began. Her palms were sweating. She couldn't understand why it suddenly seemed so important to him that she affirmed her love for him. She told him she loved him all the time, with words and deeds. They were everything to each other, all the family each one had. So why was he forcing the issue? "Mickey, I love you. You're my best friend, my brother—"

He smiled cynically, lips a thin white line, and abruptly he straightened and stepped backward. Zhara stopped in midsentence, bewildered.

"Like a brother," he repeated. *"Am* I your brother?"

"Of course you are! It doesn't matter that we don't share blood; it's the heart that matters. It's how we feel about each other that matters. You're the brother I never had, and you'll always be—"

"And I'll *always* be just your brother, right?" His cold, bloodless smile widened, frightening Zhara even more.

"Yes," she said, in a small voice. "No matter what." She waited for him to speak again, hoping that whatever he might have to say would solve the mystery of his bizarre behavior. It did, but the answer to the mystery made her immediately wish it hadn't.

Slowly, painfully, as if each word were a stone he was coughing up out of the pit of his stomach, he spoke. "You don't see me as a man, do you, Zhar?"

She wrinkled her brow. "What do you mean?"

"I mean," he said, voice rising in anguish, the cool he had struggled to maintain throughout the entire conversation falling away, like cracked plaster off a wall, "that you love me, but not as a man, as a boy. As a brother. No matter what I do, you'll never see me as anything other than the skinny little boy the bullies back at Harbourmouth used to kick. I'm still the kid you used to take care of. The funny-looking little freak you had to protect from the pushers and gangsters on the street—"

"You're *not* a freak," she intervened hotly.

"There you go again, protecting my fragile little ego . . ."

"I'm not protecting your ego, Mickey, I'm just saying it isn't true!" Her anger was growing to match his.

He went on as if he hadn't heard her. ". . . like I was still eight years old and afraid to look at myself in the mirror. You don't have to do that. I don't want you to do that. I'm a man now, Zhara."

"So . . . ?"

"So love me like one!"

Silence covered them both, shutting them in like an upside down bell jar, until all they could hear was the pounding of their blood in their own ears. Reality came as a shock, and suddenly, clearly, she could understand his behavior, his anger, his resentment toward Cole, and his insistence that if she returned to their own apartment he would be able to take care of her as well as Cole could.

Mickey was in love with her. Not the filial love that had always existed between them as they were growing up, not the childish adoration he held for her while she fought for him and stood up for him whenever he couldn't. Whatever that love had once been, it had gelled and solidified into something real and adult.

She was stunned. What was wrong with her? Why hadn't she seen it coming? Maybe Mickey was right; she *did* still see him as a child. She had never, not once, interpreted anything he had ever said to her, his insistence at being autonomous even to the detriment of his own health, his blistering dislike of Cole, as being anything other than teenage petulance. But, for Mickey, Cole wasn't only a cop with the power to sink them both; he was a rival for her affections. The possibility had never entered her mind, and now that it was reality, she didn't know what to say.

What Mickey said next drove away any last desperate hope she might have had that she had misunderstood. "Instead, you chose to love *that man*. The man who hunted you down like an animal, treated you like a criminal, put me in jail, and you in that chair . . ."

"It isn't his fault I'm in the chair," she defended Cole agitatedly. "I did a stupid thing. I'm the only one to blame."

Mickey ignored her. "There you go making excuses for your own worst enemy! I can't figure out if you're stupid or blind. What is it about him? Why him and not me?"

"I never said I loved him, Mickey," she protested miserably.

"Not with your mouth," he agreed. "But it's written all over you. You just think I'm too young or too dumb to see it for what it is."

"I don't think you're dumb . . ."

He threw his hands up in the air. "Zhara, listen. Just listen. You're not my mommy or my big sister or anything like that anymore. And I'm not a child anymore. I'm a man now, and I love you like one. All I want to know is, can you love *me* like one?"

How could she? Not only had she never even thought about Mickey in that way, throughout their friendship, but even if she wanted to, Cole filled her up. He was inside her, in her blood, in her lungs; he filled her nostrils each time she inhaled, he was her last thought when she fell asleep at night, and the first thing that crossed her mind when she got up.

Mickey didn't need an answer. Her face was all he needed to see. He pointed an accusing finger at her. "Don't bother answering. I don't want to hear it, whatever you're going to say. But let me tell you this: you're wrong about him. He's going to hurt you. He's just using you, stringing you along until he has what he needs to take you down for good. I can just see it now, a two-page spread in the paper: 'Local Boy Does It Again.' Or a book deal. Don't you think the man responsible for putting away The Cat would have a book deal coming to him? Is that what you want, for lover-boy to line up a ghostwriter on the side and make himself a fortune over your downfall?"

"Cole's not like that," she protested, hoping deep inside herself that she was right.

Mickey's mouth twisted. "Oh no? Is that what he's got you believing? I'll prove to you different." Before Zhara could speak again, he was out of the living room and making his way up the corridor.

Her hands, slippery with cold sweat, slid uselessly on the wheels, and it was a time before she was able to get a firm enough grip to wheel after him. He wasn't headed to the front door, but farther into the house, toward the rooms. "Where are you going?" she demanded. This was Cole's house; they were only visitors. The least they could do was respect his privacy.

Mickey didn't answer but started throwing open doors and sticking his head in rooms until he came upon Cole's den. "Saving you from yourself, darling," he replied, as the door slammed shut in her face. She arrived just in time to hear the well-oiled lock slip into place with a soft, wet click.

Frightened now, she hammered on the heavy door. Mickey had gone too far, both emotionally and in his actions. She wasn't sure what he was up to, but she knew it couldn't be good. "Mickey, Mickey, open up!"

There was no answer. She pounded harder. "Open up, Mickey, or I swear—"

"Or what, Zhara? I told you, you're not my pretend mommy anymore. You can't tell me what to do."

"What are you doing in there? That's Cole's private space. He doesn't even let *me* in there."

"All the more reason why this is the place to start looking," came the reply.

She didn't understand. "Looking for what?"

"Proof." Zhara heard furniture being moved and Mickey grunting.

He sounded insane. Zhara was frightened. "Proof of what, Mickey? Please come out."

"Proof of what he's doing to you, and to me, while you let him. Proof that you're wrong to trust him." There was muffled panting, and then it was quiet again.

Fingers shaking, she tugged a hairpin out of her thickly wound bun and tugged it straight. She wasn't letting this go on any longer. She was going in after him if it killed her. She inserted it into the lock, ruing her lost nimbleness, feeling for the tiny moving parts inside as they slid back one by one. The lock popped free, and almost sobbing with relief, she pushed against the door. It didn't budge.

Mickey laughed. "You forget, I know you. I know you can pick a lock in your sleep. Don't bother, there's a chair wedged against the door. You can't come in. Now, if you just give me a few more moments, I'll have what I need, and then I'll be out of here, okay?"

Zhara was beside herself. Mickey had to be stopped, before he got hurt. She wheeled back down the corridor to the living room, snatched up the phone, and held it to her ear. The dial tone was like a swarm of bees, stinging their way into her brain. Cole would know what to do.

But she couldn't dial the number. Something stopped her. Was it fear for Mickey? Of course it was! Cole would be furious if he knew that his sanctum had been breached. But there were other reasons, weren't there? What if Mickey were right? What if he did find something in there that proved to her that Cole couldn't be trusted, after all? Where would that leave her? If she did call, and he turned up in time to oust Mickey from his room, that proof, if it actually did exist, might never come to light. Reluctantly, defeated, she let the receiver fall and returned to take up watch outside Cole's den.

Inside, all was quiet—too quiet. Not even the rustle of paper. She pressed an ear against the door. "Mickey?"

No answer.

Her breath began to come in short, anguished puffs. He wouldn't hurt himself in there—would he? She called his name again, more loudly this time.

For an agonizing, endless eternity, she waited, listening to the dreadful silence, wondering what he could be doing, and then, finally, she heard the chair being dragged back away from the door, and Mickey stepped out. He was folding a small, yellow sticky-note from Cole's desk and tucking it into his shirt pocket.

"Cole will know someone's been in there," she reminded him dully.

He brushed away her warning. "I'm a professional, remember? When I'm done with a room, nobody can tell I've tossed it." His smile was tight.

She didn't bother to argue. He was right.

He patted his chest pocket, as if checking to console himself that the little piece of paper was still in it. "I suppose you know your boyfriend has a file on us in there?"

She nodded. She'd always known about the file. No surprises there.

He smiled. "Oh, he told you, did he? And did he also tell you that he's added a half-inch stack of papers to it since he arrested us in September?"

Her ears were ringing. "What?"

"Interesting reading, even if I do say so. It's kind of weird, reading things like that about yourself."

"Things like *what* about yourself?" Her interest was piqued, in spite of everything.

He shrugged and made for the front door. "Ask your lover."

She skated desperately after him. "Mickey, please, talk to me! Don't leave me like this!"

He stopped with the door open behind him. Cool air and brilliant autumn light streamed in. He waited for her to speak.

She pleaded. "Talk to me. Do you have any idea what it has been like for me, not being able to fend for myself like this? I hate this chair, and I hate having to sit in it all day. I hate not being able to help myself and being dependent on everyone else."

Mickey seemed to relent. For the first time that afternoon, he looked like his old self—calm, almost sweet. He leaned forward and kissed her hair, lightly, then her lips. "I know that, love. But don't worry. I'm doing what needs to be done. You may not be able to help yourself, but I'll help you. Promise."

He straightened and eased through the door.

Zhara called after him anxiously, liking his calm determination even less than his jealous rage. "What are you going to do?"

He didn't look back, but, instead, walked resolutely down the path and out onto the sidewalk. "Trust me!" he called after her, and left, footsteps beating a confident rhythm along the concrete.

* * *

Cole stuck his third cigarette in fifteen minutes between his lips and watched as the hands on the big brass clock over his desk crawled around. He'd taken it down twice to see if it was broken, but if it was broken, his watch would have to be as well, as they were both dragging along, driving him crazy.

But at last it was ten-thirty, time to get up and leave on a mission that could bury his career if things went badly. He sighed, tossed the half-used pack of cigarettes and a small silver lighter onto his desk, and stood up, then, as an afterthought, picked up the smokes and lighter and shoved them back into his pocket. In all likelihood it was going to be a lousy night; he needed all the calm he could muster.

He strode quickly past his son's closed bedroom door, shaking his head sadly as he did so. Omar had opted to spend the night with a friend across town. He'd said something about pulling an all-nighter for a test, but Cole knew that the boy was growing more and more puzzled and uncomfortable with the strained silence between him and Zhara and had simply opted to distance himself from it until it blew over.

He hated the idea of what his behavior was doing to his little family, but he didn't know any other way to solve the problem at hand. With any luck, though, it would all soon be over, for better or worse, and then he'd have to put everything he had into making reparations.

At the door, he shrugged into his heavy coat and patted a gray hat onto his head. It was getting mighty cold out there, and where he was headed, out in the open, wasn't exactly going to be warmer. He checked in his pockets for his keys and opened the front door.

"Take me with you."

He froze, then slowly turned. Zhara was behind him, dressed for the outdoors—and she was standing. His eyes widened.

She smiled nervously, but with a glint of pride and determination. Everything in the way she held her body said she wasn't going to be dissuaded from leaving. He stared at her, her long frame leaning against a wall for support, but the fire in her eyes showing no fear.

Briefly, every stupid comic faith-healer scene he'd ever watched on TV flashed across his mind: the wounded man throws away his crutches or leaps out of his wheelchair and shouts, "I'm healed! I can walk again!" Cole was incredulous. "You can walk?"

She nodded. "I've been practicing. I can make it all the way across the room on my own. I can go even farther, if you hold me."

He sighed, a gust of breath. "That's wonderful." He hoped that in spite of his fatigue, he convincingly conveyed his genuine admiration. "I'm proud of you."

She looked relieved and pleased. "So I can come?"

He shook his head. "You don't even know where I'm going," he protested.

She shrugged. "No, but I know that wherever it is, it's got something to do with me."

He didn't say anything.

She persisted. "Isn't that so? You're on my case again."

He couldn't lie anymore; he didn't *want* to lie to her anymore. Sadly, ashamed, he nodded. "But it's not like you think." He hoped she would believe him.

The cynical twist of her lips put paid to that vain hope. "No?" She lifted one eyebrow. "What is it like, then?"

"I'm trying to help you."

She made a gesture of exasperation with her hands. "I wish everybody would stop trying to help me!"

His eyes became suspicious slits. "What's that supposed to mean?"

She set her jaw mulishly. "Nothing."

Cole let the door fall shut and walked back across the room to her. "No, tell me. What did you mean?"

"Why is it that it's okay for you to keep secrets from me, but I have to tell you everything?" Her voice was high, and it pained him to see the hurt and frustration in her eyes. He almost relented and let her in on his plans. But he'd spent all his life playing his cards close to his chest, so he wasn't going to tip his hand now. Instead, he reached up and gently laid his fingers along her lovely, vulnerable face and leaned in so that his lips were close to her ear.

"Darling, please—" He swallowed a hard lump in his throat. "I know these past few days have been hard on you. Believe me, they've been hard on me, too. All I want to do is be with you. I wish for both our sakes that everything was just bright and sunny and normal. But it isn't. It's complicated. I'm just trying to do what's best. And what's right. Sometimes—" He paused, shocked into sudden silence by the warm trickle of moisture that dripped slowly down her cheek and onto his fingers.

"Sometimes what, Cole?" She turned her beautiful eyes up to his, begging for answers, and for a second he wanted to abandon his harebrained scheme and just lift her into his arms, take her to his room, and lock the door on the whole wretched world. But whereas time had been crawling all evening, it had suddenly sped up, and he didn't need to glance at his watch to know that if he didn't leave now he'd be late for his appointment across town.

He laid his cheek against hers, speaking into her hair. "Sometimes it just isn't that easy." Regretfully, he pulled away, out of her warmth, away from the press of her soft breasts. She didn't try to stop him.

Halfway through the door once more, he turned to look at her again. She hadn't moved but was watching him with the same huge-eyed expression of loneliness and need for assurance.

"Wait up for me," he asked. "I promise I won't be long." He wasn't much for begging, but he would if he

had to. But she nodded without protest, and he locked
the door, climbed into his car, and started the engine.

It took more than forty minutes to reach the long row
of dismal warehouses on the other side of Medusa. It was
a nasty part of town, run-down, poorly lit—a place where
people lived and worked because they had to, not because
they wanted to. The fact that it was less than ten minutes
away from the apartment where Zhara and Mickey lived
did nothing to make him feel any better. It only served
to remind him that she lived in those circumstances because everything she had, everything she earned, went
into medical help for Mickey. Sweet Zhara, putting so
much on the line for the love of one lost young boy—from
the simple necessities of life to her own good reputation.
Her sins had been many, but they were acts of love and
compassion, not of selfishness and malice. Surely God
could see that and forgive her. And if God could, so could
he.

He only wished he could take her away from that horror
permanently, find help for the boy, and somehow convince her to stay with him. He was burning to tell her how
much she meant to him, but somehow he sensed that his
words of love would not find fertile ground in her heart,
not while she feared and distrusted him. *She's suffered
enough,* he prayed fervently. *Please, Lord, let it be over soon.*

He parked two blocks away from his destination, in a
dark corner where he hoped his car would blend unseen
with the shadows. It was so chilly that he was able to see
his own breath solidifying as it left his nostrils, even in the
dark that wrapped and curled around him, making it hard
for him to put one foot securely in front of the next. This
was a warehouse district, for Pete's sake; there was probably several million dollars' worth of goods in every one
of those dark hulking sheds. Whatever happened to security lights?

As he approached block H5, his already ragged nerves

began to taunt him. Outsiders always thought that once you'd been a cop for a certain length of time, you stopped being afraid when you walked into uncertain situations, but he begged to differ. Fear made you careful; it caused adrenaline to pump. And if there were two things that would save your life if things went bad, they were caution and adrenaline. But he did regret not letting Brian in on this little outing. It wasn't strictly police business, but Brian was not only his partner, he was his friend, and if he knew Cole was out talking to a witness (he hated to call it witness-tampering) at this late hour, in a sleazy dump like this, he'd have a fit. But it was too late to call Ames. He'd just have to get through it on his own.

He paused to check the faded painted sign on the warehouse wall, to reassure himself that he was at the right place. Unconsciously, he patted the small of his back to make certain his gun was there. The hairs on the back of his neck were stirring—not a good sign.

There was a crunch of gravel and a low cough off to his left. Cole spun around in the direction of the noise, heart kicking up a racket in his chest. "Good evening, *Detective,*" Oliver Mason's voice was mocking, dragging out Cole's title like a nursery rhyme.

Cole nodded, struggling to control his revulsion at being so close to such a disgusting character. "Mason."

The heavyset man folded his short, chubby arms around his copious belly and waited. His skin was uniformly dingy, like that of someone who spent his life in dark, damp places. Bulbous, watery eyes were sunk into fatty folds of skin, and his grizzled chin stuck out from between pudgy jowls.

Out on bail, he was back on his job. His gray security-guard's uniform was rumpled, and his peaked cap was a little askew. Cole didn't need to be told that the man had been napping on duty. Not that it mattered, anyway; on such a cold and dismal night, the most Mason had to fear was trespassing by the occasional rat. The man wasn't even armed with anything more lethal than a baton.

Cole decided to make himself clear from the beginning. "Listen, Mason, as I told you on the phone, I'm here as a private citizen, not as an officer. This visit has nothing to do with the police department and nothing to do with your case or any offer the legal people may have made to you, understood?"

Mason lifted his shoulders. "Whatever makes you feel good." He was waiting.

Cole reached into his pocket, and, as he did so, Mason's eyes darted to follow their movement; his body held the tension of a man who trusted no one. For all he knew, Cole could be pulling out a weapon. Instead, he withdrew his wallet and counted out a few bills into the other man's palm. Mason scrutinized each bill carefully before putting them away, seemingly satisfied.

Formalities out of the way, Cole began. "What can you tell me about Zhara Thorne?"

Mason's jaw went slack. "Are you kidding me?"

"Why?"

The greasy man laughed. *"That's* what you wanted to talk about? You're joking. I thought it'd be one of the big guys. She's nothing. A street kid. A polliwog in a pond full of piranha. Haven't you boys got fatter fish to fry?"

"I told you," Cole reiterated carefully. Two minutes and the creep was already trying his nerves, "I'm not here as a cop. I just want to find out all I can about her."

Mason shrugged again. "Your dime. What do you want to know? I already said all I had to say back at the station."

Cole shook his head. "No, tell me everything. Everything you can remember. You knew her. Tell me about her friends, who she worked with, how often she worked. Tell me about Antonio." He stepped closer, intimidating the softer, weaker man with his hard, dense bulk. He let his voice drop an octave. "Start talking."

Mason started talking. Arms folded across his chest to ward off both the cold and the aura of evil that emanated from the other man like a bad smell, Cole listened, his face a stone mask occasionally lit up by the glow of his cigarette as he pulled on it. He would have hated to show the man any emotion; that was something he guarded like his own soul. But he *felt* a lot, and with each story, his innards tautened, twisting and wrapping themselves around his heart and pulling hard.

He listened, occasionally spitting out a question, but for the most part silent, as Mason described the world of the dozens of street children that helped him build his little empire by bringing in anything and everything that could be fenced or pawned. He described in detail the gangs that fought incessantly over turf and the way the children learned violence at an early age. One little boy he remembered got an ice pick in the temple from a rival gang that wanted to steal his shoes.

He talked about the rigors of the notorious Chicago winters, how children struggled to choose between trading stolen goods for a meal or for warm clothes. A little girl who slept with a half dozen others under a derelict pumphouse off Cabrini Green had once, in desperation, crawled into the heating vent on the roof of a diner. They didn't find her until three days later.

Cole felt a nerve in his temple twitching wildly. He reached into his pocket to discover he'd just used his last cigarette, and swore colorfully. None of these stories was new to him; every cop in every city could recite a litany of horror with his eyes closed. But the fact that Zhara—his Zhara—had endured and been shaped by all that was unbearable. His eyes stung. He spoke to prevent the burning in his eyes from becoming a more visible and embarrassing sign of pain. "Tell me about Antonio."

Mason shrugged. "He was the leader of the pack, but he had a special interest in your little friend there."

Cole nodded stoically.

"I think the little boy that always followed her around, the freaky-looking one—"

"He's an albino," Cole interjected coldly, "not a freak."

Mason went on, as if he hadn't spoken. "The boy was sick or something. I dunno, kidney, liver, cancer, something. They needed big money, and fast. Antonio was the one hit upon the idea to graduate from radios to bonds and jewelry. He was the one got them climbing into buildings. Me, I didn't care. I'da pawned their grandmother, if they'da brung her in." He smiled for the first time, as if proud of his business acumen. When he realized Cole wasn't amused, he went on.

"Antonio had the business head, too. He did the haggling over money. Drove a hard bargain. And you couldn't try to beat him down on price either—he was a big 'un. Prizefighter. He'd fight anybody in an alley for a hundred-dollar pot. Him and one or two other men on the strip. You could place bets on them, and root them on, like a cockfight. I bet on him myself, coupla times. Don't remember ever losing anything on him, neither. He used to do some kinda Japanese kicking thing."

"Kickboxing," Cole offered caustically. "Chinese."

Mason began to look irritated. "Who's telling this? You or me?"

Cole motioned him to go on with his story.

"Your girl was real sweet on him, cried up a storm every time he had a fight. She was always afraid somebody'd mark up that pretty face of his, most likely. Didn't last long, though. I heard he got killed in a shootout with the police."

Cole felt obliged to set the record straight. "He was unarmed. A rookie shot him. It was a mistake." If he hadn't liked Mason before, he sure as hell couldn't stand him now.

Mason shrugged, bored now. "Whatever."

"What else can you tell me?" Cole pressed, stepping in
on him a little. "What else can you tell me about Zhara
Thorne?" He was like a huge, hungry hole, aching to be
filled with her—details about her—good or bad. He
wanted to know everything.

Mason held his hands up as if to ward him off. "Look,
man. What do you want for eighty bucks? A handwritten
biography? I've told you all I know about her. She was one
of the crowd, nobody special. Good at her game, but that
was all. I've dealt with hundreds of no-account kids like
her. They're nothing. Just runaways. Worthless, except for
what they brought in. You lost one, you got two, three
more waiting. I used them, just like everybody else did.
Like trained monkeys—"

Cole didn't even realize he'd drawn back and punched
Mason in the mouth until he felt the impact of the blow
reverberating up his arm. The fat head snapped back, and
the eyes opened wide, uncomprehending. Shock at his
own response was instantly replaced by an overwhelming
sense of satisfaction, so he hit him again. This time the
thick body went reeling backward, and Mason hit the
ground with a muffled thud. Cole stood over him, towering, enraged, waiting for him to get up.

Mason took his own time about it, hauling himself up
and shaking his head groggily. He stared at Cole in disbelief, not shocked because he had hit him, but at the
triviality that had provoked the outburst. And the punches
had apparently knocked neither sense nor good manners
into him. "You're kidding me, man. You got pissed-off at
that? I told you, they're not even worth thinking about—"

A third enraged blow slammed his lower lip up into his
top teeth, splitting it clean through, sending blood in
spurts onto the front of Cole's coat and the cruddy pavement below their feet. Mason bellowed like a wounded
jackass, and Cole stepped away, fast, three paces, then
four, staring at him in horror. He wanted to light into

him, start swinging and never stop until the odious man
was nothing but a mass of sniveling pulp at his feet. The
hugeness of the urge frightened Cole like nothing ever
had before. Terrified at the size of his own rage, and his
willingness to use his significant physical advantage against
the older, out-of-shape man, Cole turned, breaking into
a run.

He could hear his ragged breath and see the staccato
puffs as they burst from his lips into the night. He leaned
into the wind, arms and legs pumping, wanting to be anywhere except face-to-face with his own loss of control, but
like a dog that had burst its chain and escaped, he could
hear it dragging behind him, loud and jangling. He didn't
stop until he had levered his shaking body into his car,
and proceeded to take out his residual rage, this time
aimed at himself, on the steering wheel, punching it hard,
again and again. When his fist came slamming down onto
the dash, sending a crack clean across it and shards of
hardened plastic into the side of his hand, he stopped.

He flicked on the interior light and stared at his hand,
still not feeling any pain. His hands had already been
smeared with Mason's blood; now his own coursed down
to join it. The mere idea repulsed him so much that he
threw the car door back open, stalked around to the
trunk, and extracted a plastic gallon jug, an emergency
supply for his radiator, and washed his hands thoroughly,
or at least as well as he could in the absence of soap or
disinfectant. Even when the last of the water had hit the
sidewalk, he didn't feel clean. The smell of blood was in
his nostrils and the sour taste of anger in his mouth.

He got back into the car and aggressively turned the
key. In the chill night air, the engine refused to start up.
He tried two more times, cursing and grinding the
starter—nothing. He was just contemplating stepping out
again and shooting the car like a recalcitrant horse in the
wild west when the engine turned over, and without al-

lowing it to warm up, he threw it into gear and pulled out onto the road again.

He was within minutes of home before his anger cooled sufficiently to allow him to think again. He realized that his disgust was not with Mason—no, that lowlife couldn't be expected to hold any noble opinions anyway. His attitude to the children and to Zhara was par for the course. He was angry and disgusted with himself. What had he been thinking? That late-night visit wasn't police work. He was fooling himself thinking he had gone out there to "help" Zhara. He had just gone for information; anything and everything there was to know about her was good enough for him. He had become some sort of vampire, sucking Zhara in, craving any little detail about her, thirsting for her.

And then to make things worse, he'd lost control and beat up a witness—a witness who, mind you, was perfectly entitled to press assault charges against him in the morning. It wasn't as if the spray of fresh blood that now adorned the front of his coat would lie under a simple forensic test.

He spun into his own driveway, came to a tire-squealing, skating stop, and let his heavy head fall forward to rest on the wheel, eyes closed against the brilliant colors that swirled in his field of vision. He made himself sick. So much for upholding the law! He'd gone and broken several tonight. Why hadn't he listened to his instinct and just stayed at home?

Shoulders heavy, he let himself in. The house was ablaze with light. Zhara had indeed waited up for him, as he had asked. But he couldn't face her right now, not as he was. Cain and Abel greeted him joyfully, but stopped short the moment the scent of blood hit them. Puzzled and scared, they growled, backing away. He was too exhausted to try to comfort them, so he left them to their own devices, whispering a few soothing words as he went. They watched

him go, faces the picture of anxiety, but knew their master
well enough to respect his wish to be alone.

He went straight for the shower, letting his clothes lie
where they fell. He didn't bother turning the cold water
knob, but instead settled for just the hot, forcing himself
to stay under the heated stream until his skin begged for
mercy. He watched the water as it pooled pink at his feet,
and then his blood and Oliver Mason's blood swirled
down the drain and disappeared.

His self-disgust didn't go with it. By the time he stepped
out of the steam and rubbed his scalded skin uncaringly
with a big towel, he realized that water alone wasn't capable of washing away his sins. He knew there would be
music to face over this, but nothing external could ever
be as bad as the way he felt about himself right now.

His hand stung like hell. He turned it over to look at
the underside of it, sliced open by the plastic shards of
the dashboard, still surprised that it wasn't hurting as
badly as he expected it to. But with the amount of adrenaline he had speeding through his system, he was sure
he could have lost an arm without wincing. The flow of
blood had slowed, in spite of the hot bath. By rights, he
should have poured a little iodine on it and bandaged it,
but he decided to let himself suffer a little while longer.
Lord knew he deserved it.

He didn't bother to dress, either. Instead, once he was
dry, he threw the towel aside, made his way down the
corridor to Zhara's room, and opened the door without
knocking. She was in bed, reading, knees drawn up to her
chest, with a book balanced on them. Her eyes widened
at the sight of him, huge, naked, filling the doorway, eyes
wild. For an instant, she looked afraid. He raised a single
hand in a placatory gesture. She let the book fall.

The sight of her brought a wave of need crashing over
him. Raw, physical desire brought him into instant erec-
tion, which she couldn't help but notice. Her mouth

opened and closed, moving from his face to his engorged crotch and back again with almost comical surprise. But it was more than her body that he needed. He wanted to be absolved, washed free of the stains that the hot water had failed to remove. If her body were an altar, he wanted to worship there. He wanted to prostrate himself before her and be made whole again.

He came to stand next to her bed, nudging the wheelchair out of the way. Then, kneeling like a penitent, he allowed his fingers to tug at the warm fleece nightshirt she wore, pulling it up over her head. She helped him wordlessly. He pressed his hot face against her breasts, and her hands settled lightly on his damp hair. A fat cinnamon nipple filled his mouth, and her heartbeat thumped against his lips. When he had drunk his fill of her comfort, he lifted his tormented eyes to hers. "Save me," he pleaded.

In reply, she opened her arms and gathered him to her, like mother, lover, and Earth goddess. Her body was like a place to call home. "Come inside," she whispered back, "it's warm here."

It *was* warm there, and so sweet, he sobbed with the beauty of it. She encircled him with her arms and legs and wrapped her hair around his face until none of him was exposed and vulnerable. They moved together urgently, trying to erase their need through sheer pressure, scrubbing it off each other's body. When his mouth locked on hers, he discovered he believed in the transference of souls, because hers was surely pouring into him, just as his was pouring into her. This time, *he* was the one who wept.

"Oh, my love, my love," he sighed against her throat, mouth full of her hair.

She could do nothing but call his name.

Nine

He was heavy. Zhara shifted under the dead weight of the exhausted man who had fallen asleep with her pinned under him. In order to avoid being stifled by the torso that pressed into hers like a boulder, she had to focus on her breathing, timing it with his, so that when he exhaled, and his chest compressed, she drew a breath, and when he inhaled, she allowed the force of his expanding chest to press the air from her lungs. The comfortable tandem had a soothing effect; it was almost Zen. She listened to the sound of the air escaping his lips and felt his barely perceptible heartbeat against her breasts.

She eased one of her hands out from under him, bringing it up around him to rest on the back of his head, letting her fingers curl gently around his neck, protective yet caressing. Asleep, he didn't frighten her nearly as much as he did awake. When he was like this, there was no menace, no threat. The clever eyes that somehow managed to pierce her soul, perpetually holding a question, were closed. The lips that could stroke her into frenzy or tighten like a vise, withholding answers even when the questions were about her, were soft in relaxation.

Rarely, since she had laid eyes on the man, had she felt anything other than fear. Now, she could feel compassion, longing, and sweet, sweet love, welling up, pool-

ing like warm liquid inside her, and that in itself was
frightening. She'd heard the words of love that had escaped his lips like a cool breeze whispering through the
transoms on a heated summer's night. *My love . . . my
love . . .* She hadn't returned them—at least, not out
loud—but, instead had screwed her eyes tightly closed
to shut out the folly of her surrender and mouthed them
into his shoulder, too afraid to give voice to her awesome
feelings, but too humbled by their existence to make
love with Cole and *not* release them.

The possibility that he might actually have meant what
he had said during their most urgent moments could not,
should not, even be entertained. While a man was easing
himself in between your thighs, it was easy for him to
think—or simply to say—that he loved you. Just because
she hadn't exactly had a progression of lovers over the
years didn't mean she wasn't wise to the ways of the world.
Gullibility was never one of her failings. Sometimes, beautiful words were just oil over troubled waters. Huge and
bright in her mind came the vision of a powerful, sleek,
black cat, purring loudly while its jaws were clamped
around her throat.

Then she remembered his state as he had entered her
room—eyes wide, staring, like a man in shock. He'd seen
something out there tonight, and whatever it was, it had
frightened him. And that something had had to do with
her. She felt a rush of guilt that was immediately swept
away by resentment. He'd gone looking for trouble, her
trouble, and had found it. Served him right. He just wasn't
prepared to let her sleeping secrets lie, was he? If he'd
gone out into the night and come face to face with one
of her demons, well, good. She hoped it had hissed and
spat at him for all it was worth.

She heard again his broken voice, begging her to allow
him sanctuary inside her, like the persecuted Christians
of old seeking shelter in cubbyholes in the houses of sym-

pathizers. He'd wanted to crawl into her and lie still until the thundering horses of his pursuers faded in the distance. He'd been trembling, skin hot, whispering pleas in a voice that cracked, and she'd taken pity on him and let him in.

Why not? She feared him, yes—resented him, certainly. Sometimes she knew for certain that she hated him for what he'd done and could still do to her life. But she loved him, too, and love was unselfish; it knew how to ignore emotions that were darker than itself. It could forgive.

Zhara pressed her mouth against his temple, tasting the streak of sweat that had cooled there, and stole the opportunity that his unconscious state presented to tell him what she would never be able to while he was awake. "Cole," she whispered. He shifted slightly and then settled again like a big dog in a warm spot. She let her finger trace the shape of his ear. "Cole, I love you. You're the worst thing that ever happened to me, the most frightening thing that ever happened to me, but I love you. And right now, that's enough—isn't it?"

Thick-lashed lids fluttered, and panic made her choke on her own words. He'd heard! Oh God! He would think her stupid and juvenile for even imagining that what they had was serious. Zhara felt embarrassment wash over her, and she squirmed, waiting for the sarcastic rejoinder that was sure to come next.

But Cole was far from awake. His eyes shut again, and he rolled off her, burrowing into the blankets, still pressed against her for warmth, but as oblivious to her words as he was to her presence. She was merely a source of body-warmth to the sleeping man. For all he knew, she might just as well have been a St. Bernard. She pursed her lips ruefully, settled into him, seeking out the warmth of his arms—two could play at that game—and drifted off to sleep.

* * *

He wasn't in his own bed, that much he knew. He opened his eyes to harsh sunlight and looked around. When Zhara squirmed against his chest, face creased from having been pressed against it all night, he looked down at her and the memory came back.

He smiled, remembering the generosity and openness of her embrace, and the fervor with which she had given him all he'd needed. And he *had* needed her last night. Oliver Mason's ugly face obscured his view of Zhara naked and pressed against him, but only for a few seconds. Sheer willpower allowed him to shove the unwanted apparition from his field of vision. Mason was just a bad dream. Zhara was real, and Zhara was here, stretched out alongside him, nude, soft, and beautiful.

His blood stirred, and there was a rush of glorious heat down between his legs, as he felt himself lengthening and thickening, rapidly, as if he hadn't spent his energies pouring himself into her last night. He stretched, starting with his feet, and felt the muscles along his body tense and relax in succession, getting out the kinks of sleep. Then he leaned forward and stroked her bare shoulder with his chin, letting the overnight stubble gently rasp the smooth skin. He enjoyed the contrast of rough and smooth; it was for him what Zhara was all about—prickly and resistant half the time, petal-soft and pliant the other half.

His first indication that she had awoken was the sudden buzz in his brain brought about by the presence of her fingers insinuating themselves between his thighs, seeking him out, cupping, exploring, stroking. He'd have sworn he couldn't get any harder than he already was; her touch made him a liar. Fingers deft enough to pick a lock in seconds were now coaxing from him an erratic, painful throb, and as she worked up a hypnotic rhythm, base-tip-pause, base-tip-pause, he felt a grunt burst from his mouth.

A soft, mocking laugh came from her. "I can stop, if you like," she offered slyly.

His eyes flew open in panic. "You're kidding, right?"

"Didn't want to cause you any—distress."

He let his hand capture hers, holding it fast right there, daring her to pull it away. *"Stopping* would distress me," he let her know.

She shrugged. "Well, any time you want to call a halt, just say the magic word." She grinned like a succubus, knowing he was trapped by pleasure.

He put an end to this atrocious talk of stopping by covering her mouth with his, hard, his lips and tongue preventing any further words from escaping. When he finally allowed her to draw a breath, he was smiling. Her own body had caught up with his, its desire evident by the tautness of her nipples, the rush of blood that swelled her breasts into round, full orbs of sexual tension, and the wet heat that now trickled onto his own fingers, which had decided, independently of his own conscious thought, to return the favor.

It was his turn to mock. "Still thinking of stopping?"

She pursed her lips, biting off the curse that had risen there. "Are you—" She shuddered as he allowed a second finger to follow the example of the first. She tried again to speak. "Have you lost your—uh—oh, *Cole!*"

It was getting much too hot for the blanket, so they kicked it onto the floor. Deciding not to submit to his provocation, she eased away, coming to kneel over him, taking charge, an impish grin on her face. He let her go, and, instead, crossed his hands behind his head, relaxed, waiting. If she wanted to take control, he was the last man who would stop her.

The first contact of her mouth was almost his undoing. An electric jolt all but threw him bodily into the air, like a dying man being defribulated in a desperate attempt to get his heart going again. His voice failed him; this time, he couldn't have asked her to stop, even if he'd wanted to.

Her mouth was hungry, tender, exploring, relishing; her pleasure was as great as his, and from time to time she sighed like a satisfied gourmand. He reached down to cradle her cheek, lacing his fingers through the hair that hung loose, draped over his bare hip, sending a million thrills up his spine. "Zhara, baby—you're killing me—" he rasped, and then fell silent again, unable to go on.

The sharp, hot bunching of his muscles, and the sound of distant thunder told him his orgasm was not far off. Everything around him faded into gray mist; everything he wanted and needed was right here, right now. He urged her on with his body and with his sharp, agitated breaths.

He realized with shock that the pounding in his skull was not the sound of his own blood, but was separate from them both. Startled, confused, he became still. Zhara had heard it too. She lifted her head, eyes black with excitement and shock, beautiful mouth swollen, open.

Cole drew himself up on his elbows, looking around, still confused, still painfully erect, cocking an ear to ascertain the origin of the noise that had now become so insistent that it had forced itself between him and the culmination of his pleasure. It was another few moments before it dawned on him that the source of the noise was outside his front door, hammering on it.

"Goddamn!" He swung his legs off the bed and stood up. Zhara didn't stop him, but still stared, confused like a baby roused from deep sleep. "Whoever that is, is a dead man," he promised.

He bent hastily to kiss her. "Mark that page, darling." He bent over to kiss her on that sweet mouth and then wished he hadn't—the musky scent of himself on her lips was almost enough to make him climb right back into bed and to hell with the idiot at the door. He cursed again. "I'll be right back."

He was out her door and halfway out to the front before he realized he was naked. Turning on his heel, he stomped up to his room, almost tripping on the cat, who had been sprawled outside the bedroom, shrugged on the much-maligned bathrobe, and returned to the front, anger alone making him throw the door open without first ascertaining who the culprit was. "This had better be good," he began. "There'd better be a state of emergency on, or I'll—" He stopped. Brian Ames stood on his doorstep, and he looked agitated.

Cole struggled to bite back the tirade that was keyed up and ready to roll. "Ames," he managed, finally.

Brian shoved past him and stepped into the hallway. "Man, oh man. You are hard to get on to. Wassamatter? Phone company cut you off, or you just decided you don't have to answer it anymore?" His red mustache twitched.

Cole hadn't even heard it ring. He frowned. The look on Brian's face was enough to erase any last trace of the sensuality that had been interrupted. Brian was all business. "What's wrong?"

"You've got five minutes to get dressed and into the car," Brian told him. "Get cracking."

Cole repeated the question, anxiety level rising. "What's wrong, Brian?"

"Your star witness in the Thorne case—" he began.

"Mason," Cole interrupted, dread filling him as the memory of the grotesque encounter with his own rage came back like an unrepentant ghost.

Brian nodded gravely. "Seems like—" he stopped abruptly, eyes straying beyond Cole's shoulder.

Cole turned to follow his friend's line of vision and saw Zhara standing in the doorway, leaning on the doorjamb for support, listening unabashedly.

"Should she be standing?" was the first thing out of Brian's mouth, and then he stopped again. This time, he looked a little more closely, noticing her rumpled hair, hastily donned dressing gown, and glazed eyes, and then his eyes moved back to Cole and his own state of undress. He realized instantly what he had stumbled in on, and the flush on his cheeks matched the color of his hair. "Oh. Damn."

Brian thrust his hands into his pockets and hung his head, unable to look Cole in the eye, but Cole wasn't sure if he was uncomfortable at having interrupted an intimate moment, or disappointed in his friend at having gone and gotten himself so intimately involved with a suspect. The accusing did-you-really-have-to-go-there look Brian threw him next answered *that* question. "Aw, man!" Brian muttered.

Cole shrugged and waved away anything Brian might have thought to say next. If he couldn't answer his *own* questions about this inescapable mire he'd let himself get sucked into over Zhara, then how could he ever have explained it to Brian? Instead, he tried to draw him back to the reason for his visit. *"What* about Mason?"

He held his breath. He was willing to bet dollars to doughnuts Mason had made his way to the station the moment his shift was up, to lodge a complaint against him. Wonderful. An assault charge was all his career needed right now. As if having a suspect under his roof—and in his bed—wasn't trouble enough.

Before Brian could speak again, Zhara called out from behind him. "Mason, who?" The tremble in her voice told him she already knew 'Mason who', but all the same, he supplied the man's first name, and Zhara gasped in response.

"Oh, God." She slapped a hand to her mouth, eyes wide. "I'd hoped I never had to hear his name again! He was an awful man. Awful. What has he done now?"

Cole walked up to her and held her shoulders reassuringly. "He's turned state witness in a whole lot of old cases," he told her gently, ignoring the glare he knew Brian was throwing him. "Including yours."

He wished he could take away the pain that now crossed her face. "Could this mean trouble for Mickey and me?" she asked.

He nodded. "It's possible. We don't know right now how it will turn out. But I promise you, Zhara, I'll help any way I—"

"*Was* state witness," Brian broke in. "From what I picked up on the radio this morning, I don't think Miss Thorne, or anyone else for that matter, has anything to worry about regarding Mason."

Cole frowned. "What—he's changed his mind about singing?"

Brian shrugged. "I hear he hasn't got a mind left to change. Someone bashed it in for him last night."

The silence was like a clanging of cymbals. Light pulsed behind Cole's eyelids, flaring red, stars spinning out of control. He blinked to clear his vision, but the spiral of color was too bright and insistent. Zhara's eyes flitted from one face to another, and Cole saw his own look of horror reflected in hers. He wasn't breathing, and he was pretty sure he would never be able to take another breath in life without having to fight against the bands of muscle that now constricted his ribs. "What?" he asked, although he had heard perfectly well.

Brian scratched his head uncomfortably, still ill at ease with the shattered intimacy between the two, and his own presence in the middle. "Shift changed this morning out at this warehouse where he works, and his relief turned up and found him on the ground—"

"Dead?" Cole interjected incredulously.

Brian made an elaborate gesture that said, "sure, what else?" "Beaten to death, seems like. The guy called the paramedics, and the paramedics called the station. I picked it up on the scanner." He looked Zhara in the eye and gave her a wry smile. "Seems you're off the hook again."

Air! Air! Cole struggled for some, fought for it, but couldn't seem to force any in. His feet were unsteady, and he was glad when he staggered back that there was a big, solid wall behind him to keep him from hitting the ground. Both Zhara and Brian lunged for him, and this sudden movement only served to make Zhara lose her own precarious balance and fall over.

Grunting, Brian caught her and lifted her into his arms. Cole could have kicked himself. He should have told her to sit back in her chair instead of remaining on her feet in the doorway.

"Where?" Brian asked her kindly, and she pointed the way into her room. Cole followed in time to see Brian set her down gently into her wheelchair. The room was heavy with the scent, look, and feel of sex, with bedclothes strewn about and the bed somehow managing to have shifted several inches from the wall during the night. Cole ignored Brian's pointed, accusing glance; his sins of the night had evidently not stopped with Zhara, and, right now, he was more worried about the dead man he'd left in his wake than about how his friend felt about his bedroom activities.

He plopped heavily onto the bed and let his head fall into his hands. "How could he be dead?"

Brian finally seemed to catch on to the fact that his friend's shock was way out of proportion. He dropped to his knees next to his friend and put his hand on his shoulder. "What do you mean, Cole? Why are you so upset?"

Cole shook his head, trying to clear it of the rubble of confusion, and of the awful sound of his own fists hitting Oliver Mason's head. "I didn't hit him hard enough to kill him." Zhara gasped, and he knew that she was staring at him, horrified, but he was too ashamed to look in her direction. Instead, he lifted his eyes to catch Brian's pale blue ones fixed on him, perfectly round, waiting.

"You were there—at the warehouse? Last night?" Brian asked in disbelief.

Cole nodded miserably. "Right on all counts."

"Why in the name of God would you—" he looked across at Zhara, and then stopped.

It was Zhara's turn to talk. "That's where you were last night? Speaking to Oliver Mason?"

Cole didn't see the need to answer.

She persisted. "About me?"

"I didn't hit him hard enough to kill him," Cole insisted. He hadn't, had he? He couldn't remember. There was just a shadow of memory in his mind—rage, fists connecting, him running scared, afraid of the hugeness of his anger and the passion for this woman, that had driven him to such anger. Mason had been screaming when he left. Was he lying on the ground or standing on his feet? Did he look like he'd suffered brain injury? Was he coherent? He couldn't remember.

"Why'd you hit him at all?" Brian asked.

Instead of answering his partner, he looked at Zhara. She was staring at him as if she didn't know him, horror-struck, repulsed. "I didn't like what he was saying about you," he explained weakly, hoping she'd understand and not look at him as if he were a monster. "It was just a couple of punches . . ." He was too soul-sick to go on. He had been a cop long enough to know that a misplaced punch, no matter how light, could have resulted in anything from unexpected brain damage to cerebral hemorrhaging. He hadn't punched Mason with the intent to do serious harm, but it seemed that intent had not been required for his rage to have become lethal.

Brian shot to his feet. "Damn it, Wyatt! You went out

to visit a witness without calling me? What were you thinking?"

Cole didn't know what to answer, except, "I *wasn't* thinking. I—it wasn't police business. It wasn't our business. It was personal."

Brian threw Zhara another look. "Well, I can see that. But all the same, you could have called me. I'm your partner, remember?"

Cole agreed miserably but thought that by the time this was all over, he doubted very much if Brian would still *want* to be his partner. "You'd only have tried to talk me out of it," he said defensively.

Brian snorted. "Damn right, I would have. But if I failed, I'd have come with you. How could you have been so stupid? What if you needed backup? What if he had a bunch of thugs waiting with him? Of all the—"

"Enough!" Cole roared. His head was pounding. How could a morning that had started off so beautifully suddenly turn into such a nightmare? "I've got to think."

"Think about what? What are you going to do? Head for the border?"

Cole knew that Brian's sarcasm was born out of hurt and disappointment. He didn't blame him. He was disappointed in himself. His own rejoinder left him before he could stop it. "No, no borders. And what are *you* going to do, partner? Arrest me?"

Resignedly, Brian shook his head. "No. No arrest. Let's just go."

"Where?" Zhara spoke, and the two men turned toward her; in their distress they'd all but forgotten she was there.

"To the crime scene," Cole explained, tiredly. "To see how deep the crap I'm in is."

"I'm coming with you." It was not a request.

"No." Both men answered simultaneously.

As if neither of them had answered, Zhara wheeled past

them into her bathroom. "If you'll excuse me, I have to get dressed."

Brian looked at Cole, waiting for him to tell her again she would not be allowed to come, but the fight seemed to have gone out of him. He looked like a tire that was slowly losing air. Shrugging, he left the room. "I'll wait for you both in the car."

Zhara sat next to Cole in the back seat of Detective Ames' car, sensing the other man's disapproval of her presence. She knew he wanted to play it by the book, and the book had never said anything about taking a suspect along to the scene of a crime. She brushed away her niggling sense of guilt. It wasn't that Brian Ames didn't like her, she reminded herself, it was simply that he cared about Cole, and as far as he was concerned, Cole was in trouble *because* of her. Not just now, today, but ever since he'd bent the rules and asked her to stay with him.

Well, she understood Ames' animosity, but she had news for him. She cared about Cole, too. And right now, she would have given anything to be able to take away the confusion he was going through. Ignoring the resentful glances Ames was throwing her in the driver's mirror, she let her hand caress the tense jaw of the man who sat rigidly at her side.

The black eyes stared ahead, empty, his thoughts way beyond her reach. There was no trace of the dimples she had kissed earlier. He was like a lost soul, skin cold, face a dull gray, drained of vibrancy and the spark of life that made her love him so much.

She hated seeing him like that, but she understood. A man was dead, and Cole had killed him—over her. A sense of obligation had caused him to confront Mason, and misguided chivalry had made him strike out. Now Cole bore the mark of a man's death on his soul.

Zhara squeezed her eyes shut, tears dampening the dusky fringe of her lashes, his pain becoming hers. She wondered briefly if this was the first time he had taken a life. She had no illusions about his profession; although she had never asked, there was a very real possibility that at some point during his years on the force, he might have been obliged to kill. That in itself was bad enough to have to deal with. She thought again of the newbie who had opened fire on Antonio on that God-forsaken day back in Chicago. The young cop had never been the same afterward. Zhara had even heard rumors that five months later he had resigned on psychiatric grounds.

But this was different. Even if Cole had taken a life before, that would have been in the line of duty. What could she say about Mason? As much as she hated him for his uncaring abuse of her and her friends, his death was wrongful. She knew it. Cole sure as hell knew it.

She felt the muscles of his jaw working erratically under the fingers she had laid on his cheek. Instinctively, she slid her other arm around him and pulled his unresisting body down against hers. Her lips stroked his ear. "Cole, it's going to be all right," she promised softly. She knew she was lying.

He knew it, too. He turned his eyes on her, pits of darkness that held unspeakable nightmares, and said, "My son . . ."

"He'll be okay. You won't be leaving him. You'll always be there for him. Darling, listen. You can beat this. It was an accident. You can just tell them—"

He cut across her empty protestations. "What will he think of me?"

"He loves you," she tried to reassure him. *I love you*, she wanted to add, but didn't dare. Instead, she sought his cold mouth, pressing her lips against his, not with passion, but with warmth, to comfort rather than to arouse.

For a second, his lips responded and lightly brushed

hers. His early morning stubble grazed her. Then he lifted his head. "He loves me," Cole agreed, "but can he ever respect me again?"

Before she could even begin to frame a comforting response to such a difficult question, the car slowed, and Zhara looked out the window, surprised that they had managed to make it across town so quickly. Absorbed in Cole's confusion, she had lost track of time.

Outside, a small, disorderly crowd of gawkers had gathered. Two young officers were doing their best to keep the onlookers back, but as soon as the people on one side obeyed orders to retreat, rubberneckers on the other side were closing in for another look. Excited about the little real-life police drama that was unfolding in their neighborhood, they pressed in to see the action. One or two had dragged out cameras and were busy squeezing off shots, ignoring orders to stop. A few others were prattling on excitedly about the dangerous times in which they lived.

Ames drew up beside a cop car in the parking lot in front of the row of warehouses, and, almost before the engine was off, he and Cole had thrust themselves outside and were running toward the taped-off area that was the focus of attention.

They were leaving without her! Zhara's wheelchair was neatly folded way in the trunk, and with no one to take it out and assemble it for her, she was stranded. She stuck her head out of the window and yelled at them in desperation. "Wait! Cole! Ames! Come back. I can't get out!" Frantic, she leaned forward and honked the horn.

Cole looked back, hesitated, and then looked at the crime scene again. For a moment, she was sure he wouldn't turn back for her, and then he seemed to make up his mind. He raced back to her side, and gratefully, Zhara threw open the door.

But he hadn't come to help her out. "Stay here," was his terse instruction, before he was off again.

Stay here? Was he joking? In exasperation, she decided that her only option was to take things into her own hands—or, to be more precise, her own feet. Why not? She'd filled her empty days practicing walking, up and down the length of her room, regaining strength. This was as good a time as any to do it for real.

Slowly, carefully, she eased herself out of the car and into a standing position. She looked sternly down at her feet. "Don't fail me, guys," she warned them, "or when we get back, you and I are going to have words."

Her first few steps told her that her right leg, at least, was not daunted by her threats, and was going to take its own sweet time getting her over there. Zhara tugged her flimsy coat around her against the cold and began to move carefully toward the crowd, relying heavily on her left foot, wishing she'd had the good sense to get herself a pair of crutches long before. Her slow, awkward gait soon drew stares and whispers from the crowd. She didn't blame them; she must have looked quite a sight, lifting her slow foot carefully and painstakingly to set it down and test her weight before lifting the other. As she tried to insinuate herself in between the curious group, she heard one woman, face pinched in disgust, whisper to another housewifely companion, "Damn junkies."

The short, round-faced woman in a dismal brown overcoat and threadbare scarf turned her head, arrived at her friend's diagnosis as well, and glared at Zhara, nose twitching as if she smelled something bad.

Zhara had to resist the urge to retort, or even to explain, but instead shouldered awkwardly past, face hot against the cold day. "Excuse me," she whispered meekly as she passed, squeezing toward the front. It was Cole who needed her now; she didn't have time to protect her ego.

Beyond the stretch of yellow tape, a group of uniformed

officers consulted each other, looking on as two or three other men busied themselves with the shape that lay crumpled on the ground. She inched forward as closely as she dared, eyes darting to Cole's face. He was staring at the body, transfixed. The look on his face could only be described as one thing: consternation.

Following the direction of his gaze, Zhara looked down at the battered corpse on the ground, and gasped. Oliver Mason looked as if he'd been in a train wreck. His face was a pulpy purplish mass of swellings, blood caked in his sparse hair. His arms were thrown up defensively across his face and upper body, as if, even in death, he was trying desperately to protect himself from more blows. His chest looked as if it had been crushed, with lumps and hollows in awkward places; brownish, crusty blood stained his shirt, and one leg was twisted at an angle that nature had never intended.

"Somebody sure didn't like this guy," one of the uniformed cops muttered to another. The lady cop, sucking on a cup of coffee through a straw, shrugged and went on with her duties. Her whole demeanor said, "Another day, another dead body." She seemed intent on just getting the job over with so they could all go somewhere warmer.

Zhara shook her head, unable to process the information before her. The man had been brutally and savagely beaten and had died an awful, agonizing death. She searched frantically for Cole's face. He had shifted and was now on the other side, talking to a small group of people who looked like medical professionals, paramedics, perhaps.

Her mind whirred. How could Cole have done this? This was barbaric. It was the work of a monster. She was convinced he'd said he'd only hit Mason a few times—two or three, perhaps. And she'd believed him. But this? The body looked as if someone had gone over it with a tire iron.

Cold fingers of dread clamped themselves around her neck, as she tried to find some kind of reason for this savagery. Had Cole really done this because of her? And how could he have left a man like this and then come home and made love to her?

Bile rose in her throat, and a wave of dizziness took her. She prayed silently that she wouldn't further humiliate herself by falling over into the crime scene. *Steady,* she admonished her legs, *steady now.*

Then, through some indefinable telepathic communication, Cole sensed her presence and lifted his head. His eyes met hers, and he half smiled—and then, as he read the horror in her eyes, his smile froze. Quickly, he detached himself from the huddle of men with whom he had been whispering and made it over to her in a few long strides.

"Zhara," he began.

"No." She backed away, suddenly afraid. She thought she knew him, or at least a little of him, but this—monstrous behavior, she couldn't understand it. She couldn't reconcile the man she had held in her bed with the man who had done something like this to another human being.

He reached for her over the swaying yellow police tape, and she stepped back again, too sharply this time, and lost her balance, falling into the crowd, who, instead of trying to catch her, parted like the Red Sea, and she hit the hard, filthy concrete with a thud.

Contemptuous murmurings rippled through the crowd. The sour-faced woman who had diagnosed her "drug condition" earlier shouted over the heads of others in front of her. "Sober up, lady!"

The crowd laughed, hardened by years of life in that part of town, all but inured to the misery of others.

Pain shot through the back of Zhara's head, and the

next thing she felt was Cole's arms gathering her up. She resisted, weak hands flailing, swatting him away. "Let me go!" she protested. "Cole, let me—"

"Be quiet!" he hissed. Hoisting her like an oversized doll, he worked his way back through the crowd, booming orders for everyone to get out of his way. She struggled against him all the way to the car, and when he opened the door and thrust her inside, she slapped him, hard, across the face.

"Don't pick me up without my permission!" she shouted, not caring how ridiculous that sounded.

He squeezed himself into the back seat with her, shunting her around so he could have space for himself. "What, would you rather I left you there, on the cold concrete, surrounded by a bunch of thrill-seekers who wouldn't have cared enough to help you up? I told you to stay in the car. Why didn't you listen?"

"I don't have to listen to you, Detective. I don't have to listen to anyone." She'd gotten out of the car because she was concerned about him, couldn't he see that? But now that she had, and she'd seen what lay beyond the tape, she wished she'd taken his advice and just stayed put. Still frightened and disappointed in the man she thought she understood, she taunted, "What are you going to do to punish me, Cole? Are you going to raise a hand to me like you did to Oliver Mason?"

Cole's head snapped back, as if she'd punched him in the jaw. His eyes widened. "You don't think . . ." He tailed off and inhaled to steady himself. "You think that I—did that?"

Zhara stared at him as if he'd gone mad. "What do you mean? You *told* me you did! You said you'd hit him! What, are you such a coward that you can't face up to your wrongdoings in the light of day? An hour ago you were so penitent—"

"I hit him, Zhara. I hit him, and I'm ashamed of that."

He grasped her arm, which was suspended in midair, as if she had been planning to slap him again, but somehow couldn't bring herself to land the blow. "I hit him, but I didn't kill him."

"You said you did! An hour ago—"

"An hour ago, I hadn't seen the body. I thought I'd killed him because I figured maybe I'd gotten in a bad punch. But it wasn't me. He's got a broken leg, a cracked skull, a crushed rib cage. I didn't work him over like that, Zhara."

"Oh," she sneered. She wanted to believe him, but it all seemed too unreal. "How'd he get like that? Was it, I don't know, maybe *suicide?*"

He shook his head tiredly. "No, it was murder. But I'm not the culprit. Maybe I—" He hung his head. "Maybe I contributed in some way by having been there, distracted him. Maybe if he'd been more alert on the job, or not busy thinking about me, whoever it was might not have been able to jump him." Cole's face twisted. "I'll always feel like I played a part in this man's death, and I don't know if I'll ever be able to forgive myself for coming here last night, but I didn't do *that* to him, Zhara. Someone else did. Someone who came after me. Believe me."

His eyes were on her, pleading, and his nails cut into her wrist.

Flustered, she cast around for a response. Was he telling the truth, or just trying at the last moment to cover his own tail? Had he been so shocked when confronted with evidence of his own savagery that he had convinced himself that he couldn't have done it? She struggled for breath. "I—"

"You believed me this morning!" he interjected hotly. "You were there for me this morning. Why not now? I need you now, Zhara! I need you on my side!"

Her head was buzzing. A blanket of fatigue had spread itself over her, and all she wished she could do right now was lie down and shove this whole awful mess from her mind. Could she really believe that by pure coincidence, another man had turned up on the scene after Cole and done that? It seemed so . . .

"Zhara?" Cole was waiting, face taut.

She inhaled deeply, thinking fast. Cole had come in last night looking as if the hounds of hell were after him. He had come home ridden by guilt—but, was it guilt at having landed a few ill-advised punches, or at having totally lost his cool?

He let out a short, barking laugh. "Very well, *darling*," he snorted, using the endearment she'd used to comfort him with earlier. "You're not very big on trust, are you? I thought that after all the things that have gone between us . . ." He paused, letting his eyes move slowly down her body, pausing at one or two intimate points along the way, "You'd have been more inclined to give me some credit. Looks like I was wrong. Looks to *me* like making love to someone doesn't help you know them any better. You trust me with your body, in your body, but you don't—"

He never got the chance to finish. A sharp rapping on the roof of the car was followed immediately by the appearance of Brian Ames' face in the window. "Cole," he began, raising one hand to display a clear plastic evidence bag clutched in it. "I think we've got our man."

"What?" Cole was incredulous.

"You ought to see this." He dangled the bag.

Cole held out his hand for it, but Brian hastily threw Zhara an uncertain glance.

"Just hand it over," Cole demanded impatiently, hand still outstretched.

Reluctantly, Brian released the bag into Cole's gloved hand, and his eyes came to settle on Zhara's face, waiting.

Zhara didn't like it one bit. What in the world could Cole's partner have found that he would be so reluctant to share with her? Her eyes fell to the small bag Cole held in his hands, and a sharp, agonized cry escaped her lips.

Folded in the bag, which was already neatly labeled and sealed, was a pair of thin, wire-framed glasses. One lens was shattered. The style and shape of the frames, the chewed-out ends, the chipped veneer, were instantly recognizable. The glasses could only have belonged to one person: Mickey.

"No," she began. All thoughts of Cole having been the perpetrator were swept from her mind, to be replaced by an even more inconceivable possibility. Mickey—a killer? "Never. Not him. He's incapable of anything so— monstrous." She struggled to release the door and leaped out. Cole was after her in a second, chasing her around to the front of the car, where she slumped over onto the hood, arms splayed out, feeling the warmth of the engine penetrate to her cold, cold chest.

Cole's strong hands pulled her up and turned her to face him. "Zhara," he began. He didn't even try to say, "I told you it wasn't me." Instead he tugged her toward him, hands in her hair, and, to her horror, she felt the tears, which had been threatening to fall all morning, finally well up and spill over. This time, they were for a different man, but one whom she loved just as deeply. Still, she protested. "Not him. Never."

"The glasses do belong to him, don't they?" he asked gently.

"He's a good person! And he's sick! He's too weak to have done that!"

"Baby—"

"I don't have to tell you anything!" she answered hotly, but still clung to him, sobs coming from deep inside.

"How could he have known about Mason? He couldn't have known . . ." Cole stopped and held her chin gently in one hand, forcing her to look at him. "Could he?"

Like sharp, bony fingers, the memory of the argument

she'd had with Mickey yesterday mockingly prodded her. They'd quarreled, all right—after he'd gone into Cole's study.

He spotted the cloud that passed over her face. "Tell me. What happened?"

"I—can't—" she protested.

"Zhara, tell me. Maybe we can help him . . ."

She shoved him away, her tears of pain and fear turning to anger. "Help him? How do you plan on helping him, Detective? By arresting him? By dragging him into court on a murder charge?"

"I don't know. But I *do* know we can't do anything unless you help me!"

She was too exhausted to fight anymore. "Yesterday . . ." She glanced across at Brian, who was taking in the whole scene, blue eyes sharp, mouth a thin line.

"What happened yesterday?" Cole coaxed.

"He broke into—" She looked away and then began again. "He broke into your study. I tried to stop him, honest . . ."

"I believe you," he said gently. "Go on."

"He wouldn't let me in after him. He locked me out. I heard him tossing your room."

"What was he looking for?"

She shrugged. "Anything. Proof that I—shouldn't trust you." The irony of it embarrassed her. It seemed that even in such tragic circumstances, Mickey had been right, at least about *that*.

Cole's jaw worked, muscles bulging and relaxing. "Go on."

"I don't know what he found. But he came out with something written on a piece of paper, and told me"—she stopped to glare at him accusingly—"that you'd added half an inch to our file since you—arrested us."

He nodded solemnly, with just a trace of guilt.

"And then he said it was all going to be okay, that he was going to fix things."

"What things?"

She threw her hands up. "Things! I don't know! He didn't bother to tell me. It seems like nobody bothers to tell me anything anymore. Ever since the night I fell, it's like I don't exist. I don't get drawn into conversations, and nobody, not you or anybody else, is willing to be straight with me. Well, being frail of body doesn't mean being frail of mind—"

"I know," he cut in.

She ignored him and went on. "I hurt my body, not my intellect. I'm tired of being treated like I can't understand, like I don't have a part to play in my own destiny. I'm sick of it. And you know what?"

"What?" he asked softly.

"I'm not going to put up with it anymore. I'm not going to let the world go by, or sit in that damn chair"—she pointed at the car trun—"while other people make up their minds for me what's going to happen with the rest of my life. It ends today, Cole."

He almost smiled. His hands slackened their grip on her shoulders and instead became a reassuring caress. "You don't know how happy I am to hear you say that. I'll help you in any way I—"

"No!" She wrested from his grip. "Don't help me. That's the problem. Everybody wants to help me. Well, you know what? Everyone who has tried to 'help' me my whole life has only brought me grief, so thanks, but no. I'm doing this on my own. Understand?"

"What do you mean, 'doing this'?"

Her mind flashed to Mickey. He was probably home, scared, sick, wondering if and when they would come for him, to take him back into captivity, something he feared more than death. Again, it was up to her to rescue him, just as she'd done over and over throughout her life. But she'd be insane to tell Cole that. She shook her head vigorously. "I don't know. But if I did, I certainly wouldn't be telling *you.*"

She slipped from his loose grasp and took a few slow, careful steps backward. "Thanks for your hospitality, Cole, but I think it's time I was back on my own—like a grown-up."

"What, you're going back to that *place* you call home? With the bad lighting and no insulation and poor heat? Seven floors up? In your condition?"

"Forget my 'condition'! I can take care of myself. If I have to drag myself up every flight of stairs on my hands and—"

"Cole," Ames interrupted, pointing at the evidence bag Cole still held, "I think we'd better get a move on."

Zhara's thoughts came firmly back to Mickey. "What does that mean? Are you going to send your stormtroopers over to arrest him now? Is that it?"

Cole flushed but didn't answer. Instead he withdrew from her and went over to speak softly to Brian, tugging him several yards away, obviously to avoid her hearing them. Zhara watched, as the men glanced from the glasses to the crime scene to her, and when they caught her eye, they both looked away.

As she watched them, her heart hurt for Mickey. Mason's death was ghastly, and again she was faced with the grotesque reality that someone had done something like that to another human being in a misguided attempt to help her. It was wrong, but Mickey was the only family she had. He had been trying to protect her, now it was her turn to protect him.

Without sparing another thought for logic or safety, she moved around to the driver's door as swiftly as she could and threw herself in. As she had expected, the men had been in such a hurry earlier to get out of the car that they had left the keys in the ignition.

She distractedly wondered what the penalty was for stealing a cop car, but then thrust the thought from her mind, hastily started the engine, and lurched forward. She cursed the fact that the side on which she was weakest, her right, was also the side she required to manipulate the pedals, but she was determined that if she kept a clear head and maintained control of her limbs, she would be fine.

As she pulled clumsily onto the road, she had a fleeting glimpse of Cole and Brian, both too stunned to react, staring open-mouthed in her direction, and then she was on the road, laughing out loud in spite of her dismal circumstances, just happy to be her own woman once again, not a wreck that everyone needed to coddle and "protect." All she wanted was to be back in control, to feel strong rather than weak, in charge rather than being taken charge of.

Home was a few minutes away, she reminded herself. Mickey was a few minutes away. She was going to get him, and then they'd both be off. They had nothing to keep them tied to Medusa. Blue-eyed little Catastrophe crossed her mind, but the cat had grown comfortable at Cole's house and had even begun to tolerate the presence of his dogs, so she knew she'd be well taken care of. It was time to move on.

The streets blurred by, and with them, Zhara's sense of dependency. Each screeching stop at a light was torment and the intervening spaces between them were sheer freedom. She was back in her old neighborhood, and although she had hated it, its veneer of dirt, its hordes of ragged kids in clothes too thin for the weather, the noise, the clutter, the absence of hope, it was good to be back to something she knew and understood. Familiarity gave her a sense of control, and that was what she needed now more than anything else.

She pulled clumsily up to a fire hydrant outside her

apartment, parking illegally and unevenly in front of it, and threw open the door. As she came to stand in the doorway, she tilted her head backward to spot her own forlorn curtainless window, seven floors up, and the daunting nature of her task sank in. The stairs were one thing, but in the exhilaration of her freedom run, she hadn't given any thought to what would happen next. Those seven flights were like Everest, but they were nothing compared to what she and Mickey would have to face when she finally got up there.

He'd killed someone. She hated the thought of gentle Mickey being transformed into something that could do that, but she couldn't stop to rationalize or explain. She had always been the only mother he had, and, like a mother, she wanted only to save him from himself. They'd been on the run before. They could do it again.

She shouted up to the window in the vain hope that he would hear. "Mickey! Lizard! Can you hear me?"

There was no answer, but the faint siren in the distance, growing louder with every passing moment, told her that Cole and Ames had lost no time in borrowing a vehicle to come after her. Unerringly, they had known exactly where she would come.

She cursed wretchedly, abandoning all hope of being able to catch Mickey's attention from down here, made her way into the building, and started climbing the staircase. To fuel her determination, she began counting out the number of stairs to the seventh floor, backward. The many times she had trudged up them in the past had left her with an exact figure: a hundred and twenty-six.

She counted backward loudly and confidently, her own pep-talk coming out between pants and pauses. "One-twenty-six, one-twenty-five, one-twenty-four . . ." The siren grew louder. Zhara held onto the railing for support, hoping the whole rotted thing wouldn't choose that moment to give way. "One-twenty-one, one-twenty, one-nine-teen . . ."

The strength in her right leg and arm amazed her. She wasn't sure if her new ability was the product of the huge doses of adrenaline that her racing heart was pumping into her system, or whether she'd been stronger than she believed all along, but soon she was on the second floor and still going strong.

"One-oh-two," she muttered, "One-oh-one." The siren was shrill in her ears, close, very close, buzzing around her like a huge, angry, mythical bird. She pushed harder, ignoring her wobbly leg and the knee that threatened to buckle. *Just rely on the strong leg,* she urged herself. *Let it do the work.*

"Ninety-seven, ninety-six," Her head hurt. Step, step, step. "Eighty-nine . . ." The siren-bird whirred in her ears, shrieking at her, as if she were climbing to its eyrie to steal its eggs. She forced herself to move faster.

"Eighty-six . . ." Two doors slammed and heavy footfalls sounded under her. "Eighty-five . . ."

"Zhara!"

"Eighty-four . . ."

The footsteps pounded on the staircase, thunder growing closer.

"Eighty-three . . ." The landing of the next floor was in sight. She had to reach it. She urged on her reluctant body.

"Eighty!" she shouted triumphantly, as strong hands wrapped around her, holding her back. His hard chest was a prison, and she would do anything to get away. "Let me go!" she hissed.

"Zhara, please," he whispered anxiously in her ear.

Her response was a violent kick in the kneecap. In reaction to the attack on his person, Cole let her go just long enough for her to spring forward, but Ames had slipped past him and brought her—dragged her—down in a heap onto the stairs.

"Don't touch me!" She spat at Ames like a wet cat. He let her go immediately, but she made no attempt to escape. Instead, she glowered at Cole, who was grimacing and rubbing his bruised knee. "You could at least have let me get a head start!" she said, accusingly.

Cole didn't answer but tested his knee gingerly. "You'll be the death of me one day, Thorne."

"Good!"

Without acknowledging her rejoinder, Cole was past her and continuing up the staircase, taking the steps two at a time.

"Don't hurt him!" she shrilled, near insane with fear for Mickey.

"Watch her," Cole said tersely to his partner, and then Zhara couldn't see him anymore.

It didn't mean he was out of earshot. She protested loudly. "I'm not a child! I don't have to be watched!" When all she could hear were footfalls, she let her head droop into her despairing hands, shoulders heaving, dry sobs of anger, fatigue, and bewilderment rushing out. Then she and Ames were alone on the steps.

He sat heavily beside her. She turned her head away, shutting him out.

"Cole won't hurt him," Ames tried to console her.

Zhara didn't speak. How dare Cole run off like this, leaving her with a cop who didn't like her in the least?

Ames seemed to read her mind. "I don't hate you, Zhara. Believe it or not, I don't want you to get hurt. The last thing I want is to see you miserable—"

"So let me and Mickey go."

He sighed. "You know I can't do that."

She snorted.

He let a few seconds go past and then tried again. "We got off to a bad start. I'm sorry. If I seem aggressive toward you, it's just that Cole is—my best friend. He's my partner, yes, but he's the closest friend I have. And ever since he met you—"

"So now I'm bad for him?" She turned to look at him through tear-puffed eyes. She hadn't noticed it before, but he had quite a gentle face—thin, bland, but kind.

Ames shook his head vehemently. "Not that you're bad for him, it's just that he's so . . ." He hesitated, searching. "He's so taken with you, that I think he's started making some bad decisions."

"Not as bad as the one I made to go home with him in the first place," Zhara said bitterly.

Ames let his thin shoulders rise and fall. "Maybe. But he's always had his head on, so maybe this time, I guess, his judgment isn't as far off as it seems . . ."

"Thank you," she responded sarcastically.

He didn't rise to it but went on mildly. "All the same, maybe you should just try to trust him a little more—"

"I'm not about to trust anybody!" she snapped. Trust never got her anything but hurt.

Ames sighed, thought about it for a while, and answered, "Well, maybe that's your problem right there." Before he could go on, there was the sound of feet on the stairs above, and they both craned their necks to look upward. Cole was pounding his way back down the stairs—alone.

She shot to her feet. "What did you do to him?"

He answered with the tone of someone trying to hold onto his patience. "I haven't done anything to him. He's not there."

She didn't have a clue what to say or do next. The possibility that Mickey might not be there, waiting for her, had never crossed her mind. She was speechless.

"It doesn't look like he came home since"—he paused delicately—"since last night. There's lots of clothes there, so I don't know if he's taken any with him. And I found these." He held out three small, opaque medicine bottles that rattled in his hand. Zhara didn't even need to take a closer look to know that they were the pills that Mickey had to take to survive. He'd gone to ground, evidently, and without his medicine. How long would he last?

"How badly does he need these?" Cole wanted to know.

"He's very sick," was all she could say.

He seemed to understand. "Zhara, listen," he slipped the pills into his pocket and took one of her hands, "there's an APB out on him right now—"

She wrested her hand away. "Oh, thanks a *lot!*"

"If anyone finds him, they'll bring him in, and he can get the treatment he needs."

She snorted. "I'll bet."

He insisted. "It would be the best thing. He'll get medical attention right away—"

"Sure, in *jail!*"

Cole shook his head regretfully. "There's nothing I can do about that. I'm sorry. It's not even my case; it belongs to the team that caught the call this morning. Even if I could or would do something about it, I can't."

"He'd rather die!"

"Is that what you want for him?"

It was all too much. There was no option that made sense, for her or for Mickey. When did life get so hard? There was nothing she could say. She stared at her feet, searching for answers, but found only worn wooden steps that led back up to a life she couldn't stand anymore. The sigh came not from her chest but from her battered spirit.

Cole reached out, forgetting all the angry words that had passed between them, the hurt they'd inflicted on each other, and the mistrust that stretched between them like an endless, gaping space. He pulled her tired, unresisting form closer, and his lips brushed her hair, fingers settling into the thick, uncombed mop, one hand sliding to the base of her neck to cradle her head, as he pressed it gently against his shoulder.

She was relieved that he didn't speak. Words for them brought only conflict. She let herself go limp, as he rocked her as she'd never been rocked in her mother's arms. The scratchy gray wool of his coat smelled of him, as did his throat, his open shirt collar, his . . .

Behind them, Ames cleared his throat uncomfortably. "I, uh, I'll take the squad car back to the, uh, crime scene. I'll tell the lieutenant you'll be delayed. You can take Zhara home, and I'll meet you at the station. Okay?" He waited a few seconds for Cole to answer, and when he didn't, he turned and descended the staircase gingerly, almost afraid to make any noise.

Take her home? They both knew it couldn't happen. "I'm not going home with you." Her voice was muffled against his chest. She wished she could stay there forever, pressed against him, letting him rock away her hurt, but they both knew that couldn't happen, either.

"Why not, baby? Just for a little while. Until you get better."

"I'm better."

He paused in his gently swaying motion and leaned away so he could look at her. "Stay for me, then, if not for you."

"Until what? Until Mickey gets found, and I have another cause to hate you? Until we find another reason we shouldn't be together? A reason to add to the list that's as long as my—"

"Until we figure out a way to make this work."

She wasn't letting him sway her with sweet rhetoric and fanciful dreams. "Make *what* work?"

"This," he said softly, and let his lip trace the curve of her brow. "Us."

"There is no 'us,' Cole," she told him firmly. Couldn't he see that?

"Yes, there is," he insisted, but he didn't sound that sure.

Before his arms could tighten any further, she grasped each one firmly and removed it from around her. Climbing two stairs backward brought her almost eye to eye with him, and she liked the false advantage that gave her. "Wanting doesn't make it so," she told him.

He pounced. "So you *do* want it!"

He was hemming her in with her own words. She tried again. "That wasn't wanting, it was need. It was loneliness."

"Nothing says it's against the rules to be lonely," he countered. "At least it's a place to start. Stay with me; you won't be lonely anymore."

"Don't try to bribe me!" she snapped.

He rejected that outright. "I'm not trying to bribe you. I'm offering you"—he searched for words—"refuge from your loneliness. I'm offering to take care of you—shelter, warmth, respect."

Zhara shivered. She needed all that, and more, so badly. The temptation was huge, pulling at her like a magnet. Cole would be a safe harbor. He could give her a way out from the madness that her life had been ever since she could remember. But with his gifts would come demands. She would no longer be free to hide from life as she had become accustomed to doing. If she returned home with Cole, she would have to renounce the obscurity that was both her refuge and her hell. The prospect of making that change frightened her.

Furthermore, he would want to know her. Her body wouldn't be all he claimed in return; he would ravage her mind, pillage her secrets, wanting to understand everything about her, who she was, where she had come from, everything. That would be intolerable. Her last line of defense—secrecy—would come tumbling down.

Sensing her vacillation, he pushed again, trying to sway

her permanently over to his side. "Come home," he whispered, voice trembling with emotion. "With me."

She held his dark, emotion-filled gaze, and knew there was only one way to escape the pitfall to which his seduction and promises would lead. Clearly, carefully enunciating every word, she spoke. "I . . . am . . . home."

His massive shoulders slumped, and he rubbed his brow slowly, as if a migraine were brewing. He turned away for a moment, trying to gather his senses, and then, decisively, turned back. "Would it make a difference . . ." He took her hand again. His hands squeezed her fingers much too hard, but she barely noticed the pain, so fascinated was she by the tide of emotion that ebbed and flowed across his face.

He drew a deep breath and began again. "Would it make a difference if I told you I love you?"

Her mouth fell open. *There* was something she hadn't expected! Her voice almost failed her. "What?"

He smiled, and the dimples put in an appearance for the first time in ages. "I didn't exactly have a dark staircase in mind when I was trying to find the ideal place to tell you this, but," his mouth trembled, "I love you, Zhara."

Earthquake! Her world was spinning much too fast. He couldn't be serious. Cole, love her? Sure, *she* loved *him*, and her tumultuous anger and mistrust toward him somehow hadn't succeeded in diminishing that love one iota. But for him to claim he loved her, well, surely he was either deluding himself or trying to delude her. Want, maybe. Desire, definitely. But love? Who did he think he was trying to fool?

Her lips twisted bitterly. "Did you really think I'd buy that?"

He looked puzzled. "What?"

"Do you pull that love thing out whenever you want a woman to do things your way? Does that line really still work?" She had to maintain her edge, not give in to him, or she would certainly be lost.

"It's not a line. I've never said that to anyone else . . ."

She wouldn't let him finish. Instead, she disentangled herself completely and stepped even further back. "Go home, Cole. I'm tired."

Cole leaned back heavily against the rotted wooden railing, patted himself down for cigarettes, found none, and scratched his head, not knowing what to do next. Eventually, he asked her, "Don't you care, just a little?"

She didn't trust herself to answer, so she shrugged and looked away.

"What about"—he licked his lips nervously—"what about last night? We were—"

"Two hungry people feeding off each other," she supplied, cynically. "That was all."

"Not true! We touched something deep inside. It was real!"

"It was fleeting. It's passed now. Gone."

"Let me take you upstairs, inside, and I'll show you how fleeting it was," he growled, with a hint of menace.

She couldn't afford to let him do that. It was all well and good to be firm with him several feet away from her, but if he touched her again . . . "Don't you have to get back to the station, Detective?" she asked him tautly, but inside she was pleading *Go, Cole, go now before I don't have the power to stop you from changing my mind.*

The rising tide of emotion in his face ebbed, and he nodded tightly. "Very well. Leave it at that for now. But I'll be back when my shift is over, and Zhara, you'd better be ready to talk this out."

"Of course." When his shift was over, here was the last place she expected to be.

"I'll bring your chair up for you." He half turned to go down.

She put out an arm to halt him. "Don't bother. I won't be needing it anymore."

"But it's rented out until the end of November!" he protested. "You have lots of time left."

She shrugged. "My own two feet, Cole. Good enough for me."

He nodded wryly. "It's not over," he repeated. "Tonight." She was glad he didn't offer to help her the rest of the way up the stairs.

"Tonight," she echoed, knowing that by nightfall she would be long gone.

He took a few steps down and turned, looking up at her, and was about to speak. She didn't give him the opportunity. "Go, Cole," she said firmly.

He went.

Ten

Zhara held out the small stack of bills in the palm of her hand and glared at them. No matter how she counted them, the sum still added up to much too little. Mickey had taken the corporate credit card they'd used for their security business, and all she had left was a paltry few hundred in her savings account, plus a meager overdraft. She'd emptied the account at a nearby ATM; it would be the last electronic transaction she made before she left the city, and it would spare her from being traceable by Cole and his cohorts, because she wouldn't be using her card again. The cash wouldn't get her very far, but it would get her to her destination, and after that, she'd worry about what she needed to do next.

She'd spent hours lying on her bed in the unheated apartment, trying to keep her whirling thoughts steady, but they all kept coming back to the two men she loved, and the collision that seemed inevitable between them. She tried not to think of the horrible, gnawing loss she felt for Cole, and what she might have had with him. But, then again, what *would* she have had? He claimed to love her; that made him a liar. He was a natural born manipulator, and he'd say whatever it took for him to get what he wanted. Right now, all he wanted was an answer to a riddle that had bugged him for years. Once he knew her, and once all his questions were answered, the intrigue would die, and there would be no need for the smoke screen of his professed love.

Zhara didn't think she could bear to face such pain.

Mickey, well, Mickey needed her. He could deny it all he wanted and proclaim independence till the cows came home, but they had always been together, and they'd be together now, when he needed her most. She shuddered to think of the manhunt Cole's colleagues back at the station were setting up for him, a net designed to grow tighter and tighter around its target until he had nowhere left to run.

She smiled wryly. She had news for them. Mickey had already run. Though the cops were busy staking out her apartment, as she was sure they were right now, Mickey was gone. She was the only person who knew him, knew his every thought, and Mickey was scared. In his fear, he would run to the only place he felt safe: home. But what the cops didn't know was that home for Mickey had never been their sad little apartment. Mickey's Mecca, the absolute north to his compass, his beacon in the dark, was Chicago. It was the only place he had ever sensed himself to be free.

So, here she was, in Medusa's sole airport, clutching the one-way ticket that her funds were able to buy her, trying to look nonchalant while telling the check-in clerk that no, thank you, she didn't have any luggage, save for her heavy old coat and a single change of clothes in an overnight bag. What would have been the point of explaining to the woman that she'd left her apartment in a hurry, not sparing herself the time to pack, because she was afraid that a moment's more delay would be too late, and that her bid for freedom would end in her stepping outside and into the arms of a policeman? Why bother explaining that the bag might look light, but its extra weight, in her condition, meant that it had taken her a full thirty minutes to make it back down the seven flights of stairs?

Better to be silent, smile, and make her way to the departure gate.

"Are you sure you wouldn't like one of our attendants to help you to the gate in one of our courtesy transport systems?" the clerk asked tactfully, eyeing Zhara's unsteady gait and obvious fatigue.

Zhara shook her head firmly, although the temptation was there. If Cole came looking for her later and started asking questions, she didn't want herself to be even more conspicuous than necessary. She tried to stand a little straighter. "I'm okay, really." She pointed ruefully at her right leg. "Jogging injury. It'll heal."

The clerk smiled uncertainly but politely, and looked like she was about to insist, when she was distracted by a voice behind her.

"I can help the lady to the gate, Miss. We're traveling together."

Zhara spun around so fast that only the invisible hands of an angel prevented her from losing her balance. Cole had, somehow, inexplicably, found her, and was standing so close she could feel his breath ruffle her hair. Cold shivers ran through her. "What—?" She began, but the words stuck, stillborn, in her throat.

"How did I find you? Come now, Zhara. I do a little detecting every now and then. Sometimes I even get paid for it. And, for future reference, when you book a plane ticket, it leaves electronic fingerprints all over this town. Did you forget? Or did you think I didn't know you'd run the minute you got the chance?"

She glared at him, still unable to put her shock and anger into words. Then her eyes opened even wider, as he casually withdrew a navy-and-red ticket and passed it to the clerk. "Would you mind seating us together?" he asked smoothly, the smile he gave the clerk dying the moment it settled on Zhara's face.

The clerk smiled uncertainly, noticing the crackling ani-

mosity between her two clients, but she obediently tapped
on the keys and came up with an answer. "I'm sorry, Sir."
Her ginger curls swayed from side to side, emphasizing
her regret. "I don't think I can find a seat next to your
companion. The whole row's booked up."

Zhara's rising victory was instantly shot down as Cole,
unruffled, withdrew his leather wallet, flashed his badge,
and encouraged her with one soft word. "Try."

The woman's eyes fell again on Zhara, more sharply
now, trying to ascertain whether Zhara could be a dangerous fugitive being transported on *her* airline, and hurriedly tapped out the seat changes on the keyboard. Zhara
could almost hear her mentally reciting the afternoon's
excitement to her friends when her shift was over. With
a flourish, she handed Cole his boarding pass, and, with
dismay, Zhara noted that he had indeed been assigned
the seat next to hers.

Seething, she allowed herself to be guided away from
the counter, well aware of the curious stares of the check-
in clerk, who watched them until they were out of sight.
Although every foul and vituperative thing she could
dream of saying to Cole was springing to her mind, she
pressed her lips tightly together and decided on the silent
treatment instead. Cole seemed undisturbed, willing to
play along.

At the gate, he declared his weapon, showed his credentials, and guided her into the departure lounge. It
was Halloween weekend, and some of the younger trav-
elers were getting a head start, wearing jaunty hats and
carrying lumpy parcels of costumes in clear, shrink-
wrapped plastic. For a moment she was distracted by a
little girl, who clutched a stuffed dino in one hand and
a bag of pumpkin-shaped candies in another. There was
another snippet of childhood she'd never experienced.
She sighed. She had missed out on so much of her
youth, and yet, she felt ancient.

Cole guided her to their departure gate, checked the time on his pass, and nudged her to sit. He hadn't missed the longing gaze she'd thrown the little tyke. "Never went trick-or-treating, I guess." His voice held a trace of sympathy.

Irritation rippled through her. There he went again, feeding off her history like a huge, greedy octopus—she halted her thoughts in their tracks. What good would it do? Instead, she asked tautly, "Shouldn't you be at work?"

His broad shoulders lifted and fell. "Wouldn't you know it? Today's my first day of vacation."

"I don't believe you."

"Why not? I haven't had one in three years. I put in for emergency leave, and my lieutenant is a very understanding woman. So here I am."

"Here you are," she echoed, bitterly. "Will Medusa be safe without you guarding it? Don't you have crooks to catch?"

Both their minds ran painfully to Mickey, and Cole had the grace not to answer.

Zhara spoke again. "What about your son? Don't tell me you've *abandoned* him?"

Cole didn't look perturbed. "Brian will look after him. And the cat. And the dogs. So don't bother your pretty head; they'll all be just fine."

"Got it all figured out, huh?" She hoped she injected enough sarcasm into that remark to blister his skin.

He didn't turn a hair. "Yup."

Zhara settled into sullen silence and waited for their boarding call.

Cole stared unabashedly at Zhara's profile, as she gazed out the taxi, her eyes taking in the flashy storefront windows of Michigan Avenue, the upscale department-store bags on display in the clutches of happy shoppers, the old-fashioned horse-drawn carriages leisurely taking tourists around, and cheery street-musicians trying to out-play each other on the corners. He wished he could understand what she was feeling, coming back to a city that had been both hell and redemption for her.

But, his pity was tinged with annoyance. He hadn't gotten over the look of horror in her eyes—was it only this morning?—when she had gazed down at the battered body of Oliver Mason and immediately assumed him to be guilty of the killing. That had hurt. Okay, so he himself had been worried that he might have been responsible, but the moment he saw the extent of the damage, he knew Mason hadn't died from his wild punches. But Zhara had never given him the benefit of the doubt. She had condemned him without a question or a request for an explanation.

To further rub salt into his flayed hide, she *had* showed the loyalty he would have liked to see in her—but to Mickey, not to him. She'd defended him in the face of overwhelming circumstantial evidence, and she'd given up her home and her own safety to flee town in search of her friend.

Cole's lips twisted wryly. Of course, she loved her "little brother." He could live with that. But the knowledge that she was willing to love and trust Mickey in a way that she never would him, made him bitter. And he wasn't stupid, Mickey loved Zhara back, not as a child loves his big sister, but as a man loves a woman.

Jealousy bubbled in the pit of his stomach. He felt almost foolish—jealous of a mortally ill teenager. Could he possibly stoop any lower?

In an effort to assuage his own guilt, he tried to bridge the huge space between them, reaching out and touching her lightly on the back of her listless hand. Her body tensed, and with a black look in his direction, she flattened herself against the far door, so much so that Cole hastily double-checked to ensure that the door was locked and that the pressure of her body wouldn't send it flying open.

He tried to contain his sense of powerlessness. Zhara was a clam, holding on to the pearls of her emotions with tenacity, and neither force nor gentle persuasion had worked in his efforts to get her to open herself fully. From time to time she'd let her guard slip, and he had glimpsed the complex being that she was. How much longer could he last, being tortured simultaneously by her proximity and her distance?

As long as it takes, his heart responded. He smiled ruefully. It seemed like the decision was out of his hands. All he could do was follow where his treacherous heart led.

The taxi drew up to the façade of one of the nicer hotels in the city, and for the first time since they left Medusa, Zhara spoke. "I don't know if *you* plan on staying here, but *I* certainly don't."

He lifted one thick brow. "Why not? I'm told it's very pleasant."

"Pleasant? Are you serious? I couldn't afford to pay for this!" Her sweeping arm encompassed the gilt-trimmed sliding doors and the liveried doormen. "One night in here would wipe me out!"

"I haven't asked you to pay for anything," he answered mildly, and stepped out of the cab. Peeling off a few bills, he handed them to the driver, and held out his hand politely to help her out of the car.

She sank mulishly back into the upholstery. "You can stay here if you like. I'm finding something a little more— affordable."

"But your room is already booked. And I've paid a non-refundable deposit." He tried to look disappointed.

She eyed him suspiciously. "*My* room?"

He let his eyes widen. "Yes, why?"

"You booked me a separate room?"

He smiled lazily. "Of course. It was the gentlemanly thing to do."

He watched the hesitation flit across her face. The driver cleared his throat loudly. ~~Her eyes flitted to the~~ stubby man, whose body telegraphed impatience, and back to Cole's face. Cole pushed harder. "Hot showers," he promised seductively.

Zhara said nothing.

"Magnificent view of the lake."

"This isn't a pleasure trip," she reminded him tartly.

"No," he agreed amicably, "but there's no telling how long we'll be here. Might as well be comfortable." Then he pressed home the little advantage he had left—her longing for a little luxury in her life, for a change. "Big, warm rooms. *Huge* beds—"

"Which I'll be sleeping in alone," she interrupted in a prickly tone.

"Of course," he agreed mildly, and went on. "Chocolates on the pillows—"

"I hate candy!" she grouched.

"So you keep trying to tell me." He remembered the night they'd come home from their dinner, when he'd sought to convince her that "dessert" could be quite a pleasurable thing. He could tell by her flush that she remembered, too.

The taxi driver decided that enough was enough. "Look, buddy, I got miles to go before I sleep, if you get my drift."

Wouldn't you know it: a taxi driver quoting Frost. Cole turned his head. There were taxis backing up behind them, and the occupants were beginning to get antsy. He stuck his head back into the taxi and held out his hand again. "Come on, honey, we're holding up the line. You wouldn't want that, would you?"

Grudgingly, she eased her body out of the car, swung the door shut, and, as Cole was amused to notice, com-

pletely ignored his offer of assistance as she led the way
into the hotel. He couldn't suppress a smile. Stubborn,
cranky, and fiercely independent: that was the woman he
loved.

Zhara didn't know what to do with her frustration. She
was tired, she was irritable, and she had had to tolerate
Cole at her side, sticking closer to her than her own
shadow, ignoring every barb she could think to toss in his
direction, as if they were bouncing off his Teflon-coated
carapace. Damn the man! Didn't he know when to back
down?

They'd started in the most logical place: on the north
side, where the depression hung over the neighborhoods
like a pall. Despite the changes that had taken place over
the few years since she'd sought refuge here herself, she
discovered that she still knew her way around. Problem
was, the kids she had known then had—like herself—
grown up, and had for the most part, managed to extricate themselves from their dire circumstances, and moved
on.

They had been replaced by a new set of kids, who perceived her and Cole, both adults, as the enemy, much in
the same way that she had perceived grown-ups while she
was in their position. The children of the street listened
to their questions with skepticism, and answered in mono-
syllables, only growing slightly more loquacious when a
few bills were handed over to lubricate the wheels of pro-
gress.

Furthermore, their hideouts had changed. As expected,
some of the old buildings that she herself had slept in
were either demolished or refurbished; either way, the
sleeping places she knew then no longer existed. And
what was to say that Mickey would have run to ground as
they had last time? He'd withdrawn the maximum allow-

ance on their credit card, and that meant he had money. He could afford a small room somewhere inconspicuous.

But somehow, every time they struck out, she was torn between relief and growing desperation. She knew in her heart that if they found him, he would be in trouble. Big trouble. The fact that Cole stepped away from her several times during the day to make private phone calls did not escape her. It was obvious that a manhunt was on, and he was checking in with his colleagues here in Chicago to find out if they had been more successful than he and Zhara.

Her guilt at her own treachery was hard to digest, but she kept reminding herself that if they didn't find Mickey, his fate would be a lot worse. They didn't have much time left; his health was degenerating rapidly toward the point of no return, and if they didn't get him to treatment fast, he would have worse things to worry about than being arrested.

She sat on the edge of her bed, in this lovely hotel room, with the sun dropping lower in the sky and casting a blush over everything it touched, and tried to hold it together. If only—

There was a rap on the door that was too imperious to be hotel staff. That left only one alternative.

"Come in, Cole," she said resignedly.

The door handle rattled. "I can't come in," came the muffled rejoinder. "You locked the door."

"Hasn't succeeded in keeping *you* out of my hair," she muttered, and rose slowly to let him in.

He'd showered and changed after their long and fruitless trek around the city. Zhara's eyes widened. The man was dressed for a night on the town, with a fine-looking off-white turtleneck and navy pants. He'd shaved and was smelling mighty good. One hand was hidden out of sight behind his back, and he was grinning like a fool.

She wrinkled her nose to hide her sudden longing.

"Got yourself a date? Where'd you pick her up—the bar downstairs?"

He smiled, not even falling for her barb. "Trick or treat," he recited seductively.

She scowled. "What's your problem?"

"It's Halloween. Trick or treat?" Dimples flashed.

"I know what night it is."

"So what are you going to give me?"

She folded her arms against his charm and schooled her features into a frown. "Not a damn thing."

"Then I win the right to play a trick on you," he said, stepping forward so fast that she didn't have time to take evasive action. His mouth was against hers, and the searching tip of his tongue was flicking along the outline of her lips before she had a chance to catch her breath. The sudden surprise and the uncanny heat that rolled into her like a fireball left her lungs bawling for a breath of air. But, even with her breathing cut off, and the dizzying sensation of being about to crumple for lack of it, she still found herself rising, unbidden, to press against him. Tongue reached out for tongue, fingers stroked bare nape, hips ground against hard, shocking bulge—

And then he pushed her gently away, watching her as she gasped, filling her lungs at last, heart rocking in her chest, dizzy. "Seems like your trick was my treat," he murmured. His eyes were black discs of heated wanting.

Zhara glared, more disgusted with herself than with him. "Son of a—"

He lifted a finger to cut her off. "Now, now. My mother was a saint—"

She grimaced. "What do you want, Cole?"

He shrugged, too innocently. "Nothing. Just bringing you a little something to cheer you up."

"Right now, *nothing* can cheer me up," she resisted.

He finally brought into view the hand he had been hiding. In it was a large, flashy shopping bag from one of the boutiques down on Michigan Avenue's Magnificent Mile. Her eyes grew a shade wider before she could stop them. "Not even this?" he asked seductively.

She tried to hide her excitement. "What is it?"

"Oh," he feigned ignorance. "I haven't a clue. But if you opened it, neither of us would be in suspense anymore."

Her hands knew what she wanted better than her mind did. They tore at the wrapping, revealing a luxurious long-sleeved woolen dress the color of whipped butter, a pair of fine-dernier stockings that crinkled promisingly in their cellophane wrapping, and a matching pastel-yellow, raw-silk bra-and-panty set trimmed with elaborate *broderie anglaise,* with slender yellow-satin ribbons that looped in and out of their petal-shaped cutouts. They *had* to have cost more than even the dress.

She looked up at him, puzzled. "What's this for?"

"You didn't think I'd let you go out on the town with me dressed in *jeans,* did you?" He disappeared before she could respond and was back from the hallway in a twinkling, holding an even bigger bag, which he pressed into her arms, even as she protested.

Curiosity killed the cat dead. She peered into the bag and pulled out the most gorgeous leather coat she had ever beheld. She held it against herself in shock. It fell to her midcalf and smelled divine. She ran the tips of her fingers sensuously over the incredibly pliant pelt.

"I bought it because it reminded me of your skin—soft as a child's, warm as . . ." He moved a little closer to her, and let one hand fall over the fingers that stroked the coat.

Zhara stepped skittishly backward, bringing the bag up as a shield between them. The weight of the last parcel in the bottom of the cavernous bag told her that a pair of shoes lay there.

She chased away the smile of delight playing on her

lips, like an old spinster sweeping away cobwebs in the attic. "Cole, we aren't here to go out on the town. We're here . . ." She paused. *"I'm* here, to save Mickey."

His eyes twitched just a little at the implication that his motives for searching for Mickey were less noble, and then he spoke. "I'm here for the same reason, Zhara."

Her curling lip prompted him to lay a hand on her shoulder. "Honestly," he insisted. "I don't want to see him hurt. But we've searched all day, and it's night now. A special night. So why can't we just go out together and have a good time? They've got this lovely Halloween ride on one of the riverboats. Music, cocktails on the deck, vampire waiters. I hear they're giving away free sets of fake fangs to every client."

Down deep, she knew he was right. They had searched all day, and there was nothing they could do again tonight. Why not steal a little pleasure? Would that be so bad? She almost smiled at his childish enthusiasm, but then reminded herself she was supposed to be mad at him, and sobered up again.

He persisted. "So let's just go out for a ride, okay? We can see the skyline from the boat. It's one of the most beautiful skylines in the world—"

"I know what it looks like." She dug in her heels. "I've seen it before."

"You haven't seen it with *me* before," he said softly.

She should have resisted. She should have thrown him out. But her own excitement at being out with him on such a wonderful night put paid to all her protestations. She was sunk, and she knew it. *You're an idiot,* she reprimanded herself, but to him, she said, "I can get dressed in fifteen minutes."

He smiled broadly, relief written all over his face. "I'll wait here," he said, plopping himself down on the bed.

She tugged at his ear and led him to the door by it,

292 *Simona Taylor*

firmly and without much tenderness. "You'll wait in the lobby," she countered.

He left without protest.

Chicago glittered like a Christmas tree. The cool air coming up along the river from Lake Michigan had a hint of perfume on it; it smelled of waterways and excitement and magic. Its crispness made her tug the lapels of her coat even closer around her. Seated on the deck of the small, intimate boat, with blues floating sleepily out of the sound system, and party-goers laughing softly on the upper and lower decks, Zhara relaxed, allowing her shoulder to press against Cole's.

She closed her eyes, feeling her lashes brush the satin of the mask she had been given by a smiling steward the moment they'd stepped on board. It was turning out to be a lovely evening; Cole was pleasant but not pressuring, and dinner had been wonderful. But, even so, she was uneasy, sharply aware of something missing. What it was, she couldn't say, but it was like having been forced to live her life with some sort of annoying noise continuously in the background, and now, it was gone. Only, she'd grown so accustomed to the noise in the first place, that she had barely noticed the exact moment that it had stopped.

Then her musing led her to the answer: she was relaxed, calm. Ah, that was it! The turmoil that had been her constant companion for as long as she had known herself seemed to have slipped from her like a fickle lover, stealing away while she slept. In its place, she felt something she hadn't felt in a long, long time. Peace.

She let go a long, soft, heartfelt sigh. Cole's hand came to rest reassuringly on hers.

"Beautiful," he breathed.

She looked out at the glittering lights of Navy Pier, with its amusement-park rides twirling and crowds of people scurrying about, music from a dozen bars and booths sailing to them over the water, and agreed with him softly. If he wanted to attribute her sighs to the beauty of the night, well, let him. Then, out of her peripheral vision, she realized that under the cover of the navy-and-white patterned domino he wore, he was looking at her, not the scenery.

She turned her hand palm up, allowing him to entwine his fingers with hers. She didn't speak, but ripples of excitement tied her stomach up into elaborate cloverhitches.

After a while, he asked her, "What's it been like for you, coming back here? Has it been very hard?"

She thought about that for a moment, brought her cocktail to her lips to buy her a little time, and then answered, her voice tinged with wonderment. "Not as hard as I thought it would be. I expected to be crushed by the pain, but all I feel is a quiet kind of sadness. I'm sorry I had to endure that much, so young, but I don't know— there's not much else. I should feel bitter, but I don't. It all seems so distant now."

He was silent, not intervening for fear she would get jumpy and clam up again.

Zhara went on speaking, as if vocalizing her thoughts allowed her to finally understand them. "I suppose I had a rough life, but I had some good times, too. Small things, like when we had enough money to go out and have a good meal. Walking along the pier with Antonio—" She stopped and threw him a sidelong glance, afraid of his reaction. But he only squeezed her hand and waited for her to continue.

"I just wish . . ." She stopped. Her mask had suddenly become uncomfortable, but it wasn't until she tore it off that she realized it was becoming damp with her tears. As she laid her mask on the deck between their chairs, Cole followed suit.

"What do you wish, Zhara?" His mouth was at her ear, lips brushing away the tears. "Tell me, and I'll make it happen."

"You *can't* make it happen!" She tore her hand away and slammed it against the arm of her deck chair in frustration. "*Nobody* can make it happen! It's impossible!"

"Nothing's really impossible," he soothed. "Tell me."

"I just wish I hadn't done all those things. We violated people's homes; we stole. What we did was wrong!"

He still hadn't removed his lips from her temple. "You did wrong things, but you had the right reasons. You were trying to save yourself, your friend . . ."

"That's not an excuse! That doesn't make it right!"

"No," he agreed, "but it makes it understandable. I don't know many people who would have had the courage to endure what you and Mickey have endured together. You survived."

"And my soul bears the scars," she countered ruefully.

He smiled. "Zhara, my heart, that's the wonderful thing. Your soul doesn't have to. Don't you think God understands? Do you honestly think He judges you harshly because of what you did? You've already said you're sorry. That's all it takes: repentance. You're truly sorry, so He's put it behind you. Believe me, I know. If I still carried around the memories of all those women I hurt, including Omar's mother, I'd be a ruined man now. I'd be no good to anyone—not myself, my son, or any other person who meant something to me. But I asked for forgiveness, and now I'm free of all that. I no longer feel dirty every time I look in the mirror. Trust me, that feeling of liberation is the most wondrous feeling in the world."

Zhara pursed her lips skeptically, so Cole went on. "God doesn't bear grudges. He's already put aside what you were, and now He's getting all excited about what you are and all you're going to be. And if He's forgotten all about your past, why can't you?"

She searched his eyes, puzzled. "How can I forget?"

He thought for several long moments and then stood. "Come." He held out his hands to her, and she let him help her to stand. She walked alongside him, letting his strong arm fall around her waist, not because she needed the support, which she did, but because she felt that it belonged there. Together, they walked to the ship's railing and leaned over, staring into the swirling dark waters.

"How deep do you think that water is?" he asked.

She gave him a puzzled look. "What? Um, I don't know."

"I don't either. But I'll bet you anything it's deep enough for your sins. Come." He took her shaking hands and brought them together to form a cup. "Listen carefully."

Zhara listened, mystified. She hadn't a clue what he was up to, but she obeyed, for once, trusting him.

"Now, close your eyes—"

Her damp lashes came together.

"—and think about the things you've done, and the things you think you've done. And every time you think about something you don't want in your life anymore, just put it into your hands."

Her eyes flew open. "That's ridic—"

"Shhh, darling. Honey, just do it."

She closed her eyes again and thought of her life as a climber, her life of struggle, the nights of filling the need for money for Mickey by taking what wasn't hers, and poured all those memories into her hands.

But Cole wasn't satisfied with just that. His voice was a rumble in her ear. "You didn't kill your mother, Zhara. Put that thought right in there along with the others."

With a huge effort, she did, and her body suddenly felt astoundingly lighter.

"And Antonio—his death wasn't your fault. Hold on to the memory of him, but get rid of the pain."

She put that there, too. Her hands were becoming so full, she was sure some of her sins would spill over onto the deck.

"And you've done all you could for Mickey, so stop beating yourself up over what you think you should have, but haven't."

Zhara nodded and did as she was told.

Cole gently cupped his hands under hers and held them out over the dark water. "Is it all in there now?"

"Yes," she whispered huskily.

He removed his hands from under hers. "Now," he instructed soberly, "just let them go."

She raised her eyes to his, mouth trembling. "What?"

"Let them fall. Into the water. Let them sink to the bottom and be gone. Set them free. Set yourself free."

Awed, she parted her hands and watched as her troubles and guilt tumbled like stones into the swirling water that slapped against the boat's hull. As they fell, something dark and heavy rushed out of her like a cold wind, swirling around, and it was gone. Her breath came in sharp, agitated gasps. In place of the heavy stones that had weighed upon her heart all her life, was joy.

She turned her glowing face to Cole's, and he was beaming at her, in pride, sharing her sudden happiness. "There, now." He touched her hair and then brought her now-empty hands up to his lips. "Does that feel better?"

The joy in her was spilling up and frothing over, champagne bubbles making her giddy. She swayed, and he pulled her closer to steady her. "Hold me tight, Cole," she begged. "I feel so light, I might rise up and float away."

"I think I'd like it if you floated." He lifted the edges of her hair and fluffed it about her head, just as it would be if she were truly flying. "I'd just cut myself loose from the earth and join you up there."

When they both stopped laughing, she linked her

hands behind the nape of his neck and kissed him lightly. "Thank you so much. For believing in me. For helping me find this—incredible freedom. I had no idea it was this simple. Thank you."

"My pleasure." He returned the kiss ardently, and then reluctantly broke it. Hesitantly, he asked, "What now, darling?"

Zhara took a single step away, the better to clear her head. What now, indeed? Did she dare go further and let him know how precious he was to her? Should she admit that she loved him? *Could* she? Unsure of what her next step should be, she balled up her fists and shoved them into the deep pockets of her lovely new coat—and encountered something small and hard.

She looked down. "What the—" Her words were cut off. She brought the item into her sight. It was a jewelry box, covered in pure white velvet. Her eyes flew to Cole's face.

"Gee, how'd that get in there?" he murmured.

She opened the box slowly to find a perfect amethyst, nestled in a simple gold setting, a single handcrafted leaf curling around it. It was beautiful. She lifted a questioning eyebrow.

He lifted her right hand and firmly slid the ring onto her fourth finger. "Don't panic, it's not an engagement ring. It's a ring that says . . ." He paused, searching for the right thing to say. He tried again. "It says you'll honor me with the *chance* to woo you properly. That you'll give me the opportunity to prove myself and win you over. Will you do that for me?"

Zhara brought her hand up to her face and stared at it. Cole wanted to be with her? Could he honestly mean that?

"Will you?" He was still waiting for an answer.

She found her throat too dry to utter a sound. She glanced over to where they had been sitting, where her drink still stood, ice slowly melting. She'd have given anything for a single chip of that ice on her tongue right now. Her entire head felt hot.

"And, while I'm making a fool of myself, I want to tell you I meant it when I told you I love you. I did then, and I do more now. It just keeps growing and growing inside, and there doesn't seem to be a way to slow it down, far less to stop it. I feel one day I'll just explode, pop right open under the force of it swelling in my chest and in my mind—" He halted, face darkening as blood rushed to it. "Oh, God, I'm running off at the mouth again. Bad habit."

He shut up, but waited anxiously.

Zhara opened her mouth and closed it. She opened it again.

Cole's cellular phone started up a racket in his coat pocket. He cursed like a stevedore, and flicked it open, but didn't let her go. "Give me one reason to be glad I forgot to turn this off," he barked into it.

Zhara tried to step away discreetly to allow him some privacy, but his arm tightened around her, holding her there. She watched as Cole's face grew deadly serious.

"Brian, you had better be sure about this." He was silent again as he listened, then he began barking questions. "What were their names? Who? Oh, yes, that's right. When? Who caught the squeal?"

Then she noticed that his eyes kept coming back to hers, and her instinct told her unerringly that the phone call had something to do with her. She groaned inside. Not again! Would Cole's business somehow always collide with her life? Forcefully, she disentangled herself from his grip and moved several feet away from him on the deck, her back to him. She scowled at the water below. She had felt so free, so giddily happy for such a brief moment. Did it always have to come back to this?

As Cole continued to snap questions at Brian over the

phone, Zhara distracted herself by focusing on the ship's route. They had completed their sortie into the lake and were now waiting patiently at the water lock that would allow them back into the Chicago River, where the second leg of the tour would take them up into the heart of the city. The bright lights and hubbub of Navy Pier were behind them, and, in their place was a dismal quiet.

"Story of my life," she muttered. The wind, which she had so far thought of as refreshing, now tugged tauntingly at her curls, forcing its way down the front of her dress, mockingly jabbing at her aching heart. She pulled the coat more tightly around her, to shut out both the cold and her mounting feeling of dread.

Cole finished his conversation and came to stand beside her. "Zhara?" He sounded perplexed. Grasping her shoulders, he turned her around to face him. "What is it?"

"That call was about me, wasn't it?" she accused him, belligerently.

He nodded slowly. "Sort of, yes."

"So is it always going to be like this?"

"Like what?" He still hadn't caught on.

"If you and I were"—she swallowed—"together, would I always have to dread the moment when you get a phone call about me? Or another witness turning up?"

He shook his head. "Zhara, listen. It's doubtful that anything is ever going to be done about your case. There is no evidence, nothing to link you to anything, and even your own confession couldn't convict you. You could walk into a station, here or back in Medusa, and confess for an hour, but we still wouldn't be able to do anything about it without corroboration. That's the way the law works."

"But—"

He cut her off. "And from what I'm told by my brothers in the city, Chicago police aren't even interested in reopening your file. The system is too clogged, and everyone just has such a hard time keeping up with current cases that it's doubtful if, even with a witness, they'd want to turn back the pages four years or more to hunt down an offender—not for a nonviolent case like yours. Especially since you've gone straight, have your own business, and are no longer a threat to anyone anymore. Nobody has the time to spend trying to pin you down, Zhara."

"*You* did," she accused.

"Yes. I did. I wanted to bring you down so badly, I could feel it. I was obsessed. Every cop gets fixated on a case at least once in his career—his personal campaign. The beautiful cat burglar who was too smart to leave any clues, too smart to get caught"—he smiled into her face—"was mine."

"And now?" she watched him suspiciously.

"And now I realize that it wouldn't serve any purpose. You're not a threat to anyone, and I know you're trying to make something of your life. Sometimes the scales of justice must be tempered with mercy."

"So what was that call about, then?"

His smile broadened. "Good news, actually. Mickey didn't kill Mason."

Zhara's mouth rounded. "What?"

"Brian says two of our guys collared a pair of men over on the East Side. Seems they worked for the same man as Mason, in his smuggling operation."

"And—?"

"And when Mason started to squeal on the smugglers, the boss sent them over to his place of business to plug up the leak."

"And they killed him?"

"That's the information we have. They were interrogated separately, and they ratted each other out. They were charged with murder-one an hour ago. I'm pretty sure forensics will find enough to place them at the scene."

She was perplexed. "But Mickey was there! Those glasses are his, I know it!"

Cole nodded. "There, yes. But guilty? I doubt it. He either came, spoke to Mason, and left, or turned up later and found him dead. My guess is the latter. That's probably why he panicked and ran."

"He was afraid the cops'd think it was him?"

Cole nodded ruefully. "And he was right."

"So he's out there, alone, hiding, and afraid he's a wanted man."

"Yes."

Her resentment forgotten, she clutched both his forearms desperately. "Cole, please, we have to find him."

"We're trying, remember? We've been looking for him all day." He tugged at her gently, trying to lead her back to their chairs. "Come, sit down and get some rest. You still shouldn't spend so much time on your feet. Let's try to enjoy the cruise, and then tomorrow, at first light, we'll go back out looking. Okay?"

Zhara resisted. She didn't think she had that long. Mickey was sick and frightened, and probably half out of his mind. She knew she couldn't wait until morning. She ground her teeth in frustration. Her years of friendship with Mickey had left them with a silent communication, something real but indefinable. Right now, it was telling her where he was, but her conscious mind couldn't grasp it. The image beckoned, like a half-remembered dream, ethereal, just out of her grasp.

"I know where he is," she murmured.

"Where?" he asked, softly.

"But I can't—it's too hazy. I know, but . . ." She squeezed her eyes shut. *Think, think!*

A passing ship, also filled with revelers, tooted merrily, and the occupants on board waved. Around Zhara and Cole, other passengers waved back. The deck had been filling steadily, as passengers made their way outdoors to look at the buildings that lined each bank of the river. The famous Chicago skyline. Cole had used it as bait to try to lure her on board earlier. The voice of their guide cut in on the music to point out one or two of the better-known landmarks: the Civic Opera house, with its shape like a huge armchair, the Mercantile Exchange, overwhelming in its size, and in the distance, the antenna tips atop the Sears Tower, clinging tenaciously to its title of tallest building in the world.

Click, click, click. The pieces fell into place, and the picture was complete. "God," she breathed.

"What is it?"

"The tower."

He frowned, uncomprehending. "What tower?"

She pointed at the double spires in the distance, slender, pale, sticking out against the dark sky. "That tower."

"Sears? Why?"

"Mickey's fascinated by it. When we were children, he talked about it all the time. He drew pictures of it."

"He had one stuck up on his bedroom wall back in Medusa." Understanding spread across his face.

"Right. He homes in on it like a pigeon. The time he ran away from Harbourmouth—the time I followed him— I came straight here, because I knew, I just knew, that the tower would be the place he'd come."

"But why?"

"Because all his life, Lizard has only wanted to do one thing."

Dread crossed Cole's face as understanding dawned. "And that's—"

"To climb it." Zhara could feel the panic rising. Mickey had talked about it incessantly, dreamed about it, strategized, drawn sketches, deciding which angle he'd attack it from, and what type of rope and tackle he'd need. She'd always half listened, with the patronizing amusement reserved for an amateur climber dreaming of Everest. But right now, Mickey was sure he had nothing to lose. Sears would be his last, final, crazy stunt, his swansong. And deep in her heart, Zhara knew he was already there.

She turned her dark, troubled eyes up to Cole's. "We have to go to him."

He nodded soothingly. "We will, as soon as we dock."

"No, no," she said agitatedly. "Now! We have to go there *now!*"

He thought for a few minutes, and then took her hand. "Okay, come on." Cole led her down from the deck, and as they went, Zhara cursed her body for the thousandth time; she wanted to run behind him, race off wherever he led, but her wounded body kept her spirit back. It felt like they took forever to cross a small space. On the lower deck, Cole stopped a harried-looking steward. "Who's in charge here?"

The young man grunted. "That would be the captain," he suggested unhelpfully.

"I know that." Cole struggled to hang on to his patience. "I meant where can we find him?"

The harassed steward pointed at the central passage with exaggerated solicitousness. "Down there. Straight ahead. It's the door that says 'Captain' on it."

Cole didn't waste time with a rejoinder. Instead, he led Zhara down where they had been shown and knocked sharply on the door. A slim, uniformed young man opened up.

"Captain?" Cole asked hopefully.

The man shook his head. "No, I'm the first mate. What do you need to see the Captain for?"

"We need to get off at the docking point nearest to the Sears Tower. It's an emergency."

The man looked skeptical, but he remained polite. "I'm sorry," he said soothingly, as if passengers asked for extraordinary stops all the time, "but we don't make unscheduled stops. We're about to turn around and head back to where we started."

"It's urgent," Cole began, and then remembered he had the powers of persuasion on his side. Withdrawing his wallet, he flashed his badge at the man, and then re-iterated his request, following it up with, "It's police business."

The man's eyes flitted knowingly over Zhara, took in her anxious eyes and wind-tossed hair, and returned to Cole's. His face said he was sure he knew exactly what kind of emergency this young couple had, but still, he nodded. A police request wasn't something to toy with. "I'll have a word with the captain. Wait here." He withdrew into the room, closing the door firmly in their faces, and returned a few moments later.

"Well?" Cole's body vibrated next to Zhara's, full of nervous tension.

The young man nodded. "The captain has given permission to let you off. There's a docking point a few minutes away. If you follow me to the deck, I'll see to it that you get off safely."

Zhara was so relieved, she felt that no amount of "thank yous" could be enough to convey her gratitude, but she tried, fervently, all the way to the deck. The length of time the large vessel took to carefully align itself to the mooring point seemed endless, but finally, eventually, Cole was leading her over the narrow space of water between the ship and the solid concrete of the river bank, up the endless stairs to street level, and onto the sidewalk.

"Too far to walk," she gasped. The Sears Tower was only a few blocks away, but her reluctant leg would never allow her to make it.

"I'd have carried you first," Cole smiled. Fortunately, he didn't have to. A taxi halted at his upraised hand, and the driver immediately obeyed Cole's barked instructions, setting off in the direction of the edifice, speed limit be damned.

The streets were alive, thronging. It was a little too late for children still to be out combing the neighborhoods for Halloween candy, but by this time, grown-up adventurers were hustling to the many theme parties that sprang up for the event. Warlocks, succubae, angels and Darth Mauls abounded. Young couples held hands and giggled under the glittering lights of the buildings that dominated the streets.

"Hurry," Zhara begged the driver. Everything she felt inside told her they were running out of time—that something awful was about to happen.

Cole squeezed her fingers. "If he went any faster, we'd either get pulled over or killed," he reminded her gently.

She fell silent, but her own voice rang inside her head, *hurry, hurry, hurry* . . .

The cab squealed to a stop near to the lush park that lay in the shadow of the building, and she was out even before Cole was, urging her body onward to the cluster of well-manicured trees, checking the occupants of each bench. Cole caught up with her, his voice in her ear, begging her to slow down. "Let's do this methodically, Zhara, bench by bench, bush by bush. We'll ask around . . ."

It was as if she hadn't heard him. Panting with the effort, she bent down beside a large shrub, certain that she had heard movement. The angry pair of lovers she disturbed cursed, and she withdrew sharply.

Cole grasped her by the elbow. "Zhara, listen. You're not doing him any good like this. We'll find him, but it has to be done logically, carefully. Panic doesn't help . . ."

"But, Cole . . ." The protest died on her lips as a costumed young man brushed past her rudely, almost knocking her off her balance. He was dressed as the *Rocky Horror Picture Show's* Riff-Raff, with tattered suit, pronounced hunchback, limp, thinning strawlike hair, and a ghastly complexion. He was talking excitedly to a woman who had chosen to dress like Magenta, with fuschia lips that matched her hair, and a French-maid's outfit that barely covered the curve of her bottom. From the breadcrumbs, confetti, and rice that clung to their hair, Zhara could tell they had just come from a boisterous interactive showing of the cult movie.

Riff-Raff was loudly saying to his companion, "I'm tellin' ya, babe. The damndest thing. Rope and all. Halfway up the tower. Reese says . . ."

Magenta scoffed. "Reese's yankin' yer chain, Lew. They'd never let nobody climb that thing."

The boy tugged at her white blouse. "If I'm lyin', I'm dyin'. Come on. We hurry, we might get to see him fall."

Zhara and Cole didn't need anyone to tell them who those two were talking about. Mickey was living out his fantasy for real.

"Come on," he urged. "Looks like we found him."

But, to his surprise, Zhara was rooted to the spot, paralyzed by horror. He peered at her. "Zhara?"

She was standing with her hands over her ears, trying to shut out some terror he himself could not perceive, body gently rocking. He put his arms around her, her body trembled, a low whimper that was felt rather than heard. "No," she whispered, voice a croak.

"Come with me," he urged. The foot of the tower was a few hundred yards behind them. Word of Mickey's escapade seemed to have spread throughout the park and surrounding streets, as people began streaming past them, costumes bright, faces lit up with morbid fascination. In the distance, sirens screamed. He hoped one of them was an ambulance. He tried to coax her again.

"I can't. I can't," she pleaded. "I can't look at him up there. It's too horrible. He's too weak. He doesn't have his glasses."

"Then let's talk him down," Cole said firmly, and lifted

her into his arms, striding without effort to join the rapidly growing crowd. It was only when he forced his way through to the front of the crowd that he set her down. They tilted their heads back, eyes following the direction of the collective gaze of the gawkers around them.

Mere stories above, a small figure clung to the face of the building, rope and tackle swaying gently in the wind. Mickey hadn't gone far, but something was wrong. He wasn't moving.

"Mickey!" Zhara screamed futilely. Her words were whipped away by the wind, even before they had any chance of reaching him.

"Is he planning to jump?" one excited onlooker asked the girl next to her.

"That'd be something to watch," the girl grinned, eyes glittering.

Zhara threw her an uncomprehending look. Had everyone suddenly ceased to care about what happened to others? Is this what the world had become?

The screeching of sirens was upon them, and three squad cars skated to a stop, followed immediately by a paramedic's van. Officers began trying to clear the area, pushing back the crowd, snarling at them to get back, disperse, nothing to see here. But stubbornly, the onlookers remained. No cop was preventing them from seeing this little drama play out! It was better than TV!

Cole immediately searched out the highest-ranking officer and began to whisper into his ear. From time to time, he and the other cop glanced at Zhara, and then, miracle of miracles, whatever Cole was trying to convince the officer to do seemed to be agreeable, because the man nodded, shouted instructions to his men, and Cole worked his way back through the crowd to Zhara, a megaphone clutched in one hand.

He handed it over to her. "Talk him down," Cole instructed.

"What?"

"Talk to him. Get him to come down."

"What if I break his concentration? Suppose I startle him, and he loses his footing?"

"Do it gently. Just call his name."

Zhara looked up again. Mickey had begun to move, much to the delight of the crowd. She was baffled. Why tonight? At this hour? On one of the busiest nights of the year? If he just wanted to get to the top, he could have waited until the streets were quiet, on an ordinary night, last night or tomorrow night, approached with stealth, and taken his chance with Tower security.

She didn't have to search far for an answer. Mickey knew his time was running out. He was mortally ill, and a wanted man—or so he thought. He had chosen tonight for a purpose: he wanted to go out in a blaze of glory. And she was the only one who could stop him.

The giddying height of the building made her cringe. She remembered the last time she had climbed, when her own life dangled on the end of black nylon rope—and the horrifying result. She had to get him to come down.

Slowly, she put the megaphone to her lips. "Mickey?"

Cole was behind her, solid, wide, strong, one arm around her waist, allowing her to lean against him. His strength infused her shaking body. She called Mickey's name again. There was no response from the small shape that was resolutely inching higher.

"Keep talking," Cole whispered.

She complied. "Mickey! It's me! Zhara!"

He stopped. He'd heard her! His face, a pale round spot against the blackness, turned toward her hesitantly, but then turned away, and the climbing continued, erratically, ineptly, as if he'd all but forgotten how.

"Mickey, I'm begging you. Come down! Please!"

"Tell him about Mason," Cole reminded her.

"Mickey, we know you didn't kill Mason! They got the people who did it! Honest!"

Mickey stopped again, hesitant.

"Oh, Cole, I don't know what to do next!" Her own impotence gnawed at her.

Gently, Cole pried the megaphone from her hand and brought it to his own mouth. "Mickey, this is Cole Wyatt. Zhara and I came to help you. I'm not here to arrest you. We just want you to come down before you hurt yourself."

A camera crew came shoving through the crowd, with lights and sound systems, hastily setting up their equipment. "He's still up there," one of them crowed jubilantly to the other, relieved that they hadn't come all this way for nothing.

Cole bit off the scathing tirade about compassion that rose to his tongue and tried to ignore the crew. There was more at stake here. He focused all his energies on the figure above him. "Mickey, listen. If you come down now, there'll be no charges. Trust me. What Zhara says is true. We have the people who killed Mason. We know you didn't do it. We just want you down in one piece, okay, son?"

The figure clung to the wall, true to his nickname, like a lizard. He was thinking. Then slowly, hesitantly, joy of joys, he began moving again, and, to Zhara's delight, he was moving down, not up.

Relief made her weak. She threw herself into Cole's arms, kisses of gladness falling on his surprised face. Then she turned to watch Mickey as he retraced his moves, falteringly, agonizingly, until he fell, weak, almost limp, into the arms of waiting paramedics. Scattered applause from the onlookers drowned out the "boos" of disappointment of the few who wouldn't have minded more excitement for the night.

The cameraman next to Cole cursed ignobly. "Waste of

film," he groused to the light technician, who spat on the ground in agreement.

Cole's hand snaked out to grasp the man's collar. "A little compassion next time, huh, buddy? That's a human being over there." He let the man go in disgust, realizing that his suggestion was wasted on someone so callow and insensitive.

The cameraman adjusted his collar indignantly, eyeing Cole resentfully. "Lunatic," he muttered, but had the good sense not to press the point any further. Instead, he followed his crew in the direction of the dissipating crowd.

Together, Cole and Zhara rushed over to Mickey, who was already surrounded by paramedics.

"He's burning up!" one of them yelled anxiously to the other. "Quick, get him to the stretcher."

"Have you been drinking, sir?" Another peppered him with questions while simultaneously shining a small light into his eyes to check dilation. "Any stimulants or depressants?"

Immediately, Cole withdrew the small bottles of Mickey's medicine he had been carrying around with him, and whispered a few words into the paramedic's ear. The man read the labels quickly, gave Mickey an anxious look, and shouted instructions to his colleagues, who began fussing around Mickey even faster than they had before.

Mickey allowed himself to be tapped, prodded, and manipulated as though his own body didn't belong to him. His face was like wax, and as they helped him onto the stretcher and fitted him with an IV, he neither flinched nor protested. His eyes were fixed on Zhara's.

A paramedic was about to fix a mask over Mickey's face, but Mickey softly croaked, "Zhar," and the man halted, mask in hand, eyeing Cole questioningly.

"Can we have a minute?" Cole asked, eyeing Mickey worriedly.

"Make it quick," the paramedic said.

Zhara stooped at Mickey's side. "You scared me," she chastised him gently, but she was smiling through her tears.

"Sorry. I was scared. I didn't want to stay in Medusa." He licked his blue, parched lips. "I knew they'd come after me."

"You didn't kill him."

Painfully, he shook his head. "No. I almost wanted to, though. I went there, but I didn't know what I was going to do. I just wanted to stop him from—" He glanced at Cole, and then looked away. "To stop him from testifying against us. But I got there and he was lying on the ground, with blood all over, and he was hardly breathing. I tried to give him CPR, honest, I tried, but he just looked at me and—sort of gasped out this little breath. And he died."

"Oh, Mickey, it wasn't your fault." Zhara smoothed out his flaxen hair.

He shrugged. "I didn't want to try convincing the police of that." Again, another glance at Cole. "My glasses fell off as I was trying to get away. It was dark, and I was getting giddy. I forgot to take my pills that morning—"

"Mickey, you *have* to—"

The paramedic interrupted. "Ma'am, I'm sorry, but we really must be getting along . . ."

Cole nodded at the man, who slipped the mask over Mickey's face and prepared to slide the stretcher into the back of the ambulance. Mickey didn't have the strength to protest.

"I love you," was the last thing Zhara had the chance to say before the doors slammed shut, and the agile paramedics leaped into the front. The sirens drowned out anything else she might have wanted to yell, and the ambulance screeched out onto the road.

When it finally disappeared from sight, Zhara looked around to find Cole had already flagged down a cab and was holding open the door for her.

"Let's get to the hospital," he suggested.

She nodded gratefully and allowed him to help her into the backseat. She sat heavily, weighed down by her leaden heart. Cole sat next to her, leaned back, and gently pulled her backward against his chest. "How soon do you think we'll get there?" she asked anxiously.

"Just a few minutes," he comforted her. "He'll be okay; we'll get him the help he needs. Don't worry too much."

"He loves me," she said dully.

"I know."

"Not just like a brother. As a man."

"I know," he repeated. His fingers stroked her hair, almost unawares.

"I had no idea—I never noticed. I was so foolish . . ."

Cole swallowed hard. "And how do *you* feel?" he asked, hesitantly.

She turned her head slightly, eyes meeting his. "For Mickey?" She thought about it. "I love him, but not the way he wants me to. It kind of makes me feel guilty."

"Don't be."

"But he needs me," she protested.

"You'll always be there for him. That'll never change. But you can't love someone out of obligation . . ." He paused and grunted self-deprecatingly. "But don't take any advice from me on that point. I'm biased."

"How?"

He kissed the curve at the back of her neck. "Because I want you all to myself."

The brush of his lips sent ripples down the length of her spine. Somehow, finally, she was willing to believe him, and she knew what she felt for him was real and alive with need and desire. But, still, she shook her head. "It won't work," she said sadly.

"Why not?" He paused in his sweet assault on her skin and shifted so he could face her. "Why won't it work, Zhara?"

She struggled to express herself. "Because—happiness is an impossible dream. My parents tried to find it, but they never did. The world is just too sad."

"Happiness *is* possible, Zhara. *We* can find it. You just have to give us a chance . . ."

"But the world is too cruel. People are too cruel. Look at what happened here tonight. There were people here who wanted Mickey to fall! How evil is that? And if the world can turn ordinary people into monsters, and crush dreams, what chance could we possibly have?"

He shook his head emphatically. "Broken people with broken lives. They'll always exist. There's nothing we can do about that; they'll have to find their own way. But there's good in the world, too. There were people here tonight who wanted him to be saved—"

"But will the good ever be a match for the bad? There'll always be trouble and pain in the world, in our lives, and no matter how much I love you—"

He cut her off with a joyful laugh, dimples popping, head thrown back. "So you *do* love me!"

She felt like she'd been caught by a slip of the tongue. Blood rushing to her face, she nodded shyly. To hide her embarrassment, she turned her gaze to the storefronts whizzing past.

"That's the most wonderful thing I've ever heard." He hugged her hard and kissed her lips with a loud smack.

She was still doubtful. "But—"

"Forget the 'buts,' my love. Forget the cruelty and the pain you've seen. I've seen my share, too. But if you and I work together, and strengthen what we have, we can build a space for ourselves that's safe and warm. We can shut out the cold. I'll protect you; you'll protect me. I watch your back, you watch—"

"Like partners." She smiled. It was almost conceivable. It could—almost—work.

"Yes, just like partners." He smiled back at her. He

tugged at her right hand, fingers stroking the ring that he had given her earlier.

"And what about my body?" She still couldn't believe it could be this easy.

He deliberately misunderstood her. "Oh, there are *lots* of things I can think of to do to your body, but not here . . ." He pointed discreetly at the cab driver, who was, at the moment, pretending to be deaf.

"No, no." She wanted him to be serious about this. "What if this is as good as it gets—with my health, I mean. What if I never get any better or stronger than I am right now? Do you really want to be chained to an invalid for the rest of your life?"

He sobered up a little. "You won't be an invalid, Zhara. You *will* get better. I know it in my heart. We'll work on it together. In a month, we'll both go jogging in the mornings. You just wait."

"But what if—"

"And even if you don't, you'll never be less in my eyes. God knows, I have a hard enough time keeping up with you as it is . . ."

Okay, she thought, maybe so. But she threw up another obstacle that would nag her if she didn't get it out in the open. "I've lived so much of my life away from people. I never finished school. You're an educated man. Do you really want a woman who doesn't even have a high school diploma?"

"We'll enroll you in a good program the day we get back to Medusa. You're brilliant. You'll ace it in no time, and then before you know it, there'll be a business degree with your name on it. Hell, an MBA . . ."

"Stop teasing," she protested.

He lifted a brow. "Who's teasing? I believe in you. Lord knows, I believe that you will be everything you ever wanted to be. I just want to be there by your side to see it happen."

She was afraid that if she tried to breathe, she'd be unable to. The excitement, the prospect of actually being happy with this wonderful, generous, loving man was almost too much to stand. Her hand closed around his. "Cole . . ." she began.

"Love?" he murmured.

She reached up to stroke his face, with its strong jaw, full, beautiful lips. "I love you," she began, and stopped. What did you say after that?

His eyes glowed. "You can never imagine how happy it made me to hear you say that." He leaned forward and placed his lips close to her ear. "Say it again."

She flushed crazily. "What? Are you mad? I haven't even gotten over the shock of actually saying it the first time!"

"Say it again anyway. It'll get easier, you'll see. If you practice every day," he added mischievously, "you'll be surprised how easy it gets. Come on. Try."

She was shocked to find herself laughing. This was serious business, yet she was bubbling over like a shaken-up soda. She couldn't speak.

"Repeat after me," he insisted, smiling broadly. "Cole . . ."

"Cole . . ."

"I . . ."

She tried to school her features into seriousness, but it just didn't work. She managed to get the word past a cluster of smiles. "I . . ."

"Love . . ."

"Love . . ." She giggled.

"You . . ."

"You . . ." There, she'd done it. She waited coyly for a response.

Instead of speaking to her, Cole rapped heartily on the seat in front. "Did you hear that, buddy?" he asked the driver.

The man chuckled. "Sure did. Unless you wanted me *not* to . . ."

"Oh, no, I needed a witness, in case she decides to back down later."

Zhara punched him in the shoulder. *"Cole!"*

He persisted. "Have you ever been to Medusa? They have very nice outdoor weddings there in the summer . . ."

She decided it was time to stop him before he went overboard. "That's enough. I *never* said—"

"All right, all right," he gave in. "I was just hoping."

"Well, I *hope*, you'll at least ask *me* first," she told him, severely. "You haven't even responded to that, uh, thing I just said to you." She felt her face grow hotter. "You know, the part about . . ."

"I got you. Sorry. I kind of got a little carried away."

"You sure did." But she couldn't stop smiling.

He cleared his throat. "Zhara?"

She pretended surprise. "Yes, Cole?"

"I love you, sweetheart. Will you give me the time and the chance to prove it?"

She thought about that for a bit, seriously, this time. "You don't have to prove it," she told him eventually. "I believe you."

"Good. Then will you give me the time and chance to make you happy? It's all I want to do, even if I have to spend the rest of my life getting it right. Will you?"

She stared, happiness rising up through her, tingling in her toes, vibrating like the strings of a fine harp, and it was glorious. The pain of the past blurred, receding to a place where only memory could touch, but from which it could no longer do her harm. Grief and guilt were gone in an instant. What lay ahead might be full of surprises, for no one had the power to clearly see the future, but she knew unerringly that through their love and trust she would finally find the peace that was her soul's desire.

She slipped her arms up around his neck and pressed against him so that she could feel his heart throbbing against her soft breasts, unable to answer in words, but answering him over and over again with her lips against his, her touch, and the aching tears of happiness and relief that dampened his face and hers. Her troubles escaped her in a sigh, and she let him hold her pliant body close in his huge, strong arms.

Her world fell into place.